D1488150

FAREWELL, MY GENERAL

FAREWELL,
MY GENERAL

by

Shirley Seifert

J. B. LIPPINCOTT COMPANY
Philadelphia and New York

First Edition

Library of Congress Catalog Card Number 54-6109
Printed in the United States of America

CONTENTS

Act One: KANSAS

Act Two: JOHN BROWN

Finale: VIRGINIA

Act One: KANSAS

Chapter 1. *The Name Is Stuart*

The Missouri was low, even for September. Three times between Jefferson City and Fort Leavenworth the steamboat *Polar Star* had scraped bottom. Twice only the most skillful maneuvering had got her off into deeper water. It had been a slow trip, and warm, the boat crowded—some settlers, above Westport a few Indians, but mostly officers' wives and children, going out to join their men. A slow, warm trip; and, before it was done, the steward, with permission from above, had "borrowed" from a purchase of chickens consigned to the fort. The captain was now anticipating, with relish, the post quartermaster's protest.

"Got to take care o' my passengers," he growled. "There'd be a row, sure enough, if I didn't. Trips like this, a man's hard put to find a dainty morsel to tempt a lady or a little one. Don't exactly hold with the practice myself of moving the delicate creatures around this way, but the army won't have it otherwise. Reckon they know. Reckon they do . . . mebbe!"

The captain's grumble diminished as he continued his rounds or was lost presently in a general confusion of sounds. Somewhere below a chicken cackled, demonstrating that some domestic poultry still would be left for the post, somewhere else a child wailed, a Negro boilerman sang against the heat and his labor, the engines throbbed, weary of the long upstream battle, and a woman's voice cried out:

"You, Mattie! Come right back here . . . and stay! Don't you move . . ."

Forward on the cabin deck, in a rocking chair well placed under
the shade provided by the Texas deck above, surrounded by a sea
of other occupied chairs and yet in some subtle way achieving a kind
of apartness, a pretty girl listened raptly to each note and half note
of the clamor; and, as if it all made up a well-known and beloved
symphony, a gratified smile touched her lips. She was a very pretty
girl. About nineteen, anyone would have guessed, something short of
twenty, but close. Light brown hair curled softly against her temples.
Her skin was flawlessly fair. She was slender in a way that even the
voluminous dress of the 1850's could not obliterate, in her case a
wide skirt of some dark blue silk mixture ballooning out below a
plain, tight bodice, relieved at throat and wrist by puffs of snowy
mull. The effect was immaculacy, startling at any time, but especially so against this generally rumpled boatload.

Slender hands rested, not supinely, but in practised repose on the
arms of the rocker; and her eyes were for the moment closed against
the bright afternoon light. Presently she opened them halfway and
then, at some change on shore, wide; and they were a sparkling blue.
A half hour before—surely no longer—she had closed them on monotonous flats set with scraggly willow trees and here and there a
squatter's shanty and cornpatch. Now the land rose in deeply eroded
hills and bluffs, densely covered with forest trees and looping vines.
She sat up alertly and put out a hand to touch her chaperon in the
chair pressed tightly against hers.

The latter, a matron as plump as the girl was slight, her black dress
unadorned by perishable furbelows, opened her eyes unwillingly.

"Don't tell me we're there," she said.

"We must be—almost," the girl said happily, "unless things have
changed."

"They haven't." The matron sat up now, shifting shoulders and
bosom above oppressive stays, gave her young charge a sharp inspection and collapsed again with a groan. "Oh, Lord, I'd forgotten.
What am I to say to your mother?"

If there had been no other apparent difference in their years, the
smile, becomingly shy, but triumphant, that passed over the girl's
face and disappeared would have marked it; and now two features,
less prominent in repose, were noteworthy—a straight nose and
a pointed chin, neither dominant as yet, but both perceptible

and promising at least a measure of willfulness and determination.

"Dear Mrs. Brent," she murmured, "it was so kind of you to consent to bring me."

Mrs. Brent's gentle brown eyes dilated. She flushed dangerously.

"I did nothing of the sort," she declared. "Flora Cooke, if you dare to suggest to your mother that I gave either my consent or my approval to your being here . . . I didn't, you know. You were to bring me a letter to deliver. Instead, here you were on board, with your trunks, your space taken and paid for. What was I to do?"

What, indeed? It was wicked, no doubt, to feel so smugly satisfied; but all had worked out so beautifully that it seemed to Flora almost an act of providence. Three weeks before this, when Mrs. Brent had left Fort Leavenworth to put her two daughters in school in St. Louis, Rachel Cooke, Flora's mother, had asked her please to look up her brood, supposedly safely settled in the same city, and bring back a firsthand report on their happiness and well-being. The Cooke offspring numbered four—John, an only son, who, having taken his degree in engineering at Harvard, was well placed with the Palmer and Robinson Locomotive Works, Flora, the eldest daughter, who, having been given a choice between a gay winter season in Philadelphia or St. Louis, had chosen St. Louis, to be near the rest of the family, and two younger girls, Maria and Julia, enrolled in the same school with the Brent sisters.

It had seemed a pleasant extra duty and Mrs. Brent had taken it on cheerfully. If it had not been easy, still she would have agreed. The wife of a captain, even an artillery captain, would not lightly refuse a request made by the wife of Lieutenant-Colonel Philip St. George Cooke, Post Commandant; and nobody, anyhow, refused Rachel Cooke anything she asked if he could help it. The sweetest, kindest woman who ever graced an army post, the most devoted wife and mother—all this Flora had heard repeatedly and reproachfully all the way upstream, as if she didn't know.

"But, if I had dreamed . . ." Mrs. Brent said.

When she reached St. Louis, Johnnie Cooke, in a wild gesture of independence, had thrown over his Harvard education and his good civilian job. Entirely on his own he had got himself a second lieutenant's commission in the army and was off to join a regiment of infantry in Texas. Flora, in tears over her brother's departure, but cheering him all the way, was in a matching state of rebellion against, as far as Mrs. Brent could see, musicals and cotillions and suppers and the other delights a wealthy aunt in a gay city could provide. Her greeting to Mrs. Brent was prophecy of present fact.

"Mrs. Brent, I am so glad to see you! You'll be going back soon, won't you? Then I can go with you. Aunt Lizzie, you see?"

So, here she was. The one part of her mission Mrs. Brent had accomplished correctly was helping Aunt Lizzie lock the two youngest up in school. As for the rest . . .

"Your mother," she said disconsolately, "will be beside herself, been, no doubt, ever since she got our telegram—if she got it."

The railroad at that time went only halfway across Missouri. A telegram must be carried by hand the rest of the way; but military dispatches usually went through. Poor Mrs. Brent! It was a shabby trick to have played on her; and Rachel Cooke would scold about that—gently; but, as for being beside herself, no!

"Mamma," Flora said confidently, "will understand. Just tell her the truth. Say I was homesick."

"Homesick?" Mrs. Brent snorted. "For Kansas?"

The year was 1855. Kansas, still raw, unleavened dough, was fermenting a settlers' war—something political, to do with slavery. On the far frontier, the Indians were out. Sioux this time. A settler's cow had been butchered to make a feast. A military detail sent out from Laramie to make inquiry had been massacred. It might amount to a big war. It might be only summer practice. Outside, one never knew until afterwards. Oh, there were reasons, no doubt, why parents like the Brents and the Cookes would want their children elsewhere; but none of them seemed to Flora valid. Fort Leavenworth since its founding thirty years before this had never known the threat of an attack. Look at all these young families going out for the first time.

"Dear Mrs. Brent," she said softly, still persistently, "Johnnie and I—the others, too, for that matter, were born in barracks. We grew up at army posts. We're not happy anywhere else, really. The army's in our blood. That's why Johnnie hated the engines. Did you know that Rooney Lee—he was at Harvard with Johnnie—is after his father now—Colonel Lee of Arlington Heights—and General Scott to get him a commission, too?" Maybe this choice bit of army gossip would comfort the good lady. She could see Mrs. Brent absorbing it. "I know just how Johnnie felt, because I feel the same way. It seems to me I've been away an eternity."

Actually it had been three years since her father, then Major St. George Cooke, commanding the Cavalry School of Practice at Carlisle Barracks in Pennsylvania, had been promoted to active command of the Second Regiment, United States Dragoons, and returned to frontier service. In 1852 that had meant fighting the Apache. For two years Lieutenant-Colonel Cooke and his regiment had moved from post to post in western Texas and New Mexico. Rachel, his wife, had followed when and wherever she could; but it had not been practical to move the whole family. The son had stayed on at Harvard and the three girls at school in Philadelphia, all under the guardianship of another of Rachel's sisters. None of them dreaming that the separation would be so long.

Three years—at Flora's age it was an epoch. At sixteen she had been a schoolgirl. At nineteen she was a young lady. She was even a little late in claiming that status, but she had deferred making her bow until she could do so before a society of her own preference, strictly military. In the spring of this year, 1855, it had looked as if impatient persistence were to be rewarded. The Second Dragoons moved into quarters at Leavenworth. At the close of the school term, Aunt Mary Dougherty of Philadelphia had delivered Flora and her two sisters, Maria and Julia, into the care of Aunt Elizabeth Collins in St. Louis, where John Cooke was already at the engine works. It was understood that, as soon as Rachel Cooke was settled in the commanding officer's house at Leavenworth, she would send for the girls. But she hadn't done so. The Sioux uprising or some other thing had come up. The next word was that they would stay on through the winter in St. Louis, the two younger girls in school and Flora, if you please, enjoying the advantages of a social season either there, or, if she preferred, in Philadelphia.

"I couldn't bear the thought of it," she said now to Mrs. Brent. "Not another whole winter away. Truly, I was never so homesick in my life."

Homesick for her father, her truly wonderful father—gay, wise, witty, and the most splendid cavalry officer who had ever flashed a sword on parade or parleyed with a painted Indian. Homesick for

her gentle, understanding mother. Homesick, yes, for Fort Leavenworth, Kansas. Born in barracks, as she had said, she had spent the
best of her growing years at that cantonment, living in the funny,
little clapboarded log houses that made up Officers' Row, learning
her letters in a log schoolhouse, learning to ride—first a pony, then a
sure enough horse—drinking in the excitement of life at a fort which
then, at least, stood guard over all the roads west, beside which life
anywhere else must seem dull and spiritless. Oh, she could explain
and explain; but, if a person didn't know . . .

"Mrs. Brent," she said abruptly, "was there some special reason
why mamma didn't want me at home this winter—something you
haven't told me?"

"Yes," Mrs. Brent said bluntly. "But she will have to say what it is."

"Oh!" A cloud settled on Flora's face and her spirits. She shook it
off. "But, anyhow . . ."

If Mrs. Brent had been nineteen, she would have asked her
whether she believed in inner compulsion, an urge not to be denied,
a command: "Go now—or never!" But Mrs. Brent was in every possible way not nineteen. Others on the boat, of more sympathetic
years, were still mere acquaintances—wives mostly of the company
officers of a new regiment, the very new United States First Cavalry.
The regimental command Flora could expect to know, all of it having
served at one time or another with her father in the Dragoons, but
the company men would be strangers. That's what came of staying
away, but that would be changed soon. In garrison, acquaintance
bloomed and ripened into friendship, or the opposite, rapidly. It had
to be. Locked in the tight, closed circle of the post through a long
winter, fires burning hot and bright against storms outside, everybody thrown on his own resources for amusement, young ladies, un-
attached, at a premium . . .

Say I was homesick . . . Cantonment Leavenworth, I'm coming,
coming. . . .

A scream broke into her musings—a shrill cry of outright terror. A
small boy, his red-gold hair still in baby curls, had escaped from whoever was supposed to keep him, and was running through the laby-
rinth of rockers straight for the rail. Flora was out of her chair on
the instant, but her full skirts and the other rockers were an impedi-
ment. She caught the child only just in time to save him from going

overboard. The nearness of that turned her faint; and, as much to steady herself as to make sure of her captive, she dropped to her knees and flung one arm tightly about the small wriggler.

"Peter Carey!" she gasped. "What do you think you are doing?"

"Want to see the fishes," he pouted.

"Oh, Peter!" She shuddered. "Wouldn't you rather . . ." she turned his face toward the shore. If this wasn't the hill, then she had forgotten. "Look up, Peter!" she commanded. "Way up yonder. Watch for a flag. Watch now!"

Only strong young eyes with a wish behind them could have caught the flare of bunting, but it was there. Peter shrieked his ecstasy and Flora hugged him to her. Oh, Peter, when I was no bigger than you . . . now it was the *Polar Star's* whistle that tore the air apart; and Flora scrambled to her feet, in her haste ripping an underflounce audibly. Oh, dear, she would have to take time now to mend that! Imagine arriving after all this time with a length of petticoat trailing.

She hustled Peter across the deck to his mother's rocker. A half dozen women stood away to let her through. The mother, as pale and faint as Flora herself had felt a moment before, put aside a bottle of smelling salts and looked up out of melting brown eyes clouded by incredibly long, dark lashes.

"I thought I had hold of him," she moaned. "Peter, come here to me."

Peter stood where he was. Flora, in mild irritation over her torn petticoat, stared at the limp, white hand with the wedding ring and the crystal bottle. How could a hand like that hold fast to anything? In all the years she had wasted outside, she thought, she had never seen anyone so helpless. Or, for that matter, so lovely. Dark eyes, cloud-soft dark hair, a magnolia-white skin—there was an exotic quality to Mrs. Carey's beauty, soft, pampered. Mrs. Brent—anyone—might well have asked what she was doing on this boat. Flora raised the question mentally and it might have occurred to Mrs. Carey. Her mouth had a petulant droop.

"Celie," she said in sighing explanation, "is in the cabin, packing."

Celie was the Carey maid. Mrs. Carey was rich as well as lovely. Her father, everyone on the boat knew by now, was a South Carolina planter. He was also a United States Senator. He . . . with sudden decision, Flora thrust Peter's hand into his mother's, tumbling the smelling salts into the silken lap.

"Peter," she ordered, "you stay right here now and take care of your mamma." And to Mrs. Carey, "I must go now." After all, there was that petticoat. "I'll send your Celie if I see her. We'll land in about two minutes."

"A baggage," Mrs. Brent said. "We'll all be taking care of her and her children—I mean, child—presently. You'll see."

Oh! So, that was how it was with Mrs. Carey? Not that Mrs. Brent, a matron, would tell Flora, a maid. As if everybody in the fort wouldn't know presently!

She stood now with Mrs. Brent at the rail, watching the preliminaries of landing. It had been the older woman's idea that they should wait above until the first rush was over; and it was just as well. By the time Flora had finished her toilette, complicated by the torn flounce, the broad stairway leading to the lower deck was jammed. Shrieks, scoldings, laughter and chatter still boiled up from it like steam from an overfull kettle. Somewhere in the press Mrs. Carey stood, with Peter, and again temporarily without Celie. She might faint with good cause now. Suppose she did? Well . . . suppose! There was nothing Flora could do to prevent or to cure. Nothing was required of her. She put aside the thought of Mrs. Carey, shook out her skirts, patted the puffs of her sleeves and kept her eyes resolutely forward.

On shore everything looked much as she remembered it—oh, blessedly the same. The wide, flat landing space, packed hard and dry at the end of summer, the depot, the warehouse sheds. Only people were new. Duties up on the hill that day must have been brief. A full score of officers waited near the depot to welcome the *Polar Star*. In a block of shade thrown by the buildings, a detail held their mounts. The young men themselves were out in the full sun and afoot, ready to rush forward the minute a landing plank was set down. They had paraded full dress for the occasion, and their exuberance overreached the excited outcry from the boat.

"*Oh, juba, jubilee!*" a rouster sang below decks, catching the spirit, because, goodness knew, the rousters had nothing to expect from all this but labor.

"Well, I'm thankful," Mrs. Brent said piously. "When we were so long on the way, I was afraid we might find them gone."

She was talking about the waiting officers.

"Would they be ordered out now," Flora asked, "so late as this?"

"They would and they will," Mrs. Brent said, with the satisfaction of one who bore shipwreck better if others rode the same raft. "Orders were in for them when I left. I rather think it was supplies, not families, that held them up."

Supplies seemed a probable explanation. Behind the depot, where the road from the fort came down the hill to the river, a queue of wagons also waited for the *Polar Star* to be made fast—three high ambulance wagons, to carry the officers' wives and children up the hill, then a long string of freight wagons, for enlisted men's families and general cargo. All were mule-drawn, and all had been marshaled into position and were being kept in line by an officer who sat his horse somewhat apart and to the rear, where he could watch the execution of his orders.

"Well, mercy!" Flora said vaguely, about the marching orders.

She had begun to occupy herself now with trying to select from the jigging, exuberant young men below one who might be Mrs. Carey's husband. Identification would hardly be difficult. All she needed to do was watch as the men tossed their hats into the air, as they all did repeatedly.

She was looking for a redhead, but so far none had appeared. Finally the only possibility left was the officer, still mounted, who rode up and down the long line of wagons. He had his hands too full with managing a spirited, half-broken horse to wave his hat. Unreasonably Flora hoped he was not Mrs. Carey's husband. Even at a casual glance, he looked exceptional. It might have been be cause he was on his horse instead of afoot. All cavalrymen looked better when mounted. There was something special, however, about this one. His back seemed extraordinarily straight, his shoulders extraordinarily square. He . . . he must be Lieutenant Carey. He was as interested as any other in the boat. At short intervals he turned and rode that way, then wheeled and rode off again, to cover his impatience. He turned now, as Flora watched; and his horse, weary, no doubt, of such didoes, reared, bringing himself and his rider into sharp silhouette against the sun. For a second, the two were a fluid, living statue of bronze and blue and gold. Flora tingled with wonder and delight. Never had she seen such horsemanship, never . . .

Oh, absurd! Who could handle himself on a horse better than her father? This was just Lieutenant Carey, she reminded herself, showing off for his family. She wouldn't look at him. She looked past him—and clutched Mrs. Brent's arm.

"Look!" she cried. "Yonder, under the trees. Mamma got our telegram. She's sent a carriage."

She pointed out a two-seated light wagonette, of the sort used frequently by senior officers for travel, half hidden by the branches of a giant sycamore.

"It's all over," Flora concluded. "The Sioux business, I mean. Papa's home."

"No," Mrs. Brent said. "Not possibly. What makes you think . . ."

She hushed as the driver let himself down over the near front wheel and with a leafy branch set to work to help his horses battle flies. He was a heavy man, solid as the animals. The sun picked out a patch of orange on his blouse—the Dragoons' color.

"Hosky!" Flora said, and her clutch on Mrs. Brent's arm tightened.

Sergeant Hoskins, her father's wagon master, his extra right arm in quarters or on the march, but especially on the march. If the Sioux trouble had not been settled, and still Hoskins was at Fort Leavenworth, what did that portend? Tardily she thought now of all that Mrs. Brent had not said on the journey, rather than what she had said; but it was too late to question her further. The forward landing stage swung out and was made fast. The officers surged forward. At the cargo gate the rousters sang: *"Oh, juba, jubilee!"* The debarkation began.

Mrs. Brent and Flora were the last passengers to leave the boat, Mrs. Brent making directly for the depot platform, to wait in the shade there for Hoskins to come up with the carriage. Hoskins, on the far side of the landing, still showed no sign of moving up, and would not, Flora knew, until there was prospect for a clear road. The wait, however, could hardly be long. The ambulances were loaded to capacity now. The officer escort had mounted. The freight wagons began to roll. Finally only Flora and her companion remained on foot—they and the Careys, for whom some difficulty seemed to have arisen.

The officer in charge of the wagon train must, of course, be Lieutenant Carey. Flora had not seen the meeting between him and his family, but he stood now at the tail of an ambulance, talking to them, his head uncovered. His hair was not red, just brown, with a copper overcast. Small Peter's curls could turn to that with the years. Captiously, again she turned away.

"Oh, Hosky, come on!" she complained, and did not hear the Careys moving that way until they stood directly before her and Mrs. Brent.

"Ladies," a rich Southern voice said, something higher than most and clearer, and crisped by military usage, "I know I am presumptuous, but the ambulances are full and Mrs. Carey is ailing. Would you possibly have room for her in your conveyance?"

The nerve of a brass monkey, Mrs. Brent said afterwards. Not that, perhaps, but a measure of presumption, certainly. Later Flora wished that she had paid less attention to that and had made a closer study of the man, though how she could have observed more in one meeting would be hard to say. Always her two first pictures were the clearest—man and horse outlined in gold against the sun, and then just the man, standing with a child clinging to his hand and a woman drooping in conscious prettiness near by.

Not the handsomest man she had ever seen, but certainly not unhandsome. Fairly tall, and heavier than he had looked from a distance. One felt immediately a deep reserve of strength and force. His appearance was smart in spite of the dust that settled over everyone and everything on this dry flat. His short campaign jacket and his trousers fitted without a visible wrinkle. He held his hat now in the bend of his free arm.

He was young, much too young to be a husband and father. That was Flora's first reassurance. His shoulderstraps were plain. An undistinguished second lieutenant, and that seemed strange, but not so strange as his youth. Sun and wind of some harsh climate had burned cheek and jaw an angry red; but his broad, uncovered forehead was fair and smooth; and his eyes, blue as a summer sky, were the clear, brave eyes of a boy.

No, she had to correct that at once. He had addressed his request to Mrs. Brent, as the older woman; and Mrs. Brent answered him crisply:

"The carriage was sent to meet Miss Cooke. I am sure . . ."

If she finished the sentence, nobody heard her. The young man turned to Flora; and, as if he had not seen her before, a spark flashed in his eyes, lighting a flame that was anything but boyish. It covered Flora with such pleasant confusion that she wondered to hear herself speaking coherently.

"We will be glad to accommodate your wife and child, Mr. Carey. I am sure there is ample room."

The red of sun and wind was not so deep that more color could not be added. The blue eyes burned.

"The name, ma'am, is Stuart. I have not the honor—Lieutenant Carey is occupied with duties he could not leave. I promised to look after his family."

Bells rang in Flora's ears—a mad and merry tune.

"I do beg your pardon," she said. "The mistake was natural, I hope. And now, might I suggest, if Mrs. Carey is able to walk the short distance, that we move over to the carriage? Sergeant Hoskins may not think to come for us until the wagons leave. We'll be more comfortable over yonder in the shade; and . . . I'm sure we can manage alone, Mr. Stuart, if you also have other duties."

The Colonel's daughter speaking. The blaze in the blue eyes flared up.

"I will see you ladies to the carriage, ma'am—with your permission."

When they were exactly twenty paces from the carriage, Sergeant Hoskins gave over brushing flies and stepped out ten paces to meet them. Sergeant Hoskins—lance corporal when Flora first remembered him, bringing out a batch of recruits for the Dragoons, then staying on, to teach them to stick on a horse, to ride and to shoot and to march, to pitch a tent and take it down, to read Indian sign, and all the other things that went with being a trooper. Hosky to the Cooke children, all things to them and to their father and their mother that a strong, brave, knowing man, otherwise untutored, could be.

"Hello, Hosky!" Flora said now, so glad to see him that she all but forgot the worry his presence had wakened in her. "Sergeant, we have passengers. Mrs. Brent, if you will be comfortable in the rear with Mrs. Carey, I'll ride with the driver and we'll take Peter. If that's all right with Sergeant Hoskins."

But it was not the sergeant's hand and strong arm that helped her over the wheel to her place. The hand may have lingered a second longer than needed under her elbow, or perhaps another compulsion made her turn her head. The changing light in the blue eyes was now a glimmer of mischief.

"I leave you in good hands, *Mademoiselle. Au revoir.*"

Execrable Academy French. A matter for mirth, usually; but . . .

"Isn't he nice?" Mrs. Carey cooed, as he walked away.

"You hush!" Flora wanted to cry at her over the clamor of her heart: *Not Carey, Stuart. . . . The name is Stuart.* Oh, she had been right, so right, to come home!

Sergeant Hoskins lifted himself into the wagon, settled his weight, and unwrapped the leather lines from the whip socket. His face was thunderous.

"Hosky," Flora quaked again, a little, "you haven't said you're glad to see me."

The sergeant blew.

"You've growed some, Miss Flo'. Back, you corn-fed hunks, ba-a-ack!"

On the plain, young Mr. Stuart once more rode his shining horse. The wagons began to move with purpose. A whiplash exploded, and another. Flora considered covering small Peter's ears; but, before distinguished profanity could add itself to the boy's already plentiful excitement, a clear, baritone voice was raised in song:

"*In the sweet bye and bye . . .*"

"Texas!" Hoskins growled. "Learned it off the Comanches, mebbe. A singin' lootenant!" He spat viciously over the wheel.

The singing went on:

"*We shall meet on that beautiful sho-o-ore.*"

"But . . . Hosky, a hymn?"

"The chune," the sergeant said, "don't signify nothin'. Giddap, you . . ."

Chapter 2. *Marching Orders*

The wagons were unloading now into the storehouses up on the hill. It seemed to Lieutenant James Ewell Brown Stuart, aged twenty-two and drawing for the first time extra pay as regimental quartermaster—which he needed if he was going to buy a horse that a trader had shown him down at the corral that morning—that the wagons had multiplied between the boat landing and this level. Even with the assistance of a good sergeant of his own and two corporals, he'd do well to see the goods stowed before Retreat.

What was his hurry? Never mind that now. All required of him was that he concentrate on the matter in hand and his carefully tabulated lists. So many barrels of bacon, of flour, of sugar, of dried peas, of beans . . . if he kept things in order, the task of reloading tomorrow or the next day or the day after that for the march would be less and he might find an hour or two in which to try the new mount. The horse looked good.

All required was a little concentration, but that he was finding almost impossible to achieve. The business about a horse was a subterfuge, an attempt to turn aside the demand for attention of a pair of blue eyes no less bright than his own. Not so breath-taking, perhaps, as the eyes of the languorous Mrs. Carey, but full of life, intelligent, sparkling. A straight, fine nose. A mouth—hum! It could put into prim and proper phrasing the most arrant mischief . . . soft, sweet . . . whoa, Lieutenant!

He pulled in his stomach and stiffened his chin. None of that now! Not just yet, please! Had he come safely through four years of West Point hops, his eyes steadfast on his life's ambition, only to topple over at the first encounter out here? There had been no girls in Texas, his first duty. His colonel there had supposed young men were sent to him to be dried out like buffalo meat in long pursuit of ghost Indians. Kansas had promised to be as barren as Texas until . . .

This girl now. He had recognized instantly that she was different

from any other he had known, but how was she different? Was it
her crisp daintiness of appearance in the dusty confusion? That certainly, but something more. Ah, he had it! His nose wrinkled remi-
niscently. A fragrance, delicate, elusive, but arresting. He couldn't
name it. Some flower or flowers he had known—like a bouquet from
his mother's garden of tender, but confused boyhood memory.
Strange that a perfume so light could override horseflesh and
leather, but it had.

The sun was low when the last wagoner came for special direction.
There was, the man thought, some mistake here. Household goods,
including a cast-iron heating stove, consigned to Lieutenant-Colonel
Cooke. Of the Dragoons.

"Commandant's quarters, sir. Shall I . . ."

"No," Stuart said. "Unload at the regimental depot and step lively.
I'll inquire."

He pocketed the bill of lading.

He couldn't have said why he did this. A stove was an incongruous
thing to be linked to the fragrance of an encounter too soon over;
but a man in his situation must seize any advantage offered. Besides,
a detail of the shipping label disturbed him. "Lt. Col. P. St. George
Cooke, Fort Riley, Kansas Territory." A new post farther west. How
far, he didn't know, and he would be cautious in making inquiry
for fear of what he might discover. Far enough, if he had learned
anything about western distances.

Retreat over, which she did not attend, he was still in a state of
at once pleasant and uncomfortable quandary. One thing was certain. He had no taste tonight for his bachelors' mess. He liked his
fellow officers; and usually his high spirits, set free from duty, made
their own contribution to the uproar of fun or wrangle at Bedlam—
Leavenworth's name for the unmarried officers' house—or even to
the deep discussions of politics or life in the abstract into which
young men could fall. Tonight? No.

Instead of stabling his horse, he turned him downhill toward the
wagon camp and corral of Majors, Russell and Company below the
fort on One-Mile Creek. If hunger attacked him—it regularly did—
he could manage a bit of bread and meat there. Crude fare, and
the Lord knew he'd have his belly full of it before the coming cam-

paign was over; but it suited him better this evening than soup and
vegetables and pastry and noise—and the gossip, probably already
rampant, about the charming newcomer.

It wasn't long before the smell of scorched meat was sharp in his
nose, and in another minute his horse, Dan, was picking his way
through a narrow lane between rows of cooking fires surrounded
by bearded teamsters. Beyond, in the gathering dark, stretched a
blur of wagons and shops and men and animals. He would never
forget his first sight of the place. It had been daylight, and he was
part of a detail purchasing mounts and leasing wagons with drivers.
The immensity of the thing had awed him. You couldn't see from
one boundary of the camp to the other. Acres of wagons, hills of
axletrees, whole herds of mules and oxen and half-broken horses,
to say nothing of men, all serving this business of western freight
and western settlement. He would not have believed so much could
find use in a land that looked to a casual observer as empty as it
was immense. He had marveled and bent his mind and his eyes to
searching the great emptiness. Tonight all his thoughts and desires
were right here within himself, but even more inscrutable.

A teamster recognized him and spoke.

"If it's the boss you're looking for, Lieutenant, he's at Zadok Bagnell's yonder. Zadok got in a fresh string just today—some likely
ones."

Stuart thanked the man and, on the point of saying he was not
down on army business and so was not seeking Mr. Majors, he
changed his mind. He could always look over a string of horses.
As pleasant a form of idling as he knew.

A boy stood up now from near the same fire.

"Show you the way, Lieutenant?" he offered.

"Why, thank you, boy. Walk on. I can see to follow you."

He could never endure riding a led horse.

In the commandant's house, facing the parade, the dinner hour
passed with Flora still not knowing just why her mother wanted
her to spend the winter outside—this winter above all others; and
yet, that there was a reason she was more and more certain. It was
a look in her mother's eyes—kind, loving eyes, asking of any dear
one present, "Are you happy? Comfortable? Can I do anything to

help?" It was a deepening of what the younger Cookes called her
anxious line, a mark etched lightly on her forehead actually before
any of them had been born. It was a pull at the corners of the generous mouth—almost a quiver—when she thought nobody was looking her way.

Otherwise, Rachel was, wonderfully, the same as ever—a fresh-
faced matron of early middle years, serenely aware of her position,
but making no show of that or anything else. Her welcome was
what Flora had known it would be. She came down from the porch
to the edge of the drive to wait for the carriage. She gathered Flora
into her arms, kissed her yearningly, patted her shoulder, but seemed
disappointed that Hoskins had set Mrs. Brent down at her door on
the way up.

"I wanted to thank her. I . . . well, it doesn't matter. I'll see her
tomorrow. Darling, was it a tiresome trip? Are you warm? Your face
seems flushed. Run on into the house where it is cool. I'll be along
in a minute. Hoskins, if you'll just set the trunks on the veranda,
please, Ben will carry them upstairs. And, oh, Hoskins . . ."

Flora left them talking about this and that—something about a
stove, she overheard—and went slowly up the wooden steps, her
hand touching the balustrade lovingly, then the door frame, as she
stepped inside. Lieutenant-Colonel P. St. George Cooke . . . outside, Hoskins sounded something more than disturbed now and
Rachel was rebuking him: "Sergeant, please! If that's how it is,
I'll take the matter up myself with Colonel Sumner. At once—tonight."

Flora hardly heard them. Stables sounded, and she was listening
raptly to the echoes of the subsequent stampede to the creek when
Rachel came in.

"Top quarters, mamma!" she said. "Us! What we've talked about—
it seems to me always, wondering when, if ever . . ."

Her mother and father had met and married at Fort Leavenworth.
Philip St. George Cooke was himself only a second lieutenant then
and Rachel was visiting her older sister—the Aunt Mary now of
Philadelphia, Mrs. John Dougherty. Major Dougherty at the time
had been government agent for all the Indians west of the Missouri
and had his home on the Leavenworth reservation. How long . . .

"Twenty-three years," Rachel said, with sudden, bleak emphasis;

but, when Flora looked at her in startled question, she made a face
and smiled and turned the talk to something else.

And so it went most of the evening.

"I want to hear about everyone and everything," Rachel said, but
the anxious line cut deeper into her forehead as time passed.

Now, dinner over, they sat in the parlor. A low fire burned behind
the well-swept hearth. Evenings came on cool at this season, Rachel
explained superfluously. Flora understood. The fire was for Philip
St. George Cooke absent. His chair stood before it. On the mantel
was his silver julep pitcher, flanked by handy sugar dishes and mint
phials. He had been moved about so much that he had learned
never to count on having a supply of the stuff in leaf. The shelves
of books—there had never been room before to spread them out
properly. Two volumes would be missing. In the morning, by studying the empty spots, Flora would know what her father had taken
in his saddle bags to rest his mind and spirit on long evenings in
camp. Army Regulations, of course, but what, besides? Shakespeare,
Carlyle, Dante? Pride blazed up in her, succeeded by a rush of tenderness.

Then pride, her dreams of a happy winter, went up the chimney
with the smoke from the logs, as Rachel told her. The Cookes were
not remaining at Fort Leavenworth. When the Sioux campaign was
over—it might take another month to settle everything, Rachel said
—the Second Dragoons, Lieutenant-Colonel Cooke commanding,
were to occupy Fort Riley, instead.

At first, Flora wouldn't believe it. She knew well enough how
remote the new post was. Fort Riley—out where the Kaw River
began, near the Santa Fe Trail, at the beginning of the buffalo
range. It might as well have been Timbuctoo.

"Oh!" she said, just that, going hollow inside. "Oh!"

"It's the new regiment," Rachel said. "I knew the minute I heard
they had been ordered here—before our orders came. There isn't
room at Leavenworth for both regiments and so . . ." Bitterness,
almost unheard of from Rachel, crept into her tone, and Flora ached
—some—for her, too. "Mr. Davis's pets, we call them. It does seem
the War Department favors them in every way." She rallied. "Of
course, Fort Riley is the more difficult assignment and so naturally
the senior regiment would be sent there."

"Don't excuse them," Flora said, meaning the President, Franklin Pierce, and his Secretary of War, Jefferson Davis, and all their helpers. "It's monstrous, and you know it."

Twenty-three years of waiting and dreaming and planning. She began to see, if she hadn't suspected before, why her mother and the Colonel had planned a different career for their only son—and—possibly, their daughter. Twenty-three years of waiting and giving good service and at the end—Fort Riley. Indians, emigrants, dust storms in summer, blizzards in winter, sage brush, sod huts . . .

"Oh, no!" Rachel said. "It's not that bad now. They have done considerable ' building there this summer. The quarters, Hoskins says, are generally better than they are here. The commandant's house is ready and is quite large."

Now Flora understood about Hoskins. He had been sent home to help Rachel move.

"When?" Flora asked, and Rachel sighed.

"As soon as possible. I want to be settled when your father comes back, but . . ."

She had been waiting for the delivery of a stove. The winters out on the plains were bad, and this new house had double parlors. The Colonel had said that if she would leave him his open fire in one, she might set up any sort of heating arrangement she wanted in the other. So she had ordered this stove from a foundry in St. Louis, but it didn't come and it didn't come. Finally it had been promised on the next upriver boat, which was the *Polar Star*. Hoskins, however, had not been able to locate it among the freight.

"He has an idea," Rachel said, "probably mistaken, that the stove has got in with the supplies for the new regiment and is in their warehouse. I told him I'd speak to Colonel Sumner about it and I will, if he comes over tonight."

She had said there might be callers later—Colonel Sumner or Major Sedgwick of the new regiment, both of them being adrift and so mindful of her loneliness. Old, old friends, surely Flora remembered them. Colonel Sumner's family had not come out yet and John Sedgwick was still a bachelor. Flora recalled them both, but especially Major Sedgwick. In times past the Cooke children had addressed him as Uncle John; but she thought she must be more formal now, showing respect for his rank in the new regiment.

The new regiment! Everything seemed to pivot on that theme. Disappointment, frustration, alarm crowded suddenly into the emptiness that Rachel's news had created. Flora wanted to cry and then she had to laugh.

"Oh, but it is funny," she insisted, choking back angry tears. "If you could have heard me going on to Aunt Lizzie and Mrs. Brent about coming home here!"

"I should have told you," Rachel said. "Jessie Brent should have told you, though I asked her not to. I said, 'Time enough after we've moved.' I knew you'd be unhappy for me and I was afraid all of you might be seized with the impulse to rally around. I didn't think of your breaking away like this, though I should have, when I heard about Johnnie." She wiped a few tears from her own eyes, ostensibly for the faraway, very dear, only son. "But now listen, sweetheart. Just because you are here, there is no reason why you must stay."

Rachel had thought this all out. The *Polar Star* was on its way upstream to Weston and St. Joseph. In a day or two it would be back, and Flora could return on it to St. Louis. Somebody from the fort or Leavenworth City would surely be going down and could take Mrs. Brent's place as chaperon. If necessary, Rachel herself would go.

"No," Flora said abruptly. "I couldn't. Not now."

The protest was involuntary. She could have explained it in a dozen ways, without telling the truth. Rachel tried to reason with her.

"Listen, dear. There is nothing at Fort Riley for a girl like you. All those pretty clothes upstairs, all your pretty accomplishments—you. Your father and I would be happy to have you. I'd say, take a week or a month for a visit, but at this season you might have to stay on the rest of the winter."

"I know," Flora said desolately, "but . . . no."

She got up from her chair and walked over to the window, drew the curtains aside and looked out. All she could see was the dark, picked out in scattered lights—single ones and clusters—Officers' Row, noncoms' quarters, the hospital, Bedlam, barracks. No sound that was identifiable came to her; and yet, as clearly as if the word had been spoken, the mystery of the dark pleaded, "Wait." She turned from the window and came back to her chair.

"We don't have to decide tonight," Rachel said. "Tomorrow will do."

"Hush!" Flora answered; and then, a softness creeping around her hurts and perplexities, a softness such as she had never felt before, she coaxed, "Let's talk about something else. Tell me—oh—more about the new regiment, for example. The boat was crammed with its wives."

Lieutenant Stuart and the boy from the camp sat on the fence of Bagnell's corral. It was getting pretty dark now—too dark for judging horseflesh, even with the help of big lanterns, which a stable boy hung presently on posts at the corral gate; but this was as pleasant a place as any for idling.

The string, at least the bunch in the corral, was small, but choice. Where Zadok Bagnell got his horses nobody exactly knew. Rarely, in the case of a thoroughbred, to give a tale of blood lines' authenticity, he would name a town or a state, but usually not. The pick of the string this evening was surely well bred—a filly, black, with clean, strong legs, a proud neck, small ears pricked sharply. A little nervous, perhaps.

"She's too fine for out here," the boy said.

"Yes," Stuart agreed. "Oh, you mean the filly? Yes, but you know, sometimes they make the best mounts. Arabs prefer them, I read somewhere. They claim they have stout hearts, so devoted and enduring that it makes up for the difference in bone and muscle. I've read . . ." he stopped, aware that the boy was now studying him, not horses. A small boy, hardly into his teens, all eyes and bones and hunger, too young to be hanging around a wagon camp unless he was a teamster's son, and motherless. He wasn't motherless. His jeans and shirt were patched, but clean, washed threadbare.

"You've had schooling," the boy said, again with unexpected sharpness. "You got to have schooling, before you can even think about West Point, I know. And without West Point or a heap of other schooling, you can't hardly hope to get to be an officer of cavalry, I reckon."

"You've a long way to go, boy. Time to think of several things to do or be meanwhile. Something you might like better."

But the boy was in earnest.

"I'm going on ten now," he announced. "I can do things already some men can't. I can ride a hoss. I can shoot. Antelope even. I can fetch and carry. That's what I do mostly. Or, if somebody wants to send word to somebody that's some place else. I . . . you going to stable her, Mr. Bagnell? I'll fetch her blanket."

The trader stood at the fence, the lead strap of the filly in his hand.

"A pest, that boy," he said, as the youngster made off, "but handy. What do you think of this young lady, Lieutenant? I see you looking her over. Gentle as a lamb. A child could ride her. But she's rare. Picked her up at a sale in Lexington, Kentucky. Owner hard up for a little cash. Had to cut down his stable. This one didn't show too well on the track, but she's got racing blood. What do you say?"

"Nothing, I'm afraid."

Stuart laughed ruefully. What would Zadok Bagnell say if he spoke his true thought? If she were a chieftain's daughter and I an Indian lover, I'd stake the filly at the door of her father's *tipi* . . .

"She'd be a luxury," he said ambiguously, "to a man on army subsistence."

"Can't half see her now," the trader answered. "Come down tomorrow."

"I may not find the time. Speaking of that, hadn't you better start that boy for home?"

"Got his own pony," Zadok said. "Looks out for himself mostly; and he may be staying in town. Sometimes does, picking up an odd job and an extra penny where he can. His pa took a knife in his ribs some time back and can't do much now but keep himself scarce. Lucky to be alive. Some fracas—the usual. This settlers' war you hear about. Don't amount to much yet, but will some day, if it ain't stopped soon."

Stuart understood. The rising threat of civil war in Kansas Territory between migrants from opposing sections and factions was one reason for doubling the troops in occupation. It would seem that a settler had trouble enough fighting natural enemies without being set upon by his fellow men.

"Kinda left the young 'un," Zadok continued, "with a family on his hands. His ma does all she can but she's got the farm piece and

the house and a parcel of other little ones to look after. So, if ever
you want an errand run or a letter carried special, Cody's the name
—Bill Cody. You can get hold of him here usually. Mr. Majors lets
him stay around, to see what he can find to do. Or, if you'd fancy
a piece of fresh game for your mess and haven't time to go hunting,
he's good at traps, and a crack shot. Got his first deer a few weeks
back."

"That child?" Stuart said incredulously.

"Boys grow up fast when they have to. 'Scuse me. Here's somebody looking for you."

Ransome, the regiment's adjutant, rode his horse up to the rail.
Stuart's Dan, stepping away in real or pretended discomfiture, all
but pulled Stuart off his perch.

"Had an idea I'd find you here," Ransome said, disappointed that
he had not succeeded in unseating his messmate.

Robert Ransome, Junior, as light-hearted a prankster as West
Point had ever graduated into the army; but, since he was the
Colonel's adjutant, Stuart viewed his presence with mistrust. Sure
enough . . .

"Orders, boy. Marching orders for all of us. Special orders for
the quartermaster. We're joining the Sioux hunt, after all, marching
out day after tomorrow. Reveille at dawn. What? No cheers?"

None. One day, Stuart thought. One meager little day.

"There was rejoicing at mess," Ransome rattled on. "A man gets
nowhere marching up and down on parade, you know. The only
weeping is in the married men's quarters. Say, did you know . . ."

"Did Colonel Sumner want me to report to him?" Stuart interrupted.

"Not he," Ransome said. "Your orders are all written out in my
neat hand. All you need is a light to read them by. The Colonel's
slicked up tonight to go visiting, with reinforcements—one Major
John Sedgwick. A bachelor, drawing nigh to forty, but still a hand
with the ladies; and at this house where he . . ."

Impatience swept over Stuart. One day, and that crammed with
duty.

"For a dollar I'll race you to the parade," he challenged.

"Not me," Ransome drawled. "I know your taste in hosses."

There was no shaking him off. The two climbed the hill abreast.

The barracks edging the parade were now aglow and alive from ground to roof. From Officers' Row more light pierced the darkness. At the commandant's house someone had left a window open and from it floated a sound that halted the riders.

"She sings," Robert Ransome, Junior, said in awe. "Like a prairie lark."

"Maxwellton's braes are bonnie,
Where early fa's the dew . . ."

"What do you know about prairie larks?" Stuart objected. He shivered. Ecstasy, he hoped, not ague. "Like an angel, I say."

"Know as much about larks as you do about angels," Ransome argued.

But Stuart didn't pursue the point. Ought he to ride up to the door now? "Do forgive me, ladies, for calling at this hour, unannounced. I have in my pocket a freight receipt for a stove." Was this the time? No. A man stood up in the parlor, between a light and a window. There was no mistaking the high, brushed pompadour, the nose, flattened by a war club probably, the sharp end of the beard. Colonel Edward Vose Sumner, commanding. Ransome groaned.

"Old friends of the family calling on mamma. Charming daughter obliges with a little entertainment. Outranked, as usual, fella. Come on home now. Join us in a toast: 'Ourselves on the warpath!' Oh, I forgot. You don't indulge . . ."

"Thank you," Stuart said. "I'll open my office, I think. I can do my sums better over there."

With a clearer head and so set everything in motion for the next day, to save an hour, perhaps. Tattoo, however, found him still in a sweat, trying to balance wagonloads of corn in the ear—forage against the failure of pasture—with

Her brow is like the snowdrift.

Are you serious about this girl, he asked himself. Do you want . . . yes. Like nothing he had ever wanted before. On the other hand, he knew she was too fine—a luxury on army subsistence.

Her throat is like the swan.

The way her hair curled around her ears. Especially the right, the near one . . . long march rations: sixty days of flour, ten days' pork . . .

Tomorrow, when it came, passed, Flora thought afterwards, with the fleetness of a dream. Midmorning brought Lieutenant Robert Ransome, Junior, to the house with a message from the regimental quartermaster.

"Something about a stove, ma'am? Lieutenant Stuart wishes you to know that he is giving the matter his absolute, personal attention."

"Oh!" Rachel said. "And now, with so much else to attend to!"

"Yes, ma'am, and the boy not feeling too good, besides. He snatched his supper at the wagon camp last night, and I'm afraid . . ."

Lieutenant Ransome seemed not too sad about his friend's distress. His eyes asked Rachel if she didn't mean to present him to her daughter; but, when Rachel turned to do so, Flora had slipped away to the kitchen.

"Lily, where's the ginger?"

And a half dozen other things she knew Rachel would have in store. She sniffed and brewed. She poured the brew into a pitcher. She called Ben to carry the pitcher to Lieutenant Stuart at the quartermaster's depot. She added a note.

"Do take a cup while it's hot. You'll feel ever so much better."

Now, how should she sign it? She dimpled. She flourished the pen: "P. St. George Cooke, Lt. Col., Commanding." There!

Afternoon brought Lieutenant Stuart in person, riding his big bay horse, leading another—a filly, black, with a white star on her forehead, and a sidesaddle. He tied the two horses to the porch rail.

"Mrs. Cooke," he said in earnest apology to Rachel, "I am truly distressed about your stove. No, ma'am, not yet; but the men are looking. I left orders. Miss Flora, I trust you are rested from your journey. I have an hour free. I thought . . . there's a filly a man wanted me to try. I take it for granted that you ride?"

Well, of course. Anything from a cow pony to a battery mule. How nice of him to take it for granted! She hoped he would not spoil everything by saying the filly was gentle. Even Rachel did not raise that question.

"I won't be a minute!" Flora raced for the stairs.

Then her boots made trouble. They were new. She called in Lily, the cook; but Lily knew nothing about boots. Ben, the other servant, was nowhere about. Finally she stood at the head of the stairs with the lovely, stubborn things in her hand and tears in her eyes.

"My darling," Rachel remonstrated, "surely someone . . ."

"Do allow me," Stuart said. "Mrs. Cooke, I have three sisters at home. Boots always give trouble. It takes a man, really. Please, with your permission?"

He knew how. Flora sat against the steps and pulled as he worked toe and heel, and the boots were on before Mrs. Grundy could look their way. She stood up and stamped, and he offered her his arm. They went down the stairs together and it was the most wonderful feeling. It was . . . just a feeling.

The filly was a love—and very gentle.

"I want to thank you for your kindness and the delicious tea," Stuart said, adjusting her stirrup.

"It's anything but delicious, I know," she said, "but it helps sometimes."

"It helped me. No doubt about that."

The filly had the easiest gait Flora had ever experienced. Riding her was like floating on air. Everything that day, almost, was like floating on air. As they went at a gentle trot down the road past the burying ground, she was thinking of that, certainly giving no attention to the business of riding. The filly, sensing a slack hand, shied at a tombstone; and the next thing Flora knew, she was literally floating through the air.

She landed softly in a grassy ditch. She was hurt nowhere except in her pride. No horse had ever before thrown her. What had possessed this one? Mischief apparently, not malice. After her jump, she did not bolt. She stood looking into the ditch at Flora with an expression of grave inquiry, only her eyes rolling; but that, too, could have been in fun. Stuart, on the other hand, was all anxiety, as he helped Flora to her feet.

"You are quite sure you are not hurt?" he asked over and over.

"No, really. My hat wobbles," she said finally. "I'll have to fix that."

She gave him the hat to hold while she reset her hairpins. He looked at it curiously, as if he had never seen a hat before. Used to girls and girls' fixings, he had said; but the little hat seemed something special.

"We'll exchange horses," he offered then.

"Mercy, no! I've seen your horse dancing."

Where and when was that? She would not say. With extreme care, he helped her mount again.

"Sure enough a soldier's daughter," he complimented, "but, please, never scare me like that again. Promise?"

The ride went smoothly and only too swiftly after that. Back at the post, Stuart spoke of a hop that had been hastily arranged for that night. He would like to claim the first dance and to escort Flora and her mother, if permitted. He could have his dance, Flora told him; but Major Sedgwick had bid for escort duty ahead of him. Hm!

Under the trees before the commandant's house, young Bill Cody on his pony waited to take the filly. Stuart gave him a dime and he rode off whistling.

"Thank you," Flora said from the steps, "for the best ride I've had in years."

"And I," he echoed. "See you this evening."

Then he, too, rode off, whistling at a rate that would have given Bill Cody something else to aspire to, had he been there to hear.

It could have been written into Army Regulations that young men must sing and dance away the night before a battle or a long march. The music was haphazard, furnished by volunteers from the ranks. The floor of the mess hall needed sanding, but laughter and song and the high beating of hearts made up all deficiencies.

At last Flora met Lieutenant Carey. His hair was dark auburn. He came from the southwestern corner of Virginia—"down yonder where a man has to call in a surveyor to find out whether he belongs to Virginia or North Carolina or Tennessee. I claim Virginia." Mrs. Carey had danced a waltz with him, then had retired, to sit out the rest of the evening, sending him to request of Flora the favor of a quadrille.

"Miss Cooke, I have to thank you for your kindness to Mrs. Carey, and for saving my son from death by drowning. He is your devoted admirer, though I see you have others. Will you risk my awkwardness in this set?"

He was not awkward, except by comparison.

"You'll not find me as light of foot as Beauty Stuart. Where do you reckon he learned to step like that?"

Perhaps he had never needed to be taught. A Stuart—lightness of foot could have come from some Highland ancestor, crowding all the gaiety of an otherwise austere life into an occasional fling on a patch of green to the high, mad shrilling of pipes. But . . . Beauty? What a name!

"We gave him the name when he was a plebe," Carey explained, "largely because he was anything but a pretty lad. Stocky, truculent, always spoiling for a fight and hang the odds, whether for or against him. Nobody thought he'd last out four years; but here he is, eyes front, headed for the top, and still hell-bent on getting there first, if he can make it."

Was there some truculence under Lieutenant Carey's drawl? There could be. It took a stout friendship and perfect loyalty to withstand the strain of army rivalry.

"Honor your partners!"

Stuart again, his blue eyes alight with fun, and warmer than that. Wings on his heels truly. And, after the reel, and a waltz, and another reel:

"Miss Flora, did you bring your guitar? I meant to say. I'll send for it. We're going to have to break this up at midnight. Orders. Lights out for everybody. We would appreciate a song."

The ribbon over her shoulders, strings vibrating under her hand, what should she sing? "Annie Laurie," a Neapolitan serenade? No, she'd save that. For what? Something by Stephen Foster, perhaps, sweet and halfway melancholy.

I dream of Jeannie with the light brown hair . . .

Would he? Out on the stark, treeless plains, only a blanket between him and the earth, alone under the stars, would he dream of her? Would he?

The quick rush of farewells then, and no moment alone.

"Good night. Bless your sweet heart, good night. See you in the morning."

It was the morning she would never forget. Reveille, Stable Call, Mess; and, unbelievably soon, Boots and Saddles. Assembly—the last Assembly for weeks to come, and a matter for smiles as well as tears. Lieutenant Ransome rode out to form the parade. A recruit in the front rank of Troop G was thrown. A breeze of amusement rippled down the line. He remounted and was thrown again. The breeze became a gale. Colonel Sumner barked an order. Ransome rode that way, but Captain Walker had already moved horse and would-be rider to the rear.

At last all was correct. Colonel Sumner rode down the line to the right.

". . . fours! MARCH!"

"They got a lot to learn," Hoskins growled behind a screening tree.

Flora paid no attention. There was a second forward movement now, alongside the riders—women in bonnets and caps, some in shawls, children. With no word of consultation, all chose to follow the regiment to the limits of the reservation, to stand by and watch the gray line drop down the California Road and lose itself among the cottonwoods of Salt Creek Valley. Few eyes were dry.

"I lose count o' the times I seen 'em go," a shawled Biddy mourned, "and it kicks my stummick in still, just the same."

The wagons had gone out earlier, under a sergeant wagon master. The regimental quartermaster called himself a staff officer this morning—and one with liberty of movement. As the last troop filed past, he reined up near Flora. With an extravagance of gesture, he swept off his hat and, reaching down, put a bit of paper into her hand.

"For you," he said. "Nothing, really. An excuse, to hear you say good-bye again. Will you, for me?"

She looked down at the scrap of paper. A freight receipt for a stove. "Lt. Col. P. St. George Cooke, Fort Riley, Kansas Territory."

"If we had not been ordered out," Stuart said, "I think I might have buried it, hoping that so I might keep you near. But now . . ."

She looked up through misting tears.

"Good-bye," she said, hardly above a whisper. "Oh . . . good-bye."

The brightness of his eyes swept over her.

"On second thought, let's not leave it that way. *Au revoir*, my darling. See you . . . soon."

Was it a promise or a wish? She tried to follow him with her eyes
as he rode away, but tears and the dust raised by the horses obscured
everything. He was gone, her heart said desolately, just gone.

Chapter 3. *Special Leave*

The wind blew that day—as it nearly always did in Kansas—but
with awesome ferocity on the open plains—the very open and very
empty plains.

"You're young," people said, because she did not mind the wind.

Perhaps. There were no other women as young at Fort Riley that
autumn, and no towns near. The plains were empty, but they were
also beautiful—gray under gray skies; but sometimes at morning or
evening of a clear day the low sun painted the short dry grass an
enchanting shade of rosy lavender, overlaid with gold.

"You come at the right time of the year," folks said to that. "Too
cold for snakes and too early for snow."

Yes. Riding out from the post, one had to watch only for gopher
holes. In the fine autumn weather she rode often, a number of mounts
needing exercise and a number of escorts being eager to offer their
protection. The escorts were adequate, some of them devoted. Very
nice, except that she remembered . . .

She must not remember—at least, not so constantly. Her father and
the Second Dragoons had ridden home two weeks ago. All the
savage tribes in the north country were now at peace. Colonel
Sumner, the Dragoons reported, had also turned back with the First
Cavalry, to get his men into winter quarters before snow fell. A field
maneuver, a practice march for them, and that was all. The Dragoons, having drawn blood and lost a little, too, maintained a lofty
superiority.

Flora did not relish or approve of their attitude; and, when it came
to mounts, no horse used to a trooper in the saddle was entirely
happy carrying a woman.

"It's you who have the fidgets," Lt. Col. P. St. George Cooke said,
when he rode as escort. "Steady now. Keep a firm hand. Let him

know you're in control, but otherwise loosen up some. Have you forgotten?"

"No," Flora said. "It's just . . . he wants a leg and a boot on the other side of him and a blanket roll and a carbine on the saddle."

At Fort Leavenworth, there had been a filly . . .

She must put even the filly out of her mind now. And she must get over the habit of turning everywhere she went, on the post or beyond, to look up the road that came from Fort Leavenworth. Nobody of consequence would be coming down that road now. Here it was November, and winter just around the corner.

Unexpectedly, now that she was here, she did not hate Fort Riley. Desolate the place might seem, and raw, with its ugly, four-square buildings of wood and stone—green cottonwood and fresh limestone, both cut from the hills near by—its parade and riding field stripped bare of all vegetation, except for here and there a surviving patch of short buffalo grass, now gray and dead in its winter sleep; but the very rawness and desolation soothed her loneliness. She would have hated Fort Riley had it been fairer and more companionable.

The houses were ugly, uncompromising sections of a battlemented wall. They were even uglier inside than they were outside. Since the wooden framework of the walls was green and shrank as it seasoned, no interior plastering was possible. The best that could be done for them was a covering of building paper, held fast by strips of lath, then all painted over to suit a lady's fancy. So they said; but a lady in the days when Fort Riley was new was happier if she did not yield too much to fancy.

All around this man-made ugliness then, Nature at her loveliest. Fort Riley was set in a bend of the Kansas River just below where the Smoky Hill Fork and the Republican River joined. These were mountain streams, their clear, rapid-flowing waters suggesting in no way the yellow turbulence that the Kaw achieved as it gnawed its way through the prairies beyond. Forest trees grew close beside the rivers—dense forests to the west, where the land stepped upward toward the mountains, a border of black and green to the north and the south, where, beyond the rivers, stretched the immensity of the plains.

Every day Flora left the ugliness which was the interior of the post commander's house as much as it was the interior of every other, stood a while on that porch, shrinking out of plumb like all the others, swept her eyes over the ugly reservation, then lifted them to the loveliness beyond or, if she could, rode out to be a part of the grandeur, to lose herself in it. It made no difference really which she did. Inevitably whether she walked or looked or rode, something turned her back to the east. Why?

Eastward there were roads, two of them, tying the isolated fort like cords to civilized country—the Independence Road, the fort's connection with the Santa Fe Trail, and the military road from Leavenworth. Mail came down the latter road regularly twice a week, but so far nothing had come for her and now it seemed probable that nothing would. Here it was November and winter at hand.

This was mail day and she was on her way to the sutler's store with a list of ingredients for Rachel's Christmas pudding. The courier was about due. The sutler's store was beyond the far corner of the parade and the parade was still occupied with morning drill; so she must take the long way around. If she did not hurry, by the time she had completed her errand, the flurry of the mail's arrival should be over. Then, if she were to be disappointed again, fewer people would be around to see.

Her calculations were excellent. The wind kept her from making haste. The rattle of arms drill, dismounted, went on with even monotony as she made the two sides of the parade. She turned into the path to the store. Behind her a shrill whistle broke up the drill.

"Company . . . DISMISSED!"

The mail was in. She leaned against the nearest wall. She fought hard, but the battle was short. Fortunately, when it was over, so many others were racing toward headquarters that her flight in the same direction went unnoticed.

"I have here," Lieutenant-Colonel Cooke said, "a communication from a young man, signing himself, Second Lieutenant James Ewell Brown Stuart, Regimental Quartermaster, First United States Cavalry."

"Yes, papa."

Flora had, naturally, never seen her father officiate at a court-martial. It was said that he did so most ably and justly; and yet, men preferred not to be summoned before him on charges. Flora

thought she knew how they felt. She studied the fine lines of his face
for a weakening that did not reveal itself. His eyes considered coldly
the paper under his hands. His dark blue frock coat was, as always,
immaculate, freshly brushed. All was too alarmingly, frigidly correct.

"The young man," the Colonel continued, "has the audacity, and,
I must admit, the grace, to ask my permission to address himself to
you as a suitor, in short, to come a-courting. Well?"

Flora had no answer ready. Such a glory was over everything—
even this ugly room with its paper walls, stark, in spite of the
Colonel's open fire and his books! She tried the persuasiveness of a
smile. The judge sighed.

"The letter," he said, "stabbed me to the heart, and you give me
no comfort. I'm a busy man, but not without a few tendernesses. I
. . . you can't have known Lieutenant Stuart long."

No, not long, but . . .

Her father, having admitted weakness, allowed himself to fume a
little now. He took the offending letter up in his hands.

"I wish I could put a finger on some more valid objection. The
young man's qualifications, as given here, are excellent. Cadet honors
at the military academy, quartermaster of a regiment within a year
of graduation, commended by his commander in Texas and by
Colonel Sumner. Good blood lines, the Letchers of Virginia on his
mother's side, the Stuarts going back in an impressive line of jurists
and soldiers and Burgesses. The young man, I take it, expects to
do his lineage honor. In fact, he's very sure of it, for a second lieutenant. Now, there's a thing. You would scarcely remember your
parents' early struggles."

"I remember very well," Flora said. "You and mamma managed."

"Did we?" The Colonel studied the ceiling, and his face softened.
"We lived, but," his eyes came down to his daughter's level and he
was once more sternly judicial, "you were a child. What does a child
know of difficulties?"

Nothing, if she was covered with love and laughter and general,
lively activity. It might have been then that she had fallen under the
spell of army life.

"Lieutenant Stuart has given the matter thought, at least briefly,"
Colonel Cooke said now. "Before his regiment marched, he wrote to
his father, asking his consent to marriage, in case he should be suc-

cessful in winning you. I take it the reply from Virginia was favorable, since he doesn't . . ."

"Don't you know?" Flora said. "He must have closed his letter to you before he heard. His father is dead."

"Ah?" Frowning, the Colonel studied the paper in his hand. "I'm sorry. The general impact of this missive was such that I overlooked a postscript. Possibly I was afraid to read it, not knowing what more Mr. Stuart might think of asking. I'm truly sorry. His grief seems genuine."

"Oh, it is. Papa, please . . ."

But now the Colonel was studying her, as if he had possibly overlooked a postscript there.

"Am I to understand you also have had a letter?"

"Yes, papa."

"*Yes, papa,*" her father mocked, but gently. "I don't suppose you'd care to share it with me. It might shed some light on my mental darkness."

"No, papa."

She could not share her letter with him—or anyone else. Begun on a scrap of borrowed paper, while on outpost duty in Dakota:

"What do I do, to keep myself awake? I dream of Flora with the light brown hair."

Finished at Fort Leavenworth, when he had the word from an older brother that his father was gone:

"I loved him dearly. It is hard sometimes to say, 'God's will be done.' "

He didn't sound too submissive, even on paper. Beauty Stuart, fighting against odds too great. She hurt inside—badly.

"Please, papa?"

The Colonel still studied her face, no longer frowning, just looking sad—almost as sad as she felt for young Mr. Stuart.

"The court," he said slowly, "will pursue its inquiry without the aid of other evidence. In spite of brief acquaintance, you have a tenderness for this young man?"

Tenderness? Yes, that was it—a tenderness.

"Does your mother know?"

"I think so, but . . ."

"I wish she had seen fit to share her advance information with me. I should have been better prepared. However . . ."

"But you will see him, darling, when he comes? And you will be nice?"

The Colonel was startled, even out of sadness.

"You mean you are expecting him? Here? Without waiting for an answer to this generally correct, if presumptuous epistle? You are looking for him—soon?"

"I think so, dear. I hope so. You see . . ."

. Before she could begin her explanation, a heavy fist banged on the door, heavy muscles thrust it open, and Sergeant Hoskins burst into the room. His face was dark with the wrath he kept for special people and occasions. He snapped to attention.

"Lieutenant Stuart to see you, sir. It is urgent . . . he says."

"It isn't possible," the Colonel said.

"No, sir, but . . ." he pointed to a window.

All of them looked out. There, tied to the porch rail, a large bay horse and a black filly drooped side by side. Flora caught her father's arm, drew him down to her own height, and laid her cheek against his.

"Darling," she pleaded, "be sweet to him, won't you? For my sake?"

Then she fled, leaving the field to Mr. Stuart. After all, she had things to do. Even she was overwhelmed by his precipitate arrival.

In the parlor, two fighting men faced each other warily. Their first encounter. Not likely to be the last, the younger man hoped and the older man feared. Colonel Cooke felt pretty sure that he would lose the prospective decision—that is, if he could put up any real opposition. Flora had pretty well undermined his defenses.

Not a bad-looking soldier, he thought, this first suitor—the first, that is, to his knowledge. Becomingly modest now that he had come in through a breach in the wall. He waited respectfully for Colonel Cooke to open the interview. But how? The Colonel felt no special animosity, only a general unwillingness. On the other hand, he felt no warmth of welcome. Again he looked out the window.

"Your mount is exhausted," he said crisply.

Mounts, he should have said. Why two? Animosity became more possible. No good cavalryman, with a heart . . .

"I rode them both too hard, I reckon," the young man said. "My time was short. I hope a good feed and a rubdown will restore them."

Soft-spoken resistance, but definitely resistance.

"Have a chair," the Colonel said, taking the one he had abandoned at the visitor's arrival. Fidgety young animal. Well, of course. He had something very much on his mind. His eye kept roving toward the letter on the Colonel's desk.

"I had your letter," the Colonel said. Might as well open fire. "I can't say you allowed me much time to formulate a reply. You must believe in surprise tactics."

"Yes, sir. No, sir." Becoming confusion, but then, "I hope you have no objection."

"Objection? Of course, I object. You are asking me to give you my daughter."

"Yes, sir." Fellow couldn't stay sitting. Had to get up and move about. "Believe me, I think I know how you feel. She is the loveliest . . ."

"Oh, no!" the Colonel said. "I can, having a fair memory, judge your present feeling; but you can't know mine. You won't, until you have a daughter of your own to cherish—and keep, while you can."

He'd hardly realized the girl was grown, admitting, however, to a certain change he'd noted in his brief renewal of their acquaintance during the past two weeks. This young man, if encouraged, could recite Flora's charms by rote. All he, the father, knew was her dearness.

"You speak of objection," he went on—heavily, he admitted to himself. "None to you personally if all you ask is permission to pay attention to my daughter. As to anything more serious—do you mind a practical question? Have you any means of support beyond your lieutenant's pay?"

Pretty abrupt that, but he must establish some sort of advantage.

"None, sir." A brave, honest answer. Thirty-three dollars and thirty-three cents a month, plus subsistence and forage. A few dollars extra as quartermaster. Wouldn't keep a girl in dancing slippers. "But I mean to apply myself, Colonel Cooke. I hope to win honors, to advance as rapidly as circumstances permit."

"Circumstances and the War Department," the Colonel reminded him. "The road to promotion, Mr. Stuart, is a bit longer than from Leavenworth out here. Honors are hard to come by, except in time of war."

"Yes, sir. We discussed that—my father and I—while I was a cadet at West Point."

Ah! The Colonel felt himself trapped in a blunder. He should have begun the conversation by expressing regret over the elder Stuart's death. That would have established a proper paternal attitude. He retraced his steps.

"I am deeply sorry to hear of your bereavement. I lost my father before I was old enough to appreciate him. Still, nothing ever filled the place he would have had in my life."

"No, sir. I am sure of that."

Tears filled the young man's eyes. He made no attempt to conceal them. For the first time the Colonel warmed to him. The fellow was likable enough, if only he had not come courting Flora.

"I can hardly realize," he went on, "that I'll never see him again. You asked about my means. I think his estate was not large. Divided among us—we are four sons and four daughters—well, there it is, sir. I am richer for having known him, but that's all of it, I am afraid."

"Well," the Colonel said, somehow ashamed of his question, "we'll talk about it another time."

And then the scoundrel, seeing an opening, gathered his forces and charged.

"No, sir. I must settle everything now. I am here on short leave— seven days. I have asked for a longer leave, time to go home to Virginia and assist personally in the settlement of my father's estate. If the long leave comes through, what I want is to marry your daughter and take her back to Virginia with me as my wife. Whether it comes through or not, I still want . . ."

Now it was the Colonel who couldn't stay sitting. What he actually said he could never recall. The whole idea was preposterous, unthinkable.

"You are strangers," he stormed.

"No, sir. I can't agree to that. An aeon of time would not alter my feeling, or hers, if she feels as I do."

"No!" the Colonel went down fighting. "No. You are here. I will

put you up at this post, as my guest, for your seven days. You may
address yourself to Flora; but as for anything in the way of an understanding, an engagement, no! No, indeed."

"I never blustered more," he told Rachel afterwards, "or with less
effect. He just stood there, smiling, saying, 'That's how I want it,
sir.' "

"Yes, dear," Rachel said.

"There is no defense against such an attack," the Colonel concluded.

"No, dear. I saw that at once."

Flora, meantime, in her room prettied herself, and schooled herself into a pose of starchy primness meant to carry her through the
moment when she, reinforced by Rachel, should make the visitor
welcome; but, when the moment came, she stammered.

"This is s-surely a surp—prise, Lieutenant."

She couldn't manage another word. His warm, strong hands surrounded her small, cold ones. His presence filled the room—the rear
parlor, Rachel's. His eyes, dark with feeling, commanded her to look
up at him before he spoke.

"You must have known I would come."

Yes. In her heart she had known.

The next day was one of glorious sunshine and the minimum of
wind—for Kansas. There was a morning ride—on borrowed horses.
That command Colonel Cooke could enforce. The bay horse, Dan,
and the black filly must rest in stall and paddock, to recover from
their journey.

"Did you bring her all that way for me to ride?" Flora asked of the
filly.

"She is yours to keep, if you will have her."

How could she keep the filly unless . . . she stroked the soft, dark
muzzle.

"What do you call her?" she parried.

"What we named her that day, if you remember, Mischief."

They mounted then and rode. They explored the Smoky Hill Fork,
the Republican. They ended with a sharp gallop, coming to rest on
a bit of high ground overlooking the post and its immediate sur-

roundings. Below them, the barren clearing was all but hidden by trees, only a few streamers of smoke betraying its location. Everywhere else were the plains.

"It could be the end of the world." Flora pointed to the far horizon.

"Will you ride with me there?" Stuart asked.

"Where?" she said.

"To the end of the world—the moon, perhaps?" Then, before she could answer, he was off his horse and standing beside her. He reached up to lift her down, but then kept her waiting. "What I mean is," he said presently, so earnestly that she felt a slight chill to hear him, "will you ride Mischief back to Leavenworth with me next week—as Mrs. Stuart?"

The night before, she had wondered, waking and dreaming, when or how or whether he would speak to her today of marriage, without ever arriving at her answer. She had no answer ready now. She looked down at him, then away. By chance, her eyes picked up the trace of a narrow, empty road.

"I don't know," she said, "except . . . I think I could not bear it if you rode away alone."

With a cry of poorly restrained exultation, he swung her to the ground, held her a second with his hands, then crushed her to him.

"My darling, my own darling," he said, "I promise you'll never be sorry."

How could she ever be sorry? To be the object of such open, blazing, unabashed adoration as he lavished on her then and, more quietly ever after, set her on a dizzy pinnacle of happiness.

"It frightens me," she said unsteadily, "to be so happy."

He considered the preciousness of her in the circle of his arm. He touched her fine, soft hair reverently with his hand. He lowered his head and sniffed, to catch the elusive fragrance that had haunted his dreams out on the prairie, even with the air full of wet wood smoke.

"It would frighten me," he said, "if I were in my sober senses, which I am not likely to be ever again."

When he kissed her, she thought, if he were not holding me, with his strength, I could not stand.

But he could be a most thoughtful, she learned, as well as a tumultuous lover—studiously thoughtful when he seemed most mad. He had chosen her with his mind as well as his heart.

"You are, you know, a rare person," he said that afternoon in the front parlor. The wind was up now and the Colonel's fire felt good. Flora was arranging tea things on a table and wondering what had become of her father. Rachel was in the kitchen talking to Lily, but where was the Colonel? Stables had sounded an hour ago. She and Stuart had an announcement to make that could not wait.

"You're different," Stuart said, "from any other girl I ever knew."

"How am I different?" she asked.

She would want to cultivate that distinction.

"Just different," he said. "You don't fuss and flutter and sigh and put on. You are just yourself—proud and spunky and sweet . . ." He glanced obliquely toward the rear of the house and sighed. How far off was that kitchen? He and Flora were on their good behavior. He could maintain decorum when the occasion demanded it and wanted that to be plain. "In some ways you remind me of my mother."

"Oh!" Proud, spunky, sweet—was she not beautiful in her own right or even a little charming?

"You don't look like her," Stuart said. "There's no outward resemblance. It's a quality, I think. You'll like each other, I'm sure." If he had only been content to dwell on flower fragrance! "I . . ." he sensed that his compliment was not well directed, "love my mother very much."

He loved a host of people and a host loved him. She never reached the end of the list.

"You . . ." she looked at him, her eyes wet with feeling; and that would have been the end of cold decorum, had not a door opened audibly at the rear of the house and even more audibly a voice outside the front door said,

"Brr! Step inside, Captain, and share a pitcher of toddy?"

Oh, no, Flora thought, he mustn't, whoever the captain was.

He didn't. A few minutes later, while Colonel Cooke was still warming his hands before the fire, she stood beside Stuart and together they announced that, if it could be arranged, they would like to be married the following Tuesday.

The parents took the blow steadily. Rachel wiped her eyes, but between wipes looked beseechingly at the Colonel. He frowned, then turned to Flora.

"Is that how you want it, chick? You are sure?"

"Yes, papa." She went into his arms then, Stuart fidgeting.

Afterwards, Colonel Cooke made one of his funny stories about her *yes, papas*. That was all her argument, he declared. "Yes, papa," and she got into those two words more telling opposition than any lengthy debate he'd ever heard.

However, he sputtered violently when he offered his prospective son-in-law a glass of toddy, and Stuart refused.

"You don't?" he said incredulously. "Not any? Well, I . . . water? You can't always be sure about water. Learned that when I was a subaltern. Now, Bourbon, or good Monongahela . . . well, you must say."

He looked hopefully out the window. How could a man drink a toast, with everybody else taking tea?

"No good to call in Hoskins," he grumbled. "He doesn't, either. Put himself under restraint years ago, standing guard over the whisky barrel at Leavenworth." He waited for Stuart's excuse.

"It was a promise," Stuart said, "I gave my mother when I was a boy."

When he first went away to school. The significant thing, more significant than the mother's reason for asking the promise, was that, having given it, he kept it.

"Damned teetotaler," Colonel Cooke complained later into what he had hoped would be sympathetic ears.

"A young man has to decide *muy pronto*, entering the service," Colonel Sumner answered. "You can't object to him on that score. I wouldn't."

"Didn't decide," Colonel Cooke argued, and told of the promise. "I suppose that's no objection, either. That's my trouble. Can't lay a hand on anything that is. Rides like a centaur. A good shot. Took him hunting one day when the women were busy with a sewing bee. He was the only one of us that bagged a bird. Don't laugh. It isn't altogether funny. Any good at drill?"

"Exceptional." Sumner chuckled. "A pleasure to see—and hear him."

"I'm sure you can hear him. He's a trifle subdued right now. His recent bereavement. But I'll wager he's noisy when he lets go. Sings, you know."

"So do you. I seem to remember . . ."

"Never a circumstance to him. In chapel yesterday he laid into a hymn. Everybody else hushed and let him have it. Did he stop on that account? He did not. Sang solo right through to the Amen."

Stuart hardly knew that he sang alone. Singing, in sorrow or joy, defeat or triumph, was his great release. He had a beautiful voice—clear, melodious, vibrant. His raptness on the song again made little shivers run through Flora. Alternately she felt herself reduced to nothing beside him and then lifted with great pride. She could hardly wait for chapel to be over so that she could present him to the few who did not yet know him.

"This is my young man. This is Lieutenant Stuart."

It was his fervor in so simple a thing as a song that made her shiver. Her adoration was another peril. Rachel, indirectly, spoke to her of that.

"Life will be different, dear. How will you like sitting with the chaperons? Never dancing with another man?"

"I will love it all," Flora answered. "I wouldn't want to dance with anyone else now."

There was one dark thing in the picture, but it took shape so slowly that at first she was unaware of it. The week, for all its enchantment, was a quiet time. Out of respect for Stuart's sorrow, no dancing parties were arranged. The dictum, even Flora perceived, expressed other people's feeling rather than Stuart's. He could have danced without forgetting his grief, with no irreverence to his dead. If he sat quiet too long, with no release, a restlessness built up in him that was likely to escape in strange ways. His invitation to Flora to ride with him to the ends of the earth was one expression of this unbounded energy. Every day he rode with Flora, then again alone. In that way, when evening came, he could just manage a quiet time beside the fire.

Fair evenings to remember, filled with the exchange of talk—army talk mostly, gossip, speculation . . .

"Promotion's a funny thing," Colonel Cooke said one evening. "You take me. There never was a man could capsize a loaded raft or mire a battery or ammunition wagon in better style. I lived in daily anticipation of being cashiered. Fact. One day I picked up a rifle to clean it, and all but murdered my wife."

"Colonel Cooke, really," Rachel protested, "if you would not insist on telling that tale! To begin with, it wasn't your gun."

"My dear, there it is on the record: 'Lieutenant Cooke, special leave, to take wife to hospital.'"

Through the laughter and protest, the implication was clear: "If you, my young friend, would only oblige with a few colossal blunders!"

"When your father talks like that," Stuart commented, "he's only screening the truth. He is a remarkable man, isn't he?"

"Yes," Flora agreed, awarding a smile to both dear ones. But, perhaps, now there had been enough talk. She took down her guitar.

"Shall I sing for you, Mr. Stuart?"

There was music, too, those evenings, Stuart attempting to pick up her songs, but soon abandoning the effort.

"I can't fasten my mind on the words," he said, worshiping her with his eyes. "Later you can teach me. I'll just whistle the tune now."

She was quicker at learning his favorites.

"My father taught us that one," he said more than once, then went on to talk of his father. Then he would have a tale of his mother or a brother or sister. Then friends, all in the distant land of his youth.

"You love Virginia, don't you?" Flora challenged finally. "Better than anything anywhere?"

"Better than anywhere," Stuart admitted. "It's home, my darling."

The way Leavenworth had always been home to her. If only they had been going to stop at Leavenworth!

"I'm jealous," she warned, and laughed, but meant it.

"You absurd little thing! I thought you were a Virginian, too."

"No. Just papa. And he was only fourteen when he went off to West Point. He's been out this way most of the time since he finished. Mamma's people are from Philadelphia originally, but she's all western now. As for the rest of us—Johnnie, Maria, Julia and me—I've told you were all born at western posts."

"I'll readopt you," Stuart promised, "in the name of Virginia."

She was not sure she wanted to be adopted or readopted. She developed finally a state of near panic over Virginia—its various and unknown qualities and quantities. As her wedding day approached, the panic grew. Suppose, she thought, she had been wrong in accepting Stuart's statement that his father, Judge Archibald Stuart, while apparently a delightful person to know, had not been a man of means. Suppose his estate, after all, proved to be a large one, rich enough to provide even for the youngest son the easy life of a Virginia gentleman. Suppose . . . she tried not to think about it.

But the feeling persisted, a reluctance, a foreboding, opposing sweet desire.

The spices, stored, borrowed and bought, intended for a Christmas pudding, went into a wedding cake, instead. Every day someone went hunting—the funeral baked meats, Colonel Cooke sighed, himself assembling ingredients for a bowl of punch. Gifts began to come in—canned fruit, precious bits of linen or glass or silver from army treasure chests, Indian jewelry and pottery, a blanket from Saltillo in Old Mexico.

"It will cover a lot of wall," the donor said.

Colonel Sumner came over from Leavenworth. He brought Stuart's long leave, and a buffalo robe.

"Tuck it into your carriage," he advised. "You can't trust November weather. Highly hazardous."

Precious old fusser! When the time came, the robe was tucked into the carriage, but over Flora's trunks. The carriage was to leave Fort Riley early in the morning of the wedding day. The driver was to proceed nineteen miles east by road to the crossing of the Big Blue River, stop at the "commodious residence of Mr. and Mrs. Elzey Bingham," and there await the arrival of the bridal couple, following by horse. The plan seemed to Flora and Stuart entirely feasible. There were four possible stops between the two forts, the accommodations for travelers never commodious; but at each place a room could be had. The carriage would be sent ahead each morning and each evening be waiting for them with the trunks. If riding proved too arduous or the weather turned foul, they could always descend to the ease of cushions and buffalo robe. However, they did not anticipate bad weather or any other difficulty.

Sure enough, the fourteenth of November dawned with a mere hit and miss scattering of woolly clouds in an otherwise bright sky. Stuart, who slept at the Big House, Riley's Bachelors' Hall, was awake, as always, at the first note of reveille. He scrubbed himself with a pail of water an orderly brought, and hurried off to the stables, to make sure Dan and Mischief were fit. Hoskins was in the filly's stall, fussing with straps on a new side saddle, a beautiful affair of Spanish leather, his wedding gift to Flora: "I taught her to ride, sir."

"I've exercised her twice with it now, sir," he said, taking the saddle away and making room for a man with brush and curry comb. "She takes to it easy."

He had not yet shown the gift to Flora. His attitude toward Stuart and the marriage remained stiff, unyielding, a curious replica, for his station, of the attitude of Lieutenant-Colonel Cooke: "I must, I suppose, make the best of what I can't stop. They tell me you are a splendid young man, but I dunno . . . yet."

Stuart examined the saddle again, admired it, and went on to see about the carriage. The driver had the horses hitched to it, and was ready to pick up the trunks.

"Well, get along," Stuart said.

His impatience was on his own account. He was not due to report for the marriage service until shortly before eleven. That was an eternity of hours away and how would he fill them?

"Hello, there. Where do you think you've been? I couldn't imagine . . ."

Captain Richard Anderson of the Dragoons, who had offered to be best man, stood in the wide door of the stable. He was a kindly-spoken, level-eyed, likable man, but over-conscientious in the performance of duty. He had seen Stuart to his quarters the evening before and now here he was this early in the morning. Bugle notes split the frosty air. Breakfast call, but the bridegroom wasn't hungry.

"Well, I am," Anderson said, and took him firmly in tow again.

At five minutes before eleven, still under escort of the tall captain, himself and attendant shaved, shined, brushed and pressed to the last half inch, Stuart knocked on the door of the post chaplain's residence. They would walk with him to the chapel.

"Had no idea so much footwork was involved," Anderson grumbled gently.

At a quarter past eleven, Stuart stood near the small wooden altar, decorated with artificial greenery and pine boughs, facing forward, and saw, as nobody else could, his exquisite girl coming toward him, a vision in white silk and lace, her face pale, but composed. Just before she reached the altar, she raised her eyes; and the color of the sky—blue depths and gray shadow—was caught in them. His flower—his—now and forever.

To Flora, the day had no laggard hours. Her wedding day, and it rushed by. Chaplain Clarkson read the marriage service, she thought, with indecent haste. When it was over, she turned and saw for the first time how the chapel was packed with people. Outside there were even more. They lined the way clear to the door of the Colonel's residence; but Stuart now rushed her past all of them, as if he didn't want anybody else to see her but himself.

At home, dinner was served immediately. Colonel Sumner had his watch out and was still fussing about the hazards of November. Dinner over, while the toasts were still being drunk, she was upstairs and changing into her riding clothes; and there, all at once, the panic she had fought off through the week crowded in upon her. She wanted to sit right down on the floor where she was and say she couldn't go on. She couldn't. Truly she hadn't realized . . .

Rachel came over and put her arm around her.

"Dear, I had Lily fix you a cup of tea, with milk. Drink it now and try to eat the biscuit, too. I don't think you took a mouthful at noon. You must eat, you know."

But downstairs, where the horses waited, Rachel's eyes, too, were bright with tears. Hoskins stood at Mischief's head. Colonel Cooke helped Flora mount, brushing Stuart aside with a brief, "My privilege still, sir." Flora leaned forward and said her last good-bye to the sergeant:

"Good-bye, Hosky. It's a beautiful saddle. I'll keep it always."

And they were away, leaving everybody just standing there. It wasn't until they had left the fort well behind, the bare plains stretching out ahead, that Stuart came close and spoke: "My darling, are you crying, too?"

"No," she said. "At least, I can't think why I should." Her hand groped for his. "This really is the end of the world now, isn't it?"

He covered her hand with his, strong, warm, reassuring. He swung it to and fro boyishly, squeezed it, and let it go.

"Close column!" he said huskily. "Forward—at a trot—MARCH!"

Chapter 4. *Virginia Honeymoon*

Alec Stuart met them at the Wytheville, Virginia, depot. William Alexander Stuart, the oldest of the brothers.

"Alec, I reckon," Stuart said toward the end of the journey, trying, at Flora's insistence and because he liked to talk of the family, to tell her a little more about this one and that, "will sort of take pa's place now."

Alec had his home and a law office in Wytheville. He was married, his wife the widow of a cousin—Cousin James Ewell Brown, from whom James Stuart had his imposing given name. They had two children, boys. Alec, Stuart said, had other interests besides law—leather tanning, a sawmill; and lately he had taken a hand in improving and expanding the production of salt at a village named Saltville, southward, in Patrick County, near the family home, Laurel Hill.

What astonished Flora was her husband's tone of reliance, almost dependence. Was Alec so much older?

"Well," Stuart said, "I remember him as a man grown when I was still a bleating lamb, crying for my mammy."

His mammy, Alec, Saltville, Laurel Hill—Flora conned the lesson and snuggled closer to her dear love in the little railroad coach, not too clean and alternately steaming, then frigid.

It was dusk when the engine chuffed to a stop at Wytheville, and a light snow was falling. Steam from the locomotive spread a frozen fog over the platform. It was cold and windy. Not like Kansas, where the wind could knock a person over. This was a sly wind, with a cutting edge. Then out of the frozen fog came this man, looking twice his natural size because of a long, rough overcoat, to which had been added a plaid shawl, muffling him to the edges of his hat.

"Jeems?" The first time Flora had heard that. "Missed you—almost."

The two brothers embraced; and then the big man was holding Flora's hands and, even in that poor light, making an appraisal.

"Welcome to Virginia," he said.

He had a pleasant, slow way of speaking, not a drawl, just deliberate. There was a buggy and team waiting, he told them.

"We could walk," James Stuart suggested. He stood now with his face turned upward, his mouth open, tasting the snowflakes, as if they had a special relish.

"Get there faster if we ride," Alec said.

They rode, Flora, in spite of her full skirts, tucked between the two brothers on the seat of the buggy. The horses were colts and skittish; but Alec controlled them easily. There was, at least, that point of resemblance.

"Have a hard journey?" he asked.

"It was long," Stuart conceded.

Had it seemed long to him? Flora had wished that some of it might be longer.

"How's ma?" James asked then.

"All right," Alec answered. "She misses pa."

Ah, poor thing, Flora thought. To have been married all these years to a man as delightful as Judge Stuart seemed to have been, and then to lose him!

"Is she here with you in Wytheville?" was the next question.

"No," Alec said. "At home. None of us could persuade her to leave."

Well, of course not, if that was where memory lived on.

"It would have been easier," Alec continued, "if she had been willing to be here for a while. A good many legal quirks to settling an estate. It will mean a lot of traveling back and forth for others this way. However, that's how she wants it. I wouldn't argue the point."

He didn't sound irritated. He was just saying how things were.

"I must get down to Laurel Hill soon," James said then.

"Yes," Alec agreed, "she will be expecting you."

In the dark Flora felt him turn, to look at her. Unaccountably, at least to herself, she shivered.

"Are you cold?" he asked.

She declared she wasn't. Then she knew she was—like ice from head to foot. Alec stopped the horses, handed the lines to James, and began to unwrap his shawl. She protested. He ought not to expose himself now, having had his ears covered. There was really no reason. He laid the shawl around her shoulders.

"It could be your jacket's too thin," he suggested.

It wasn't a jacket. It was a mantelet of velvet, warmly lined, one of her most fashionable pieces. She had hoped . . .

"A shame, too, when it's so pretty." He lapped the shawl and tucked in the ends, so that she was fairly pinioned. Then he took back the lines and they went on. On the other side of her Flora felt her husband chuckling. The scoundrel! Why hadn't he told her Alec was like this?

Perhaps he had thought he was telling her. At home, divested of outer wrappings, Alec was in appearance an older, more settled version of James Stuart. Not quite so colorful, certainly not so noisy. His eyes were a less vivid blue, his hair thinning on top, and his limbs were strung more loosely, but that could have been due to the lack of military drill in his life. When he was amused, laughter was a twinkle in his eye, a twist of his lips; but she was glad, she found, that he could be amused. There was too much sober seriousness in his face; and it wasn't just lately, she thought, that a restraint had been put upon him or a burden given him to bear. Probably it had always been like that—a born responsible person. The only reason why he had mellowed instead of souring was that he took most things as they came and bore them the best way he could, without fussing. Flora had an idea that his sweet brown-haired wife had wrapped the shawl about him when he set out for the depot, and he hadn't wanted it but accepted it to please her. No need in making her unhappy over a little thing like that, was there?

"I think," Flora said at the end of that first evening, "I'm going to like Brother Alec very much—when I get to know him."

"I told you so," Stuart said. "But what makes you think," he teased, "that you'll ever get to know him? Alec's deep," and he added, "like you."

Was she deep, she asked in surprise.

"Deep as a well," Stuart informed her, but fondly.

The snow delayed their visit to Laurel Hill; but it was a beautiful day when they finally set out, a light wind chasing the last patches of cloud from a dazzling winter sky, the mountains sharp and clear,

blue or snow-covered, against the horizon, the colts—Alec's naturally
—dancing in anticipation of a run. Virginia in her Christmas best,
Stuart said, noisy and cheerful with a fresh lot of happy anticipa-
tions. So was Mrs. J. E. B. Stuart dressed in her best, Flora reminded
him. At the last minute she had decided that, regardless of freezing
temperatures, her coat must be the velvet mantelet. She would accept Alec's shawl for extra warmth; but, at the end of the journey,
when the peelings came off, she, Flora Cooke Stuart, must be there
underneath all.

"I surely hope so," Stuart said, kissing her on the mouth right out
in front of Alec and his family.

"Mr. Stuart, you scandalize me," she whispered.

"Ha!" he said. "Don't you believe it. The family is just meeting
you but they've known me a long, long time."

A beautiful day. The miles were nothing to the strong legs of the
young horses. Still, what with stopping to water and breathe them,
stopping so that the Stuarts could exchange greetings with everybody from preacher to blacksmith along the way, it was midafternoon when they turned off into a narrower lane, barred presently
by a wide gate, opening into the dooryard of a snow-thatched farmhouse.

All the way up the lane, their approach was heralded by a wild
screaming, not of pain or terror, but excitement. When the horses
were visible through the trees, an extra loud shriek climaxed the
screams and the gate was flung wide by a strapping young Negress,
who had posted herself there to give the first word of their coming.

"Bellors?" Flora asked uncertainly. "Is it Bellors?"

Among the reminiscences exchanged by Alec and his brother
while the snowstorm held the younger Stuarts at Wytheville, were
tales of two Negro playmates of "Jeems's" childhood, named, incredibly, Dollors and Bellors. Their mother, it seemed, the cook at Laurel
Hill and a woman of sentiment, had conceived a great admiration
for a visiting lady of Spanish extraction, and had vowed that her
next girl baby should have her given name—Dolores. When the baby
came, however, it was twins. Hence Dollors and Bellors. And Dollors, because she had been expected and had a welcome waiting,
was always a tractable girl; but Bellors from the beginning had
been a rip.

"Just harum-scarum," Jeems said, his eyes shining, "and fun."

Alec hemmed a little. There was a story that Bellors had indirectly caused her mother's death, that, following an argument, she had threatened the cook with a stick of firewood, causing her to fall down the steps to the spring house and crack her head on the stones.

"I never believed it," Jeems said. "No matter how many sticks you found lying about. Poor Bellors! Everybody always ready to think the worst of her!"

Alec shrugged off the story. There was, possibly, some doubt about it.

"You wouldn't want to take her off ma's hands, would you?" he said the next minute, in his slow, easy way. "It's a thing we're going to need to consider. I mean—generally. There are more people at Laurel Hill than the farm needs or can support. Ma won't sell anyone born on the place, if she can help it."

He was just talking, surely. In the new household Flora and Stuart were planning, a servant could have a place, preferably a body-servant for Stuart, but never, in any case, a potential murderess.

So, now, this was Bellors, the wild creature screaming like an African priestess gone mad, dancing and leaping. Twice it looked as if she would fling herself into the path before the horses and be trampled, but each time she bounded clear. Then a clear voice called from the house steps.

"Bellors, stop that noise. Be still."

The capering ceased. Stuart, seeing a boy now at the horses' heads, dropped the lines, and was out of the buggy instantly, and running up the walk to the house, where his mother waited.

"Jemmie! Oh, Jemmie!" The clear voice broke on the cry.

Tears stung Flora's eyes. To see her dear love holding his mother so! Tenderly, as only he knew how to hold a woman, his generous heart expanding to enfold all her pain or sorrow or longing. All hers for that moment, at least.

All hers. Protective instinct dried Flora's tears; and she stood up, to unfold the shawl. *When the peeling is off, I want to be there—me.*

"Joe's got tight holt on de hosses. You don' need to be skeered to step down."

Bellors leered at her from beside the buggy. Meaning to smile, no doubt; but Flora shrunk away.

"Thank you," she said. "I'll wait for Mr. Stuart to help me."

Trying to prepare her child for some of the difficulties she might face, Rachel Cooke had said to Flora back in far-off Kansas:

"Dear, you will be a stranger in a strange land. Lean upon your husband. Then remember to think of others before you think of yourself. Their feelings, not yours, when they see you for the first time. Mr. Stuart's mother in particular. She has had a great loss and your husband is her youngest son."

How had Rachel known? Flora's first reaction to her mother-in-law was that she would never be fond of her. She couldn't get near enough to her. The awe she felt was almost equal to that of the servants, all of whom showed a measure of the wild Bellors' instant obedience.

The elder Mrs. Stuart—ma or Mother Stuart to a large family—was a tall woman—almost as tall as her Jemmie. Her hair was brown, fading into gray. About her eyes Flora couldn't be sure. They seemed hazel in some lights, sometimes gray—faded, too, perhaps. She was a well-fleshed woman, her face not so much wrinkled as lined, her mouth strong and tightly held, though it could quiver and soften with emotion. All in all, she was too strong and self-sufficient for a stranger's well-meant sympathy to find much encouragement; and her strength was double here at Laurel Hill, where she ruled, entrenched behind undisputed possession.

The pleasant, comfortable home, spacious until the family began to pour in, admirably served by its too numerous but well-trained hands, was hers, Stuart had explained, an inheritance from her own people. She had managed it herself always, the Judge, her husband, having little time for such business and being much away from home; and she had managed it well. The farm had taken care of all of them, Stuart said. Did "all," Flora began to wonder, include the Judge? It was only a fancy, but it gathered force now that she had met Elizabeth Pannill Stuart face to face, and more when she saw a portrait of Archibald Stuart, Judge, Burgess, Member of Congress and all else that he had been.

The portrait hung above the fireplace in the large common room. The painter had got to the life the ruddy complexion, the bright blue eyes, the high good humor of the subject.

"Well?" Mother Stuart said, when Flora stood quiet before the picture.

Out of the many thoughts that occurred to her, Flora chose the one on which she and the older woman would most surely agree. "There is a strong resemblance."

It was more than resemblance. It was almost identity.

"I could ask nothing better," Mother Stuart said, almost defensively, "than that Jemmie should follow in his father's footsteps."

Oh, but she had asked something better. There was that promise she had demanded when Jemmie was a boy going off to school, a promise that in manhood made him still a firm abstainer from alcoholic refreshment. There was no stern abstention in that face over the mantel. There was James Stuart's devoutness at worship. That, too, he must have been taught by his mother. Again Flora chose her reply with care.

"Don't you think he is well suited now by a military career?"

"Is he?" the mother said, just as cautiously. "I wonder."

She crossed the room then to a cabinet of small treasures standing against the far wall, unlocked it, and brought out a framed daguerreotype.

"Jemmie, when he was a cadet," she said, superfluously, as she opened the frame and handed the picture to Flora.

"Oh!" Flora said, ecstatic over the boy's face—so young, so fiercely solemn. "Isn't he sweet?"

"Yes," the mother agreed, "he was. Jemmie was always a sweet lad—even when he was in trouble."

Oh? A sweet lad, but possibly a little turbulent? Flora's expression must have betrayed her question. His mother smiled indulgently.

"Jemmie was impulsive," she explained. "We never knew when he was away what whim would seize him. Like when he joined the Methodist Church during a revival meeting, all of us at home being Episcopalian."

Yes, he had told Flora about that. What troubled her now was— did his mother think of a wife as a whim? It seemed possible.

"You spoke of a military career just now," Mother Stuart went on, not noticing. "I had as well tell you that wasn't my choice for him."

No? Then it had been his father's idea? Not even that, it seemed. A friend in Washington, thinking to do the Judge a favor, had got the appointment to West Point for Jemmie. Even then the Judge wasn't sure, but he said Jemmie had as well give the Academy a trial. If he didn't like it, he needn't finish.

"And the funniest part of all is," Jemmie himself said, coming in right then, fresh and cold from a bit of outdoors, "I didn't like it at first. I wasn't sure right up to graduation; but now," he put his arm around Flora and drew her to his side, "I like it fine—all of it."

"Do you, dear?" his mother said, and took the daguerreotype from Flora and locked it away in the cabinet. Flora had an idea—absurd, no doubt—that she would have liked to do the same with her son, had it been possible.

"Your father," Mother Stuart said to Flora that evening after supper, when the three of them sat together before the fire, "getting acquainted," "has a peculiar name."

"St. George?" Flora loved the name, the high, proud sound of it, and the story behind it. "His mother came from St. George in the Bermuda Islands. She loved her home and named her first son for it." Lovely, legendary Catharine Esten Cooke—had she, too, been homesick in Virginia?

"You should know Colonel Cooke," Stuart said to his mother. "Now, there is a real soldier. The *ne plus ultra*, really. I do wish you could know him."

"I doubt," his mother said—coldly, as Flora's spirits rose, "that I shall ever have the privilege. Kansas is much too far away.

Stuart had already spoken of their wedding journey. Now, teasing her, he went over the route again—across Kansas by horse, down the Missouri by boat to St. Louis, another boat to Memphis, finally the railroad across Tennessee into Virginia.

"And when we go back," he said, greatly amused by her horror, "it will be worse. We'll have to cross most of Missouri by stage. No boats are running now."

"Don't talk about going back," his mother said sharply.

The next day one of the sisters, Mary Stuart, came down from Staunton, where she taught in a young ladies' seminary. She was, again, a graver edition of James, a little starchy in manner. She brought a Richmond paper with a report on Kansas. It was snowing out there. It had been snowing ever since the first of December. Thirty inches covered the ground when the report had been sent in and more was falling. A longing for the clean, stark whiteness swept over Flora. She could almost not bear it. Stuart, seeing her pinched face, put his arm around her and tried to amuse her and the others with a tale of Rachel's stove.

"Well, I'm thankful we manage without them," his mother said.

They managed, Flora thought, but not too well. In spite of the general comfort of the house, she was always cold—unless she sat practically in the hot ashes.

"Will you live in a house like that?" Mother Stuart asked, meaning commandant's quarters.

Stuart shouted at the idea and drew her a picture of the clapboarded log cabins that made up Officers' Row at Fort Leavenworth.

"We'll be lucky to have one at that," he said. "A second lieutenant doesn't rate very high. We may have to double up with another couple."

All bright and brave and meant to be cheery, but Flora didn't like the look on her mother-in-law's face. She meant to do something better for her Jemmie.

Upstairs, in what had once been the boys' room and now had been given to her and Jemmie, Flora complained of a headache.

"That darling head?" Stuart said. "Does it hurt—terribly? Rest it here and I will kiss the pain away. So and so and so!"

She slept finally, but fitfully, dreaming once that Bellors was chasing her down a long road, brandishing a knife. Again Stuart soothed her and quieted her. In the morning, however, her eyes were glued shut and her throat ached. Every bone in her head ached. Finally she let go with a great sneeze.

"Horrors!" she gasped. "I'm taking cold."

She had a cold. A frightful one. Stuart was beside himself with anxiety. He called for his mother, for Mary. When did they expect John? John was a doctor brother. Not till tomorrow? Well, what was that stuff his mother used to give them when they had colds? He left Mary in attendance and Dollors at the foot of the steps to call him if he was needed, and disappeared into the kitchen quarters.

Some time later he tiptoed back into the bedroom carrying a pitcher of the vilest smelling stuff. It could well have been poison. Flora would have been sure of it if he hadn't brewed it.

"My turn," he said, managing a weak grin. "Down with it—every drop."

She downed it. The reek was the worst. Almost immediately she began to warm up inside. She looked up at Stuart and, on the verge of a smile, had a better thought. She closed her eyes and squeezed out a tear. It wasn't hard to do that day.

"Don't leave me," she begged.

Stuart stood by the bed in an agony of inaction until he could bear it no longer. He made a sudden swooping motion and gathered her, with a pair of blankets, into his arms. A wide chair stood before the fire. He carried her there and sat down, still holding her, covered her feet carefully, and tucked a trailing end of blanket carefully around her.

"Poor, miserable little suffering thing!" he murmured, then, feeling that something special was required, "*Ma petite . . . ma povere petite Floore!*"

That awful French! She couldn't help laughing. She began to shake again, frightening him afresh. His arms tightened. He thought she was having a chill. Fortunately her face was hidden. It would not do—it would never do for him to know.

"I'll be all right," she sighed. "Just—just go on talking."

How could he, he demanded, worried as he was. But he tried. Presently in desperation he broke into a song.

"In the sweet bye and bye . . ."

"Ah-h-h!" she sighed.

What would his people think? Well, what? What was Stuart thinking? That was more important. Possibly that he was a husband first and a son second? Presently, soothed by the warmth of his arms and the fire, or it could have been the nauseous syrup, she drowsed. Cautiously he rose and carried her to the bed. She opened her eyes sleepily.

"Don't leave me," she sighed.

All that day and half the next she held him captive. She could almost see him pondering the gravity of his responsibility—a thing he had taken perhaps too lightly before this. If he had been a tender lover before, anxiety made him doubly attentive now. He was not easy if he had to be away from her for more than an hour. Such a hush was now on everyone and everything that Flora, on the point of declaring herself cured, again thought better of it and took her time. Alec Stuart, riding over a few days later, with a stack of legal documents, found her enthroned in the best chair, her face peeking out from a zephyr shawl, her feet on a stool.

"I hear you've had a cold," he said gravely. "I hope you're better."

When she thanked him and said, yes, much better, unexpectedly he patted her shoulder before going on about his legal business.

There was a general gathering of the clan over the Christmas holiday, some staying at Laurel Hill, the rest at Wytheville. Virginia, after this, was to Flora largely a matter of people coming and going. She herself remained at Laurel Hill, contenting herself with short outings to this and that remembered place near by, always in the company of her husband. In the family discussions involving a partition of Judge Stuart's so-called estate, she carefully took no part, usually carrying a book off to her own fireside.

So, finally, under Alec's patient guidance, a settlement was made. For his share, Jemmie was given title to some questionable St. Louis real estate, apparently acquired by his great-grandfather, another Judge Stuart, who had spent some time in Louisiana Territory when Thomas Jefferson was President. The claim had lain dormant so long, Stuart said, that he didn't believe it would amount to much. He was sorry.

"Aunt Lizzie Collins will know," Flora said, so happy over a number of things that she could hardly trust herself to speak. Here it was January, their leave almost over, and Stuart making preparations to depart with her for the West. Whatever else had been planned for him, whatever his mother wanted, the plans had come to nothing. Flora studied his face now, trying to tell whether he was glad to go or regretful. A little of both, she decided; or, perhaps, he was reluctant only to tell her of lesser bequests.

"Jemmie thinks you must be leaving now," Mother Stuart said.

"Yes," Flora answered. "It wouldn't be safe to wait any longer."

Mrs. Stuart had the daguerreotype in her hands. Oh, poor dear! She mustn't really . . . but she didn't, after all.

"Jemmie thinks you would rather have this than anything else here; and so I have put your name down for it. It is to be yours some day, but not now. I can't give it to you now. I hope you understand."

Yes. Flora had a moment of shame.

"Mother Stuart," she said, "believe me, you'll never be sorry. About your Jemmie being a soldier, I mean. He will make a splendid name for all of us some day."

"Well, time will tell."

Mother Stuart put the picture away again, but brought out another packet. Flower seeds, of all things!

"Some of everything I grow here at Laurel Hill," she said. "Jemmie may have told you about my garden?"

"Often," Flora said. "Oh, Mother Stuart, what a lovely thought. I will carry them home myself. When spring comes I'll get help and plant them carefully, and keep them watered."

"Well," Mrs. Stuart said, "you are welcome, I am sure. I haven't any idea that they will grow and bloom—in Kansas; but . . . you are welcome."

If that had been all; but it wasn't. Jemmie, it seemed, was now gravely concerned lest his dear little wife's strength might prove unequal to the rigors of the life she faced so bravely. So, his mother, who was giving each of her children someone among the surplus hands at Laurel Hill, had given him his choice.

Oh, no! Flora thought. He wouldn't. But he had. Bellors.

"She's wild," Mrs. Stuart agreed, "but a good girl, really, and devoted to Jemmie. He knows how to handle her. She's strong, excellently suited to the primitive conditions of your life out yonder."

But they weren't that primitive. My punishment, Flora thought, for something.

"Surely," Mrs. Stuart said, "you're not afraid of the girl."

Surely Flora was afraid. She tried to tell Stuart. He laughed. Was his wife that kind of a goose? Look! He felt he had to take Bellors. He felt sorry for the girl. Nobody here seemed to want her. She would be all right out west, he thought. Was she willing to go? She was overjoyed at the prospect.

Finally Flora asked him if he thought it wise to take a slave back to Kansas right now. With feeling so excited about that? Both the Cooke servants were free people. It was exactly what she should not have said to Stuart. Did she think for a minute, he wanted to know, that any man—Border Ruffian or Jayhawker—would molest an army officer because of his property—whether man, woman, horse or dog?

Flora began to see that her idol was not a man with whom one progressed far through argument. They took Bellors. She was quiet enough when the day came for them to board the chuffing, snorting train, westward bound now from Wytheville. While Stuart put Bellors into her place, Alec had a few last words with Flora.

"You're quite sure, I hope," he said in his slow way, "that we here in Virginia have your best interests at heart out yonder."

"Oh, Mr. Stuart," Flora began.

"Brother Alec," he suggested; and this time his unexpected gesture was to brush her cheek with his lips. "Sister, come see us again . . . real soon."

Chapter 5. *Married Quarters*

"And, after Virginia, to come home to this!" Lucy Carey said.

This was a house, Flora's and Stuart's first, and all their own. While they were away, a Captain McClellan, who had been only a name on the regiment's roster, he himself being absent on leave for foreign study, had resigned. This had meant two promotions below the rank of captain, and Stuart had now his first lieutenant's bars.

And a house. It was a two-room log cabin, clapboarded outside and roughly plastered within. The plaster was cracked, but the Saltillo blanket covered the worst crevice. The furniture was meager—mostly barrels and boxes brightened with calico cushions; but it sufficed. The house was cold. It was the coldest winter that anyone in Kansas could remember; but the buffalo robe kept them warm at night and made a luxurious divan of the bed by day; and, taking a tip from Rachel, they had stoves. Wonderful, everyone said, to be the wife of the quartermaster, with first go at supplies and command over guardhouse labor.

Wonderful, Flora thought, to be the wife of First Lieutenant J. E. B. Stuart. It seemed to her that, with his promotion, he had grown an inch taller. Certainly the gravity of new responsibility was most becoming.

Sing jubilee, jubilo—tonight, to celebrate the promotion, the Stuarts were having a party. They had begged for a week of grace, just one week. As it was, their guests must bring their own plates and cups and cutlery; but most of a young pig was now roasting in the iron stove in the kitchen. Stuart would bring home fresh bread from the post bakery. There would be coffee, canned peaches—he had seized them the day before—and cucumber pickles. And music and talk—they were months behind on regimental gossip.

Sing jubilee—crash! A terrific downfall of some sort kitchenwards. The stove? Or Bellors?

Most probably the latter. Flora knew she ought to investigate, but she rebelled. A short while before, lost in happy dreaming, she had forgotten Bellors. She didn't want to be reminded now. Also she was afraid of what she might discover in the kitchen. She . . .

"Surely you're not afraid of the girl?"

Her mother-in-law's incredulity brought Flora to her feet. She laid aside her work—a rag rug she had been braiding—and listened. From the kitchen now came scuffling noises. The back door opened. A minute later it was closed, with another crash. Now, really, she must go. If anything had happened to her supper! No, not just yet. Wait.

From the direction of the parade, a thin sound of whistling promised reinforcements. The cheerful notes gained volume. Heavy boots crunched over the frozen snow, with a muffled jingle of spurs. The next minute Stuart was pounding ice off heels and spurs against their door jamb. Flora, weak with relief at his coming, remained in the shadow of the door as it swung back and he entered, shaking himself like a big dog. He dropped an oilcloth-covered bundle on the table, beat his hat some more against his leg, still whistling, then, assailed by the seeming emptiness of the house, broke off.

"Flora!" he called. *"Ma pet . . ."*

"Good sir," she said behind him, "you startled me. I thought from the sound we had a flight of bobolinks."

"Bobolinks, eh?" He smothered her in his arms, kissed her hungrily. It had been four hours since their last parting.

She hated then to bring up the subject of Bellors but there was no help for it. Whistling a graver tune, Stuart gathered up his bundle

of supplies and went out to see. In a few minutes he was back, half
laughing, half angry, buttoning his coat and reaching for his hat.
"The coffee boiler," he reported. "Smashed. I'll get another."
"Stuart, how . . ."
"Dropped it. Broke off the lid."
"But we could still use it."
"Not this one," Stuart said. "She threw it out."
In a fit of temper—that was the door opening and closing—bang!
It was the custom at the post, not too elegant but expedient, to dis-
pose of refuse by stepping out the back way and flinging it as far
as possible. Dogs, rabbits, and time reduced the deposit and every
so often a scavenger detail cleaned the premises. This was the part
of housekeeping Bellors enjoyed most. The Stuarts shuddered to
think what a sudden thaw might reveal behind their cabin. Now
the coffee boiler had been added, sunk, no doubt, because of its
weight and heat, in the depths of a drift.
"We could borrow," Flora began, but did not go on. They must
not borrow any more, not while they had Bellors.

The party, everything notwithstanding, was a great success. The
girls sat on the bed and the two barrel chairs. The boys folded their
overcoats for cushions and sat on the floor. Where else in the world,
Flora wondered, could a person find such easy, joyous comrade-
ship?
The food was hot, delicious and abundant. Everyone's appetite,
even fastidious Lucy Carey's, was sharp. Talk, however, especially
to one who had been away for three months, was the best of the
feast. In its more serious phase, it dealt chiefly with promotions.
Who would be the next lucky dog or dogs? These things were hard
to calculate with a group of men very even in their claims, but nobody present hesitated to figure out a few answers. Sometimes a hot
spark of dispute had to be quenched before it blazed into uncomfortable argument; but it was good talk, rich, and lusty as the young
men who tossed it back and forth.
From promotions to whiskers. There was more fierce competition
in the regiment that winter over those. The idea, aside from prevailing male fashion, had been inspired by an army ruling: "No whiskers
below the jawline except for the cavalry." So the cavalry felt bound

to take advantage of the exception. Stuart, who had scraped his chin
for his wedding and his visit home, was off to a late start; but, even
so, it looked as if here, too, he might give his brother officers a race
for final honors. His rivals, again setting themselves up as judges,
thought a beard was what his face needed. That chin was all right
for a bulldog, but it was not a pretty feature. Flora, seeing nothing
whatever wrong with Stuart's chin—they said it was too short—wondered how much older a beard would make him look. Already
brown stubble seemed to be holding an argument with the clear
blue eyes and the broad forehead above.

Promotions, beards, and finally the weather. Each guest coming
in had announced with a groan that it was still snowing; but a few
thought, hopefully, the night seemed not quite so bitter cold. Sure
enough, as the evening passed, the room seemed to grow warmer.
The stove was allowed to cool to less than red heat. At last, when,
unwillingly, the boldest man present opened the door to let the
company file out for home, he announced with wonder that icicles
were forming on the eaves and beginning to drip. The air was mild.
Downright mild.

"A sirocco, do you think?" he suggested.

Not a sirocco, but the bitter weather was over. By early March
ice was moving in the river, Stables was again a signal for a joyful
stampede to open water, on a stretch of level ground near the fort
Colonel Sumner was marking off a regimental cornpatch, and Flora
was laying out her flowerbeds. At the same time morning and afternoon drill were stepped up; and presently there was another warning that summer held more serious things in store.

A fort was not located and garrisoned just to be a military decora-
tion. It was a salient of the nation's ramparts and the men who were
stationed in it literally kept watch and were forever ready to up
portcullis and ride out to answer an alarm. Jefferson Davis, the Secretary of War, had not asked for and obtained two fine new regiments of cavalry, handsomely officered, because of his delight in
alert soldiering or in horseflesh, though those were part of his nature.
More mounted guards were needed—the Second Cavalry in Texas
to protect settlers there against Comanche and Apache attacks, the
First Cavalry and the Second Dragoons in Kansas to protect settlers

also from Indians, but even more from raiders more terrible than savages because they were men of their own kind, hired and often led by bitter partisans, ordered to burn, to kill, to terrify.

Settlers' wars were not a subject of light talk in social gatherings, and, Stuart said, not much discussed among the men. Partisan politics had small interest for soldiers except as they affected the disposition and movements of troops. It was possible that Eli Thayer and Henry Ward Beecher and others of New England, organizing and arming their Emigrant Aid Society, had no idea of the kind of men who would lead their anti-slavery forces into the territory; and gentlemen from the South, grim-faced over a dwindling majority in Congress, realizing now that a bill dividing Kansas Territory might well give the nation two more anti-slavery states—Kansas and Nebraska—in place of one, had no idea of the reprisals Border Ruffians from Missouri would take against the abolitionist zealots. Whatever the sympathies of the national government, orders from Secretary Davis to the officers commanding the regiments in Kansas were clear. The troops were to engage in no conflict with settlers of either party. They were to arrest and confine men guilty of violence. They were to prevent bloodshed. They were to keep the peace.

It was a task not much to a soldier's liking. Violence and bloodshed could not be forestalled. Squadrons of cavalry and dragoons were moved about like pawns; but, before summer was well begun, death and conflagration hung over the green land like a smoke pall. Stuart, who, with his promotion, had begun to fret over his quartermaster's duties keeping him out of his place in the line, having now no ardor whatever for police work, gave over fuming and settled down almost contentedly to making out requisitions and commanding supply trains.

One morning, still in early March, he appeared unexpectedly at the cabin with a dispatch for Flora to translate. Colonel Sumner's request. "Will Mrs. Stuart be good enough to help on the underlined passages, being more familiar than anyone else here with her father's handwriting:"

Flora sat down at the table, her eyes blurring. Had she missed her own dear people so much—even here?

"Can't you make it out, either?" Stuart asked.

"Plain as print," she said softly. "That's what papa would say—plain as print. Well, I'm ready."

Stuart took out memorandum book and pencil. She read the dispatch to him, raising her hand as she approached the passages in doubt:

> "To prevent hostile collisions . . . not to interfere with people who may have come from a distance . . . behaving in peaceable and lawful manner . . . last resort the effusion of blood of citizens . . ."

Was she prejudiced or were these rather noble sentiments set down in the process of interpreting military orders? Had Stuart noticed? No, he was still writing. When he finished, it was Flora he admired, for being able to read her father's script. He saluted her gravely and, tardily, offered a reward—a letter from Rachel.

"Stuart!" she reproached.

Her way of addressing him. When he became a first lieutenant, Mr. Stuart was not respectful. Lieutenant Stuart was too long. Any variation of James seemed to belong to Virginia. Just Stuart had a sound. So that was it. Always.

He laughed at her from the door. "If you've a mind to write an answer," he teased, "a rider will be starting back this afternoon," and went off, whistling like a blackbird.

That was one thing the summer of fiercest fighting in Kansas meant to Flora—letters to and from dear ones, separated more by circumstance than distance, a rare glimpse of her father, none of Rachel. Travel was too hazardous. Even in the more settled country around Leavenworth, Flora was not allowed, except under escort, to ride Mischief beyond the post limits.

However, aside from restricted movement, life at the fort went on much as usual. Babies were born—among them Lucy Carey's, an exquisite girl child this time—children played, women sewed and planted flowers. Flora put in her Virginia seeds and watered the green sprouts and brought most of them into flower. All, except the China asters. Bellors, having been told to pour all waste water on the garden, threw lye from a soap kettle over the asters. Well . . .

Between times, the women watched their men ride off into the pall of smoke and wondered and waited for their return, and saw them come back, tired, disgusted or grimly silent or full of chatter about everything except what they had seen or experienced.

"Darling, I want just to sit and look at you, and forget."

Some talked in their sleep. Not Stuart. He might ride in at any hour of the day or night. Wide-awake, alert until he had made his report and given his orders, he would end with another sort of report to Flora, unbelievably tender even at his weariest, deliver any messages he carried, then drop like a stone and sleep like the dead, to awaken the next morning, all new, ready to ride wherever his orders took him. He, like the others, talked little, and evasively, of what went on under the dark smoke pall.

"If papa's at Lecompton now," Flora complained one day, "and likely to be there for a while, why can't mamma be with him? It's nearer, and it's a town, isn't it?"

"Lecompton?" Stuart said merely, with high eyebrows.

"Dear me, another sink of iniquity?" Flora guessed.

Stuart smiled. Had she any idea how those words, select and chaste though they were, seemed, coming from her fresh, clean mouth? He kissed them away.

"Sodom and Gomorrha rolled into one," he said lightly, dismissing so that assemblage of grogshops and shanties. "Your father's looking fit. The *ne plus ultra*, really, of commanding officers."

She was as pleased as a child with a sack of candy at his tribute. The *ne plus ultra*, he said again of his father-in-law, and he, Stuart, was glad to learn from him. He had been present, for example, when Colonel Cooke had confiscated a wagonload of "Beecher's Bibles" near the Nebraska border. Now, how had he known that wagon was filled with new rifles? Those had been Free-State lawbreakers; but with fine impartiality the Colonel could stand just as firmly against a partisan mob from the other side.

These bits and scraps Stuart brought home to Flora, knowing she was a soldier's daughter; but the dark scenes he kept to himself. Bloodshed and misery strewed the path of civil strife and much of both fell upon the innocent. Many a weary, ragged child he carried on his saddle that summer, to ease an impossible flight. Many a pale, sorrowing woman he coaxed back to hope, stopping at her lonely cabin for a drink of water, telling her the soldiers were near and she had no cause for alarm, at least, not right now.

"Your husband will be with you shortly, ma'am. There is an order for all militia to disperse, and the men to return to their homes."

That was a good order—to disperse the militia. If the ruffians who led them had no followers, there must be an end to sacking and killing and burning, and the question as to whether Kansas should be a free state or allow slavery would be decided lawfully by vote of the settlers, though this peaceful conclusion still seemed remote. For one thing, you could never tell about the settlers. There was that man Brown, for example.

Stuart's first encounter with the man was early in May, on the main street of Lawrence, another unfortunate town selected to be the seat of uneasy government, temporary at best. The latest territorial governor had got wind of a threatened attack on the town and had asked for military aid. Grudgingly Colonel Sumner had detailed two companies, "to disperse any mobs and arrest anyone making a show of violence." This man and his wagonload were not a mob; and whether their presence was offensive or defensive could not be told on sight. Probably the latter, since Lawrence was a Free-State town. The wagon drawn up before the entrance of a shabby building flaunting its name—"Free State Hotel"—was an arsenal on wheels. It bristled on four sides with home-made pikestaffs—poles with bayonets attached. Of the five men in it, four wore heavy broadswords, the inevitable Bowie knives, two revolvers apiece, and carried rifles, as well. The fifth man, much older than the others, on this day at any rate went unarmed; and yet, he was the most warlike of them all. Seeing him once, a person would never forget him, never confuse him with any other.

Seated beside the driver, his long arms hanging idle over his bony knees, his pale eyes curiously veiled by heavy lids, he was like some strange bird of prey, brooding, just brooding on the scene. Grizzled, tangled hair grew unnaturally low on his forehead. Stuart, riding up to the hotel with a message for a marshal said to be sojourning there, stopped his horse at the far end of the hitching rail and slowly dismounted. He thought, as he tied the horse and turned away, that the driver of the wagon said something to the old man, but the latter gave no heed. He just sat on, brooding.

Then, as Stuart reached the door, the clatter of hoofs announced the coming of more soldiers—Lieutenant Carey with a small detail.

What struck Carey, he said afterwards, was the pikestaffs. This looked to him more like a warlike assembly than anything he'd seen that morning. So he rode up to the wagon to execute his military orders.

"Sorry," he said, politely enough, "you'll have to move on."

The driver of the wagon took up the lines, but the old man stopped him.

"Stay where you be, Solomon!" He raised the curtains of his eyelids to transfix Carey with a glare, perhaps only to get a good look at him, then lowered them again. "Why should we move?" he asked. "We are doing no harm."

"Orders, sir!" Carey said, with more snap.

"Whose orders?" The old man could raise goose pimples on a body with a word.

"Governor Shannon of this territory and Colonel Sumner of the United States Army."

"I recognize the authority of neither," the old man said. "We have met in free assembly and elected our own magistrates . . ."

"You will move at once," Carey interrupted, his dander up, his red hair rising, "or I will place you and your men under military arrest."

A man in the rear of the wagon spoke then, calling the old man pa, and advising him that they had better do as directed. The old man turned to protest, but the one called Solomon took up the lines again and the wagon began to roll.

"Fall in!" Carey said to his troopers and proceeded to escort it out of town.

"The funny thing is," he said to Stuart afterwards, "he went peaceably enough after that. I didn't let him stop until we reached a creek ten miles out. He read me a final curse out there—told me what I might expect if I interfered with the march of righteousness . . . did you get a good look at him?"

"Yes," Stuart said. "I asked about him, too. His name is Brown— John Brown. He's from New England, by way of Iowa. The men with him were three sons and a son-in-law."

"Settlers?"

"The young men are. Farmers down near Pottawatomi Creek. They've been here two years and gave no trouble until the old man moved in with them last winter. A sort of self-constituted missionary, they say. Wields fearful authority over his sons."

"He told me I'd hear from him again," Carey said.

"I shouldn't wonder," Stuart allowed.

John Brown, the farmer of Pottawatomi Creek. But land was not tilled with pikestaff or broadsword. No, nor with proper tools, either, that late spring in eastern Kansas. It was not a year of planting or growing.

John Brown—he made mock of the army's neutrality after Lawrence was sacked and burned by a pro-slavery mob later in that same month.

"With armed might you drove out the lawful defenders," he cried out, "and let in the forces of unrighteousness. You are no protection to the innocent. You are the minions of a government that oppresses the poor and the defenseless and favors holding men and women in bondage."

He was everywhere in his armored wagon calling out to his followers—and he had more and more of them—in his mad, impassioned way, to meet force with force and throw off the yoke of oppression. Slaves began to disappear in western Missouri. It was said but not proved that he helped them get away. He preached violence, but so far he had not been seen to carry a torch in any of the reprisal burnings that followed the sack of Lawrence; and the army hesitated to lay hands on him.

"Not prisons enough to hold all the exhorters," Colonel Sumner said.

And Stuart, who had seen the man only once and felt more and more a squirming of dislike inside when his name was mentioned, had to admit that the Colonel was right, if he meant to abide by orders.

But now it was the pro-slavery partisans who had no patience with a neutral army. Having destroyed Lawrence, they sent a warning to John Brown and his sons on Pottawatomi Creek: "Get out—or we're coming after you."

They set a day—the twenty-fifth of May. On the night of the twenty-fourth John Brown made the rounds of several isolated cabins near the settlement of Osawatomi, forced into the open five leaders of those who had threatened him, and murdered them. Butchered them. Hacked them to pieces with some kind of heavy knife, those who saw the victims said. Broadswords, Stuart thought, broadswords.

Osawatomi Brown, they called the madman after that; and the squirming of dislike in Stuart was a sick loathing.

"Will you arrest him now?" the governor of Kansas asked Colonel Sumner.

"Him and his sons," Sumner answered, stiff with outrage. "We will not rest until we have him."

He had most of the First Cavalry with him at the time down that way, patrolling the Missouri border near by; and he might have made the capture, except for one thing. Stuart as quartermaster had to tell him what that was.

Supplying troops that were called hither and yon without warning was always a problem in the pillaged, fought-over and burned-over country; and stores in the present camp were running low, particularly feed for the horses. Grain which had been purchased in Westport, Missouri, was being held by the partisans whom Sumner had been sent to keep out of Kansas. They would release the grain if Sumner let them cross the river with it now. Otherwise, no!

"No!" Colonel Sumner echoed, just as firmly. "I will not be dictated to by a civilian mob. We'll do this job in an orderly fashion. Keep the grain then. We'll get some down from Leavenworth if we must."

Stuart shook his head and held up two fingers. Two days' supply in camp, no more, he meant.

"You will ride after it yourself, Lieutenant Stuart, to make sure that it comes promptly."

"I . . . yes, sir. At once."

All the way north the spectre of John Brown rode with him, the long arms, the ugly weapons dripping blood. With him or a little ahead of him. He was hampered by heavy rain as night came on, and a tale could spread faster than he could ride. Near Fort Leavenworth an Indian farmer who helped pull him and his weary horse up from a flooded ford asked him if he had heard.

"An awful thing," the Indian said. "All my life I never heard nothing like it. Glad to put you up for the night, Lieutenant. You got another mean crossing between here and the fort. Better wait for daylight."

"Thank you, no," Stuart said wearily, peering through the dark. "I'll push on."

Every man in the saddle, Sumner had said, out hunting old Brown. Stuart wished he might share in the capture. Or . . . did he? Still the grisly story haunted him. What could come of a thing like that finally?

Barracks were dark, the post buried generally in sleep, when Stuart identified himself to a surprised sentry, and rode on to rouse the wagon sergeant at the stables and tell him what he needed in the early morning.

"As many wagons as you can find mules and teamsters for, up at the forage yard at seven sharp. We'll load tarps and axes, too. A mean road, narrow, full of mudholes . . . what time is it now?"

"Ten o'clock, sir."

"Better than I thought." Stuart rested his hand on Dan's shoulder. The horse shivered. "Unsaddle this boy and give him a rubdown before you feed him. He won't want water, but I do—to get some of this muck out of my eyes and ears."

"Yes, sir. If you're for your quarters then, sir, I'll ready a mount."

"Why, thank you, but never mind. I'll walk."

"You'll have to go the long way around, sir. The parade's a lake."

"I'll walk—to clear my head."

To conjure away that horror which still haunted him. He must not take such a thing near that clear light shining yonder. He had caught his first glimpse of it while he was still arguing with the sentry on the outer fringe of darkness. In his mind's eye he saw it often when he was miles from home, knowing that it burned always in vigil for him.

"Every evening, darling?" he asked, when she told him. "What do you do? How do you pass the time?"

"I read," she said. "Sometimes I sew, but usually I read."

Bless her well-stocked little head!

"Is my wife a blue-stocking?" he teased.

"I will be some day if you're away so much. Do you mind?"

Did he mind? Had she any idea how proud of her he was? Daily he drew comparisons, always to the disadvantage of other women. Some inherent quality of distinction was hers, a blending of her father's keen intellect and her mother's gentler wisdom, this seasoned with her own special sweetness, the lift of her voice in song, her soft speech, her utter exquisite cleanliness. She smelled like a posy always.

His girl, his flower. His steps, which had quickened as he approached the house, slackened. Noiselessly, he thought, he sidled up to the window through which the light came, and looked in.

It was a heavy book tonight. It rested on the table, tilted against a pile of others. Bless her healthiness, she munched an apple as she read. Her dress was calico, with a neat print in red. The light from the lamp was for the book presumably; but to Stuart's hungry eyes it served only to illumine the whole picture. He shaped his mouth to whistle a warning; but, before he could make a sound, she turned to listen. She laid down the apple. She stood up. He must warn her about standing like that in an area of light, and all dark outside.

"I dream of Jeannie with the light brown hair . . ."

"Stuart!"

With her warm and sweet in his arms, his soaked coat draggling her now with the dirty business of being a soldier, he thought with a groan of his orders to the sergeant. Seven sharp? To be sure, when the wagons were loaded, he could snatch another hour, for breakfast and good-bye, and still overtake the lumbering train. An hour? To measure time like this in hours? Flora stirred in his arms, blissfully unaware of wet or filth.

"Stuart, my own! I miss you so when you're away."

Chapter 6. *Indians!*

Neither the First Cavalry nor the mob that broke over the Missouri border after the Osawatomi murders captured John Brown. How he made his escape, who helped him, nobody knew; but he got

away—he and all but two of his sons. Of these one was killed by a
posse, the other, in a state of near imbecility over the horrors he had
witnessed, made public repudiation of his father's crime. But he was
not likely ever to forget it. Not he or anyone else. The shadow of
Osawatomi Brown was part of the smoke pall that hung over Kansas
all that weary summer.

By contrast then, the routine of life at the post offered sweet refreshment to a dusty or bedraggled officer riding home for a day or
a week, finally to stay. Flora had always some change to report to
Stuart. Early in the summer, when it seemed that Colonel Sumner
would be away most of the time, Persifor Smith, commanding the
Department of the West, took over at headquarters house. Because
he was a general in rank and an old dear, besides, with a charming
wife, social life sharpened in punctilio. In August two junior lieuten-
ants from the class of 1856 at the Point reported from summer fur-
lough, Lunsford Lomax and George Bayard. The former, a Rhode
Islander of Virginia parentage, was as south as if he had never seen
New England; but Bayard, from Pennsylvania, was an out-and-out
Yankee. A short, stocky fellow, who talked too much about his ambi-
tions and his determination to get on by one route or another, he
irritated Stuart because he was named to Stuart's company. Stuart
had been hoping for a year that the place would be given to Fitzhugh
Lee, Colonel Robert E. Lee's nephew.

"That's why he didn't get preferment," Stuart said. "The old man
bends over backwards not to seek favors for his kin."

"Like papa with Johnnie," Flora said. "I know."

Winter settled down finally on the harried land. Not an iron winter
like the one before. Streams and ponds froze sufficiently to add ice-
cutting and storage to other post duties; but hardships, by comparison, were few. There was work to fill the days, and the nights were
variously merry with theatricals and dances. Sometimes girls from
outside came, to add that kind of variety to the picture. On New
Year's Eve balls were given by two rival hotels in Leavenworth City,
one sponsored by Free State citizens, the other pro-slavery. The
army, declaring stoutly for neutrality under such circumstances,
attended both, and danced until everyone had to make a break and
run for it to be back at the post in time for reveille.

"Stuart," Flora said, snuggled down in furs in a hired livery stable cutter, which her lord drove with his usual skill and abandon, "who are the Misses Ege of St. Joseph?"

The night was calm and clear, the stars still bright against the faint promise of dawn.

"Just that," Stuart teased. "The Misses Ege of St. Joseph." He whistled a measure in waltz time. "Why? Did I seem over-attentive?"

"A little, perhaps. Oh, it isn't you or anything you do. It's those silly girls." Not just the Misses Ege. A half dozen others, flushed, bright-eyed, their hands reaching toward her husband in the figure of a dance. "Darling, I can't help it. I don't like . . ." Abruptly she hushed, conscious all at once of her surroundings, the runners singing over the frozen snow, Stuart large and comfortingly close beside her. "What nonsense I'm talking!" she said brokenly. "It's a beautiful night, isn't it? A beautiful world, really."

Who, indeed, were the Misses Ege? Who or what?

"A New Year beginning," Stuart reminded her. He, too, sounded solemn.

"Stuart, if you had everything to choose from, what would you ask for first, for this year to come?"

"Just what I have," he assured her. "Why? Do you want something else?"

"Yes, dear, I do." But she wouldn't say what it was.

She wanted a child. It was the only thing lacking, she thought, to make their life together perfect. She wanted a child now . . . very, very much.

A good winter to hold in one's heart and remember, though shadows still hovered. Would there be more bloodshed and sorrow and military patrol the coming summer? Probably. The new governor—none lasted out a year—had asked for a bodyguard. A troop of soldiers to act as military escort. Who wanted that assignment? Nobody.

The old trouble was still there, waiting under the snow, with less justification than ever. Free State settlers, bona fide settlers, outnumbered others now five to one. If a true election could be held, without sacking, burning and terrorizing, the thing would be done; but the day seemed still not near. Not while Missouri said defiantly that she would save Kansas if she had to bring in ten thousand armed

men, not while the Free Staters were led by convicted murderers
and other fugitives from law or by mad zealots like old John Brown.

There! The name still could produce a chill that all but put out a
fire on the jolliest of evenings; and, if one didn't turn the talk quickly,
the chill would spread and a dark shadow cover more than Kansas.

"Please," Flora begged, "why do you mention him now? He's gone.
Let's try to forget him."

He was gone. But where? A person couldn't be easy, not knowing.

Still, in spite of shadows, it was a good winter. Friendships that
had been new a year before seemed old and firmer now. Circles
formed within the larger grouping of the regiment. Names were
grouped—the Stuarts, the McIntyres, the Careys—though Lucy Carey
had the homesick blues that year. Lieutenant Stanley was another in
that circle. He was engaged to a girl Flora had known at Carlisle
Barracks, when Colonel Cooke had commanded there. And young
Lunsford Lomax—a good winter; and then, suddenly it was spring.

General orders arrived. No sooner were the seals broken and the
sheets out of their stout envelope than a breeze entered headquarters
through a crack in door or window, ruffled them, snatched at the contents, and carried the news out to the parade. Somebody out there
whiffed the breeze, stared, shaped his mouth to whistle, and changed
to a yell.

"Indians! Ya—hoooooo!"

Kansas, in spite of everything, grew. Settlers came now from the
west, backtracking from California, where only those who found a
bonanza prospered. The land out there, they said, was no good for
farming. Kansas had it beat every way for that. The Cheyenne tribes,
directly in the path of this new tide, took fright for their buffalo
range. They threatened now to outdo their white brothers with sacking and burning and driving off horses and cattle. Were they fighters,
someone asked. Hellions on the warpath. Well, never mind that. Had
someone else mentioned buffalo? Hunting rifles came out of their
corners, down from their racks, for cleaning and oiling.

The orders were posted finally, for serious study. Stuart, his eyes
shooting sparks, brought a copy home to Flora.

1. *The 10th Infantry to leave Minnesota and move to Leavenworth.*

"Stuart, a whole new regiment? But . . . where?"

"In tents under the trees, I reckon." Stuart sailed his hat across the room. "Read on."

Also six companies of Dragoons from Fort Riley.

"Stuart, papa and mamma here?"

"To keep the lid from blowing off Kansas," he explained, "while we hunt Indians. Read on, pet. You haven't come to our orders."

Unwillingness closed Flora's throat. That morning she had experienced a round of dizziness. It was the first sign that her wish for a child might be granted. Breathless after the spell passed, happy, she had not thought how it would be if Stuart were away during much of her waiting.

2. *Lieutenant-Colonel Johnston with two companies of infantry and two squadrons of cavalry to proceed south to run the southern boundary of Kansas Territory.*

Joseph E. Johnston, the First Cavalry's lieutenant-colonel. So far he had not put in appearance at Leavenworth.

"On recruiting duty," Stuart said." You must have known him somewhere. Your father surely does. He's an old hand, and one of the finest."

And at last:

3. *Two squadrons of the 1st Cavalry to proceed up the Arkansas River. Companies D, E, G, H . . .*

G Troop was Stuart's company and its captain was away, to marry a girl in Florida. There had been an exodus of officers that early spring, on matrimony bound. David Stanley among others was off to Pennsylvania to marry his Margaret. He might be back in time to march with his company, but Captain Walker? Hardly.

"Stuart, if he doesn't get back, you could have the company command."

"Not if I keep my quartermaster post." His eyes darkened.

Flora hoped her trembling did not show.

"Stuart, you would like to change now, wouldn't you?"

"I thought of it. Old Sedge will lead the Arkansas column. But I don't know. Quartermaster duty will mean the biggest job I've handled so far. Colonel Sumner is taking a third column out over the California Road by way of Fort Kearny and Laramie. Each column calls for its own supply train—fifty wagons at least, with six mules apiece, and its own *caballard* of spare animals. Bill Cody has asked for a place with one, as cavvy boy. I'm off to Missouri tomorrow to look at horses and mules and cattle. A big job."

"Yes, I know," Flora said, "but . . ."

"What's the matter with you?" Stuart held her off at arm's length. "You're white as new plaster. You're not afraid surely? You? What an idea!"

He hugged her to him. She hid her face for a minute.

"Not exactly afraid," she said then. "When do you think the march will begin?"

"Well, you know Sumner. He'll want grass a foot high, for green fodder. Besides, the new garrison has to move in. My guess now would be early May."

May . . . another month. By then she would be sure. Anyhow, what difference would it make about Stuart's going?

"Stuart, if you don't take back your place in the line, who will lead the company?"

"Why, young Bayard, of course."

The pushing new second lieutenant.

"Oh, no! Stuart, I won't have it."

He laughed uproariously.

"I will consider that aspect of the situation," he promised, and went off singing.

The cavalry went into tents on the plain below the post the first of May. Married men, of course, kept their families in quarters and visited much with them there, such as had families. The Carey quarters had new tenants now. Right after the regiment encamped, Lieutenant Carey obtained leave to escort his wife and family to St. Louis, to see them off to Mrs. Carey's home in South Carolina. For a visit, it was said, though few in the regiment expected to see any of them again. Lieutenant Carey in St. Louis would hand in his resignation to General Smith, and go on east with his family, to grow fat and lazy and rich as a planter. The end of a good soldier, but not many blamed him. Since the New Year, Lucy had been after him to resign.

She was quite frank about everything when Flora went over to ask if she could help in the preparations for the journey. Quite frank and rather bitter, so that a person knew there had been strain in that household and there might be more.

"I've endured everything," Lucy said, "just to be here with Peter Carey, to let him be what he thinks he wants to be; but finally there comes a time . . . I'm glad you came while young Peter is away. You see, he doesn't know. He's been packing his toys—for storage. He thinks he is coming back to them; but we're not, you know—not small Peter, the baby and I. I'm leaving the blocks and things for the other children at the post. Goodness knows, small Peter will have everything he can ask for where we're going. A loving grandpa and grandma, who hardly know him." She looked at Flora doubtfully, through lashes gummed with tears.

"Small Peter loves it here—the school and all," Flora said softly. "Doesn't he?"

"That's one reason we're leaving," Lucy said. "I want to get away before the thing gets too tight a hold on him, too. Big Peter, you see, didn't have much of a life before he went to West Point. His folks were gentry, but poor. It's different with the boy. Other things are possible for him, and I want him to know about them while he is young enough to forget this."

But it might already be too late for that, Flora suggested. Children remembered remarkably. Yes, Peter Carey had mentioned that, Lucy said. It was his great hope that his son would remember; but small Peter, she thought, was hers as well as his father's. He should come to know the other possibilities and then make his choice.

"I suppose," she said a minute later, "even if you don't ask, you are wondering about big Peter. I don't know. He says he is coming back. He likes the army, fair weather or foul, and means to stay with it. Well . . ."

The baby tired suddenly of thumping with a spoon on the arm of a chair where Lucy or Celie had tied her and began to fuss.

"Imagine," Lucy said abruptly, "her in Utah!"

There was a miserable last line in the general orders, which every wife was trying to forget: "The regiment to march fully equipped and prepared for distant places." Distant places meant Utah, surely. There was trouble now in that territory, the settlers in their mountain land defying the laws of the United States, refusing to comply with rules for territorial organization, and, possibly, most important of all, refusing to pay due revenue into the national treasury.

"Just talk, Lucy," Flora said, still softly.

But strong talk. A new governor was being sent out under military escort. Some of the troops now gathering in and around Leavenworth would form that escort. Separation might mean to their wives not months, but a year, or more.

Lucy said, "You're not afraid? Not even now?"

Flora was startled. By this time she was quite sure that she was going to have a child. Early in the next year, as well as she could calculate; but she had so far not told anyone. She answered Lucy's question indirectly.

"Horribly afraid—always," she admitted.

She wakened almost every night cold with fear, even with Stuart warm and real beside her.

"If they should build a fort off there," Lucy persisted, "would you go?"

"I'd rather go than stay, if Stuart was there," Flora answered.

"Well, you're a braver woman than I am."

But that was not true. No woman had ever any right to say of another that she was naturally braver or stronger. If finally what one did, how one lived, looked braver, that must be credited to some force other than physical make-up.

"I must be going," Flora said abruptly, standing up to take her leave.

"Celie!" Lucy called. "I asked her to pack up some things especially for you," she explained. "Evie's baby things. She's outgrown them and they would be just so much unnecessary plunder to carry away."

"Lucy . . . those lovely, lovely things you brought with you?"

"Some of them you girls made here," Lucy reminded her. But not the choicer pieces. "Please take them. Evie won't need them, nor I. Not now, or ever any more, I think."

Poor Lucy! Breaking her heart and big Peter's, smashing them like pieces of crystal. It was useless to try to tell her what she was doing. She knew, and still she had to do it. The promise of this Flora had seen when she had first laid eyes on Lucy Carey; but later, liking both Peters so much, and then the baby, she had made the family a unit in her heart, taking in even lovely, indolent, selfish Lucy.

She was in tears herself when she left the house. To hide the tears, she ran. Also she could hardly wait to be inside the simple orderliness of her own quarters. No dark corners there, if she could open and scour and air them. No dark corners in her heart, or Stuart's. There must never be. No secrets, to breed misunderstandings. A shared loyalty always, a sharing of all desire.

"Whoa, there!" a gay voice shouted behind her. "Where are you running to or from? Oh, I see. Do pardon me."

David Stanley fell in beside her. A nice fellow, very happy in his new marriage. His bride, too, was a dear, army through and through. Flora had been proud to present her to their small circle.

"I've something here," Stanley said, "I think you might like to see. A piece in the paper about your husband. No names used, of course, but you'll know. So will others. Here it is; and thank you, Mrs. Stuart, for being sweet to Margaret. It makes things awfully pleasant for us. See you later."

The piece in the paper concerned the preparations for the western campaign. The writer had got hold of figures on troops and supplies and, his own eyes bulging, had put down his amazement in a way to astound the reader. One thousand mounted men, three thousand infantry, three hundred wagons with six-mule teams. Thousands of dollars spent. Seated, breathless from hurrying, in her own rocker, Flora read the items and steadied. She had been wondering how she would tell Stuart all she had to tell him. Now she knew.

> "Put my money on the bob-tailed nag . . .
> Somebody bet on the bay."

He was home; and her first words were, after all, unpremeditated.

"Pugh!" Her nose wrinkled. "Where have you been? The mule corral?"

Stuart's nightingales, young Bayard called them.

"Fine greeting for a cavalryman, from a cavalryman's wife!" Stuart kissed her again, and headed for the kitchen, bellowing for Bellors and hot water and lye soap. His lady found him objectionable.

He told her that he'd come from looking over Zadok Bagnell's latest string.

"I hope you found nothing you wanted for yourself," Flora said.

He turned from working a comb through wet hair and whiskers. His eyes were round with surprise. He needed an extra horse, if Dan was to survive the campaign.

"I mean," Flora hurried to explain, "you can have Mischief, if she'll do. I shan't be riding her for a while."

Stuart pocketed the comb. He started to say something and stopped. He took a step toward her; and, deep down, his eyes began to glow.

"My pet," he said, softly for him. "My pet!"

She reached for him blindly.

"Hold me," she begged. "Tighter, foolish. I won't fall to pieces."

His arms tightened, but cautiously. How could a man be sure? Then another thought struck him and he freed a hand to turn her face to the light of his searching eyes.

"Did you have any idea of hiding this from me?"

"No." A small fib, and, she hoped, her last. "I was waiting to be sure."

"When?"

"Sometime this winter."

"I'll be home."

"Mercy, yes." As if there were no Utah.

Behind them Bellors banged a dish on the table.

"Dinner's ready," she snorted, and slammed out of the room. Stuart laughed.

"Madame, will you dine?" But in his eyes a glow persisted. "I see you've had the paper," he observed, placing her in her chair.

"David Stanley gave it to me," she told him. She had left it spread for Stuart to see. "Darling, you have done wonderfully with your quartermaster assignment, I know; but, still, you'd rather ride with your company, wouldn't you?"

"Old Sedge's vagabonds will have good hunting," Stuart answered thoughtfully. "More excitement, more fun, but . . . well, no. It seems I'll still be quartermaster when we break camp. I mentioned the possibility to Colonel Sumner of my changing back to my company and you should have heard Old Fussbuttons roar: 'Leave all this to a novice now?' So-o, that's how it will be. I'll stay with the headquarters column, of course."

Flora sighed.

"I won't pretend I'm not relieved," she said, "but I still must have my say. Dear heart, if on the march things should change, if circumstances should arise to make another choice preferable, you are

not to let any thought of me keep you from what you think is your
first duty."

Drawing battle lines with his fingers on the checked tablecloth, he
answered still in jest. She wanted to see him decorated with arrows?

"Sweetheart, don't!" She closed her eyes, then opened them and
renewed her plea. Finally he gave his promise. The only way he
could for a soldier.

"Relieved of quartermaster duty until further notice . . ." Stuart
carried his release in his shirt pocket, along with Flora's prayerbook.
The first sign of hostile Indians had sent him hot-foot to Colonel
Sumner demanding it. Early July, and their column had made Fort
Laramie and doubled back, then gone into camp on the South Platte,
to wait for Sedgwick's column; and a restlessness had developed
among the animals at night.

"Injuns, Lieutenant, sir," Bill Cody said. "It ain't wolves or cats."

The restlessness, he pointed out, began at the outer edge of the
corral and it didn't come right with the barking of a coyote, which
sounded itself not just right and was too evenly answered by another
animal in another quarter. The restlessness began when something
stirred close by and down on the ground. No, sir, it warn't a cata-
mount, either. Horses went wild over cats. Injuns. This day he was
sure he had seen the faint print of a moccasin in the dust.

"Come with me to headquarters," Stuart said.

A day or two later, sure enough, a band of Arapaho had come into
camp, pleading starvation brought on by drought and the frightening away of game by the armies. The Arapaho, too, were frightened;
and that was why they had come to show their rags and their bones
to the white chief, so that they might not be mistaken for enemies
like the foolish Cheyenne, and shot down by the white man's roaring
guns, they having done no wrong. The Colonel had them fed, showing them the extent of his sprawling camp, then asked what about
the foolish Cheyenne, their reputed brothers.

No brothers, the Arapaho said, and surely fools, even though
bands from the north had joined with bands from the south and all
had ponies and rifles, most of them stolen. The Cheyenne were many
in number and flaming with anger; but they should know that they
could not fight a battle against white warriors, who, if they were not

so many in number, still were trained to stand and shoot iron from guns until even the Cheyenne must turn and run before them. Surely the Cheyenne were fools and led by fools.

"Sir," Stuart said then to his colonel, "with the supply trains moving steadily between us and Laramie, anyone could take over my duties now."

It was the right time to ask.

"I may need every fighting man in line," the Colonel agreed, and gave him his release.

A few days later Sedgwick's vagabonds rode up on the opposite bank of the river, their bellies full and their wagons empty. They came with a whoop and a halloo—good hunting, awful heat, but no losses and no signs of Indians. Bayard rode with G Troop and Peter Carey with his own company. He had chosen, after all, to rejoin the regiment. He was the same reckless, devil-may-care soldier as before when on the move; but, in an idle hour, with time for brooding, his disposition soured quickly.

"Glad to see you, Pete!" Stuart greeted him; and then, almost immediately both were called to headquarters.

Major Sedgwick and the Delaware Indian who was his chief scout waited in Sumner's tent with a different report from that given by the company officers. There had been plenty of Indian sign, too vague, too uncertain for Sedgwick to institute action, but still undeniable. He had chosen instead to bring a warning to Colonel Sumner. The tribes, he thought, were moving toward some prearranged rendezvous. What action they planned after that was anyone's guess. They might have heard of the battalion preparing to march into Utah and would wait to attack it in some lonely pass. There was another possibility. Strip western Kansas of troops—how strong, for example, was the garrison now at Fort Riley?

Colonel Sumner could not say. Two, possibly three companies of infantry.

"And women and children?" Peter Carey spoke up.

Colonel Sumner cut him down promptly.

"Your turn is coming, Mr. Carey. Why do you suppose I sent for you?"

"If you are thinking of sending a courier, I want to volunteer."

"We haven't time to exchange messages, Mr. Carey. We won't wait to hear that Riley or any other post is in distress. Neither is your courage or your willingness in question. I will give you work to test both. You and Stuart, with the Major's help and mine, will choose each a patrol of twenty men. You will take the best of the Indian guides and ride out ahead and to the right of our main column, which will break camp tomorrow and begin moving to the south. Your task will be, first, to locate the drift and, if possible, the rendezvous of the Cheyenne nation, second, to draw the attention of their scouts away from us. The danger lies in the fact that you are likely, one or the other, possibly both, to find the Indians, it being their way to become invisible when large bodies of troops are on the move, but to act more boldly against a handful. It will be to your personal interest to achieve a similar invisibility. That's all. Detailed orders will be given you later."

It was hot that summer on the plains. Even the rivers went underground, Speck-in-the-Dust, the Pawnee guide said, contemptuous of the trickle of water beside which he and Stuart had stopped to refresh their ponies. The little draw was indifferently screened by stunted shrubbery and sparse cottonwoods. On both sides stretched the usual great emptiness. Two weeks of patrol, and Stuart could only hope that his detail had remained as unseen as the Indians it hunted.

Two weeks, and this day no different from any other except that each morning one felt that there must be a change some time and this could be when it came. Behind him and the Indian, too far off to be seen but near enough to be reached quickly in case of sudden need, his patrol followed. It, too, was strung out as thinly as safety permitted; and the last man was as important as the first, even though the first was Hoskins of the Dragoons. Satiated with taking guns and pikestaffs away from belligerent settlers, and defrauded two years before this of his due share in the Sioux campaign, Hoskins, too, had asked for his release from guard and wagon duty. Sumner had picked him up at Fort Kearny with a squadron of Dragoons, and now here he was—worth any twenty others usually but just today of no more importance than the last man in the string, who rode the fleetest pony and would be the one, if trouble came or Indians were seen, to make at breakneck speed for Colonel Sumner at the head of the slow-moving main column.

Stuart squatted beside the trickle of water in the draw, cupped his hands to hold a mouthful, sloshed the brackish stuff over his tongue and upper throat, and spat it out. The taste was unspeakable, but . . . in the act of shaking his hands dry, he froze, his eyes on the guide. Speck-in-the-Dust, his hand on his pony's mane, stood motionless, too, his head forward, his whole posture tense with an effort to identify something he thought he saw.

Ahead, less than a mile away, the tracing of the draw turned to move around the base of one of those sudden upthrusts of rock that stand like outposts of the mountains on the western plains. Stuart and the Pawnee had had their eyes on it all day, thinking that, when they reached it, they might climb to the top, to take a general look at the country around. That was why they had stopped here to water their ponies. Once they undertook the climb, they could stop for nothing.

The cover looked scanty enough, gray patches of dry brush against a tawny barrenness as deserted as it had seemed all day. Even when Stuart drew himself upright and catfooted over to the Pawnee, he could, for several long minutes, see no change. Then, suddenly, a scrap of brush swayed and, seconds later, changed its position. It was, of course, no rooted bush or tree he saw, nor any trick of tortured watching. Five minutes more and he made out the fuzzy outlines of a man on a horse, both tawny in color, so nearly matching the sandstone of the butte as to have made them invisible if they had not moved.

Stuart's first impulse was to shout his relief. Springs within him that had dried up in the heat flowed again. The Indian he saw must be a scout. But for whom and where were his people? Were they in force? Thoughts, calculations, raced through his head as he and the Pawnee watched the Indian move through the brush to the base of the butte and disappear.

"Shai-ene," the Pawnee said.

"I hope so." Stuart licked his lips. "Over there behind the hill?"

The Pawnee nodded. "Water," he said. "Grass, maybe."

"How many, I wonder," Stuart muttered to himself, busily writing a message for Hoskins. "Here," to the scout, "take this to Boss Man back yonder. Tell him to have young soldier ride like anything; but the paper says it."

The Pawnee took the paper.

"You ride like hell, too," he suggested. "Shai-ene bad medicine for white man now. You see him—he see you, maybe."

"The boy on the pony? If he did, I'll know in time to follow you," Stuart said. "Be off now and come back quick. I'll wait here."

Until dark. Hoskins would bivouac where he was and keep watch until Stuart and the Pawnee scouted that hill. He had to see what was on the other side.

Chief Fire-in-the-Eye, the Pawnee named Stuart that night. They had climbed the hill without disturbing stick or stone and lay now on the summit, looking down on the Cheyenne camp. The light in Stuart's eyes might have been the reflection of the cooking fires below; or it could have been the excitement that burned through him, while outwardly and generally he was cool as ice, counting, calculating. He counted the *tipis*—ninety-three or just about that. He swept his eyes over the horses, restless and bunched, for easy catching. Anywhere from three hundred to five hundred warriors, he estimated, and touched the Pawnee.

"All right. Let's go."

> *"If you want to have a good time*
> *You must jine the cavalry . . ."*

The song was a soft growl in Stuart's dry throat, but a true report on his state of mind. It was good to feel the powerful reach of big Dan under him, good to be riding with his fellows again, his colonel's curt, "Well done, sir!" warm in his heart alongside Pete Carey's grudging, "You lucky cuss!"

The cavalry—six companies, with a light battery and an ambulance and surgeon bringing up the rear—rode detached from the more unwieldy bulk of the main column; and G Troop was all Stuart's now.

So now the pursuit. The troopers rode two by two at a fast walk. Hats were pulled low and handkerchiefs were tied over their noses. Men and horses rapidly became one shade of yellow gray; but they felt good. Action at last. Action—the reason for months of monotonous drill. They would catch those Indians and soon. It had to be soon or these would be more spook Indians, appearing one day to vanish the next. But they weren't spooks, Stuart knew. The pursuit was hot.

It was hard to see through the thick haze of dust, but the cavalry had now crossed the little draw. Almost any minute the shock of battle could come.

"If you want to have a good time . . ."

His first battle, and how would he take it? Old-timers said a man could never be sure. Those with the least fear in advance sometimes went to pieces in a crisis and those who were afraid were the coolest under fire. Stuart acknowledged a crawling something within him that protested stubbornly against that purposeful movement toward what might be his last hour. It could be fear.

And then it came. A trumpet sounded. A dusty trooper on a rearing horse rode down the line.

"Form fours! Double up there! Fours . . ."

He recognized the voice if not the man. Peter Carey, who had been given the consolation prize today of taking the forward patrol.

"Pete, we've caught 'em?" Stuart yelled.

"Naw," came the mocking answer. "This is just practice drill." But then Pete added tensely, itching with his own excitement, "Line 'em up, Beauty. Here we go!"

Never, Stuart thought, if he lived to be a hundred, and over and over saw ten times that many men drawn up in battle array, would he forget the picture the Cheyenne tribesmen made that day as they stood to face the white chieftain and his braves. They had chosen the open plain for battle. Perhaps they hadn't the choice. It hardly mattered. Who said Indians would not stand? Their line, varying in depth, fanned out over the dun-colored land, and you couldn't be sure you saw the true end of it in either direction. It was a fluid line, its movement rhythmical as the slow balancing of monstrous birdwings. With the brief cessation of movement, the dust cloud between the Indians and the troopers settled into scattered whirls, and Stuart saw the whole spectacle clearly and his heart was gripped by it. It was hard to remember that those naked, yelling men, controlling their ponies with the sinews of their thighs in a way many white men could not learn, so that their arms would be free to brandish their white men's guns, were savages, that it was their way to fall upon white men, unprotected, and rob and kill, that they spared neither man nor woman nor child when they made war. This band could truly have been on its way to plunder Fort Riley with particular hideousness, if Colonel Sumner had not discovered it and thrown his soldiers into its path.

Remembering all this, Stuart took his eyes from the fanning, undulating, howling line and turned in his saddle to examine his own troop. Not beautiful, those seventy gray spectres with the burning eyes, but ready. Their carbines ready, too, for there could be only one maneuver under the circumstances. A short advance to within sure rifle range, a smashing volley from the front line, to panic the Indians' ponies and bring down a few horses and men, then a thundering charge with drawn sabres, to finish the job when the Indian line broke in confusion and helter-skelter flight.

But the Indians moved first. They came on at a gallop and a trumpet blared. But the call was wrong. It reversed the expected orders:

"Draw sabres! CHARGE!"

No preliminary volley. No orderly change of pace to gather momentum. Everything was now. "Draw sabres, CHARGE!" The shout went down the line. Stuart's voice swelled it. His sabre flashed. His next shout was lost in an ear-splitting yell. He felt Dan gather his muscles for the gallop; and off he went, G Troop boot to boot behind him. It was magnificent and it was all wrong. If the cavalry could have reached the Indians, they would have smashed them; but the Indians with a matching yell whirled their ponies and fled.

"Come on!" Stuart roared, and the pounding pursuit continued. The noise and the yelling and the confusion were beyond description. Dust blinded him but he would not or could not halt. He had no thought of halting until his brave Dan coughed and faltered. That brought him to his senses and he stopped. He threw a leg over Dan and dismounted. A great gray hunter loomed up in the dust. He put out a hand and caught the bridle.

"I need your mount," he said to the trooper astride the animal. "Fall back."

He was off on the hunter. Up ahead, it seemed, the Indians had halted to give fight. That, perhaps, had been their intention all along —to keep clear of the mad rush of the charge, then to engage the men who outran their comrades. Stuart rode the gray into the choicest kind of a melee and was just in time to spoil the designs of an Indian on foot aiming his gun at young Lomax, who was very busy shooting another warrior. Stuart thrust at the Indian after Lomax, meaning to run him through; but the hunter plunged and reared, spoiling his stroke, so that he only grazed the savage's leg. The Indian turned with a howl and fired at Stuart, but missed him. A voice behind Stuart shouted, "I'll get him!" and David Stanley rolled off his horse, to get a steadier aim, he said afterwards; but in the great haste of everything, his gun went off and the Indian still had the best of things. He grinned evilly and aimed his revolver now at Stanley, now at Stuart. "Look out!" somebody else shouted, as Stuart, meaning to sell his life dearly, swung his sabre and brought it down on the Indian's head. The Indian sagged to his knees, firing as he fell.

Stuart thought the hunter had reared again, except that no horse in years had rocked him like that. Something struck him a fearful blow.

"Stuart," Stanley called from the ground, "he got you, didn't he? Stuart?"

Someone with more authority spoke through a rushing as of many waters: "Mind the horse. Get him down when you can. Watch him."

Stuart opened his mouth for a gasping breath and his ears cleared, but something seemed to give in his chest and his shirt was wet with blood, soaking through the dust and spreading. He was able to throw his leg back over the hunter and slide to the ground, in not too good form, perhaps; and then he wished he were back in the saddle, for his knees sagged like the Indian's. But McIntyre had a blanket ready and eased him down on it, while Stanley grimly planted sabres to hold an awning above him, to keep the sun off. The pursuit thundered past, parting like a biblical sea. Some time later Rally sounded.

And this was the end? This was glory?

"Flora . . . *ma povere petite* . . ."

Afterwards Stuart, too, could laugh, but still with a solemn note.

"The battle, before it was over," he said ruefully, "was several miles ahead, and the surgeon farther than that to the rear. Good man, though. I like him. Name's Brewer. Ticketed for New Mexico, but we hope to keep him here."

Flora's hand moved over him, for reassurance. Her fingers rested on the spot where the random bullet had entered his breast, by God's providence burrowing through soft flesh well to the left of a vital area. It could so easily have been farther to the right, and fatal. There was still an angry scar. Did it hurt . . . now?

"When you touch it?" Stuart kissed her fingers. "No. It never did much, not after the first day. The worst was the sick wagon. The ambulance had broken apart crossing a gully; so they fastened the tongue to the hind wheels and rigged a pallet on the spring. A cushioned pallet, they said, but . . ."

Sick camp, still out on the burning plains. Himself, aching from the bruising ride, burning inside to match the heat without. The young sawbones finally, going over him with strong, sure hands and no mercy. Smiling when his work was done.

"You'll live—to draw a real one some day."

Four days on that pallet bed in that camp. Nothing to do but think. Nothing to read but the prayerbook and Army Regulations. Six other pallets there besides his own. Hoskins on one of them, with an ugly wound in his side; but he, too, would live, Doc Brewer said.

"I'd hate to go home to my family," Stuart said, "with word of it, if he didn't."

Four days, and on the fifth that subtle stir that meant movement. How and how far would they be moved? The doctor would say, the green young lieutenant in charge of the camp told him. Those who could mount would ride. The rest would travel by Indian travois.

Hoskins, conscious by now and only too lucid, was giving instructions for weaving the travois. He was indecently profane about it, but the work proceeded. Stuart listened and watched. Presently, smothering a groan, he turned over and got to his hands and knees, then, dizzily, to his feet. Where were the horses? He had no mind to wait on the doctor's verdict. He would ride.

The next morning their little group set out, with the young lieutenant in command and two Pawnee guides, their destination Fort Kearny; and the riding was bad, but nothing so bad as the rain. It rained now, to make up for all that had not fallen through the rest of summer. They lost their way. Even the Pawnee guides disappeared, fearing that the blame would be put upon them. The young lieutenant had no compass and his confusion began to look disastrous; soon

Stuart, who at least could sound loud and certain, took over. He had nothing to go by himself except instinct and the stars, when they shone. Each night he ordered the guard to wake him if there was a glimmer of starlight. Then he would establish his directions and set stakes, to sight by the next morning. Northeast should bring them finally to Kearny. It brought them near to death by drowning.

They bivouacked one night in the dark and the rain at the edge of a rising river on what seemed safe, high ground, only to waken to some vague alarm and find the water halfway up the horses' legs and coming after all of them. They got the horses and themselves out of the way, then gave up the illusion of sleeping.

There they squatted on their saddles, under the dripping trees, as miserable a bunch of men as anyone could imagine. Hoskins presently got up from his pallet and borrowed a seat next to Stuart.

"If I got to drown," he growled, "I'll take it vertical."

There they sat until morning. By then the river had crested and was beginning to fall, but there was a lot of water still.

"Hurrah!" Stuart yelled, defying the foaming river. "I know where we are now. That's the Big Blue. We'll have to swim but the road's over yonder."

He made the first try at the crossing and got over, then went back, to help Hoskins and the others. Four times he crossed that river, going and coming.

"But God was with us, I reckon," he said to Flora. "We got over and the road was there. That night was the worst. If I believed in omens or signs . . ."

"Darling, hush!" Flora begged. "Don't talk about omens and signs, and please don't laugh at any of it. I had a dream while you were away. I saw you so clearly! You were alone and on a horse. It seemed a darker horse than Dan, but everything was gray and obsure except just you. You were in uniform; and this creature—he never came out of the shadows altogether—must have been afoot, because he struck at you from below. He struck and you went down . . ."

"My foolish darling," Stuart soothed. "It was only a dream, because here I am. Now, there is just one other thing."

"What for pity's sake?"

"Our weapons. Our cavalryman's gear. Somehow we're hooked up wrong. Never mind. I'll work on that this winter."

Chapter 7. *Family Man*

The baby was a girl, tiny but perfect, with promise of her father's curling hair and his bright blue eyes. She was born at Fort Riley, to which six companies of the First Cavalry and most of the Second Infantry were moved in November—the Second Dragoons under Colonel Cooke remaining in occupancy at Leavenworth.

Nobody minded the move much, least of all the Stuarts. Their associations with the far post were only happy ones. With Utah now part of general orders, Leavenworth was too crowded for anybody's comfort. They had a much better house at Fort Riley, with a leanto, where Bellors slept, thus giving them full use of the two main rooms.

Ah, Bellors! If they could only have left her behind! During the first six months at Fort Leavenworth, in spite of sundry mishaps, she had shown a measure of tractability; but after that a change came—a tendency to spells of sullen brooding. She still gave obedience to Mast' Jeems, but she resented any orders from Flora. The change had begun, Flora sometimes thought, with her outcry over a ruined flowerbed. Or the woman might have picked up some seed of revolt in that generally dark and awful summer. Certainly, after John Brown had come and gone, there was unrest among slaves everywhere, even on military reservations. Most probably the woman had room in her primitive mind for only one devotion. Giving that to Mast' Jeems, she hated Flora.

"She'll do better at Fort Riley," Stuart said, still unwilling to admit that he had blundered in taking her from Virginia.

But she didn't do better. When the baby came, she extended her jealousy of the mother to include the child. How could she, Flora thought, how could she?

They named the baby Flora. "My two flowers," Stuart said, and would hear to no other choice. Not that Flora objected, though she did feel a small pang when he stole her other name to give it to the child. Little Flora became now *Lar Petite*, as he said it, Flora, the mother, being then "darling little mommie," "my darling wife," and so on. These were proud titles and she was silly, she told herself, to feel the loss of the old ones.

The year 1858 was a crowded one, its events, large and small, not seeming too important at the time, but the least of them achieving significance in retrospect. Flora from the beginning felt a richness of promise, but that could have been due purely to happiness. She was radiantly happy in having her baby. She dressed her in the sheer muslins and nainsooks and zephyr wool that Lucy Carey had given her and wished that Lucy could see. She wished she could see Lucy —or small Peter—or big Peter, for that matter. Would she ever see them again? Lieutenant Carey, after the battle with the Cheyenne, disgruntled over a lack of mention of his part in it in Colonel Sumner's report, had handed in his resignation, after all. One of the saddest things about that was that at parting he and Stuart exchanged bitter words.

"A man's place is with his family," Peter said, meaning he longed for them beyond telling. "Who knows? I may like being a planter."

"You won't," Stuart told him. "You'll hate it, and you'll hate yourself finally." And to Flora, "Well, *obit* Peter Carey, First Lieutenant, First Cavalry, U. S. A. Cross him off the roll and forget him."

"Oh, Stuart!" Flora pleaded. She had never heard him speak so harshly.

"What good is a man," he ranted, "who is a slave to the woman he loves? A captain? When he can't hold his own household in line? From now on everything he does will be to her ordering. Everything he has . . . oh, pshaw!"

A richly happy spring, nevertheless, full of laughter and sunshine, with only an occasional thunderclap. By the end of March Flora was again riding Mischief, though her riding habit was a snug fit. Then she was dancing, and the fit of her clothes improved. All in the garrison were now old friends, as those things went in the army, and decorum was not so rigid. She danced as freely and gaily and as lightly as Stuart himself; and nobody sang more sweetly to a guitar.

But there remained Bellors. Flora could not with any peace of mind leave the baby with her for more than a short while. By day she would take the child with her wherever she went. By night she depended on a friendly understanding in Officers' Row that those at home in a house would look out every once in a while to see that all was snug and quiet in the others.

Stuart called this foolish fussing. Granted that Bellors was less than perfect as a servant, he still did not believe that she was dangerous or mean. And how could she have a spite against *Lar Petite*? See here, if Flora was going to worry so about one child, what would she do when she had a sure enough family?

The picture of Stuart as the head of such a household was captivating, but it did not remove the fact of Bellors. To her other sins she had now added drinking. Stuart gave her a little money, and almost any of the men who served the Stuart rear door could be bribed to bring her a bottle of whisky. Some probably enjoyed bringing the stuff to the house of such an outspoken temperance man as the Lieutenant. Flora could only watch, and hurry home from parties and pray that, if Bellors ever did turn violent, Stuart would be on hand to deal with her.

Fortunately, he was on hand. One evening in April, at post theatricals, during an interlude of buck and wing dancing, an orderly made his way to Stuart's place, touched Stuart on the arm and muttered something in his ear. Flora, seated close beside him in the packed hall, felt him stiffen.

"Sit still," he said to her. "I'll be back in a minute."

But he didn't come back. Finally Flora spoke to David Stanley, sitting beyond her.

"Please, I can't wait any longer. I must go."

The three of them—Stanley, his wife, and Flora—left the hall together.

It was with the help of Aggie, the Stanleys' maid, that Flora afterwards pieced out the full story. Told by the Stanleys to keep an eye and ear open, she had heard the Stuart baby crying. Then she had heard Bellors talking "loud," and had waited for nothing more, but had run with the word to the hall. Running back then to the house with Lieutenant Stuart, she said she could hardly keep up. When they got there, they could see Bellors standing over the baby's crib. Stuart burst open the door, "shoved" Bellors aside, and went to look at the baby. She seemed all right, but was still crying. And he put Bellors out. Right then.

When Flora in her turn reached the house, Bellors was muttering in her leanto and Stuart's face was still white. His eyes blazed.

"I'll send her away tomorrow," he promised.

And he kept his word, even though, when the two women un-
dressed the child, there were no marks upon her. Plainly Bellors had
not struck her. She might have shaken her. Certainly she had frightened the baby. They would never know just how. Her screaming
quieted, little Flora sobbed, then sighed, and once in a while shivered in her mother's arms.

"Tomorrow," Stuart said again.

When morning came, he got a place for Bellors in a wagon east-
bound for Westport, then mounted his horse and, using a leave he
would have preferred to spend otherwise, rode off with her.

"You goin' to take me back to Verginny, Mast' Jeems?" she asked,
otherwise showing no particular emotion.

"No," he said. "You know I can't do that. Missouri, maybe."

"Missoura's a nice place. Ef I don' lak it dar, mebbe I'll git wo'd to
Parson Brown."

"Who?" Stuart asked.

"Parson Brown, de black folks' frien'. I'll holler an' he'll year me."

There was only one Brown she could mean—old Osawatomi
Brown. Sure enough, at Westport Stuart learned that he had been
seen again in Kansas, that he had a cabin near the Missouri border
and was organizing a new underground route for the delivery of
fugitive slaves from the region to Canada.

And that was the burden of anxiety that Stuart brought back with
him, in so far as it was in his nature to wrestle with burdens. He had
found a good home for Bellors on a farm in western Missouri; so he
wasn't worried about her, although Flora gave some thought to the
welfare of the farmer and his family; and he had obtained in exchange a boy of nineteen named Ben, who, born in Kentucky and,
therefore, well acquainted with horses and horsemen, made an excellent personal servant. This was a luxury Flora had wanted for
Stuart more and more as his importance in the regiment grew and
another promotion became increasingly probable. He had his differences and disagreements with his brother officers and even his su-
periors, but nobody denied his worth as a soldier. Uncle John Sedgwick, the most critical of observers, who talked usually in terms of
horses, pronounced him one "of the best the army had ever foaled."

Also on the way back Stuart had stopped at Leavenworth long enough to secure, with Rachel's and black Lily's help, a maid for Flora. This was a girl named Tilda, daughter of freed Negroes, another pure aborigine in appearance, but all sunshine in nature. The baby accepted her immediately. So Flora thanked God for a reward beyond mere deliverance, but Stuart brooded still over John Brown. How, he pondered, had Bellors heard he was back? That seemed to him significant.

"You've never seen the man," he said to Flora. "I have."

"I wish we had never heard of him," Colonel Cooke said. He was paying Fort Riley and his daughter a visit at the time.

"Oh, stop!" Flora begged. "I won't have him spoil things for us here. It seems too bad."

Stuart's eyes snapped.

"Hear that?" he said to his father-in-law. "That's how she spoke to me, sir, the day we met: 'If you have other duties, Mr. Stuart, I'll excuse you.' A very pert young lady, I thought." But a wholly desirable wife, his eyes added.

When spring was at its height, before the regiment took to the field again, Flora and the little one and Tilda went back to Fort Leavenworth, to spend the summer there with Rachel Cooke. Flora's younger sisters, Maria and Julia, were there, too; and the prospect of a long family visit assuaged the pangs of parting, though it could not stifle them.

Utah was openly the objective of this year's campaign. A whole army was massed in Kansas to bring the recalcitrant Brigham Young to terms. Regiments of infantry, as well as cavalry, among them the Sixth Infantry, including Second Lieutenant Rooney Lee, John Cooke's classmate at Harvard. Everybody's regiment but Johnnie's, it seemed to the Cookes.

Another Johnston reported—Brigadier-General Albert Sydney Johnston, up from Texas. He had the over-all command; Colonel Cooke commanded the cavalry. Colonel Sumner, in a pet over Johnston's preferment, went to Jefferson Barracks in St. Louis, to command the Department of the West. The old heartburn over promotions, Flora thought, but oh, it was good to see her father parade his command.

"Like old times," she said. "Dear papa, you will watch out for my darling a little? You won't give him everything dangerous to do, will you?"

"I promise you I shall not spare him," Colonel Cooke answered. "I never saw a young man better able to care for himself. I hope, in turn, you didn't ask him to keep watch over me. Ah, I see you did. Well, what did he say?"

"He said," Flora sighed, "just what you say—that you were able to take care of yourself and several thousand others, or he was no judge."

"Hah! I thank him for the tribute. I'll tell him I left you looking well and the child beginning to show signs of awakening intelligence."

Flora was not at Fort Riley when Stuart left with his regiment, but she meant to be there when he returned. That would be September at the earliest, she calculated; and, as the time came near, she grew restless. In vain Rachel reasoned with her. It was too early. Riley was deserted—a skeleton guard.

"I know, I know," she said to every argument. "It's just a feeling. The house empty, everything covered with dust. He will be tired, hungry. Such a long march, and all we have heard is bad."

Not to be there when Stuart dismissed his troop and threw himself off his jaded horse, his eyes two glowing embers in his dusty face, his arms open to gather her in and draw her close to him, dust and all! Not to be there!

On a day in early September she and her sisters and the baby, in charge of Tilda, spent the late afternoon—as they had spent every afternoon for a week—as near to the western limits of Fort Leavenworth as decency and regulations permitted. Sixteen-year-old Tilda played with the baby on a comforter on the ground. The others had campstools. Julia and Maria were sewing. Flora was reading aloud —Maria Sedgwick's new novel, "Married or Single." An enchanting story and highly appropriate, but Flora could never remember what it was about. She read mechanically. Every time she turned a page she raised her eyes and looked out over the valley. Suddenly she stopped, her lips parted, her hand motionless.

"Well?" Julia said tartly. "Are we to hear what Uncle said to Miss What's-her-name?"

"Be still," Flora said. "I see something."

A speck of something, too far away to have shape or semblance, but moving on the road. A horse and rider presently. Still too far off. Then . . . it was not an Indian, not an Indian's pony. A soldier, an army horse. Now, how could she know that? She knew. The next minute her book dropped to the ground and she was on her feet. She looked, the girls said, as if she might fly off into space; and each of them seized an arm.

"Sister," Maria said, "it could be almost anyone, you know."

No. She would know him in the darkest dark, astride a pack mule.

"Even if it is Lieutenant Stuart," Maria went on, "you can't run down the road to meet him, like any common trash."

No, she couldn't do that.

"I'll stay right here," she promised. "I won't move. Take the baby and go home. Tell mamma he has come and I am waiting. I'll wait here."

There she stood, fresh as a rose in her sprigged dimity, when he rode up over the hill on a borrowed nag.

"Oh, Lemuel, my love; oh, Lemuel, my beau . . ."

Her tears wet the dust on his coat and left blobs of mud on her face.

"I'll never leave home again," she said. "If I have to wait a year, I'll be right there."

He wiped the mud off her face but could do nothing to save her dress. The horse sighed and began to crop grass.

"All those extra miles, and you so tired!"

"There were orders and dispatches for here," Stuart told her. "I should deliver them now."

But she couldn't let him go just yet.

"Darling, was it a hard campaign? You're thin."

Square and sturdy and strong, but his cheekbones showed through sun and windburn.

"Utah's no land of peace and plenty," he said, "except to God's anointed, which we were not. A barren land to an invading army, but, heigh-ho, we learned how little a man can have to eat and survive. Harder on the horses than on us. Dan's used up, I'm afraid; and I'm glad I didn't take Mischief. Come, I'll walk with you as far as the

parade. I'll tell you everything later. How is *Lar Petite?* And your
mother? I've messages for her, and something for Maria from Doc
Brewer. I think he's sweet on your sister. Did you hear that they've
discovered gold in Colorado?"

Flora had heard, and she heard more about Utah both before and
afterwards than Stuart ever told her. The great snorting, trumpeting
army that Albert Sydney Johnston had led out so proudly had proved
unequal to the task in hand simply because in the wild mountain
country it could not be supplied. Headquarters troops ate their own
mules for meat. The commander of the expedition escaped censure
only because his losses in men were less than they might have been
and other, graver matters presently engrossed people's attention. By
comparison, even gold in Colorado was an incident.

To the Stuarts, again snug in their tight little house at Fort Riley,
the winter following held no great events but was rich in smaller
happenings. They took no part, except as observers, in the rush to
Colorado after gold. Thousands of prospectors passed the fort that
year on their way up the Smoky Hill trail to the mountains. Bill
Cody was one—weedy, starvation thin, bent on making a fortune fast
this time. He was back very soon, thinner than ever, sick from priva-
tion and exposure, mostly from disappointment.

Stuart would hardly ever talk gold. He took the position and held
it that there was more wealth to be dug from the fertile Kansas
prairies than lay hidden in Colorado. He defended his views more
stoutly than ever after an encounter with a lanky, redheaded ex-West
Pointer named Sherman, a dozen years his senior, who had settled in
Leavenworth City. Mr. Sherman had left the army to practise law;
and his handling of settlers' claims sent him out over the territory in
frock coat and buckboard wagon, drawn by a team of excellent
mules, all in the best form and most impressive. He had been with
the army in California in 1848, when gold was discovered there, had
prospected unsuccessfully himself on short leaves. Later, as a civilian,
he had represented a St. Louis bank in San Francisco. He painted a
sombre picture of what went on at the diggings. He might not be
accumulating wealth now at law; but, for a man with a family, law
seemed to him better than gold hunting. He had a charming manner
with ladies, and Flora liked him.

"Law," Stuart said after Mr. Sherman's visit. "There's another good thing. Kansas can do with a lot of lawing." And he had Alec send him some law books.

He talked land investment and he read law. Flora would look at him, sometimes hopefully, trying to picture him as a western farmer, or in a frock coat in a dusty courtroom; but she had to admit that either image was hard to establish.

He was more nearly her own Stuart when he worked at that military belt and sabre attachment that puzzled him so. A simple thing when he had finally solved the problem, it had troubled him ever since the battle with the Cheyenne Indians, when it had taken four cavalry officers to dispatch one Indian.

He would sit at the table, surrounded by strips of thong leather, wire, metal hooks, sharp knives, strong pincers and sheets of paper. Flora would be in a low chair with a bit of sewing or knitting in her lap. The baby would be in her cradle, cooing to herself, or, perhaps, in a chair that Hoskins had fashioned for her—a marvelous chair with broad arms and rockers, cut out of one piece of wood and painted to represent trotting horses.

They would be all together in the small, bright room, but Stuart in his mind back on Solomon Fork, seeing again that Indian aiming his gun at Lomax on foot, seeing himself swinging his sabre to cut the Indian down, but not killing him, seeing Stanley roll off his horse and popping off the last load in his revolver; and there he, Stuart, sat with a useless sword in his hand and no time to sheathe it and draw his gun. There never was time, he explained to Flora; and a man could not, of course, throw his sword away. That was the problem. There had to be a rapid, sure way of dropping it and keeping it. Fastening it to the swordsman's arm was no good. That way a man could mutilate his horse and himself. No, there was some other answer.

For months he pushed things this way and that on the table, sometimes sweeping everything into a heap and abandoning the problem in near despair; but finally there came a time when he sang as he worked. Later, a triumphant evening when he fastened to his sword belt a simple metal ring and to the ring a more carefully fashioned metal hook, to hold his sheathed sabre.

"Draw SABRES!"

His sword flashed out. His silhouette extended up the wall and doubled back on the ceiling. The baby crowed ecstatically. To oblige her, he made a few passes in the air.

"Prepare to DISMOUNT!"

The sabre was sheathed, hanging from his belt. The next minute it and the detachable hook hung on the back of a chair and he faced the same imaginary enemy with drawn revolver. The chair back, he explained, was the pommel of his saddle, and there you were. All very simple, once a man got the right idea. His face was flushed, his breathing rapid.

"Stuart, I am so proud of you! What will you do next?"

"I don't know," he said. "Suppose I ask Alec his opinion?"

Flora was hardly surprised at Alec's reply. What James had written about his invention sounded to Alec most promising, and a radical departure from the old way of sabre straps permanently attached to the sword belt. Was James thinking of applying for a patent? Was there any chance of his coming home this year? They could talk the whole thing over at length then. It had been going on four years, Alec reminded him, and closed with love to Flora and the baby, whom all of them in Virginia were most anxious to see.

"Stuart?" The old unwillingness stirred in Flora.

"I've considerable time coming," Stuart said, not noticing.

A month later to a day Flora was in the kitchen showing Tilda, as teachable as Bellors had been otherwise, how to make a ginger cake, when a noise out on the parade made the black girl drop the hot pan on the table and crouch in a corner, her apron over her head.

"Injuns!" she said. "Is't Injuns, Miss Flo'?"

"No." Flora was startled herself. "Of course not. Our men singing."

"My name it is Joe Bowers . . ."

A promotion, a new baby, new orders?

"I come from County Pike."

Stuart crashed through the door. His color was high even for him, his hair on end, his eyes blazing. He seized Flora by the waist, whirled her around the room in a giddy waltz. He kissed her until her color matched his.

"Stuart, for pity's sake!"

"It's come," he shouted. "My leave! Six months."

Six months? She didn't believe it. She didn't want . . .

"Get out the trunks," Stuart ordered. "We're off for Virginia May first."

Virginia. Half a year this time. Virginia . . .

Stuart chided Flora for her lack of proper comment. She drew off behind a screen of trivialities.

"My clothes! I never supposed—I haven't a thing to wear. No, but really . . ."

Stuart went off into happy laughter. How could he know, how could anyone know what she was truly thinking? She was a little uncertain herself; but she had a feeling that here was something momentous, pregnant with the promise of great change. She would not have been surprised to see the walls of their house crumble and disappear. When they returned from the long leave, would the house still be standing?

All this because of a simple metal ring, and an ingenious, detachable metal hook.

Act Two: JOHN BROWN

Chapter 1. *United States Patent, Number 25,684*

As if in reproach, Virginia was never lovelier than that summer. Laurel was in bloom when they went through the mountains, and the air at the Wytheville depot was soft as a caress when they left the train. Alec met them, as before, but even that was different.

"Welcome," he said to Flora in his slow, easy way. "Welcome home," and smiled, and kissed her. "Seems to me you're looking mighty pert."

For the pertness Rachel Cooke was chiefly responsible. About the time that Stuart's leave had come through, Colonel Cooke had been ordered to Europe to observe army maneuvers over there before completing a book he was writing on cavalry tactics. The Colonel and Rachel and the two younger sisters were now on the ocean, outward bound. However, before that point had been reached, much shopping had to be done by the ladies; and Rachel had included Flora. There had been a glorious three weeks in St. Louis, and a very orgy of buying. Even Stuart, who had packed and stored their belongings at Fort Riley, came on in time to have a new uniform tailored.

"This is no time to be counting pennies," Rachel said—Rachel, the practical one. "We have a position to maintain."

Not since that summer when she had thrown over the outside world and its supposed delights to return to the army had Flora owned so many pretty dresses. No wonder Alec admired her. As for the kiss of welcome—

"I wanted to the first time," he told her, "but, not knowing you, I was a little overawed. You seemed a little starchier then, somehow."

"Scared," she confessed; and a valuable friendship was carried forward.

The gay, mad interlude in St. Louis had put an entirely new aspect on the Virginia journey. Flora wondered now at her misgivings. She and Stuart were both at their best. The new uniform and hat had dug deeply into the price of his servant Ben, whom he had sold back to Kentucky. One servant had been enough for them to carry along and Flora had to have a maid because of the baby. Even Tilda was helping to maintain the family position.

And, of course, there was the baby. Pet, the Virginia Stuarts called her, shortening Jemmie's *La Petite*, to suit their tongues.

"She looks like you, Jemmie," the grandmother said—her highest praise.

"Except that she is small and finely built like Flora," Stuart answered. "A Cooke in that respect."

His mother turned the conversation.

"You have changed, Jemmie."

He had changed. Flora could see that, using the eyes of those who had not been by to watch time's processes. It was not that he looked older. She doubted that James Stuart would ever have lines in his face like those showing now in Alec's. His eyes, his high spirits, his restless, abounding health of body had not altered and probably never would. A person could not think of him as anything but imperishably young. And yet, there was growth and change. Maturity, some settling influence had smoothed the jutting edges, the roughness, the insistence on recognition of first manhood.

"You have changed, Jemmie," his mother said, her own hair now all gray under her lace cap; and Flora could have sworn there was relief in her tone. Some doubt or mistrust that had followed them westward four years before this had been removed by what she thought she saw now in her turbulent youngest son. Things had turned out better for him than she had been willing to believe they would. Here he was, seeming quite settled, for him, with the beginning of a nice family; and she was thankful.

"Well, I'm thankful, too," Flora thought, "but I could have told her."

A lovely summer. No mourning. Daytimes, at Laurel Hill, if

Stuart was about, Flora had little rest. He must show her where the hornets took after him long ago, the pool where he had learned to swim, the tree that had the best apples, the one he fell out of for fear of more hornets. They would ride their horses to call on his friends, to spend the day, to invite the friends in turn to take a meal and spend an evening at Laurel Hill. If the evening was fine and they sat out of doors, Flora would play her guitar and sing.

And then she would quiet the strings under her hand and sit back and listen to Stuart answering questions about Kansas. He talked with sureness and authority, telling them of the changes that had come about out there, of the towns now springing up under the blessings of peace, of the Pikes Peak or Bust gold rush. But the wonder was not in Stuart's manner of telling these things, it was the respectful tone of the questions. She thought it was not only Stuart who had changed, or Kansas. While they were away, something had happened to Virginia.

"And now," Alec said one evening, his interruption as sudden as a bull frog's booming in the soft dark, "Kansas will come in a free state, after all; and Eli Thayer and Beecher and their New England Emigrant Aid Society have won the decision, as we might have known they would."

"Kansas will come in without slavery," Stuart answered, "but no one man, more than another, is responsible. The fertile soil would tempt anyone to settle there, but the rigor of the winters makes it a white man's land."

"You mean," Alec went on deliberately, thoughtfully, "it would have come out the same if nobody had lifted voice or hand to direct the course of nature? Meddlers, then, have shed the blood. Meddlers, one of the seven abominations of the Lord."

Flora wished it were not quite so dark, so that she could have seen Stuart's face or Alec's. However, if there had been light, a shadow might have fallen across the friendly gathering—the shadow of a man named Brown or one of those others. Gently again she touched the strings of her guitar.

> *"When the swallows homeward fly,*
> *When the roses scattered lie . . ."*

Another day she was talking to Mrs. Stuart about Bellors.

"I wondered at the time how you would make out with the girl," Mother Stuart said. "Oh, dear, if we had kept her here, we, too, might have had to send her away." She smoothed the hem of a fine handkerchief with her fingers. "That is our problem in Virginia— how to take care of our people. They come to us naturally, as inheritance usually. There is little buying or selling, until they increase in number by marriage and births and there are too many. What can we do then but send them away? We don't like to do it, but what else can we do?"

"Ask Harriet Beecher Stowe," Mary Stuart said, "or her brother. Either of them could tell you."

"Mary, I wish you would not mention that woman's name in my hearing. I have asked you not to. As for her brother . . ."

"Massachusetts," Mary insisted, "always could tell Virginia what she ought to do, better than she knows herself."

"I suppose so," Mrs. Stuart agreed, hearkening back to some old, old memory or tale. "They never did get on too well. Still," she thought another minute, then drew herself up proudly, "we were here first." And, to clinch the argument, "George Washington was a Virginian."

And that was about as close as ladies came to the troubled talk that drew men together in bunches on almost any street corner, among the columns of a county courthouse, at the races, even in church porticos that summer of 1859; but the trouble was there, in the hearts of everyone.

The sabre attachment, then, took the Stuarts to Carlisle Barracks in Pennsylvania. In after years that was a thing to contemplate—the potency of small things. Stuart himself spoke of his invention so on that day in Alec's law office, when the three of them settled on a plan of action.

A new sword belt of leather, equipped with Stuart's ring and hook, a drawing in detail of the new device, another of the old-style belt and attachment, and a neatly written manual of instructions, lay spread out on Alec's desk, under Alec's eyes and hand. James Stuart, a restless sitter on chairs at any time, stood by a tall, narrow window. Flora sat, expectant, silent, in a consultant's chair.

"It's a small thing, I know, Alec," Stuart said, "but, if it is good, it can be important. If it has any possibilities," he knew it had, "for my family's sake and my own, I should like to make the most of them."

"Well," Alec, too, was maintaining an attitude, his manner carefully noncommittal, "it could amount to something. It is presented now in good style, and I will take the proper steps with the Patent Office. Meanwhile, although it is not desirable to show it around generally, had you thought of consulting some higher army authority?"

"We wondered," Stuart favored Flora with a slow wink, "about the Cavalry Board at Carlisle."

"Excellent," Alec said. "The least they can offer is an endorsement."

However much he knew of law, how little he knew the army! Lieutenant Stuart and his army wife should have known better what to expect. At Carlisle, they stayed with friends, and the visit on the whole was happy; but Flora so far had never spent a more anxious day than the one on which Stuart by special appointment demonstrated his invention before the Cavalry Board in full session. He was gone for hours; and she, waiting just where he had told her good-bye, knew from the manner of his dismounting at the curb that the experience had been trying. Just let him swagger noticeably and there was bound to be trouble. She was down the steps and into his arms on the instant.

"Stuart, was it awful?"

He made a face.

"Just like the examining board at West Point. I . . . had forgotten."

"Stuart! But then you did all right. You didn't mind."

"A man never gets past minding, I reckon. I must have given six full demonstrations."

"My darling, I wish I had been there."

"It would have helped," he said. "Nobody else cared about anything but thinking up new questions. One old fuddy-duddy in particular made a game of trying to trip me. I wanted to spit him on my sabre."

"Stuart . . . and what then? What did they say finally?"

He drew away. He swelled out his chest.

"They said . . . 'Hmmm!' "

"Oh, no!" But she had to laugh. Stuart laughed with her. Her eyes were moist before she finished and so were his. "That couldn't be all."

"Couldn't it?" he asked. "They said it was. 'That is all, Mr. Stuart. We will render an opinion later.' "

It was the end of the week before the opinion was stated. The officers were impressed, to the extent that they regretted they had no power to act officially on the invention. They advised Lieutenant Stuart to submit it next to the War Department in Washington.

So, they went on to Philadelphia; and Stuart left Flora there, with the baby and Tilda, at the home of the Doughertys while he went down to Washington to interview the Adjutant General. His good friend and classmate, Custis Lee, had offices in the same building. Custis would tell him how to present his case properly.

And the Adjutant General said, "Put your application in writing and leave it here with me. I will let you know."

Custis Lee made Stuart sit right down in his office and write the letter, then carried him off to Arlington for a visit with the Lee family.

"He sounds like a wonderful person," Flora said, hearing the report. "Captain Lee?"

"Captain Lee," Stuart agreed, with no grudging, "and a prince of the blood royal."

"Was Colonel Lee at home?" He was more her own Stuart, recalling Arlington, than when he spoke of his disappointment. "You think so highly of him!"

"No, he was away," Stuart said. "Court-martial duty somewhere. But Mrs. Lee was kind enough for two. She said when I came back to Washington, I must bring you and *Lar Petite* and stay at Arlington. I thanked her, of course, but I don't know. She is not well and seems anything but strong. Miss Mary Lee says when her rheumatism is bad, she suffers horridly."

"Oh!" Flora said. "There is a Miss Mary in that house, too?"

Stuart laughed.

"And a Miss Mildred, and Miss Agnes, and Miss Annie, and young

Bob. Those were all who were at home then, beside Custis and me."

"Mercy, what a household!"

Two months passed. It was now October, the last month of the long leave. The Stuarts were in Richmond, attending a national gathering of the Episcopal Church, and visiting relatives and friends. It was a happy climax to a busy summer and gave them something to do while they waited to hear from the War Department.

But why didn't they hear? Alec in Wytheville had their Richmond address. So did Custis Lee in Washington have it. If there was a communication, they should receive it without too much delay. There was the telegraph, besides. Flora was afraid her petitions in St. Paul's had narrowed to one subject. She did so want Stuart to carry some official recognition of his worth back to Kansas!

Then, quite suddenly, when they had just about given up hope of ever hearing, there it was—an official document, heavy with seals, the address scratched and written over in Alec's fine script—waiting on a tray in the front hall of their boarding house.

The Secretary of War had written. Would Lieutenant Stuart please report at his earliest opportunity to the office of the Adjutant General to discuss the possible adoption of his military belt as cavalry equipment for the army? The letter arrived Saturday afternoon. Sunday Stuart boarded a train for Washington.

Monday morning he awoke with the capital, and was out at the columned entrance of the long, brick barracks at 17th and Pennsylvania so early that the guards, in spite of his uniform, looked on him with distrust. He turned his back on their glassy stares and took to pacing the sidewalk. Wore a visible path on the bricks, he said later, before the doors officially opened and someone was good enough to take his letter of summons as a card of admission and let him in. Some time after that he found himself once more in the anteroom of the office of Colonel Drinkard, Chief Clerk of the War Department. The Colonel, glancing at the letter, remembered him.

"Stuart—First Cavalry—the sabre thing. Very interesting. You are prompt in reporting."

"The letter is almost a week old," Stuart pointed out. "I telegraphed from Richmond Saturday saying I would be here today."

"Saturday? Yes, of course. Please sit down. Make yourself comfortable. Monday is a busy day. Many things to pick up. However, I
will arrange for someone to see you presently."

Presently? It was past eleven o'clock before Colonel Drinkard
summoned him. Stuart rose gauntly and the two men started for the
hall door. An orderly appeared and stood at stiff salute.

"Colonel Drinkard, sir, the Commanding General asks you to come
to his office at once. It is urgent."

The orderly faced about and disappeared. Colonel Drinkard followed, leaving Stuart once more stranded. But not for long. Urgent,
the orderly had said; and footsteps multiplied now in the corridor.
The situation seemed to call for reconnaissance. Again Stuart went
to the door. Down the hall a young man in an ensign's uniform
waited outside a similar closed door. The door opened presently and
a clerk handed the ensign an envelope. He saluted, and hurried
away. Two minutes later Colonel Drinkard appeared.

"Lieutenant Stuart? You're still here? Good! You are acquainted
with Arlington, the home of Colonel Lee? Fine! We need a courier.
The orders are confidential. If you . . ."

"I'll be proud to ride to Arlington for you, sir."

He still had no idea what the disturbance was about, but the
urgency was a beating of drums in his ears.

"You see," he explained to Flora afterwards, "besides old General
Winfield Scott, Colonel Lee was the only high ranking officer within
call."

"Oh, darling," Flora said, "and your invention?"

"Nobody thought of that," Stuart said.

It was a beautiful October day. Dogwood flamed scarlet against
the white pillars of Arlington. The Negro major-domo was also in
fine contrast.

"Colonel Lee is in his study, Lieutenant. If you will step inside . . ."

"I'll wait out here, Ned, if I may. I've been indoors all morning."

He never wanted to be commanding general of the United States
if it meant being cooped up . . .

Colonel Lee even in fatigue coat and slippers was the taut,

immaculate gentleman that Stuart remembered from the military academy. He approached his former cadet with outstretched, open hand.

"Mr. Stuart, I declare I shouldn't have known you, except that Rooney and Custis have in a way prepared me. Rooney came home from Kansas with a prodigious beard, but, as he said, no match for yours." A glimmer of amusement lighted the clear, straightforward eyes. He was smooth-shaven then himself, except for close-trimmed side whiskers. "I'm sorry I missed you in August."

Then he took the order from the War Department and read it, Stuart thought, twice. He turned to the servant and said quietly,

"Have a horse saddled for me, please. I shall be riding back to the capital with Lieutenant Stuart."

"And all the time," Flora said, "you had no idea what had happened?"

"I am not sure that Colonel Lee knew," Stuart said, "but that was when he asked me to be his aide."

They were riding along, Stuart a respectful pace or two to the rear, Colonel Lee pondering something thoughtfully. Suddenly he turned to Stuart.

"I may have to undertake a small military assignment," he said. "In that case, I should, I think, have an aide. Would you oblige me?"

The warning drum beat more loudly in Stuart's ears as he replied that he would be proud to serve the Colonel so.

Five hours later he sat beside Colonel Lee in the dusty coach of a train bound for Baltimore, Maryland. Five hours—the time had been spent by Colonel Lee in conference with various top authorities in Washington, up to and including President Buchanan. A steadily accelerated rushing about had attended all the conferences, giving the impression of rising panic. Panic, it seemed to Stuart, was absurd, disgraceful, and a waste of time. Action, prompt and decisive, was what the occasion demanded, even if the wildest rumors flying about everywhere were true. Clinging to his official status as Lee's aide, beating his heels in impatience against the floors of a dozen anterooms by now, he had had no trouble in gathering information. Boiled down to the terms of a news dispatch, what the crisis amounted to was that a mob of insurrectionists on Sunday evening, the day before, had invaded the town of Harper's Ferry, Virginia, had fired upon and killed several unarmed citizens, taken others captive, and seized the government arsenal. They were in possession of the arsenal now, were holding their captives—all prominent people—there as hostages, for what purpose, nobody exactly knew.

"A mob," Stuart said to Colonel Lee on the train, "armed with clubs and rifles. That's the kind of thing we had in Kansas. I didn't suppose it could happen in Virginia."

"I'm afraid it has happened," Lee said. Over the clack of wheels his tone seemed extraordinarily quiet, though he did not minimize the situation or its seriousness. The delay in Washington seemed to him legitimate. He himself had wanted as many facts and as clear orders as possible before he set out for the scene; and verifiable facts were hard to secure since by now telegraphic communication with the town had been cut and the Baltimore and Ohio Railroad was not sending trains across the river. The railroad, which had given the first warning of the uprising, reported that firing was still heard in Harper's Ferry, and another source had stated that one of the hostages held was Colonel Lewis Washington. Lee hoped for more detailed information when they reached Baltimore.

He hoped also to overtake a detachment of marines which had entrained at Washington earlier in the afternoon. Ninety men, under a Lieutenant Israel Green, with a Major Russell, paymaster of the corps, to lend him countenance purely, a paymaster not being eligible to take a command. A glimmer of amusement sparkled in Colonel Lee's eyes.

"There seems to have been a lack of fighting men, as well as of ranking officers, at the capital." Then he was once more quietly solemn. "I think ninety marines will be sufficient. Maryland and Virginia are sending or have sent militia. The situation is grave, but I anticipate that the nearer we come to Harper's Ferry, the smaller the mob will prove to be. You may have heard talk of a slave uprising. I put no stock in that. However, we do have certainly an insurrection and it must be dealt with."

They did not overtake the marines at Baltimore, in spite of an order Lee had sent them from Washington. When the train carrying him and Stuart stopped at an engine relay house outside the city, he was told that Lieutenant Green's company, together with a contingent of Maryland militia, had left an hour before.

There was no humor in the clear brown eyes then. Crisply Lee called for the yard superintendent.

"Is there a way station this side of Harper's Ferry with a telegraph operator?" he demanded.

There was a place called Sandy Hook, one mile this side of the river.

"Order the agent to flag that train and hold it." He added a second order to Lieutenant Green: "All troops detrain at Sandy Hook wait for me there. Colonel R. E. Lee, United States Army, Commanding."

"And now," he said to the yard superintendent as the telegraph keys began to transmit the orders, "please clear the tracks and send me on without further delay."

The superintendent scratched his ear. There wasn't another train . . .

"It is imperative that I proceed at once to Harper's Ferry—by a handcar, if nothing else is available."

They made the journey in the cab of the railroad's newest locomotive. Early autumn dark had fallen before they got away. Stuart, begging now for active duty, was given authority over the engine's whistle and managed to drown out conversation and, it was possible, any complicated thought. A few more details had been gathered at Baltimore about the trouble Lee had been sent to settle. The insurgents were led by a man calling himself Smith, who, a few months before this, had leased a farm in Maryland. It was plain now, of course, that he had no intention of raising a crop there. So far as anyone knew, he had not planted one. He had gone to work at once to gather his force of conspirators.

He had black men in his band as well as white. He had led them into Harper's Ferry on a Sunday evening when folks were going home from church, looking for anything but trouble. That was how the mob had been able to seize notable prisoners. Time anybody got to a gun, it was all over. The man and his mob had hold of the arsenal and the hostages were locked up inside.

A man named Smith . . . black men and white . . . Stuart bore down on the whistle cord.

Whoo-oo-oo! The whistle shrieked its alarm, clearing the right of way through the dark for the pounding locomotive. At scattered stations lanterns waved it on and blank, staring faces watched it pass. Whoo-oo! How far Sandy Hook? Those are Virginia gentlemen shut up in that arsenal at the mercy of the mob. How far? Not far now. Eight o'clock, nine o'clock, ten o'clock. Campfires speckled the dark. Is this Sandy Hook? That's it, sir, just ahead. We made it.

A young man, taut and correct in the poor light, stiffened to a salute beside the engine cab.

"Lieutenant Green, sir. My marines are at your disposal."

An older man in army blues removed his hat and extended his hand.

"Major Russell, sir. Colonel, thank God you've come! This is a mess."

In the background, others, representing the militia of two sovereign states, waited to be recognized.

"Sir," someone, indubitably a Virginian, said, "we beg to inform you that, whatever you may have heard to the contrary, loyal militia is now in full possession of the city of Harper's Ferry. Aided by the citizens, who were taken at a disadvantage yesterday evening, we have established patrols. Every road leading to and from . . ."

"The bridge over the Potomac?" Lee prompted. There was an edge to his question. In the mad ride just completed, he had had no whistle cord with which to relieve his mounting tension.

"That, too, is now in our hands."

"And the armory? What is the situation there?"

"Well . . . ah. . . ."

"I take it this man Smith still holds the government arsenal."

"Well . . . ah, not precisely. This evening, seeing that the forces surrounding him were increasing, the leader of the mob saw fit to shift his position. He . . . ah . . . moved from the arsenal to another building on the armory grounds—a smaller building housing a fire engine and . . ."

"Why did he do that?"

"The engine house is fairly impregnable, sir, having stout stone walls and double doors, but no windows."

"I see. And he made this move unmolested?"

"Well . . . ah . . . by then Smith and his followers were well supplied with arms. There were the hostages to be considered. None of us wanted to be guilty of shooting down a fellow Virginian."

Deep silence held the night for a full minute; and then . . .

"Lieutenant Green! Call out your men. We will march at once into Harper's Ferry."

The town of Harper's Ferry nestled in a sharp triangle made by the union of the two mountain rivers—the Shenandoah and the Potomac. Just beyond the bridge, on the Virginia side, lay the armory grounds. A little farther along stood the small railroad depot. In the depot building in the small hours of the morning, Stuart wrote out by lamplight Lee's ultimatum to the insurgents. Outside, Lieutenant Green had broken the lock on a tool shed and was issuing sledge hammers to his marines. This was Lee's consideration of the hostages. He would take the engine house without the firing of a gun.

The ultimatum was brief and clear. Colonel Lee of the United States Army, commanding troops sent by the President to suppress insurrection at Harper's Ferry, demanded surrender of all in the armory buildings. If they would surrender peaceably and restore stolen property, he promised them safety, under guard, to await further orders of the President. If they refused, he called their attention to the fact that the armory was surrounded by troops, that they could not escape and, if he were compelled to use force, he could not answer for their safety.

"Lieutenant Stuart," Colonel Lee looked up from a final study of the wording, "your service with me continues on a purely voluntary basis. You are under no obligation to carry my order to the leader of the insurrectionists. Although his followers, considering the size of the engine house, must be far fewer in number than rumor states, they are desperate men. You run a great risk, even showing a flag of truce."

"Colonel Lee, I consider carrying your order part of my assigned duty, and I accept the risk."

"Well, good! You understand there is to be no parleying. If the answer is no, you will step outside at once and wave your hat where Lieutenant Green can see you."

"I understand." Excitement was mounting in him, other emotions beating below it. Colonel Washington, other gentlemen, of no hostile intent toward anyone, shut up in that brick shed, no comforts of any kind, their lives threatened.

What remained of the night was given to assigning all participants to their various stations. Daylight came at half-past six, and showed the militia set in a wide circle around the level green of the armory grounds, with citizens of the town on every rising slope and housetop and tree to the rear. On the green itself, Israel Green's marines in three companies, the first armed with sledge hammers, the second and third with bayonets fixed, waited for Stuart to deliver the ultimatum and to give them the signal for attack. They were very sure, and so was Stuart, that the signal would come.

At seven sharp, Stuart left Lee standing on a small rise of ground about forty feet from the engine house and, with a white handkerchief waving from the tip of his sabre, marched across the green. Two thousand people, at least, watched him go. He had no realization of fear; but his objective, the stone engine house, did increase in size as he approached it. The doors, he saw now, were formidable —double doors of oak, nail studded, with a stone abutment dividing them. No windows, as he had been told, but surely some opening that would allow him to be heard. He drew out Lee's order and in loud, ringing tones read it through.

There was a sound of a bolt being drawn, and the door to the left of the abutment moved. It opened about four inches, no more. The barrel of a carbine was thrust through the opening. Stuart waited, breathing hard. The opening widened and a face appeared above the menacing gun—a grimy face, a long, tangled gray beard, pale wild eyes, more tangled gray hair low on a furrowed forehead. Stuart could not help a short step backward. Osawatomi Brown! That he, James Ewell Brown Stuart, should have been sent here to make identification certain. It looked like Fate.

At the same instant, the carbine wavered in its aim. John Brown did not recognize Lieutenant Stuart but he did the uniform. Desperate he might be, but not desperate enough to shoot down a United States regular. He began now to bargain for terms. He wanted to take his wagon and his prisoners across the river to the Maryland shore. He named a place where he would set the captives free. Out of the gloom behind him one of the captives spoke up:

"Never mind us here. Shoot!"

But others were not so brave. They begged the young man, whoever he was, to urge Colonel Lee in person to come to the engine
house to confer with Captain Smith. The darkness, the groans, the
plaints, old Brown's whining insistence brought Stuart's disgust to
a boil. No parley, Lee had said, no parley. He stepped aside, waved
his hat and the marines came forward with a rush. The old man and
the carbine disappeared. The door slammed to.

There was still no firing inside or outside of the engine house.
The hammers in the hands of the marines beat upon the doors but
with as little visible effect as the drumming of woodpeckers in the
spring. They'd never break through at that rate. On the green near
by lay a ladder. Israel Green's eyes fell on it and brightened.

In seconds the ladder was in the hands of his men, twelve to each
side. The lieutenant let out his breath in an explosive order. The ram
drove against the wood. Weakened, perhaps, after all, by the sledge
hammers, the boards gave with a splintering crash. With a roar of
triumph, the marines pulled back the ladder and young Green, with
sword drawn, went through the gaping hole. He went in so instantly
that nobody had time to shoot him down. The first of his men to
follow him, however, fell, and the second. Then there was a groan
and thud. Somebody called, "He's down. You got him, sir. That does
it."

Presently the doors opened wide. The marines carried John Brown
out, bleeding from a shallow wound in his neck. They laid him and
their two fallen comrades, one dead, the other badly wounded, side
by side on the grass. The attack on Harper's Ferry was over, but
this could not be the end of it.

"Osawatomi still had his gun and his knife when they laid him
down," Stuart said, walking the floor as he relived the day for Flora.
"They took them away, of course, finally. I asked for the knife and
got it. I mean to keep it."

"Stuart?" Flora begged. Never before had she seen hate in his
eyes.

"He'll never use gun or knife again, I promise you. Two men he
had with him in Kansas, the kind of men who followed him out
there, were with him at Harper's Ferry, too. They'd gone north with
him to Canada. He hatched this plot while he was still out west."

"If it had happened anywhere except in Virginia!" Flora said, she and uncounted others.

"That was part of the plot," Stuart said implacably. "He can say he was not an incendiary or a ruffian, that he had come only to aid those suffering a great wrong; but . . . Colonel Lee sent me over to his place in Maryland the next day and there was his wagon—his Kansas wagon, I could swear, with pikes and cutlasses, just as I remember it."

"Stuart, what will they do with him now?"

"Hang him surely. He seized United States property. He shot down two men sent by the President to arrest him. Maybe it would have been better all around if Green had run him through instead of just nicking him. They'll hang him, and the North will have a martyr and the South a cause. You'll see."

She saw too clearly. A day or so later John Brown said it in his way from prison: "Men of the South, I warn you, prepare. The end is not yet."

"Stuart," Flora said, "kiss me. Try to forget, if only for a little while."

She would coax him back to smile and song, using every loving way; but it would be, she knew, only for a little while. They would go back to Kansas and the blessed routine of a prairie fort, but no place was sanctuary now.

"Men of the South, I warn you . . ."

Chapter 2. *A Man of the South*

The blessed routine of a prairie fort.

They stopped in St. Louis on their way home and Stuart bought Flora a velvet jacket. It was a sure enough jacket this time, short, with flaring tails, and most impractical for the plains in winter; but it was a love of a wrap, the sleeves bordered with soft, brown fur. Otter, the furrier said.

"Darling," Flora protested, "we shouldn't, you know. We've spent too much money as it is this year."

But Stuart would listen to no words of thrift or prudence.

"It will give folks something to talk about besides—you know—old John Brown," he said.

"They will buzz about the jacket," Flora agreed, preening before a long mirror, "and, when we're not within hearing, about your extravagance; but I'm afraid, dear, they will still want to know about John Brown."

And she wanted him to tell about it, because of late he had developed a tendency, strange in him, toward reticence. When the Harper's Ferry tragedy—she could never think of it otherwise—was new, he had talked freely about his part in the action, especially to her, as if he might so expel the memory of it from his consciousness. Now, never forgetting it, no matter how he tried, he studied it alone, leaving her outside and wondering. This was a new thing in their lives together; and it frightened her more than the event itself or any significance that the world might attach to the capture and execution of a madman and a martyr. The pretty jacket was to make her smile, when Stuart couldn't. Not with quite the gay abandon of before, at least.

"We'll have to bear with the questioning, I suppose," Flora said. "If it gets too tiresome, I'll help you turn it aside. We can show them your patent. We should frame it, really."

A handsome document, complete with drawings. J. E. B. STUART —BELT. Seeing his name in bold type heading the page made her jump every time she looked at it, which was often. A paper could not give her love distinction, but it told the world he was extraordinary.

They went on to Kansas then, and everything was much as Flora had foreseen—a buzz over their arrival and all that had happened while they were away, admiration and envy for the jacket, congratulations over the patent. And after that, John Brown. What a thing that Stuart should have been in Washington when it happened!

"We should have caught him at Osawatomi," Captain McIntyre said.

"You can't stop what he stood for that way," David Stanley objected. "I mean, there would have been some other. Sorry, Beauty. It must have looked bad at the time."

"Yes," Stuart said, his eyes like coals.

Then, blessedly, routine enveloped them with the others—mail escort, drill, guard, patrol—work and fun, fun and work; and the outside world receded as the year wore away, only troubling echoes drifting in with newspapers and periodicals; but they were few and still not too bad.

One of the things that had happened during the Stuarts' absence was the acquisition of a full-scale, uniformed regimental band. It played for the Christmas and New Year's dances and, almost before winter was over, when wind and weather permitted, gave concerts on the parade on Sunday afternoons. People from all the county attended. Nothing was beyond the range of the leader's ambition, though many pieces seemed out of reach for his musicians. Practice nights were more fun for the post than concerts. Everybody sat or strolled out of doors, to listen and offer comment.

Early in 1860 the Cookes came home from Europe; and Maria married Dr. Charles Brewer, the young and personable surgeon attached to the First Cavalry. The Brewers moved into quarters at Fort Riley; and, with two girls out of three in residence, Rachel and the youngest sister, Julia, spent much of their time also at the same post, especially after Colonel Cooke was given command of the new military department of Utah.

Eighteen-sixty was a great year for Cookes generally, Stuart said. The Colonel's book on cavalry tactics was finished, the last annotation made. It was now in the hands of the War Department, being edited for printing and official issue. With a department to command, and his name on everyone's lips, Colonel Cooke could count now on the star of a brigadier-general.

"High time," Rachel said, considering the gray in his hair.

Flora, too, thought that her father, for the first time to her knowing, looked older, and a little tired. His step was as firm, his back as straight as before; but this was a conscious tautness. He said he was weary of travel and study, and glad to take active command again. Utah? Yes—the farther, the better. There were times when a man needed to be alone, to set his thoughts in line.

He set out with his staff for Utah Territory in August, leaving his family at Riley. He left with a smart salute and a jest: "If you need to get word to me, send a line by pony express."

There was that, too, this year of years. Bill Cody rode part of the route, taking on the dispatch bag at Kearny. Before the regular rides began, he came to Riley to tell the Stuarts of his appointment. A handsome boy, with his blond hair and keen hunter's eyes. Just fourteen, but sure now that he had attained full manhood.

And that summer it was the Kiowa Indians, blood brothers to the Comanche, who went on the warpath. These were savages—primitive, blood-lusting—among the cruelest on the Great Plains. They fought still with bows and arrows. The First Cavalry rode out to deal with them. Lieutenant Bayard took a stone arrowhead deep in one cheekbone. Stuart and Charles Brewer brought him back to Riley, to send him on by ambulance and steamboat to St. Louis for better surgery than the young doctor thought he could compass; and, protectively, neither would let Flora say a word of good-bye to the poor fellow, or even encourage her to ask questions.

Their reason was that Flora was now expecting her second child. Stuart cupped her chin in his hand and searched her face with his eyes.

"How are you?" he asked.

Clear eyes again and new sun and windburn. Oh, better a battle with Kiowa Indians than the dark, evil thing that could eat a man's heart away!

"I am very well," she assured him.

"Is she?" Stuart turned to Rachel for assurance.

"Yes," Rachel said, "but she will be better now that she has seen you."

However . . .

"Any news?" Stuart asked in the next breath; and joy faded. There was plenty of news—too much. Fist fights in the national Congress. There were men in that body who would have done well to take themselves to a salt desert, to set their thoughts in line.

"Any letters from home?" That was better. If only there were enough slow, easy-going, shrewd men like William Alexander Stuart! Alec, too, thought it was a time for cool heads, not hot ones, to rule.

Stuart read his brother's letter and pocketed it without comment, but he hadn't time to go through the accumulation of newspapers.

"Make a bundle of them, will you?" he asked Flora. "Here, I'll help you roll them."

All that he could carry, wrapped in oilcloth, strapped to his saddle.

Now, if the Kiowa set the plains afire, let it be the papers that burned, not her dear one.

It was the Kiowa and their brothers, the Comanche, that took Stuart away again over winter. The fighting companies had barely time to rest and remount and pass on the improvement of the band at Riley before new orders came, this time for a detail to proceed to Colorado, equipped to pass the winter, their purpose being to locate a new fort near the headwaters of the Arkansas.

Again the tenderness of parting was an opiate for the pain of separation. Stuart held Flora long and close that blustery October morning.

"If it's a boy," he said, "we will name him for your father."

"Not Jemmie?" she asked. "That's what I've been calling him."

As foolishly fond as another proud woman whom she knew.

"If you want to please me," Stuart said, "I'd prefer the other."

And that, as always, was the end of debate.

"It will please me, too, darling," she answered. "I hope you know that. And papa, though he will make a joke about it. When did you think of it?"

That seemed important.

"That summer when he and I were together in Utah." So long ago? "I never talked much about that campaign. It was a bad time, but he made even the bad look good. I said then that if ever I had a son, I should want him to be such a man—and he could be, with you his mother. Your father never lost his way or his head or his power of command. He . . . well, really," he finished with the old tribute: "the *ne plus ultra!*"

Flora drew his head down and kissed him—his brave eyes, his forehead.

"My darling, you make me very happy and proud. God bless you, and keep you. I don't suppose we can look to hear from you often?"

"Not often," he said. "When there is a courier, I'll send you word; and you must do the same, telling me all the news. Promise?"

"I promise. And you will think of us always—three of us—back here, waiting?"

This time, when he rode away, his eyes were wet, not hers.

Their son was born in November, again a healthy child. Pain was forgotten in a fierce, glad pride of possession; and, if she could not send word immediately to Stuart, why, then, other news, for the same reasons, could not go forward. Her last letter from him had come shortly before the birth of the baby. He was well. They had got log huts built in their camp ahead of the first deep snow. Hunting was excellent. He sent love and kisses to his two sweethearts.

December passed. January brought news from Washington. South Carolina had led off in a movement toward secession. More states followed. February came. Six seceded states set up a provisional government for the Confederate States of America at Montgomery, Alabama, and named Jefferson Davis President but snow still drifted deep in all the mountain passes. March, and the swift mountain streams broke through their barriers of ice. Now, one could look for floods. April—there was a loud "Halloa!" from the parade; and, before Flora could reach the door of their house, Stuart had opened it.

"My dear, my dear, my dear!"

Warmed and dry, he knelt by the sleeping baby's cradle, properly awed.

"He looks like you," he said.

"Do you think so?" Flora answered. "We couldn't be sure."

"You knew it all along, you rascal. Brigadier-General Philip St. George—Stuart!" He grinned with delight, then, frowning, got to his feet. Carefully, because of the sleeping child, he tiptoed over to the fire and sat down.

"Where's *Lar Petite?*"

"Tilda," Flora explained, "usually puts her down for her nap in the kitchen. Then, whichever baby wakes up first doesn't disturb the other. Often both of them sleep right through to Stables."

So easy to regulate a house when all about was regular.

"Ah-h-h!" Stuart stretched his legs out to the warmth, and leaned back against the chair. "Don't ask me to move for a week," he said.

A week? But surely . . .

"Stuart?"

He turned his head to smile at her. The tenderest smile, she thought, that he had ever given her. Yes, because of what was to follow.

"Come here," he ordered. "Sit down. No, not way over there. Here, close beside me. That's right. Now. How brave are you?"

She began at once to quake.

"I am not brave at all. Surely by now you know that. Any pretense otherwise is just pretense."

"A brave pretense then, I call it." He took one of her hands and held it between his. "You didn't send on any papers after I left, as I asked you to," he accused.

She shook her head.

"I thought . . . did you . . . ?"

"Yes, I did," he said gravely. "I know everything that has happened. Never mind how. I don't suppose you've had a late report on Virginia?"

Nothing within the week. She was now cold with apprehension.

"I have two letters here that I wanted to show you before I sent them on."

He didn't say he wouldn't send them if she disapproved. Simply he wanted her to know about them. One was addressed to Mr. Jefferson Davis, United States Senator from Mississippi; but Mr. Davis was no longer a senator. He . . .

"I wrote the letter in January," Stuart explained.

And then he hadn't sent it, perhaps because he could not. He had held it—it hardly mattered why. What did matter was what the letter said:

> No sane man can fail to calculate on a rupture of our national bonds . . . I beg leave in such an event respectfully to ask you to secure for me a position in the Army of the South.

He gave references—Colonel Lee, General J. E. Johnston, Colonel Cooke.

"Stuart, have you consulted papa?"

"I would if I could, dear heart. You know that, but I am sure he would give his approval. How could he do otherwise?"

"Will you wait?"

"No, I have waited—longer than I thought I could."

The second letter was to Alec and just finished.

> I feel I must tell you my course of conduct. Naturally I go with Virginia.

Naturally. There was something then about a legion of cavalry. Alec was to begin enlisting it in Wythe County.

"But, Stuart," Flora said faintly, "Virginia still doesn't know . . ."
"I know," he said.

Surely, she thought, the walls will go down now, and I have been living in a fool's paradise. No. For months she had been anticipating this day, merely pushing her foreknowledge aside.

"Darling, is there no other way?" she asked even now. "You—all of us have so much to lose."

He knew that, too. Protest in his own heart was the fire in his eyes, the bitterness of his words as he walked the floor presently, talking wildly of coercion, of invasion, of sacred rights. He knew. In a way his heart, too, was breaking; but his mind was made up.

The baby awoke and cried. Flora took him up.

"Don't tell the others just yet," she begged. "Must you?"

"Maria knows," he said. "I brought her a letter from Doc. He's staying in Colorado, of course, until camp breaks up."

"Stuart, Charles Brewer—who else?"

"Well, most of us. Beale, McIntyre, Lomax . . ."

"Not Uncle John?"

"No, not Old Sedge," he admitted. Some older heads, he supposed, would hesitate. Not all. There was one who would act with promptness and decision. One of these days he, too, would come riding from the west.

No, it would not be like that, Flora knew. If the day came when Brevet Brigadier-General Cooke felt that he no longer cared to have a place in the army he had served so long, he would take his leave in high style, observing the last rite of punctilio. If that day came, but would it? "There are times," he had said, "when a man needs to be alone, to set his thoughts in line."

"Stuart, wait until we hear from papa," she implored. "Wait a little longer. Nothing is certain."

She was beating puny hands against inexorable destiny. How he chafed under the waiting!

"If Virginia goes out, and there is war, I want to be among the first in line. Don't you see?"

Two things broke the spell finally. One was the bombardment of Fort Sumter. How fast that news traveled! The other was a letter from John Cooke in Texas. Rachel brought it to the house for them to read. Practically the entire Eighth Infantry was marching north and east, under a Major Longstreet.

"I don't seem to recall him," Rachel said unhappily; and now she, too, began to show her years.

And Stuart would wait no longer, even though there was still no word from Colonel Cooke or from Virginia.

"What do they find to argue about this length of time?" he fumed.

They were anxious men, sorrowful, too, east and west, north and south.

"It can end only one way."

"Yes," Flora agreed and began packing.

"I must go now," he said. "You can wait here until I send you word."

No. Not possibly. They were his family. If he left, they left with him, even to Tilda.

"You don't have to go with us," Flora said to the black girl. "Nobody knows what will come of all this. You'll be better off in Kansas."

"Don' you wan' me, Miss Flo'?" Tilda looked disconsolate.

"Of course, I want you."

"I wish the Brewers were going with you," Rachel fretted.

"We'll be there almost as soon as they are," Maria assured her. "It's you, dear, we all will hate to leave here alone."

Orders brought the Colorado detail to Fort Riley just before the Stuarts got away. That made the good-byes no easier. Good-bye for always to the Stanleys, see you soon to the McIntyres and young Lomax. Where would they see them?

Leavenworth City was in a furore when they got that far.

"Mob tried to board me last night," the captain of the *Polar Star* informed the Stuarts. "Don't know what they were after. I ordered them off and they left. St. Louis—they've set Federal troops about the arsenal there."

Stuart was still in uniform, still Lieutenant Stuart of the First United States Cavalry. He answered the captain politely, but kept his arm around Flora, who was watching the rousters lift the hawsers from the posts at the landing.

"It's just a rope, dear," he said, as the last one splashed into the water.

A rope. A mooring cable. Flora closed her eyes and leaned against her husband.

Finale: VIRGINIA

Chapter 1. *The Big Move*

It was absurd then to cry over a saddle. Adams Express had shipped it from St. Louis but would not guarantee its arrival in Virginia. Now here it was. A dray had delivered it that morning to Alec's office in Wytheville.

"Is that all now, I wonder?" Alec said. "Now, now, sister!"

Everything in Flora gave way at once. She dropped on the floor beside the lovely, ugly object; and her tears came with a rush that would not be stopped. The smell was part of Stuart, coming in from a long ride or just a day's duty. The scratches were marks of his spurs. He would never admit to weariness but once in a while, swinging a leg over, he must have raked leather.

"It brings to mind so many things," she said brokenly. "Nobody knows."

Alec sat down helplessly in his swivel chair. The thing, he supposed, was to let her cry it out. The storm presently did lessen.

"I don't often do like this. Just . . . sometimes."

One other time had been over Stuart's captain's commission. It came while she and Stuart were in St. Louis, straightening their little affairs, telling friends good-bye. Stuart mailed it back to Washington, with his resignation. She had cried out over that. Six years of waiting and striving and loving and hoping—you couldn't let them go without tears.

Stuart had been sweet. Unshaken outwardly, perhaps inwardly, but not unmoved. Certainly not unsympathetic. When she was exhausted from her crying, her head aching more noticeably than her heart, he had soothed her as only he could, taking the pins out of her hair, letting it fall over his arm, bathing her eyes, kissing away the new tears that started, kissing her swollen nose.

"Looks like you'd fallen into the Smoky Hill and drowned and we hadn't found you for a week," he chided.

Sending Tilda away, or trying to.

"Take care of the children yourself this evening," he ordered. "Mrs. Stuart must not be disturbed."

Tilda had looked at him, her mouth twisting uncertainly.

"Mist' Philip ain' had his suppah," she said finally.

"Oh, that's it? Well . . . fix him a sugar-tit and tell him supper will be late this evening."

He roared at Tilda, to cover his own discomfiture. Time had been when Tilda would have thrown her apron over her head and run before the storm. Now she rolled her eyes, said "Yassah" with considerable dignity and left slowly. Stuart's eyes twinkled, but he bristled until she was away.

"Stuart," Flora said, "I shouldn't act like this. I mustn't, for the children's sake."

"And your sake," Stuart said, "and mine. Come here, you poor, sad little thing. Come here!" They stood together by the window of their hotel room and he held her chin in his hand and turned her face to the fading light. He looked deep into her eyes. "It isn't as if you hadn't known," he said. "You did know, didn't you?"

Yes, she had known. It seemed to her that she had always known. Not just since that happy summer and autumn in Virginia, which had ended so unhappily. Before that. A warrior husband, as gallant in battle as he was in wooing his lady, brave, devout . . . ah, there it was. Devout. Whole-souled in all he did, giving without stint, withholding nothing. Yes, she had known, and loved him, knowing.

"And surely," he said then, "you think what I am doing is right?"

Oh, right! There was no right and there was no wrong. When the world was going to pieces, their world, everybody's, it helped little to cleave the wreckage into two halves. But he was waiting for her answer.

"Darling, I know you are doing the only thing you could do."

She felt his arms slacken.

"And that's as far as you can go?" he asked.

"My poor reasoning," she pleaded, "will take me no farther."

"My own darling." He kissed her again, sadly. "Dear, unhappy little wife."

The next day he was gone. Within an hour of his going, she knew what was right for her. He had left her a dozen trivial matters to put in order. More important, he had left her to make her choice, whether to remain where she was or follow him. He had made the suggestion at Fort Riley in all seriousness as a possible solution to practical difficulties. "You can come on with the others," he said now, boarding a boat for Memphis; but the choice was hers.

As before, her decision was instant. She and the children would follow Stuart, and immediately. She would wait for nobody. She dried her eyes and went to work, tying up all the frayed ends of their old living; and now, here she was—she and the saddle. Almost the last instruction Stuart had given was, "Be sure and ship the saddle. It's mine."

It was his, in every way. She touched its hard, insensible ugliness again, and stood up, facing Alec. Oh, poor Alec now! Each time she saw him he looked older, less hair on top, another crease somewhere in his face, not bending under his burdens, but settling down under them, his eyes more quizzical, a droop taking shape at the corners of his generous mouth.

"Alec, I'm sorry," she said again. "I am not regularly this kind of coward."

"I'm sure you are not." His smile, inspired by the same shrewd insight which gave her father his reputation for wit, but gentler, touched, too, by the fun that in his younger brother would have been unrestrained laughter, brightened his face. "It is the women," he reminded her, "who will suffer most if there is heavy fighting."

"Oh, no!" she denied swiftly.

Heavy fighting—the shock of massed men meeting other massed men, men who didn't wheel their ponies and scamper to a spot from which they could shoot their arrows or their Sharps rifles with small danger to themselves. Heavy fighting—the sort of combat that Stuart and Stanley and McIntyre and Bayard and the Lees and others had studied at the Academy but had never really thought to see. Heavy fighting—her father had seen some in Italy. She turned now from

Alec's bluntness, but even more quickly from the thought of her father.

"It's just that now everything is so different," she said. "So new and strange. I don't suppose anyone who hasn't lived at any army post can know how different. Everything there, you see, is regulated." So beautifully, so securely regulated! "We wake up to a bugle call. We time our cooking, our sewing, our meals that way. We even see the doctor at sick call. Really. It's quite unhandy to be ill at any other hour. We use hot water or paregoric or common sense and fortitude and endure until sick call the next day. If we want anything, it's issued or there's the sutler's store. We get along with mighty little, some people think; but really we have everything and right at hand. And . . ."

She hesitated. It wasn't even a lonely life, as some claimed. If she had gone out to Colorado to live at the new fort, she wouldn't have been lonely. Next door would have been Margaret Stanley and others. All with children and housekeeping problems, blessings and difficulties to share. There it was—to share. Lonely? She had never been so alone in her life as she was now.

But it wasn't polite to say that to Alec. By his definition, it wasn't true. She and the babies were welcome in Wytheville. They could make any Stuart home their home for as long as they might need to stay. Here was a refuge as safe and secure as any in the world, Alec would think.

"I must sound dreadfully ungrateful," she apologized. "You—everyone has been most kind. Well . . ."

She turned back to the saddle because Alec was considering it now with a rueful distaste that matched her sorrow.

"I suppose," he said, "since he went to the trouble of shipping it out, he will want it forwarded to camp. I really can't see why. If we can't equip our fighting men, we are in a sorry state."

"All the men took their saddles, Alec. It's a kind of superstition. Yes, he does want it forwarded. I have directions here in a letter."

Stuart's latest, written from his first command. At Harper's Ferry, of all places. She hoped her hands looked steady as she unfolded the sheet.

"*Marching orders . . . I leave at six a. m. Colonel Jackson . . .*" oh, bother! Where was that bit about the saddle? Well, finally!

"When my saddle comes, send it on, care of Spotts, Harvey and Company."

"But that's Richmond," Alec objected. "If he's at Harper's Ferry . . ."

"Orders change," Flora said. "Spotts, Harvey in Richmond will know where to forward the saddle, I suppose. Harper's Ferry, or wherever the cavalry is. Things are a little confused right now."

"I only hope they are equally confused," Alec said soberly, "on the other side of the line. I'll take care of the saddle, sister. And . . . is there anything else?"

Yes, but how could she say it?

"Brother Alec, you're very good. I don't know how we'd manage without you. We'll be coming to you always for help, I'm sure . . ."

"What I'm here for," Alec growled.

"Yes, I know." The Wytheville depot, with wet snow falling. Alec in the murk, steady as one of the props that held the roof. She smiled at him fondly and he blushed. "But, after all, we're not children any more. Your young brother is twenty-eight years old, a colonel in the Provisional Army of Virginia. If things clear up presently and he knows where his command is likely to be, I should like to be near him."

"My dear Flora, do you think that's wise?"

No, not wise, but . . .

"We talked it over," she said. "That's the way we want it."

"You'll leave the children with us here?"

"No. They belong where we are. We are a family, too, you see."

That was one advantage in Virginia. After the distances of the West, it was a snug area, with railroads running every which way, and towns all about.

"I don't know how you can think of such a thing," Alec said. "It sounds like Jeems, but even he ought to know better. It would hardly be safe."

"It would be perfectly safe," Flora insisted. "Brother Alec, do you think for a minute that, with Colonel Stuart patrolling the border, there is any chance of an invasion?"

"I do," Alec said. "As many chances as there are fords in the Potomac, to say nothing of inlets of the sea."

"You don't talk like other people around here," Flora reminded him.

The war would be over before it was well begun, they said. It couldn't last. The North might have numbers and money; but the South had its men and its righteous cause—the defense of its sacred soil, its sacred independence of thought and action, defying coercion. Its brave sons would rally to the new flag. Alec did not sound so blindly confident. She thought of the long wait before Virginia had finally voted to leave the Union. There must have been many William Alexander Stuarts present at that convention.

"A few of us," Alec said now, "try to face facts. Where do you think . . ."

"I don't know, but finally the army must go into camp somewhere." How else could companies drill? How could the men know one another or their leaders? "And there'll be a town, and James will send for us. When he does, I'll want to go. Don't try to argue me out of it, Alec. That's what I am asking of you now. Don't argue."

Alec shook his head. All the fervor of patriotic rallies, the rolling of wheels, the marching of men—all of them couldn't hope to ride—must boil down finally to a situation like this. This fastidious, carefully reared, carefully educated young woman, her life and future tied to the destiny of his brilliant, headstrong young brother. For every man a woman somewhere.

"How old are you?" he asked.

"Twenty-five," Flora said. "Why?"

"Then, I suppose you must have your way, too. As it happens, I had a letter myself from Jeems this morning. He mentions Warrenton as a suitable place of residence for you. What do you think of Warrenton?"

"Alec, Warrenton will be lovely."

She had never seen the town, and presently she forgot Alec's kindness. It had been a month now—more—since she had kissed Stuart good-bye in St. Louis. There had been letters, rapturous, when he knew she was in Virginia; but a person could subsist only so long on such fare. Never had any separation—of miles or circumstance—seemed like this one. If she did not see Stuart soon, she felt that, like a plant deprived of sun, she must just naturally shrink to nothing and die.

Warrenton, Virginia, was a pretty town, set against low mountains, brave in summer green, from which sparkling, spring-fed creeks, called most appropriately "runs," raced down to unite in broader runs and finally become a river that hurried on to find its outlet into the Chesapeake Bay and the sea.

It was a town of some consequence this late June in the year 1861. From it a wide turnpike ran northeastward by way of Gainesville, Centreville, and Fairfax Courthouse to the Potomac and Washington. Leading off in another direction, southeastward, a spur of railroad track connected at Warrenton Junction with the main line of the Orange and Alexandria Railroad. What with its situation and these excellent lines of communication, the town was now and might be for the duration of the war a middle meeting ground for those rallying to the defense of Virginia. Many companies of volunteers went to Richmond to be assigned to posts of duty; but others, especially from the mountain counties, were more direct in their approach. One day Flora, walking uptown to make a purchase, was delayed by a company of horsemen, all in gray homespun, lolling easily in their saddles in the way of men who rode horses as if saddles were rocking chairs. Young men they were, some with dark beards, some too young to have any. All had laughter in their eyes and gay quips on their tongues.

"Which way's the fightin'? Reckon if we keep ridin' north, we'll meet up with a few Yankees? Howdy, ma'am. Remember me to all the folks."

Gray, Flora thought, was a good color for men defending their homes. An army of men in gray . . . then something called her attention to the leader. It was the way he sat his horse. No lolling there. Ease, but a disciplined ease. Cavalry, she thought, West Point drill. A man never lost the way of it. He must have noticed her staring. As he rode on, he lifted his broad hat and flourished it about his head; and there was a gleam as from burnished copper.

"Peter Carey!" The cry escaped her before she knew it was coming.

A trooper, passing, looked at her curiously, then away politely; and she put her hand over her mouth. Whatever did she mean? If it was Lieutenant Carey, she had never in her life called him by his given name. But madness persisted. She wanted to run alongside the troop now, calling still, "Peter Carey, stop! Wait! Where are you going? Where did you leave Lucy . . . and the children?"

How many years had it been? Only four? It seemed much longer. But then, it seemed almost as long since she had seen any of the old crowd. My kinfolk, she thought. As surely as if the same blood had run in their veins. The man at the head of the dusty troop need not have been Peter Carey. Four years and a full beard made the likeness vague. It was just the auburn hair and the set of his shoulders and . . . longing.

She must ask Stuart when she wrote. No, he would be with her this Sunday. She would ask him then. That was, perhaps, the most favorable feature of Warrenton. It was far enough from the front lines to be safe and near enough so that a man might occasionally take a short leave from duty and ride down to spend a day or two with his family. Stuart had suggested Warrenton while he was still at Harper's Ferry. He was, Flora thought, farther away now, but still somewhere vaguely to the north. Still in Colonel—no, General Johnston's command, still working with a commander of infantry named Jackson. Colonel Jackson of the Institute; and he, too, was probably something higher than a colonel now, being an older man and having begun with a colonel's rank.

"An odd man," Stuart said of him, "but I like him. We get along all right." Suggesting that others might not have his luck.

The Saturday of Stuart's projected visit—his third since Flora and the babies had settled into a "room" in Warrenton—dawned clear and warm. It was, to be sure, July; and warm weather was to be expected. Flora was up early, laying out fresh clothing for the children and herself, tidying the room. Used as she had been always to close quarters, a room, she had learned, even a large one, with a deep wardrobe and a capacious bureau, could get out of hand if not continually tidied.

"I often wish," her hostess said, "that my other ladies had been brought up in the army. You give the least trouble. I do appreciate it."

But did she, really? Flora sometimes wondered. She might seem more elegant to some if she were not so particular or so briskly industrious. But there, that was how she was made and how she had been trained. And, of course, she had Tilda to help her. Whatever would she have done without Tilda?

Anyhow, today everything must have a special shine. It was hard to make one room and that in another's house have the air of home, but she did what she could. Fresh flowers in water on the center table. A newspaper, the latest obtainable. Windows darkened, if he came in the heat of the day, curtains back to let in the cool of evening if he arrived late. A rocking chair . . .

Stuart would ride up to the gate, with the pleasant clatter of a cavalryman's gear. He wore it all, partly to please folks, partly from expediency.

"I've just one of everything," he would say with appealing ruefulness, "and I daren't leave a piece behind. The equipment for our army is a little slow in coming through and I wouldn't want to tempt a brother officer beyond his strength."

"Your husband's such a jolly man, Mrs. Stuart," the ladies of the boarding house said after his first visit. "Is he always in such high spirits?"

"He isn't given to melancholy," Flora said conservatively.

The truth was she had never seen him so exuberant. It was as though, in championing what a few admitted to be a fairly desperate cause, he had achieved freedom from a restraint that had irked him overlong. However much fun he made over his first command, jubilance began there.

"Three hundred men and thirty-one officers," he whooped, "but I'm on top. Hardly a one of them has ever had to curry his own horse or black his own boots, but they all know how to ride. With a bit of drill—a good bit of drill—they'll make a showing. You'll see."

"Such a jolly young man!" the ladies said. The dear ladies!

"Somebody's expecting somebody today," they said to Flora this Saturday at breakfast. "We can tell."

They certainly could tell. When Stuart rode up, they would be on the porch or scattered about on the lawn. They would camp there all day, to be sure. And they would see him first, and such a flutteration! Bless their hearts, Flora understood. She would even hold back, to give them their borrowed pleasure. Stuart stood for their own absent loved ones, scattered here and there. Beyond that, with his laughter and gay talk and snatch of song, he was a symbol.

"So heartening!" the ladies said.

So, Flora would keep herself in the background, with the two children, and let the ladies have their flutter. Stuart would have a greeting for each, often a letter in his pocket. He would make his way gaily through the gathering, and come finally to his own. He would marvel at *La Petite*, as if he had never seen her before. He would measure with his hand the amount of her growth since they had been together last. It couldn't have been more than a hair's breadth, but he made the most of it. He would take the boy then—cautiously at first, because the child was still a little uncertain about this man with the great brown beard—but presently he would be tossing him in the air and Philip would crow, then shriek with delight, and kick and fuss if his father paused, to look him over, his son.

"He'll send that child into convulsions one of these days," the ladies said.

Of course, he never did. The romp over, he would give the baby back to Tilda, standing there, one foot trampling the other, her dark face aglow with pleasure and embarrassment.

"Are they good children, Tilda?" he would ask.

"They's tol'able, Cap'n Stuart," she would answer, almost inaudibly.

Grades and rank were always a confusion to Tilda.

Laughing at her reply, Stuart would turn to Flora. There she would stand, as fresh and fragrant as starched dimity and crushed rose petals or powdered orris root could make her, looking a model of patience and forbearance, but not feeling that way at all. Her heart would be clamoring like a bell with its cord caught. Before they touched each other, their eyes would meet and hold. Something would flash across the space between them. "My own!" one said to the other at the same instant; and that was it. "My own!" "Darling wife," Stuart called Flora in his letters. That, too, said everything. Each was to the other what he or she could be to nobody else.

The delayed meeting, the quick embrace, to be followed by a longer one when they were in the house, in the cool, shaded tidiness of the room, were worth waiting for; but today, this Saturday of mid-July, contrarily, for no particular reason, Flora had a whimsical desire to be first instead of last. By ten o'clock she had her plans made. The children were outside with Tilda. She was dressed. The room was the best she could make of it. She took a bonnet—she had trimmed it to wear to church with Stuart the next day—and a parasol from the wardrobe, put the hat on, gave herself the usual not too flattering, "I hope this will do" examination, and set out, leaving by a rear door and a back gate, to avoid either questioning or offers of companionship.

She had reasoned that, because the weather was warm, Stuart would rise early wherever he had spent the night, to make the most of this day's ride before sun-up. She could look for him almost any time now. She hurried from the house, through the gate, down the side street; but, on reaching the turnpike, she slowed to a stroll; and with the first horseman who appeared in the distance, she came to a full stop and waited. She might, she thought, already have come too far. Stuart, if it were he, would dismount, to walk back to the boarding house with her. A short walk would be absorbed in his pleasure at her coming to meet him; but, like most habitual riders, he tolerated a long march poorly.

In another minute she knew that the man approaching was not Stuart. Not even a trooper. The horse was big and handsome and that had fooled her; but the rider was some nondescript bundle of something, certainly not military. This swift conclusion put such a different complexion on everything, emptied the horizon of hope so effectively that she hesitated and then did a complete about-face, meaning to retreat over the way she had come. Whatever had she been thinking of? She might have been fifteen instead of twenty-five. What would Rachel say of such behavior?

"Dear child, it makes me tremble for you."

But the rider had now seen her. He whipped up his horse. Again Flora quickened her pace and again forced it down to a slow stroll. It could not be because of her that the rider urged his horse to a trot. This was Virginia. She was still in town, not on a country road. Still the man came on, and faster than ever. There was something rhythmical about the horse's gait, she thought; and then he hailed her.

"Hi-ya, Miss Flo' . . . oh, Miss Flo', hit's me."

He passed her and reined up. Flora let out her breath in an exhausting sigh. What an idiot she was! Not Stuart, but his man Joe, whom his mother had given him recently out of the few people still belonging to her, that he might have his own body-servant in the Army of Virginia. A faithful creature of something more than Stuart's years. Not too intelligent. The boy Stuart had once had from Kentucky would have done better; but . . .

"You can have Joe," the elder Mrs. Stuart said, and so . . .

He had dismounted now and stood, fumbling a nondescript cap in his large hands, waiting for Flora to speak to him.

"Well," she said, over an obstruction in her throat, "Joe! I . . . you startled me."

"Yas'm. I musta. Kunnel Jeems sent me. I's to say he sorry, he kain' mak it right now. I . . . gotta lettah . . . yere."

He tucked the funny cap under his arm and from inside his shirt drew a brown paper packet. Flora all but refused it.

"My darling," her heart cried, "I don't want a letter. I want you. You promised . . ."

She steadied and put out her hand for the packet. Inside was a single sheet of paper, well covered with writing, folded over a pressed rose, still fresh enough to have retained some color and much fragrance. Back at the boarding house, in the room, in the center of the bouquet on the table was a rosebud, also red.

"I seed a bluecoat, Miss Flo'," Joe said, fearfully excited. "A Yankee bluecoat, mo'n one—day befo' yistiddy."

He pulled his precious cap from under his arm now, to show it to her.

"What?" Flora said. "Oh, yes, I see."

The cap on closer inspection was blue, an infantryman's cap, United States Army. *I seed a bluecoat, Miss Flo'*. The letter would tell her. She forced a smile.

"Come on with me to the house, Joe," she said. "You've had a long, hard ride."

"I kain' stay, Miss Flo'. I promised Kunnel Jeems I'd come straight back. Ef I don', I won' know whah to fin' him."

No?

"Well, but you must have a bite to eat," Flora said, "and feed your horse and rest him. That much, anyhow. I want to send an answer to Colonel Stuart."

"Yas'm. I was to wait fo' dat."

A letter, and the rosebud.

"I cut this for you this morning, my darling, thinking I would fasten it in your coat when you came . . ."

I seed a bluecoat, Miss Flo'—mo'n one.

"God bless you and keep you safe—for my sake . . ."

Chapter 2.   *Colonel Stuart*

"Before the enemy,
July 4, 1861

"My darling wife—"

If Stuart had wanted to tell Flora more exactly where he was on the evening he wrote to her, he would have found it difficult to name the place. Northeast from Winchester, Johnston's lines about three miles to the rear. At least, he had been assured that they would maintain that distance and stand ready.

Northeast from Winchester, a little south of Martinsburg, the advance force consisting of Stuart's cavalry, five good companies now, and a contingent of infantry under Colonel Thomas J. Jackson, West Point class of 1846, breveted for gallantry in various engagements preceding the capture of Mexico City in 1848, newly resigned from the principalship of Virginia Military Institute, a dour eccentric, if Stuart had ever seen one, but every long inch of him a soldier. Stuart couldn't have named a man now in the Confederate forces whose support he would rather have when he took his still fairly green cavalry afield.

His troopers were being put to the test right now. A Yankee army of undetermined size, commanded by a seasoned general named Patterson, had crossed the Potomac near Williamsport. This in itself was no great accomplishment. Crossing the Potomac in July was easy in a number of places, but there was question as to Patterson's intent. General Johnston's command at Winchester was in itself an outpost, guarding the Shenandoah Valley. The main Confederate forces

were massing farther east, around the important railroad junction at
Manassas.

It was Stuart's scouts—Stuart was proud of that—who had discovered Patterson's presence in Virginia. Immediately Johnston had
ordered a reconnaissance. That was what Stuart and Jackson were
about now. They were not to engage in battle with Patterson's army.
They were to watch its movements, feel it for strength, and keep
Johnston informed. If a battle was shaping up, Johnston preferred to
choose the ground and the time.

Stuart, riding alone across country in the warmth of a July afternoon, had to smile. Jackson had felt Patterson's strength sharply the
day before, a hot skirmish on the outskirts of Martinsburg losing him
a handful of men. The cavalry had helped pull the rest of the detail
so entangled out of the fire.

His cavalry, Stuart thought, was doing all right, but the men
needed more drill. He was troubled, too, about the company officers,
all the officers. It happened too often that a leader popular with his
men knew practically nothing about forming or breaking a line or a
column and was inclined to be more obstinate than the troopers
about learning. Today for example, mistrusting the caution, skill or
judgment of most of his subordinates, he had chosen to make himself a sort of one-man advance patrol. It steadied the troopers in the
ranks to know that he was out front. Better yet, it steadied him.

He rode alone, the disposition of the following column clear in his
mind, his senses otherwise sharply alive against any surprise contact
with a Yankee detail. About midafternoon, riding across country
for a change, he stopped at a farmhouse, ostensibly to ask permission
to cut through a wooded pasture to a road skirting the property,
really to ascertain that the road was where he had been told it was.
He had ordered a company under a young Captain Blackford out
that way earlier.

An angular woman in calico answered his knock on the door.

"Evenin'," she said to his pleasant greeting, then sharply, "Be you
a Yankee?"

He had to laugh. He was wearing gray breeches and shirt, but
his old army hat and his old army coat, with eagles that Flora had
embroidered on the shoulder straps. He had a uniform on order in
Richmond, but . . .

"What do you think?" he asked.

She looked at him and at his horse, a bay hunter that Alec had sent from Wythe County.

"You ain't," the woman said. "Now, what can I do for you?"

He inquired about the road. Surely, she said, he could ride through the pasture. Most wouldn't have asked.

"Just keep on like you're pointed," her last words were, "till you come to a rail fence. Turn right then. The road's close by."

As he trotted off, his spirits rose unaccountably. He wanted to throw back his head and yodel. Lieutenant Stuart would have done so. Colonel Stuart was another matter.

The trees in the pasture became denser. Could the woman deliberately have directed him into a patch of brush? No, before the thicket grew too dense for penetration, he saw a corner of the rail fence. Sunlight poured down into a clearing. Song did rise to his lips then as he rode out of the cover of the trees, but it died in its first flight.

On the other side of the fence, nothing more between him and it than that, he saw a patch of blue. Army blue—soldiers, infantrymen —no time to count them, but fifty at least. He had no time to think what they were doing there. They had seen him as suddenly and plainly as he had seen them. Infantrymen, with new rifles, loaded, he had no doubt.

"You there!" he said gruffly. "Who's in command?"

A man with a lieutenant's bars saluted—a young man, about the age of the captain Stuart had thought to meet on the road, and more frightened, because he was in strange country, where he didn't belong—saluted shakily.

"Fence in your way?" Stuart asked. "Take it down."

The lieutenant gave the order. Two lengths of fence went down. By then Stuart had his gun out and had cocked it. He thought he smelled dust off to the right in the direction of the road.

"Lay down your arms," he ordered next.

The young lieutenant turned to him in question. The men stared.

"Lay down your arms at the peril of your lives!" Stuart roared, and showed his gun. The smell of dust was stronger. To his surprise, the rifles were dropped. "Forward, MARCH!" He motioned, with the gun, toward the gap in the fence. In a daze the men obeyed.

Captain Blackford's troopers were filing down the road. That was the dust. At Stuart's hail they turned off. After the first shock of unbelief, they made short work of surrounding the discomfited Yankees.

> Today I captured one whole company, "I," 15th Pennsylvania, officers and all—two privates of 2d Cavalry and a surgeon, including 48 stand of arms of ammunition . . .

Colonel Thomas J. Jackson sat on his sorrel mare, knees high and elbows sawing, to receive the prisoner detail and its escort, also the young colonel of cavalry commanding. He peered at Stuart from under the visor of his Chapultepec cap. Throughout Stuart's detailed report no trace of expression touched his gaunt features. At the end, his eyelids flickered once.

"Good!" he said. "We'll smoke out more of them tomorrow."

Tomorrow—only then Stuart recalled that tomorrow he had thought to be on his way to Warrenton for a visit with Flora. He had promised.

As it was, it was evening before he could settle down to writing her a letter to explain his absence. He was resting in his tent—a matter of two blankets, one tied by its corners to convenient limbs of trees above, and one spread on the ground, both Indian red.

"But . . . red, dear?" he could hear Flora question, and see her delicate eyebrows go up in points. "Isn't that a little conspicuous?"

It was, after the manner of a chieftain. Well, that was what he aimed to be now—a chieftain.

He rested in his tent, seated on a folding stool beside an up-ended packing box, and chewed a pen, composing the letter. He couldn't set down full details, wouldn't do; and, besides, he didn't want to frighten her. Still, it would do no good to hide the truth or try to. She had a shrewdness about seeing through omissions. He would tell her—oh, high cockalorum, he must tell her about that company of Pennsylvania infantry.

He wrote furiously, in short, swift, impatient strokes. Then he stopped, nursing his pen again, thinking what next. That went down to the accompaniment of chuckles.

"Why don't your pa come? He's missing most of the fun."

He sat back, frowning. Sometimes he wondered about Colonel Cooke. Of course, Utah was far off; and the Colonel, as Flora said, would be very correct about delivering his command to properly constituted authority. Still, he wondered.

He wrote now more slowly, whistling a random tune. Outside somebody put words to the tune and sang it softly, and others caught it up until finally the grove beside a chattering spring-fed stream where the advance guard bivouacked pulsated with song:

> "*If you want to have a good time*
> *You must jine the cavalry . . ."*

He cocked an ear to listen. A pleasant sound, and tribute, of course. A pleasant sound—presently if the noise got out of hand, he— no, let them sing. Caution was all right in its place. Boldness and high courage were, perhaps, even more important. Brave as lions those young men out there in the dark. They needed to be brave. The time was coming . . . his letter finished, he thought, he took a drooping rose from his lapel—he had broken it from a roadside hedge that morning—blew the dust off its petals, kissed the center of it, wondering at its surviving fragrance, and laid it on the sheet of paper. Then, on impulse, he added another line:

"Pray for me, my darling.

> Yours ever,
> J. E. B. Stuart"

Chapter 3. *A Victory Lost*

There was little of song that lowering July day almost three weeks later, when Stuart's cavalry formed in a gully—not enough of a gully to conceal a foot soldier, let alone a man on a horse—on the extreme left of the force massed to meet McDowell's Army of the Potomac thrusting down the Warrenton Pike toward Manassas Junction. Coming from mountains into this open farm country, a body was put to it to find cover.

Not that the cavalry was hunting cover exactly. In the rough region about Martinsburg they had learned to work behind a screen if Nature provided one. Their courage and their spirits were as high as ever. The action they had seen at the head of the Valley had been just enough to make them feel their oats. Not much fighting actually. After losing a whole company of infantry in one afternoon, Patterson kept his Yankees on tighter rein. Could be that his orders were not to fight, just to threaten. 'Y Gad, before the fun was over, he could hardly have told who was threatening whom. Didn't know when Jackson pulled his infantry out of line. And, on the day when Joe Johnston at Piedmont put his army on the cars for Manassas, the woods between him and the Yanks had swarmed so with Confederate cavalry that Patterson must have thought Johnston was preparing an attack.

All the time Stuart was waiting for a signal that the last company was on the rails, Manassas bound. When the word came, he threw his hat in the air and, with a yell any of his men could scarcely equal, cried out, "Let's ride!"

Out came that light, keen sword he carried. He never wore the regulation sabre. That might have been a matter of weight. Riding at the clip he did, all his horse could carry was Stuart himself—say a hundred eighty to ninety pounds, bone and muscle. Out came that sword and the order, clear and sure, carrying so that Patterson could have heard if he'd his ear cocked that way: "Forward—open column of fours—MARCH!"

Off they put; and it was walk, trot, gallop, then trot again, then halt. For five minutes only, to let the horses blow and the men walk about. Then off again, then a longer rest, time to unbit the horses and let them graze and drink while the men stretched on their backs and the column was checked to be sure none had strayed. None had. A battle was shaping up ahead. They aimed to beat the railroad cars to it.

They mighty near did so. Some time after midnight of the twentieth, they crossed the Warrenton Pike and in a woods unsaddled and picketed their horses and dropped where they stood. Reveille jarred them out of deep sleep, but there was hot breakfast. Before it was over, orders were snapping and there was a rumble in the air— the big guns beginning to speak. Very soon after that, Stuart's cavalry was in position. A two-squadron front, and the rest in a second line in reserve. From time to time through the day Stuart shifted the squadrons, to rest them; but that generally was the formation.

Stuart? He never rested when anything was going on. Didn't need to. Twice he took a different horse, but that was all.

So, here they were in this low spot behind what folks in these parts called a ridge. On the other side somewhere was Bull Run. If you knew the place you knew where. Otherwise it was hearsay. Most of a battle to a man in the ranks until he went into action was hearsay. He couldn't see much. Now and then a column on higher ground moved forward, with flags flying and sometimes even a band playing. The guns would speak and kick up dust and the marching men would hesitate, and sometimes fall back, sometimes keep on and be lost finally in the smoke. Sometimes the fighting was so far away it would be only rolling echoes. Sometimes a ball whistled by—but that one had missed you.

So there they stood most of the day, waiting. They stood to horse. The word to mount would be given in time. Stuart would never let them be caught afoot—unless he had to hold a position. Then he'd send the horses back out of range of the hot fighting. But he'd try something else first. On their right a battery of guns he had got from somewhere roared out occasionally, warning somebody off. Guns were good—the big fellows. Old Jack south of Martinsburg had only one battery, but he made it tell.

Where was old Jack? Did anybody know? A man kept hearing about others. There was General Longstreet. He and an infantry division had stopped the Yanks a couple of days before. At Blackburn's Ford. That was when the call had gone out to Winchester for reinforcements. And there were Ewell, and Bee, and Bartow, and Hill, and the man on top—a Frenchman from New Orleans, named Beauregard. Where was their corps commander—Joe Johnston? And where was old Jack? Why, there! To the right front. See that hill, with the farmhouse on it? The men and the guns massed there were Jackson's brigade. There they were and there they meant to stay. If the Yankees wanted past that hill, they'd have to go around. They'd never go over it. Now, God grant there were men to Jackson's right and his left to stop that! The cavalry in position stiffened. They were the left flank or most of it—they and a small bunch of infantry under a man named Elzey.

And they waited. And waited. The worst of the waiting was thirst. Whether that was heat and dust or being more anxious than he knew a man couldn't say. He only knew his mouth was packed with cotton. All the water in the branch—hardly drinkable by now—wouldn't have quenched it.

They waited, Lieutenant Beckham's light battery barking on their right, nothing on their left. Nothing that is, except Stuart. Easy in the saddle, steady, alive to all that went on around him, on a small knob all his own, with a thin cover of trees—much too thin to suit those who watched him—he, too, waited. Now and again he would set a spy glass to his eye, but not often. What went on tolerably close—that was most important—he saw unaided. Every half hour he would send off a dispatch rider. As often as that or oftener a rider from some other section would dash up to him and then dash off again. When the riders rode both ways desperately and thick and fast, things were tightening up, the men knew—that and that the day was hot and muggy and they were thirsty.

Stuart, too, at times during the day felt his tongue like flannel in his mouth; but usually he was much too busy to notice. Also at times the thought came to him that Warrenton and Flora and the children were only twenty miles to the rear. What had he been thinking of not to move them? The first place General Lee had fortified, before he went off to take command elsewhere, had been Manassas Junction. He had known what to expect.

However, it was never Stuart's way to waste time in idle regret or useless reflection; and today he had little time to waste. To an on-looker he might appear motionless, even idle; but he was busy every minute studying the shifting panorama spread out before him. It was, as the mists of morning cleared, just that—a panorama, though real. Hot, smoking, bloody, real; and something very wrong in the picture. A confusion, he decided early in the day—a confusion over and above the backward and forward movement of divisions he could not always identify.

There was a confusion, first, of uniforms. Zouaves from New York looked much like Zouaves from Louisiana. A confusion, second, of flags. Red and white stripes and a blue field with stars at a distance were too much the same. A person couldn't stop to count. Something would have to be done about that—a new flag immediately, at least for battle, and uniforms of one color that could be recognized. Otherwise you could turn your guns on your own men. Once a melee just within his range of vision made him think that had happened. He frowned and concentrated his attention the more sharply on nearer action. A man couldn't afford on a day like this to let feelings override his judgment. He must keep cool. He must face facts and issues squarely, so that he could give a true report and know what was best to do.

The picture at midmorning looked none too promising. On the eighteenth, three days before this, McDowell had tried a frontal attack and had been thrown back with a jar by Longstreet—infantryman, the man Flora's brother John had followed up from Texas. So now McDowell was doing what any good general with a large force ought to have done. He was marching his army across the Confederate front in a flanking movement, meaning to encircle the left of the main line and attack from the rear. Only two things had kept him from carrying out his plan. The man in command on the left of the Confederate line as it had stood early that day saw what was coming and sent warning; and the line could be lengthened on the left by Johnston's men just down from Winchester. "Good!" Stuart could have said over that and his part in it, but again there was no time for felicitation. The issue was by no means settled.

He saw two regiments sent by Beauregard to halt McDowell's advance across the turnpike hurled back, swept away like wheat before men with scythes; and he could only send word that this had happened and where he thought the poor devils were trying to rally. And wait.

When Jackson took Henry House Hill, he would have liked to raise a cheer, but he did not. The situation was too desperate. He saw the lines forming in the lee of the hill, away from the advancing Federal troops. He saw the guns go into position. A glimpse of Jackson himself made his heart swell fondly, then collapse with dismay. He ordered up a courier to carry a warning: "Do not expose yourself so!" then thought how absurd that was. Four times the Federal command charged Jack's guns. Twice the bluecoats seemed to have them, to

penetrate Jackson's front line; but finally, when the scramble un-
scrambled, the Yanks were falling back and there sat Jackson on his
sorrel, apparently untouched.

"Hold fast!" was Jackson's reply to Stuart's warning.

It seemed to Stuart that was all he did that day—hold fast and
wait and wriggle. His impatience at times rose to the boiling point.
Why didn't the command order an advance over yonder at the center
front or to the right—to break through McDowell's column, to make
him halt and, perhaps, call back some of the regiments moving on
and on, aiming still to turn the Confederate left? McDowell still
thought he could get around the line there. Well, he almost did.

Jackson saw. Shortly after noon another regiment of Virginia
cavalry, Colonel Radford commanding, took position close to Henry
House Hill, to be an extra flying wedge against a sudden thrust at
Jackson's flank; and Stuart shifted to draw his small force still farther
to the left. He was really in the air now, but under tolerable cover.
The men grumbled, thinking all the action was going to others; but
Stuart knew better. Finally there came a time . . .

He ordered his men into the saddle. Again he shifted position.
Down one of the lanes that threaded the terrain like a web, he had
spotted a column of infantry advancing rapidly in a direction that
would bring it right past the knoll he occupied on forward lookout.
He sent word to Beckham to hold his fire. He drew his sword. The
column came on. Red fezzes, white breeches—more Zouaves. How
many regiments did McDowell have?

He moistened his dry lips with his hot tongue and tightened his
grip on his sword. He waited until, unmolested and almost in position for an attack, he heard their commander order them front into
line. And right prettily they began their oblique.

Cavalry's defense is a spirited attack. If the enemy can be surprised while shifting position . . .

Up went his sword.

"Draw sabres. CHARGE!"

A trumpet blared—he'd forgotten that boy. From the roar that followed, anybody would have thought a thousand men were behind
him. Walk, trot, gallop—yelling like madmen, his two squadrons

knocked the Zouaves' front line off its feet. Their reserves broke and ran. The impulse naturally was to follow; but . . .

Cavalry without support cannot make a sustained attack . . .

"HALT! Sound the recall," he said to the eager trumpeter.

For a dizzy second he thought he couldn't hold his men and take them back. Then, just as shakily, he realized that they were pulling up their horses.

"Carry SABRES! To the rear—at a trot—MARCH!"

Cursing softly, they followed him back to their old position. They had turned aside a vicious thrust, gained a respite, no more. What now?

Panic came next. A ripple almost visible, certainly perceptible, ran the full length of the Confederate positions. It was unreasonable panic and yet, not without reason—an emotional reeling compounded of heat, weariness and, to green troops, intolerable strain. Stuart sent a courier to Johnston to ask the reason and learned that a column of infantry, with some cavalry, out of Stuart's vision, but within that of others to the rear, had been sighted moving toward the battle from the west. Patterson's army from Winchester, panic said. Yankees from somewhere.

"No!" Stuart said furiously. "No!"

It couldn't be Patterson. He couldn't have brought his army down through the gap, not any portion of it, in the wake of the cavalry at any such rate. They had left him sitting. Time he got up and started . . . it was not Patterson. He wouldn't have had any orders—oh, there were a thousand reasons. Finally, not being able to endure impotent, self-contained denial, Stuart wrote out his opinion and dispatched it to Johnston.

"If," he concluded, "the advancing column should prove to be our own men, I beg to inform you that, barring a more vital need elsewhere, this end of the line would welcome reinforcement. It might decide the issue."

It would decide the issue. He was sure of it, and just as sure that finally the issue would be decided as he wanted it. But how to put his faith into the hearts of others? His line—the men had got over their healthy, seething fury at being drawn back from the charge and shared now the general strain. How could he relieve that? Something

was needed to take their minds off the waiting. A song, perhaps.
Something they all knew. A line came to him—right out of a Virginia
fence corner. How did it go? He took off his hat, rested it on the
pommel of his saddle, to let the thick, wet mass of his hair cool, if it
would. He hummed the line softly. The young trumpeter looked at
him in surprise, and smiled shakily.

"*Mr. Frog would a-courtin' ride . . . hmmm!*"

he supplied.

"Louder!" Stuart said. "Louder!"

And sang with the youngster. The sound carried to the waiting
troopers. Hesitatingly, then lustily they caught up the refrain. Tension melted. Behind the low ridge, between Stuart and the hard-
pressed anchor of Jackson's line the Zouaves were reforming. Now,
God send . . .

From far to the rear came a faint cheering. It swelled to a roar.
Stuart threw back his head and roared with it:

"*Mr. Frog would a-courtin' ride,*
Sword and pistols by his side . . . hmmmm! hmmm!"

Within minutes he was reading an answer to his dispatch. Johnston
sent congratulations and begged him to keep up his good work. He
himself had ridden out to meet the troops advancing from the north-
west. As Stuart had suggested, they had proved to be a Southern
column, General Jubal Early commanding, who fortuitously had
happened to be near enough the battle ground to lend support. He
had requested General Early to take up his position at the extreme
left. Would Colonel Stuart oblige with exact directions?

Hastily Stuart gave his instructions to the courier. He wanted
Early's support on his right, between him and Jackson, but hurry!
If they acted promptly . . .

Then everything seemed to happen at once. Elzey, Jackson's man
at the base of the hill, sent word to Stuart to hold his fire. It looked
to him as if a handful of their own men had got to Stuart's front. He
was sending the same word to Early. To wait and be sure.

Stuart was beside himself. He didn't know what Elzey saw, but
any columns advancing in front were Federal troops. He had kept
them all under observation. If Elzey would rally his men and with

Early make ready to support the cavalry in a spirited assault, he thought they might turn the tide.

For a few minutes he was sending one messenger out on the heels of another. And all the time keeping his eyes on the advancing Yankees. Two columns now from across the turnpike, but somehow not seeming to have the heart for their duty. Now, what did they know that he did not? He sent an order to Beckham to try a shot that way.

And just like that, it happened. The blue lines wavered, broke, turned and melted away, lost in a general backward movement. A message came from Jubal Early. His men were tired. They needed time to breathe. No time, Stuart flashed back at him. Climb out and see for himself. The Yankees were on the run. Shock paralyzed even Stuart for a minute, but only that long.

"Mount!" he yelled to his men in line. And to the trumpeter, "Call them up. Everybody out. Sound the pursuit. We're off. Forward, MARCH!"

It was no march. It was a tearing gallop, stopped only by the need to round up prisoners and send them to the rear under guard. He cut through the hapless Zouaves and half a dozen other units, not knowing who they were, except that they had been Yankee soldiers, bent an hour ago on destroying him. At a bend of Bull Run above the Stone Bridge he lost his supporting infantry. Some time later his cavalry had dwindled to nothing. They had not stopped for loot. The infantry had halted for lack of legs and he himself had used up the cavalry as prisoner guards.

Twelve miles from the starting point, Stuart caught up his stumbling mount, looked about him, and knew he was alone. No, not entirely. That gunner lad, Lieutenant Beckham, on a battery horse, as blown as Stuart's, was right behind him. After that there was nobody.

He rubbed the back of his hand across his eyes and looked about him again, unbelieving. There was no pursuit? It seemed impossible. Surely one regiment or another by now could be making organized movement forward. On the basis of his own captures, half the fleeing army could have been made prisoner, and the rest driven back clear to the Federal capital. Who had halted the pursuit? Who—this was more probable—had failed to realize the possibility?

He dismounted stiffly. Beckham did the same. They turned their horses rearward and, too bewildered for words, began their individual retreat.

The litter about them was indescribable—ambulance wagons, sutlers' wagons, carts, overturned tents, cots, guns, hats—the pike was strewn with gear. Presumably back from the road there would be the dead of both armies. If there were wounded, they were too far gone to cry out or they had been carried away. The stillness of early evening covered everything. There was a feel of thunder in the air, but no sound of it. Not even a bird sang, the roaring guns having driven all wild things from the scene.

Once Stuart stopped to turn over with the toe of his boot what remained of a lady's parasol—ivory and mother of pearl and lace and silk, trampled and broken and torn. He had seen tracks of carriage wheels all along on the road and beside it. So, the ladies had come out from Washington to watch the show? Well, ladies were like that. He raised his hat in salute, and thought of Flora and his early morning qualms over her safety back in Warrenton. Bless her, he must get word to her now, see her . . . presently. Not immediately. Surely, whatever the present cause for delay, plans must be forming to follow up the great victory—or it was no victory. He turned to his companion. Grimy work, shooting guns. Stuart doubted that he would recognize Lieutenant Beckham after he had found time to wash.

"Good fun while it lasted," he said.

A grin opened a gash in Beckham's face.

They led their horses until they came to a branch with a good flow of water, and stopped to let them drink. They rode on then at a slow walk. Cooking fires were going now behind Confederate lines. Stuart stopped to ask for news and the first grim report of the day was given him. The commanders of both those regiments that he had seen thrown back, by weight of numbers only, across the pike that morning had been killed. Brave, good men. Could they be spared? No, but they were gone. And others with them, no doubt. As to prisoners, all were being sent promptly to the rear. It was good to know that something was being done promptly.

A little later he was recognized by a group and a cheer welcomed him. Jackson's men. How was the new brigadier-general, he asked. Safe, they said, and sound except where a Yankee bullet had nicked him on the hand. Pizen mad, though, giving thanks to God one min-

ute and in the next breath asking why his friends and comrades had
not been emboldened to go on and make mincemeat of the Yankees.
Would Colonel Stuart relish a stick of sugar candy? A Yankee sutler
had spilled a wagonload and they had picked up the jars that weren't
broken. It was fresh, and tasty. It really was, Stuart agreed, and sent
his respectful congratulations to Jackson. He'd see him later, he
hoped.

Early's men next, flat on their backs still with weariness. Jubal
Early, soft-spoken like his one dispatch, but hearty in his handclasp
and felicitations. A beautiful job, by all accounts, he said Stuart had
done with his small force of cavalry. He regretted his late arrival and
that his men had been too exhausted to show much fight. They had
been marching all day. Stuart said they had come just in time. He
didn't need anyone to tell him later how it might have been if the
Federal army had held on two hours longer or if Early had not come.
Battles, it might be, were always decided by ifs. The Army of Virginia, the Army of the South—it lacked even a certain name as yet—
sprawled in a scattered, disorganized mass, each unit close to where
it had fought; and, as the men rested, a person could almost see the
fine ardor that had carried them through the day ooze off. The major
generals might be gathered in council now, debating the advisability
of pursuit tomorrow; and there was nobody to say with authority that
tomorrow would be too late, that the time was now or never.

A drop of water splashed on Stuart's nose. A streak of lightning
tore the sky apart. Thunder rolled now, and he could hear the rain
advancing.

"The weather," he said wryly to Lieutenant Beckham, "has come
out on the side of the Yankees. We'd better hunt cover."

Chapter 4. *And Women Must Weep*

To Flora, in the boarding house at Warrenton, cowering at the
echoes of the big guns, from time to time burying her head in a
down pillow, the rain was heaven-sent. She opened her ears to the
sound of it in the night and her eyes with equal eagerness the next

morning on a world sloshing wet and knew that the fighting, for a
while, at least, was over.

It rained for two nights and a day between; and, on the second
morning, when the sun came through the clouds shortly before noon,
she was able to come forth with a shining face and join in the general
rejoicing. By then the news of the victory, of the Yankee retreat to
Washington, was on everybody's tongue. A Richmond paper had
come, giving a full account of the battle, even to a black-bordered
list of the known slain, which Flora did not take time to read, Stuart's
name being mentioned elsewhere in the paper. It was no more than
a mention and not prominently placed: "Among those contributing
heroically to the brave stand of our army was Colonel J. E. B. Stuart,
commanding the First Virginia Cavalry"; but it told her what she
wanted to know. He had come through unharmed.

"What do you hear from your husband—directly, I mean?" one of
the ladies asked.

"Why, nothing so far," Flora answered, surprised, in view of the
weather, at the question. "I expect to hear from him soon, of course,
now that the rain has stopped. That is, as soon as the roads dry out."

Being himself, Stuart did not need thoroughly dry roads. He came
that afternoon, with a companion—an officer of artillery. Flora saw
the patches of red almost as soon as she recognized Stuart. Behind
the two men Joe rode a third horse, sitting sloppily, as usual, even
more so—sideways.

Flora was disappointed. Stuart's visits were so infrequent that she
hated to share them with anyone. Today, thinking he just might appear, she had dressed early and taken a chair on an empty veranda,
this being the hour when most people who weren't expecting visitors
napped. Now this stranger. She waited until the riders were almost
to the gate, then rose, meaning to welcome them at the porch steps;
but Stuart raised a shout.

"A surprise for you, pet. Come and see."

A friend? A relative? Surely nobody that she knew well; but she
went on down the walk to the gate, then stopped. Stuart was laughing at her for some reason. The other man was dismounting. As he
did so, something about him did look familiar. He turned.

"Johnnie!" the cry stuck in her throat. "Johnnie, I didn't know you.
I never thought . . . oh, dear!"

Then he, too, had been at Manassas. Of course. That Major Long-street, General Longstreet now.

"Johnnie, you look wonderful. You really do. I wish . . . come on up to the house where I can really see you. I mean . . . I must sit down. I . . ."

Stuart's arm steadied her.

"We brought a horse for you," he murmured in her ear. "We thought that way we could have a little time alone. Look up yonder."

Sure enough, on the veranda the chairs were already being filled. She laughed. How clever of Stuart to think of a ride! The only possible solution. But she'd have to change; so they'd as well march on and be presented.

Happily, proudly she went up the walk, arm in arm with the two men.

"Here he is!" she cried, producing Stuart first at the head of the porch steps. "Bring out your questions, ladies. And this is my brother, Captain Cooke, of General Longstreet's division."

Was ever a woman prouder? Johnnie did look well. He was a little quieter than she remembered, but then, she had chattered so wildly that he hadn't had time to say much. So handsome in his new uniform—so handsome in any case, fair like Rachel, but with his father's trim erectness and easy lightness of speech and manner.

"Don't disturb yourselves, ladies, please, or disarrange the chairs on my account. I'll ride the rail here quite comfortably."

Flora flew into the house to change. Was ever a woman more blessed in her men?

Probably she was too proud, riding off, with one on either side of her. It was just her good fortune to have a handsome brother as well as a dashing husband. Her mount was an extra delight, a gentle, light footed mare, Stuart's latest acquisition, a gift of friends and well-wishers. Lady Margrave, he called her, and said she was almost pure Arabian.

The day was warm, the air after the rain heavy with the scent of summer. Except for this and that about the horses and the roads and had she heard lately from the Brewers, and the like, they rode in near silence for a while; and at first that seemed quite natural, and re-laxed, and enjoyable in itself. Then it seemed strange. She looked at John on her left, and his fairness wore a scowl. Not since his battle

with engines had she seen him look so baffled and angry. She looked
at Stuart on her right. Bless him, he looked as if he had lost a night
of sleep.

"Now, what is it?" she said, her voice sharp with anxiety. And
the two men looked across her at each other.

"I'll tell you in a minute, pet," Stuart said, "as soon as we can get
off the road."

So, they hadn't come just to pay her a call. No, this was a mission.

"But I can't wait now," she said. "Is it bad news? Mamma? Papa?"

"Your father," Stuart said, and then, "he's not coming in on our
side, dear. He's keeping his command in the other army."

The time came when Southern officers who had served in it called
it, some with nostalgia, the old army. Now the break was too new
and words were harsher.

"Oh!" Flora's first sensation was relief. "Stuart, why did you
frighten me so? I thought he'd been hurt, or even killed."

"This," Stuart said, "is, I think, worse."

No, he didn't mean that. He couldn't. But he did. They had come
now to what should have been a small, fordable branch but was, instead, a brown, foaming river. The road stopped and so did they,
and sat their horses looking at one another, trying for words to put
to a circumstance that each in his own way saw as tragic; but no
two of them saw it alike.

"I was afraid of this," Flora said finally. "From the first. Stuart, I
should have warned you. I wanted to—back in Kansas, when he first
went out to Utah."

"I wouldn't have listened," Stuart said, his eyes smoldering. "I
couldn't have imagined it."

No. That was why she had never finished the warning.

"Johnnie, you might have known."

"No." Johnnie flushed to the roots of his hair. "A person could
always count on his doing the unusual in the most unusual way, but
I never thought of this—that he would betray Virginia!"

"Oh, Johnnie!"

"He was born here. I wasn't—but I didn't hesitate."

But the older man had hesitated. He had gone off into the desert
and the mountains to be alone and set his thoughts in line. And this
was the result.

"Do you mean to say you are not ashamed?" Johnnie demanded. No, not ashamed. Sorry, but not ashamed. Even a little proud.

"Well, I am," Johnnie said. "When you introduced me to your friends back in town, suppose they had known. They would have got up and left the porch and I shouldn't have blamed them."

"Johnnie, what are you saying?" Now, God give her patience! "Stuart . . ."

"We named our boy for him," Stuart mourned.

"Because you loved him, and admired him," Flora said. "You do still. You always will."

"No," he said. "Never again." And then, "I'll never forgive him as long as I live." Forgive him for what? "I counted on him. We all did. He could have had a top command. We needed him."

Ah, there it was! Disappointment, alarm, though Stuart would be the last one to admit it.

"Mind you," he added, "it will make no difference who he is or was when we meet, as we must some day, on the field of battle. He is my enemy now. He chooses to have it that way, so that is how it will be."

And she thought she had known heartbreak before. She turned back to her brother.

"When did you hear? How?"

A man in his command had picked up a newspaper on the battle-field—the Washington *Star*.

"If you'd seen his expression when he gave me the paper!"

"Johnnie, hush! Do you still have it? Let me see it, please."

A grimy, tattered sheet, the story a few paragraphs on a page devoted to army reports. Colonel Cooke, commanding the Department of Utah, accompanied by several members of his staff, had arrived in St. Louis, reporting, presumably, for new orders.

Yes, that was how he would do it. Tears blurred the page—proud, loving tears. Bless him, oh, bless him, too! Asked then by the newsman, who must have known something of his personal history, for a statement, he had made one—brief for him, but in his best style. Brave, beautiful words:

> I have served too long in the Army of the United States . . . I cannot abandon the standard now.

"Johnnie," Flora said, "did you read this? Stuart?" Both had read it.

"He always had a command of language," John said.

"Words don't alter facts," Stuart said.

And then they were at it again: betrayal, never a true Virginian. Flora had said so herself, Stuart remembered. He had ranged himself on the side of the enemy. He would live to rue the day.

"Oh, stop it!" she cried. "Stop it! I won't have it. Why did you come here if this was all you planned to say to me?"

If you please, they had come to give her the news gently, to comfort her, thinking she would need help to bear up under the blow.

"But now," Stuart said, as coldly as he had ever spoken to her, "you actually seem to be defending him—you, my wife."

"I never heard such nonsense," she told him. "He doesn't need defending. He has made a fair, honorable choice. Do you think it was easy? It wasn't—not nearly as easy as your choice or Johnnie's. You saw only one thing you wanted to do. It would have been easier all around if he had been able to look at things your way; but he couldn't. So, hard as it was for him to make his stand alone, knowing that all his family—all of it, not just we three—would be on the other side, he made it. What is there to defend in that? Or be ashamed of? I never was more proud of my father than I am now. I never loved him so much. I only wish I could tell him so. I wish . . . never mind. I won't say it. I'm going now. Don't follow me, please. I'll find my way back to town. Joe will bring the horse to you. I don't want . . . I . . . good-bye!"

She turned the mare. She slapped her. Lady Margrave broke and ran.

It was a swift run while it lasted. A whistle ended it. Oh, of course! All his mounts were like that. Even Mischief, hers. More amazing, the mare stood while Stuart pounded up alongside and halted. Immediately he was down in the road, lifting Flora, stiffly resisting, from the saddle. His arms went around her. He held her, just held her, until finally with a sigh she, too, gave way and leaned against him.

"There!" he said. "Feeling better now?"

No.

"So blind, so cruel!" she said.

"Floss," Johnnie said now, from somewhere near, "I'm sorry."

She shook her head and clenched her fists.

"There!" Stuart said again. "We'll just not talk about it any more—this evening."

"Perhaps, I'd better go on," Johnnie said unhappily.

"No," Stuart said. "Stay. We'll all go back to town together presently. I think we'll have to do that, don't you, pet?"

Yes, she supposed so. She stood away, and began to smooth her hair.

At home in Warrenton, Tilda had the children dressed and ready to greet their father and the uncle they had never seen. They took command of the situation and gave what remained of the visit a suitable, merry aspect.

"My conscience, Floss!" Johnnie said, in the best bachelor fashion. "It doesn't seem possible."

Laughing at that, Stuart put little Flora, her best dimity, best blue hair ribbon and all, up before him on his big hunter and cantered off with her for a ride. Both came back, looking flushed and happy, Stuart holding his daughter at arm's length, then pulling her to him to kiss her as he set her down.

"You tickle!" she squealed unexpectedly; and Flora was startled, but Stuart was enchanted.

"Growing up, do you suppose?" he asked.

Then she watched him wistfully as he held his son, but all he said then was, "A broth of a boy, don't you think, Uncle John?"

And it was time for good-bye. Stuart held her close.

"We botched the parley, I'm afraid," he murmured. "Never mind. Sleep well, anyhow, my darling. Don't spoil those pretty eyes with weeping over what can't be helped now. Promise? After all, if I have you . . ."

"My heart," she said brokenly, "all yours. Always."

"That's all I want to know."

They left with a song.

> *"Oh, Susanna, don't you cry for me."*

And Tilda, listening and watching until they were out of sight and hearing, said something about Master Philip and bed.

"You know," Flora sighed, "before he was born, I never called him that. He was Jemmie to me, for his father. I've never been satisfied that the other name was right for him."

She loved the other name; but now, if it was to be a thing between her and Stuart whenever they met, or, worse, between him and his son . . .

"Miss Flo'," Tilda said unhappily, "you had trouble today? Too much trouble to talk about?"

"No," Flora said. "I'll tell you."

Simply she did so, and found her first relief in telling.

"Yore pore ma!" Tilda commented, unerringly. "I'll bet she jes' . . . Miss Flo', how're you an' yore ma goin' to manage dis?"

"I don't know," Flora said. "Somehow, I suppose. Tilda, don't put the children to bed just yet. It's such a pleasant evening. I'll stay here with them while you get a blanket from the house. We'll play here on the grass until the mosquitoes and the stars come out. Don't fret about me—or mamma. We'll make out."

Somehow—just somehow.

Chapter 5. *A Very Merry Christmas*

"I never in my life," Maria Brewer said, "saw so many things made out of a few yards of red flannel."

Red flannel covered her lap and it covered Flora's. It covered the bed, the bureau, the center table, two hassocks and the floor. It made the room, a spacious one for wartime Richmond, with an alcove, seem smaller than it was.

The room . . . Flora pushed aside her sewing, blinked her eyes to rest them, and sighed.

"I could do a history of this war," she vowed, "in terms of rooms."

August, 1861. The room an airy chamber in a spacious house known as Machen's near Fairfax Courthouse. After Manassas there had been a general shifting of command, Jackson returning to the Shenandoah Valley, Beauregard going to Richmond and farther south, Johnston assuming command of the Army of Northern Virginia and moving his front line nearer to Alexandria to keep watch over a new Union army assembling before Washington. Stuart remained with Johnston; and Flora, still grieving over the family break, had insisted on moving nearer to his headquarters. It was the only way finally in which she could "make out." One heart, one first allegiance; but it would help to be close to Stuart, where she could see him oftener.

"Fairfax Courthouse will be close," Stuart said, hesitant to the last about the advisability of the move, "but I doubt that you'll see me much oftener. I'm going to bc busy," he warned.

Very busy, Flora saw at once, driven by fresh restlessness now, impatient, as if he had been shown the dimensions of a great undertaking and knew he had no time to waste, as perhaps he had not. General Johnston had recommended him for the command of a brigade; and, while the promotion itself in August had not come through, he was doing the work of organization necessary. New units joined his forces continually.

"You'll never guess whom I saw today," he said one evening. "Pete Carey. Captain Carey now, self-constituted. Brought his own men up from the Virginia-Carolina border. They've not just come. Been drifting around before this, looking over the prospects. Grumble Jones brought him up today. Wants to include the company in the First Virginia. Well, there are two kindred homespun characters."

Grumble Jones, Flora understood, was the man elected to active command of the First Virginia as Stuart moved up, but . . . about to make some glad comment on Peter Carey's presence and to speak of the troop she had seen in Warrenton, she hesitated. Stuart lolled in the grass on the Machen's lawn, his horse almost within reach of his hand. He twirled his hat on his forefinger and studied it frowningly. When he spoke, it was on an apparently different subject.

"Would you," he asked, glancing at her sideways, "have a feather somewhere for this *chapeau?*"

Pshaw! She watched him too closely, she thought, always looking for something. This was her Stuart as she had always known him—that intimate look, the French word in his ridiculous, inimitable intonation.

"I'll look," she said, then added on impulse, "When you are a brigadier-general, I'll give you a plume. Would you wear a plume?"

"Would I?" His eyes glowed, then darkened.

"Tell me more about Pete Carey," she said quickly. "Has he changed?"

"No. Not for the better, at any rate. His men call him Rusty. He wears farmer clothes and so do all in his company." Then, that was the troop she had seen. "Grumble Jones would fancy dressing the entire regiment that way."

So that was why he had thought of the feather? The men in home-spun, possibly Grumble Jones himself or even Peter Carey, looking askance at Stuart's preferment, might have made a disparaging remark about his new uniform, with its braid and bright buttons; and he could think of but one answer—another touch of elegance.

"Did Big Peter have anything to say about Lucy and the children?"

"They're still in South Carolina. Look! If they should happen to come to Virginia and you should meet, you will be friendly, of course; but . . ."

Her stricken expression stopped him. Could he, she wondered, bear a grudge so long? Did he still blame Lucy for drawing Peter out of the service?

"My darling!" Stuart was up, squatting on his heels, studying her face. "Forgive me. Are you lonely—still? I come as often as I can."

She had to smile at the simple conceit of the remark.

"Dear, you are very good about coming," she said quickly. "And even when you don't, I know you are on the other side of one of the hills hereabouts. I shouldn't be lonely. I get to see Johnnie now once in a while, after so many years of not seeing him at all. I have the children and Tilda—and the Brewers in Richmond, which isn't far." A distance less than a hundred miles still seemed to her hardly worth reckoning.

The list ended too soon. Stuart's eyes were still anxious.

"I'm afraid," she said lamely, "that I am a person of narrow attachments. So many new people here. They come and go. I can't begin to know them . . ."

That she should long so absurdly to see Lucy Carey! Of whom she had disapproved, she would have said, more than Stuart could. Impulsively she passed her hand over the thick, warm sweep of his hair. What could she say to make him smile? It was one thing for her heart to ache, but he wasn't Stuart when he looked as he did now.

"It's your fault, really, I sometimes think. I mean it. People are a little surprised when they meet me. Nobody seems to reckon on there being a Mrs. Stuart. They're surprised; then they are curious; and finally, if they are women, they are not happy until they find something in me that they can dislike. I've caught romantic young ladies looking at me with positive loathing."

The ruse worked. He laughed. What an idea! He made up a bit of verse;

> *"I am the beau gallant,*
> *For whom the ladies sigh and pant."*

Machen's near Fairfax Courthouse, a pleasant place, a roomy mansion, a grassy lawn, a beautiful countryside, Stuart near—except for the ache that persisted in her heart and one other circumstance, the month could have been a summer's holiday. That circumstance was the nearness of the two opposing armies to each other. Outposts and patrols met in frequent small skirmishes. When they did, at Machen's Flora could hear even the firing of small arms.

Stuart's young men, however, took those adventures lightly.

"We nearly always get the better of 'em," they assured her. "When we can't overpower 'em, we outsmart 'em; and we can always outrun 'em."

They were very young men who came trooping to join the cavalry that year. Alternately it soothed and sharpened the ache in her heart to see the devotion with which they followed their young commander. There was no doubt about it, Stuart's star was rising. Each time she saw him there was some added mark of distinction. She herself sewed a feather in his hat, that he might be recognized at first sight. A lady from Winchester sent him gold spurs. She had meant them for her son, slain at Manassas. Others gave him, from Yankee plunder, a pair of high boots, Boston made, ornamented with stitching of gold thread. A glittering combination with the gold spurs, and he saved them for dress; but somehow even in hours of work there was a shine about him.

August at Fairfax Courthouse; and, if the young men chose to make an hour of waiting look like a summer's holiday, it would have been a poor-spirited onlooker who would deny them their fun. Sev-

eral times a week there were dances, hastily arranged, with musicians from camp; and, when there were visitors, with hampers of
food, a picnic could be got up even faster. Chin up, eyes bright,
heartache disciplined and subdued, Flora, with Stuart, joined in
many of the frolics; but, better to remember than any of that were
the days when a sidesaddle was put on Lady Margrave and she rode
with him to visit one spot or another where, according to legend, he
kept watch at night, still not trusting the safety of his force entirely
to the vigilance of others. He had now a second blooded mare, the
gift of admirers, named Skylark; but Lady remained Flora's favorite.

"So this," she quoted from gossip one day, looking at a great tree
and a scrap of tarpaulin, "is where 'Stuart sleeps without blanket
over or under him'?"

He turned to her, his eyes alight with fun.

"August is right warm in Virginia," he reminded her.

On another late afternoon he showed her from Munson's Hill the
city of Washington. They rode nearly to the crest of the hill, then
dismounted. To cool the horses, Stuart said; but afterwards Flora
knew it was because they would be less conspicuous on foot if their
outlook should be under observation. Slowly, leading the two mares,
they made their way through the trees and stopped at the edge of
them, looking out; and there in a green valley beyond the glimmer
of water was the city. The declining sun flashed on the dazzling
white Capitol, on a gold cross topping a church spire.

"They told me you could see," she said in awe, "but I had no idea
it was so near."

Stuart did not answer. She turned, and saw that he hadn't heard
her. He stood, lost in a dream in which she had no part. His head
was lifted, his face exalted. Where had she seen him look so before?
Only at divine service. He comes here often, she thought, and alone.
He was alone now. Timidly but insisting that he be aware of her, she
put out her hand and touched his arm. Absently he covered it with
one of his and drew her to his side.

"Some day," he began, "I shall . . ."

"Don't say it," she begged.

He let her go. Ah! Without meaning to, she had pricked his dream.

"You don't believe I can take that town?"

"Darling, I believe you are equal to anything. Just don't say it, please. It's silly superstition, but there it is. I wish you wouldn't."

It was more than superstition. It was foreboding. She would not look again at the sunlight on marble Washington.

Consequently, she had difficulty in persuading him to show her another spectacle which she really wanted to see. Between dances that evening, young Captain Blackford, knowing that Stuart in the afternoon had showed her Washington, asked if on the same ride he had showed her McClellan's army.

McClellan—where had she heard the name before? A saddle, a regiment's roster? Captain—no, General McClellan now.

"You can't be serious," Stuart said when she came to him with her request. "If Washington frightened you into a near fit, what will you say to the enemy camp? It's a big one," he warned.

"I know." It wasn't Washington that had frightened her; it was Stuart's dedication to a vow; but she couldn't hope to make him understand that. "If I know what I'm going to see, I won't be frightened."

He didn't understand that, either; but he still objected.

"Please. I've a special reason."

She wouldn't say what the reason was, and did not until after Stuart had yielded and taken her to that other hill.

It was their last ride around Fairfax Courthouse. The next day she and the children were moving into the back country. Johnston was shifting his army now, drawing in his lines, tightening them. After she saw the Army of the Potomac, she understood why.

Their last ride probably for many a day. They had too much to think about to indulge in idle chatter. Even the horses' hoofs made hardly a whisper of sound over the soft woods turf. Presently they looked out once more from a screen of trees; but this time a wide plain spread out below them, with the sparkle of water in the distance; and all the land between the low hill where they were and the water was covered with tents. Now it was Flora who had no words for what she saw.

"Well?" Stuart said.

She raised her hand.

"I am telling papa good-bye. Do you mind?"

For answer, he put his arm around her and pointed.

"The cavalry, most of it, is over there."

She thought, as she looked where he directed, that she could make out a special orderliness in the rows of company tents, the picket lines for the horses, the space for cooking fires, the grouping of officers' quarters, as she had seen it diagrammed for the book on tactics.

"He is there, too," she said. "You know?"

"Yes," Stuart said, "he is there, when he is not in Washington. They have given him a cavalry command." A mischievous smile crinkled his eyes. "Brigadier-general, and he is not too well pleased. Well," he snorted softly, "it serves him right. He would have been a major-general with us."

"Oh!" Flora said, assailed now by pity.

Brigadier-general. In time of war the one grade promotion, long since earned and expected, was a slight. Why, she asked herself, but knew the answer. Army politics. He had never courted favor in Washington. And it could be because of us over here, she thought, and that he was born a Virginian. They might think that his heart wouldn't be in his work and they could be right to an extent, though he would never give less than his best. But mostly what he lacked was youth. Her father, her brilliant, accomplished father—but his hair might now be all white. General McClellan, all promise so far and no great achievement, except the invention of a saddle, was a young man by comparison.

"I can't help feeling sorry," she said. "Sorry that he is unhappy."

"Not unhappy," Stuart said, still brusquely, "just disgruntled." Then he changed the subject and his tone. "Your mother and Julia are with him in Washington. They're at Brown's Hotel. All are well."

"Stuart!"

There was gratitude in her cry and a plea for forgiveness. He was offering atonement, she knew, for any pain he had helped to cause her.

"But your mother was heard to say she wished she could hear from her daughter Flora. The others, too, I suppose; but she mentioned you in particular. So, if you will write a line on a scrap of paper that can be folded quite small, I'll engage to deliver it."

"Stuart . . ."

"I'll have it placed under her plate some morning at breakfast."

"But how?" she questioned.

One or another of his young men, it seemed, visited Washington often. Spies.

"I wouldn't want anyone to take that risk for me," she faltered.

"*Ma povere petite,*" Stuart said; and, for once, she did not laugh, "that risk among others will be nothing. What will you say in the note?"

Flora thought, her eyes never leaving him.

"Just that we are well," she said finally, "and we send our love. I can say that, darling?"

"Love," he conceded, looking out over the plain, "but no mercy."

Later, at Machen's, when he took the note, it was, "This is as near as I ever hope to come to compounding treachery." Then he kissed her. She had never loved him more.

Orange Courthouse then, and Culpeper, and, briefly, another time at Warrenton. The Army of Northern Virginia shifted position continually, always on the *qui vive*, expecting an attack by the Northern Army, which was still growing until, some said, presently it would be too ponderous to move. That was a forlorn hope. If McClellan were minded to retrieve honors lost at Manassas, he must stage a grand attack soon. With each shift, Flora would move to a new town. The place would have been recommended by General Hill or General Longstreet or someone of equal prestige. Their wives had stayed there or were there and found the place agreeable. As her acquaintance with official kin grew, so did Flora's sense of importance. Remembering Rachel, she wore now an air of gentle dignity, calculated to carry her past any pair of cocked or questioning eyebrows.

Stuart was delighted. He sang, going and coming. The world, with his help, was forgetting; his darling wife was forgetting the whole sorry business of Brigadier-General Cooke, U. S. A.

Flora was not forgetting. The heartache was still there, but reduced now to a smaller spot of pain, easier to hide.

November, and they were back near the front lines, the house a bleak, bare structure known as Mellon's, the town Centreville. "Camp Qui Vive," Stuart called the place when he made it his headquarters.

"I don't know," he said uneasily, helping to settle them into that room. "We're in a better position generally here than at Fairfax, but I don't know."

Flora had no idea from the first that their stay at Mellon's would be other than temporary. They had hurried out of Warrenton because of a scarlet fever outbreak, but the threat of grippe and pneumonia in this cold house seemed almost as bad. November, and winter coming on, and no stoves. Tilda went about so blue with chill that Flora saw no difference in her that gray morning when she tiptoed into the dining room with a warning.

"Miss Flo'!" Her teeth were chattering, but even that was no sign. "I looked out a winder upstairs jes' now, an' I seed a bluecoat. 'Mongst de trees."

"No," Flora said. "You must be wrong."

"No'm, I ain'."

Glass splintered somewhere. The Negro serving breakfast set down a dish and his eyes rolled. At the end of the table an elderly gentleman—Captain Blackford's father, up from Lynchburg to visit his son—said without thinking, "That was a bullet."

It still seemed impossible.

"Tilda," Flora said, surprised at her own continued calm, "dress the children and bring them down here to me. No, I'll come help you."

In the hall they met Captain Blackford coming through the front door.

"Mrs. Stuart." He stopped respectfully, but she could see his anxiety. "We are having a small raid outside. Colonel Stuart sends word to bar the doors and keep away from the windows. We . . . we'll drive them off presently."

It wasn't presently. All day Flora sat with her children and others in a sheltered corner made by the staircase and a piece of wall and listened to the barking of guns and the rush of horses, and ran through and through her repertoire of song and story.

"And Little Klaus walked on and on . . . Once upon a time a duckling was hatched in a farmyard . . . 'Then I will,' said the Little Red Hen . . . Mr. Frog would a courting ride . . . There was a man in our town and he was wondrous wise . . ."

In the late afternoon, when Stuart came, as she knew he must soon, spattered with mud, she was too hoarse to give him suitable welcome.

"My pet," he said, "was it as bad as that?"

Tilda came to her defense.

"She ain' skeered, Cap'n Stuart. She ain' bin skeered. Jes' talkin' an' singin' all day, playin' wid de chillun, to keep um quiet."

He was tremendously proud, he said, tremendously; but Flora could feel the tension in his arm.

"You will pack tonight," he ordered. "I'm sending you to Richmond tomorrow. I've wired Doc Brewer and Mrs. Duval, ordering a room for you."

Mrs. Duval's, the select boarding house, where Flora and Stuart had stayed during the church conclave in 1859, waiting for word from Washington on the patent. A smaller room, costing twice as much now as then; but she must not look askance at it. Only an order from Colonel Stuart of the cavalry, backed up by General Johnston, had cleared it for her and the children.

Here it was December and here she was, enjoying a visit from Maria—sweet, steady Maria, more like Rachel than any other of her children—and sewing like mad on yards of red flannel. The first garments she had made were finished—riding habits for herself and little Flora, modish Garibaldi jackets to top sober black skirts, caps to match the jackets, lined with china silk and finished with silver braid. Stuart had kept his promise about the little one's pony. A brigadier-general, he pointed out, was allowed five horses.

"I would like to see his face when you two appear before him in those rigs," Maria said of the habits. "He'll hold a grand review."

There would be a grand review presently, Flora told her. That was why she had made the costumes. General Stuart's wife and daughter must do him honor. It was understood that they would attend the review when Stuart was ready. Flora was expecting word any day now. Here it was December . . .

Here it was December and she had his plume laid by and he had his brigade. Six regiments, five colonels and one major to command. Flora blinked her eyes again and proceeded to take the final stitches on the garment spread over her lap—a circular cape of gray worsted, lined with the red flannel, and topped by a collar of soft brown fur.

She stood up presently and flung the garment about her hips, swaying to make it swing and show its bright lining.

"Wonderful!" Maria said. "You should keep it for charades in the
parlor. You could borrow Stuart's fancy boots and be a Cossack
dancer."

His boots? Flora could put both feet into one of them.

"Idiot!" she called her sister. "Pretending you don't know what this
is meant to be."

She lifted the cape to her shoulder and went over to the bureau, to
study it in the mirror, particularly the collar. Whatever would she do
if she ran out of fur and feathers? She threw back a fold dramati-
cally.

"Seriously," she said, "how does it look?"

"Wonderful!" Maria said again. "Until some hungry soldier thinks
he sees a squirrel and takes aim."

"Oh!" Flora turned back to the mirror. "Do you really think . . ."

"No," Maria said quickly, "and I wish you wouldn't think so much.
Does Stuart know about the cape?"

"Yes," Flora said. "I had to know whether he could wear it or
would. The plume in his hat was a great success but I wasn't sure
about the cape. To tell you the absolute truth, I had to speak for the
privilege of making it." She made a wry face at her image in the
mirror.

"You mean," Maria asked, "everybody is wanting to give him
things?"

"Everybody," Flora agreed. "His sash, his shoulderstraps, his
battle flag. Every romantic girl in the South is embroidering a banner. There aren't enough regiments—or heroes—to go around."

"I know one girl," Maria said slyly, "who sewed her tippet to a
military cape for a brigadier-general."

"That's different," Flora said, and came out of her slight pet into
dimpling laughter. "That girl also made her true love some bright
red underwear. What do you suppose Stuart will say to that shirt and
those drawers?"

"He'll be enchanted," Maria said without hesitation. "Likely as not
he'll belt his sword over them, step into his boots, and hold a viewing."

"They're awfully red," Flora admitted, "but I've heard nothing keeps off rheumatism like cochineal dye. It snowed at Centreville after we left."

"Darling!" Maria, whose charm was a warm sensitivity to others' feelings, jumped up and put her arms around her sister. "Do you ever have him off your mind?"

"Never. I might just as well be where he is."

She let the cape fall from her shoulders and clung to Maria.

"Honey," the latter protested, "how long will you last at this rate?"

"Oh, a long time," Flora assured her. "The Cookes are tough. Hadn't you heard?"

She dried her eyes, picked up the cape, dusted it critically and added it to the flannel on the bed.

"Sister, you're wonderful!" Maria said now. "And the cape is a masterpiece."

"The tailor who made Stuart's uniform helped me," Flora confessed. "Sweet of him, wasn't it, after Stuart had had to put off paying his bill, in order to settle with Mrs. Duval for this . . ." she shuddered, "palatial room. Really, making the cape wasn't a circumstance, compared to those drawers. If it hadn't been for Mrs. Lee's sewing circle, I never could have managed them."

In Richmond, society—ladies' society—had already divided into two widely separated groups. The thing both had in common was devotion to the cause of the Confederacy, a feeling which from the first marching away of son, husband, brother or lover, had passed right out of reasoned belief into passionate prayer. The difference was in the expression of anxiety. One group gave itself over to a seeming intoxication of fun—balls, parties, theatricals. If the ladies of that group sewed, it was on battle flags or silken sashes. The whole effect of such activities was a glittering display of high spirits which, some people said censoriously, only went to show how little some people realized the seriousness of war.

The comment seemed to Flora extremely unjust. It wasn't choice altogether that made her drift into the second group, exemplified nobly by "Mrs. Lee's sewing circle." It hurt to know that people said of her, "Wouldn't you think General Stuart's wife would be someone very light-hearted and merry and just ravishingly pretty? She's young enough and sings nicely, I'm told. Bookish—but we need people like that for getting up tableaus and charades. A Cooke, you know, first cousin to John Esten Cooke, the novelist. There's a gay fellow. And she has a most attractive brother, unmarried, just named colonel of the 14th North Carolina Infantry. But . . . well, she is just the Lee type, I reckon."

Not altogether the Lee type. Everything young and buoyant in her inclined toward the gayer crowd; but, well, living in one room, though in the best of boarding houses, living on Stuart's pay, knowing his unsettled debts, she couldn't keep up appearances. Her silks lost their shimmer, her slippers wore thin, and what fun was dancing, anyhow, with Stuart away? He, that year at least, would have nothing to do with Richmond frivolities. Did the ladies know?

Still it hurt, rather, when Lucy Carey, up from South Carolina for the winter, older, with a couple of lines marking the sides of her petulant mouth, but prettier than ever, went into the gay set like a duck settling on feeding ground.

"Dear me!" Lucy said. "Life in the old army was never like this. Come along with me this afternoon, Floss, won't you? Everybody of consequence will be there. That British newspaper correspondent—what's his name? Russell—is going to talk about Mason and Slidell. The Davises promised to attend—well, at least Mrs. Davis and her sister. I'll lend you a dress. Celie will fix you up."

No, that wouldn't do. Pride forbade borrowed finery, though it was common practice for people to exchange clothing. Pride . . . perhaps she was the Lee type, after all. To be allowed to join Mrs. Lee's circle was in itself a distinction. Lucy Carey wouldn't be given the privilege—nobody was given it offhand. Custis Lee called on Flora at Mrs. Duval's and took her to see his mother.

"My dear, do you sew?" Mrs. Lee asked. "A few of us gather here one or two afternoons a week to make bandages and sew up a few homely comforts for our men. We'd be pleased to have your help and the delight of your young company."

Except for Mrs. Rooney Lee, still known to Richmond as "little Charlotte Wickham," Flora was the youngest of the group that met in the quiet house on Franklin Street, where no effort was made to keep up with the social swim. Mrs. Lee's health would not allow it, had she wanted to do anything of the sort. A slight woman, with fine eyes and a manner that could be as vivacious as anyone's if she was feeling well, too often she was pale from a sleepless night and sometimes she had to be excused from attending her own gatherings. Then one of her daughters, Mary or Mildred or Agnes, must do the honors.

Of the Lee girls—all beauties, with their father's handsome, clear brown eyes, and a lurking sense of mischief, now subdued—Flora's favorite was the eldest, Mary, possibly because the latter had come to have considerable acquaintance with Stuart. Being the eldest daughter, and the men of the house being occupied with business of government or of war, Mary had taken upon herself a kind of supervision of the family's estates. Arlington was now, of course, confiscate to the Northern government—and there was reason enough for one's sense of fun to be subdued, but another estate, Ravensworth, was close to the battle lines and Stuart had more than once been called upon to give her safe conduct.

"I think," Flora complained to her gently, "you see him more often than I do."

"I fancy there's a difference in the meetings," Mary answered.

There were other fine women in the sewing circle, Mrs. Joseph Johnston and Mrs. Longstreet, for example. The latter also had been a colonel's daughter, and had married, against strong paternal opposition, a young lieutenant. She knew John Cooke. She had three lively children. She was older than Flora, but they had so much in common that a difference in years should not have mattered.

It was a privilege, Flora admitted, to associate with such women; but new acquaintance still could not replace old attachment. Lucy Carey, through her father's influence, settled into the Spottswood Hotel, where nobody in months had been able to secure a room, let alone a suite. Much the same Lucy. The differences between her and Flora were what they had always been. Their husbands were no longer friends, new resentments building on an old misunderstanding that would better have been forgotten; but the two women fell into each other's arms with moans of delight. One hour with Lucy was to Flora as refreshing as a summer shower on a parched flowerbed.

There was nobody, for example, Flora told Maria now, who could match Lucy's comment on Richmond society: "Did you ever see so many women?"

And right there someone knocked on the door.

"Gentleman to see Mrs. Stuart, if she is at home to callers."

It was Mrs. Duval's exceedingly correct mulatto parlor maid. Flora took a card from the tray she offered.

"John Esten!" she cried. "Down from camp!"

John Esten Cooke, her favorite of all the Cooke connections in Virginia. Novelist, littérateur—she knew him as a charming gentleman, an incorrigible tease; and now that he had joined Stuart's staff, he had added importance.

"Coming, Maria?" she called, already halfway to the stairs.

In the parlor her distinguished relative was warming himself before a coal grate. She held out both hands in welcome.

"Cousin John!"

He took her hands and drew her to him, to kiss her cheek.

"Just to maintain the family tradition," he said.

"What family?" Flora retorted.

"Ah!" He let her go and turned to the door. "Cousin Maria, how are you? I must say you are both looking well—for stay-at-home war ladies. Cousin Flo' has actually two locks of hair out of place, and look at her cheeks!"

"I've been fussing with some sewing," Flora said. "Cousin John . . ."

Maria laughed. "You should see the sewing. Sister, I'll step outside to watch for the children. They've been out with their nurse, John Esten. They usually bring up at the railway depot to watch for a choo-choo, and come home nicely sooted. I'll rush them up the backstairs, Flora, for a quick wipe before I bring them in."

"Don't!" John Esten begged. "I should like to see a child of Flo's under a layer of dirt."

The most dreadful tease! As far back as Flora could remember.

"It's the first time I've seen you in uniform," she said, as Maria left. "I like it."

"Well, to be absolutely truthful," he said with a wink, "I don't. The prevailing fashion, you know, or I wouldn't. I mean it. Ask your husband some day his opinion of my military qualifications. He's having a devil of a time knowing what to do with me. Right now I have the choice of two positions—both honorary. Honorary aide to General Stuart, whose staff has already outgrown his rank, though he may rise to it presently, or honorary lieutenant of the new Stuart Horse Artillery. So unnecessary in both places that, when a courier was needed on Richmond business, I qualified instanter. While here, I should have a stripe set in my breeches, but I'm blessed if I know what color."

"John Esten, hush!" Flora begged. "Tell me at once what brings you."

"Business with the Quartermaster General," he insisted. "We are short on a few items up north, and a few days ago we got caught in a sort of ambush. Oh, nothing too serious," at Flora's look of alarm. "Stuart pulled us out and they didn't get him, which I think was what they intended. Sit down, hadn't you better? He's all right, but still smarting. We suffered some losses. I think you would have been proud of your husband, my dear. Knowing that he had been ambushed, he calmly ordered his empty wagons to the rear—it was a foraging expedition, you see—then held a bunch of Joe Johnston's green infantry along the beleaguered road, staying with them until he had pulled out his guns and they could be released to skedaddle also. Early the next day he went back with a fresh detail, to bury his dead and gather the wounded, also to recover the harness from his slain mules and horses, so that the Yankees couldn't count that in their plunder. Besides, he needed it."

"John Esten," Flora said, "I know you have a letter for me."

"A letter?" he said hazily. "And that man with everything in the world on his mind?"

"He wouldn't send you here without one," Flora insisted. "Give it to me this minute."

John Esten with a shake of his head and a sigh surrendered it. Flora tore it open.

My darling wife—

Peace settled on her spirit, and fluttered away in a panic. She had been sure that the first line would read, "I am sending John Esten with a conveyance to fetch you and the babies." But it didn't say that.

My darling wife, I am sending your Christmas present by John Esten—fifteen yds. I had hoped to give it to you here . . .

A present? Fifteen yards of what? She didn't want a present.

myself, if the roads ever became passable. They grow worse instead of better. I can't think of coming to Richmond because I dare not leave this place even for a few hours. We look for the enemy to attack at any time.

It is quite cold here. Our mess is short of many things, especially coffee and sugar. Send me something nice by John Esten, will you?

And then,

XXXX and XXXX to you my darling. Kiss the babies . . .

Flora closed her eyes and fought a hard battle with herself. When she opened them, John Esten had a murderous Bowie knife poised over the knotted string around a brown paper parcel which he had managed up to now to conceal.

"Don't!" she cried sharply, and, when he looked up in surprise, added weakly, "I need the string. Anyhow, I do think I might be allowed to open my own present."

Pecking and picking and poking at the knotted twine gave her more time but not enough to prepare her for the shimmering mass of silk that met her eyes when finally she laid back the brown wrapper and the protective white tissue paper lining. Taffeta silk, changing as the light fell on it, from sea green to sea blue—the loveliest color she had ever seen.

"Oh!" That was her breath coming and going. "Oh!"

"I was to tell Stuart," John Esten chattered, "how you looked when you saw the stuff. It would require a man of my literary gifts certainly; but I believe I can give a fair idea."

"Oh!" she said again, and again. How had he known? The one thing in the way of a gift she wanted most. She could attend an occasional party now in the best of style. She had in her trunks a length of Brussels lace. She would take that and the silk to a dressmaker. There must be a full, swishing skirt, an off-the-shoulder bodice. She had shoulders as white and as dimpled as any in the city. She would dress her hair high with a comb . . .

"John Esten, how in the world? Where did it come from?"

"Baltimore. Now, listen, Flo. You're not to question me. If you do, I'm not to answer."

So, she knew. A scout, with a special order. Stuart had told her how they ran the lines. But this was a scout extraordinary. Smoothing a fold of the silk, her hand came upon something hard. It was a packet of thread—two spools of sewing silk, matching the material. No man would have thought of ordering those; no man would have added them to the purchase.

"A woman," she said.

"Possibly," John Esten admitted.

A young woman, of excellent taste.

"Stuart should not burden his messengers with errands for me. I've said so before this."

"She was enchanted," John Esten said unwarily. "At least, she said she was. Look here, if you will ask questions, you deserve to hear the truth. A widow, young, with a pass through both lines, enabling her to visit aged relatives in Alexandria. She was enchanted because Stuart is always warmly grateful for such special service . . ."

Flora pretended not to hear him. She was busy replacing the wrapping about the handsome silk. She didn't want the dress at all now. Stuart still in debt to his Richmond tailor. Lacking such simple comforts as coffee and sugar.

"John Esten, how did you come to Richmond?"

"With a wagon train. Didn't I tell you my business was with the Quartermaster General?"

"When will you be going back?"

"Tomorrow, if I obey orders."

"Could you carry a few things for me?"

"Yes." Then he grew wary. "How much?"

"It could come to a hundred pounds or even a little over. You had better bring a wagon past the house."

"Flora, for heaven's sake!"

"I've been accumulating things for some time. When do you expect to start?"

"Early in the morning."

Early. She remembered how that was. "Wagons at the depot at seven." Time for loading, time for the drivers to snatch breakfast.

"I'll have everything at the front door here by nine," she promised.

At nine the following morning, there she was, in her warmest wool dress, with the scarlet flannel short petticoat under a number of others, with a doubled cashmere shawl around her shoulders, its points deep behind and before, with a tight, quilted hood over her ears, and mittens to match. Two boxes rested at her feet, along with a folded camp cot, Charles Brewer's admonishing gift to his brother-in-law. One box held the new flannel underwear and the cape, neatly folded, and Stuart's plume. The other, larger and heavier, contained four pounds of loaf sugar, four of coffee in the bean, a jar of honey, another of molasses, a tin box of cakes and one of nut-filled candy. Maria had given her the cakes and candy the evening before when she took Tilda and the children over to the Brewer house.

John Esten's face, when the army wagon, with a top—Flora had counted on his seeing to his own comfort—rolled to a halt before the stone steps, was something to contemplate.

"I might have known," he said. "Cousin Flora, I can't do this. If anything I said yesterday, about a widow or anybody else, is behind this mad resolve, please dismiss it from your mind. It is of no consequence. No, I won't listen. It's cold. The roads are bad. Stuart will tie me to the mouth of a cannon and shoot me at the Yankees. Flora, I beg of you!"

She wouldn't yield. She was ready. He had no idea how many layers of warm clothing she had about her. She had ridden army wagons before over horrible roads. She was going.

"My God!" John Esten said, shouldering the heavier of her two boxes. "Come along, then."

For the first twenty miles he didn't stop grumbling.

"You could write a book on tactics yourself. Is this how you took Stuart? A mere man hasn't a chance. You'll be sorry."

She may have had a qualm or two in the course of the hard journey, but nothing to make her wish she might turn around and go back. Not even when, at the end of three long days, she stood with her plunder in the entrance hall of the bleak house styled "Headquarters, Camp Qui Vive," waiting for Stuart to be told she was there. Outside, a battle flag, scarlet with crossed blue bars, slapped in a sharp northeasterly wind, a sentry stamped and marched to keep his blood running, and another trooper blanketed a courier's horse. Indoors, in the comparative warmth of sheltering walls, Flora shivered as she had not done out in the wind. In the adjacent parlor, she heard a pen scratching and the young officer who had brought her to the house coughed hesitantly. He was a stranger to her, until he gave his name—Captain Pelham of the Stuart Horse Artillery. Then she remembered Stuart's mentioning him often in recent letters.

"Excuse me, sir. Lieutenant Cooke has arrived—with three wagons. He will report presently in person, he begged me to say." The pen stopped scratching.

"Three? Couldn't possibly carry what I asked for in three wagons."

"No, sir. It may be there are more to follow." The pen was scratching again, and Captain Pelham risked all. "Meantime, there's a lady to see you."

The pen scratched on. "Tell . . ." it stopped with a sputter. "What did you say? A lady? Here?"

"Yes, sir. In the hall."

"Did she give her name?"

"Yes, sir. She says she is Mrs. Stuart."

"What?"

A chair creaked, released from the weight it had borne. Spurs struck the bare boards of the floor. In the hall Flora tussled with the ties of her hood. A warm thing, but she doubted its becomingness. She had time only to fling it back off her hair, to pray that her nose might not be as blue as she feared it was. Then Stuart was in the door.

"Flora!" Maybe John Esten was right. Maybe she had done a rash, impetuous thing. But oh, the blessed satisfaction of being where she was, of seeing Stuart, so square, so strong, so brave in his gray cloth uniform, not yet stained beyond the possibility of repair by loving hands!

"To wish you a very merry Christmas, my darling!" she faltered.

The cry of welcome Stuart gave then was so hungry, so rapturous, that every doubt fled in disorder. Seconds later, snug and warm and safe in his arms, she didn't give a fig how many ladies wove him sashes or embroidered him flags or ran his errands. It didn't matter if he kissed their hands in homage, as John Esten said he did, especially if they were young and beautiful. What was that, compared to her utter, complete possession?

"My own Stuart!" her heart cried wildly. "Mine, mine, mine!"

Chapter 6. *Panic at the Capital*

Surely no spring was ever lovelier than the spring of the new year—1862. One day everything was gray and cold and bleak and people were going about in overshoes and overcoats. The next, or so it seemed, the trees were bursting into leaf and flowers were budding.

"It's always like that," Richmond ladies said. "Always comes with a rush. First thing you know the magnolias will be in bloom. Then summer, and nobody ready for it."

"Beautiful!" Flora sighed, her eyes catching some of the blue of the violets the children were gathering—her two and little Evie Carey. Young Peter, going on nine now, was much too old to gather flowers. The two families—widows and orphans, Lucy Carey said —were picnicking in a wooded glade off the Brook Road north of the city. Peter, at the edge of a little run, wrestled with a toy boat his mother had bought him. The two nursemaids chattered to each other as they minded the smaller children. Flora had spread a blanket for herself and Lucy, but Lucy perched herself above it on a folding stool. Bugs and things. She had never really enjoyed picnics, Flora remembered; but the children did, and this was the only way she, Flora, could compensate for the gay and sometimes elevating parties she attended with Lucy, for the loan of Lucy's dressmaker, for the goodies Lucy shared with her out of hampers and boxes up from Carolina. The picnic supper for this evening Lucy had provided, but Flora had provided the picnic, knowing the spot for it, secluded, charming, near to town and a good road, safe from vagrant prowlers.

"And I'm everlastingly grateful," Lucy said, "for all but the bugs and the freckles. But then, I'm bound to have some and it may be as well to commence early."

Flora smiled at the exaggerated concern over a few freckles. More beautiful than ever, this older Lucy; but Flora could see, now that their friendship was re-established, a change in her. Some current of deep feeling stirred under the determined light-heartedness. Flora didn't know about the years after Big Peter had left the army and before he returned to service; but she was sure there had been more bitterness than joy in Lucy's victory.

"That man of mine," Lucy said now. "There is only one way to endure him—that is to let him run his life to suit himself."

But she was in Richmond with the children, when she could have been far safer and more comfortable at home. She would be Lucy Carey to the end of her days, light and lazy and indolent and lovely, but she had suffered and had known remorse and would find a way, if she could, to make amends. Possibly that was why she clung to Flora, hoping for help or a hint as to how. And Flora, in turn, gathered strength from her dependence.

Flora turned now to look at small Peter down by the brook. He was all but in the water, struggling with his boat.

"Remember the time he nearly went overboard into the Missouri?" Lucy asked. "Our first acquaintance and you didn't like me a little bit."

"I was horriby envious," Flora answered. "I didn't see how anybody would ever notice a plain little thing like me, with you around."

"Awful, arrogant little snip I thought you," Lucy countered. "So neat and fresh and equal to everything. A colonel's daughter, besides. Your Stuart's first impression was the same, but I had his arm and I felt him jump and tighten up all over. If you had been just another pretty girl, he would have bowed and flirted a little and forgotten you. You weren't. So, he jumped and took a second look; and well, that was the way of it."

They looked at each other and away, each thinking of the same thing—their husbands as unharmonious as they were friendly. At the beginning of the year, the various volunteer regiments of the Army of Virginia had held elections. Colonel Jones, Carey's superior, had lost the First Virginia to Fitzhugh Lee. Jones, then, too valuable an officer to waste, had been given a command under

Turner Ashby in the Shenandoah Valley. Carey had asked to be transferred with him and his request had been granted.

"My fault, Flora," Lucy said of that. "If I had behaved as I should and Peter had stayed in the army, he and Stuart would be out in front together now."

Carey possibly outranking Stuart, though that might be questioned. Flora put her small, strong, needle-scarred hand over Lucy's.

"It's because they are so much alike that they quarrel," she said. That, and Carey's unquenchable resentment. "They will be friends again some day."

"They will," Lucy agreed, "unless . . ."

She did not name the condition. A roar from young Peter prevented.

"Peter!" Her scream made Flora jump. It was so like that warm day on the Missouri; but the boy was older now and the branch was shallow, though he had waded out after his boat, what remained of it. He came up stained and dripping, but unhurt except in spirit, and brought his wreck to show to Flora and Lucy.

"It was a nice boat, mamma," he said ruefully. "I'm sorry I spoiled it. I wanted to give it a proper launching, and it sank. Too top-heavy, I reckon, for running water; but, if you can't put a gunboat on a river, what good is it?"

"Well, I'm dreadfully sorry, Commodore," his mother said. "It doesn't look to me like it was much good. What will you do now?"

The boy studied the shapeless wet mess in his hands.

"If you don't care," he said finally, "I'll take it apart and see what's wrong with it. Then I reckon I'll have to try to make a better one."

"Darling, that's a fine idea," Lucy said; and off the boy went.

"My son," Lucy said to Flora. "Would you believe it? That little log schoolhouse at Leavenworth, I reckon. You said he'd never forget and he never has, not for a minute. Today everything is Navy with him. Tomorrow he'll be a scout, or a general. He'll grow up to be something military, you can be sure. Not all the tutors we could hire will change it, nor any power of circumstance. I should never have taken him away. You were right."

"I was just talking," Flora said, impatient now with her primness of that past time. "I don't like prophets or prophecies. I never will . . . again."

Unbidden, as always, a spectre crossed the bright April picture, a man with burning eyes and the sepulchral voice of doom and a patriarch's beard. It was said that the Yankee soldiers marched now to a chant about him: "His soul goes marching on." The visitation fortunately, was brief, dispelled by a child's laughter. The little girls and toddling Jimmie Stuart were bringing up their booty now for examination, but only the Stuart children carried flowers. Exquisite Evie Carey had an angleworm.

"Evangeline Carey, put that reptile down!" Lucy screamed. "Don't bring it one inch nearer. Put it down, I say! That I should have two children," she moaned, "and neither one any more like me than if some other woman had mothered them!"

"The wrong one of mine is most like me," Flora answered, picking up her Jimmie, and holding him close.

James Ewell Brown Stuart, Junior; and he was too small for anybody to be sure, but she was more certain with each passing month that taking his original name away wouldn't keep him from being mostly Cooke. If Stuart noticed, so far he had made no comment; but he saw the little ones only too rarely. An afternoon's romp on a blanket like this or on his own red one at camp, a melee of man and children and dogs—two setter pups had now been given to him—or a practice ride. The red-jacketed lady's habits had been a great success, particularly *La Petite's*. Stuart loved both children deeply; but, if he had a favorite, it was his daughter. He was pestering Flora now to have the child's portrait painted and Flora was in despair. No artist alive could produce a likeness that would please the doting father.

"Time to wash up now," Tilda said. "Miss Flo', dis yore sewin'? Good Lawd, look dar! I'll shake it good befo' you wrap hit up."

They were on their way home in the hired hack that Lucy had engaged for the expedition—two tired and slightly rumpled mothers—"I can be one just so long," Lucy said—four exceedingly tired children, little Jimmie sound asleep, and two still chattering maids; and suddenly, with the journey almost done, their carriage came to an abrupt halt, its way blocked by a column of soldiers marching across town. Not recruits. Veterans from somewhere marching to a new front. Their colonel, mounted on a black stallion, was a dark, heavy

man and a stranger. He and his adjutant looked fresh enough in neat
uniforms but the soldiers tramping behind them were travel-stained
and weary. They had come a long way. Stubble of unintended
beards darkened young faces. Flora stood under the new green of
trees at the edge of the sidewalk, young Peter on one hand, the little
girls on the other, and watched the soldiers pass. Lucy was too tired
to mingle with the crowd. There was some cheering, to which the
soldiers replied with salutes and uncertain smiles and, now and then,
a meaningless sally. The band played "Maryland, My Maryland"; but
all the South marched to that tune now. Names of places were tossed
into the air. Finally she caught one.

"They say," she said soberly to Lucy, back at the hack with her
charges, "that McClellan has landed at Yorktown, but I don't believe
it. It seems to me I would have heard."

What she did believe was that there would be no more picnics in
the woods near Richmond.

"Where is this place called New Madrid?" a lady in the sewing
room asked. "Does anybody know?"

Flora waited for someone else to speak up; but, when nobody did,
she answered.

"It's on the west bank of the Mississippi, near the mouth of the
Ohio. Coming east, we used to take a boat down to Memphis. That's
how I know."

Was it a large town, important? No, just a steamboat landing.
Then, why did the dispatches make so much of its fall? Another
feather in the hat of that Yankee—Unconditional Surrender Grant.
Nobody could answer that.

Few in Richmond, if any, had ever heard of Shiloh Church or
Pittsburg Landing; but it did seem that the Yankees were taking
every battle out yonder. More of that man Grant? Had the South no
army out there to stop him? Yes, a fine, brave army. Its commander
was one of the Confederacy's best generals before he died at Shiloh.
Albert Sydney Johnston. Flora remembered his great camp on the
plains the year he marched out to Utah. Now, compared to the Army
of the Potomac, that camp was nothing. She had seen McClellan's
tents again at Christmas. A Leviathan, she had called his army.
Could anything so ponderous move into battle?

It had moved. Leaving part under General McDowell, the one who had been sent running in full flight at Manassas, Little Mac had brought the rest by water to Fortress Monroe, not Yorktown, and had made a landing. His purpose was evident—to move up the Peninsula between the James and the York Rivers, and attack Richmond from the east while McDowell moved against it from the north.

Both must be stopped. More troops poured into Richmond than the capital had seen since spring of the year before, and went on through, to stiffen the defenses at Yorktown, where the Peninsula was narrowest. Miraculously, aided by General McClellan's instinct for caution, the defenses held, at least for a while. The grace of God, anxious folk said, still not easy in their minds. Less than a year ago all the talk had been of a march on Washington, the Federal capital. Now it was how to defend Richmond. General Joseph Johnston was moving his army southward, solidifying his lines, keeping his cavalry out to scout McDowell, but definitely retreating. All this, taken with the bad news from the West, made it seem that the star of the Confederacy had come under some sinister influence.

One evening in May General Stuart of the cavalry, splashed with mud above his high boots, but looking otherwise very jaunty in his red-lined cape and plumed hat, reined up before Mrs. Duval's select boarding house in Richmond, and, with no apparent cessation of movement, dismounted, handed his reins to a following aide and strode to the door. Mrs. Duval, handsome in black silk and jet beads, herself opened the door. He swept off his hat with a flourish.

"Madame, I must say you are looking well. Am I fortunate enough to find Mrs. Stuart at home?"

"Yes," the landlady answered, drawing the door back full width now. "I heard her come in a short while ago, with the children. I'll send upstairs for her."

That proved not to be necessary. Stuart, making a rueful face at his muddy boots, removed his spurs before he entered the house. Carried loosely in his hand, they made still a pleasant jingle. He laid them down carefully under his cape and hat at the hall tree and turned; and Flora stood at the head of the stairs. One hand gathered the fullness of her skirts out of the way of her feet; the other was white against the dark of her snugly fitted and buttoned bodice.

What a lady she was always, Stuart thought. What a lady—there could be no hour when, coming upon her without warning, he would find her retreating in confusion to remove curl papers or to change from whatever she might be wearing. Even what she called disarray had still a sweet orderliness about it.

Longing beat up suddenly from deep inside him. That it found expression in laughter of voice and lips and eyes made it no less longing.

"Madame!" he teased. "Is it possible that you were not expecting a visit from your husband?"

A door to his left closed gently but with emphasis. So, that was what had kept her aloof at the top of the stairs? Laughing again, he strode toward them; and she was in his arms before he could begin the climb.

"No!" she protested, when she could speak. "Of course, I was not expecting you. You said . . ."

Nothing but the exigencies of war . . . but she could wait to ask about that. She put up her arms in a rare movement of invitation, and drew his head down to hers, laying her cheek against his.

"My dear, my dear!" she said brokenly.

Tears stung his eyes as he held her.

"You smell so good!" he said, absurdly. "I hope you never run out of whatever it is you use."

She laughed now. Not while roses bloomed and she had a sunny windowsill. And spices, she recollected. She had enough for this summer—well, she must guard her supply. Plenty for now, anyhow. She laughed again, recalling how every time she sent Stuart anything from her store of possessions, like a feather for his hat, for example, those young rascals on his staff swore the bees followed him, looking for nectar. But not finding any, to be sure.

"You'll stay, now that you're here?" she asked. "For supper, at least?"

He kissed her questioning eyes, her tremulous lips.

"Not this time, sweetheart." He told her about Blackford outside. "I was passing and stopped by for *a big hug and a squeeze.*"

A magic phrase he had delighted to teach Jimmie, complete with responses; but he must answer her other question now.

"Stuart?"

"We've been moving troops into the Peninsula," he said. "And a number of men in my brigade were born and raised there. We'll be serving as guides and escorts, to get everybody where he has been ordered."

"Stuart?" she asked still.

"Everything's just all right," he assured her. "Don't let anybody try to tell you different. Aren't we here all around you?"

Literally, wonderfully present. She relinquished him slowly.

"You'll want to see the children," she said, then prattled to him all the way up the stairs about them. Jimmie would be asleep. He had reached the age when he began to fight off naps; but Tilda had kept the two youngsters on the Capitol green while Flora attended a church meeting; and, as always, by the time the young man reached home, he was ready for bed. Pet was well, growing . . .

Small Flora waited at the door of the room, Tilda behind her. Pretty as a sunbeam, Stuart thought, with a thundercloud on guard. She flew at him with a glad cry, then drew back, wrinkling her nose and rubbing it with her hand. It had got to be a game between them, her objection to his beard. He paddled her lightly before he set her down on the floor, then said to Flora,

"You know, lately one or two others have raised an objection. Ho, what a face! The beard flourishes, you'll observe. If I should shave it, or even trim it a bit, you might worry. But I won't; so fret about everything else, if you must, but not about that. Good evening, Tilda. How are you? Seems to me you're thinner, and you never were fat. Don't you get enough to eat, or do these young'uns run the flesh off you?"

"I eats awright," Tilda said, squirming. "Things is skeerce yere an' dar, but we make out."

He stood still then an appreciable minute inside the room. He looked at his yearling son, spread-eagled on the wide bed. His guardians had had barely time to get a protective scrap of quilt between him and the counterpane, and to remove his shoes. He dared not kiss the boy, not wanting to stir him out of a delayed nap; but one doubled fist lay over the edge of the bed. He knelt and touched his lips to it.

"Dear Lord, it is for such as these . . ."

"Papa's praying," little Flora whispered.

"Sh!" her mother said.

"Grant me courage and strength and bless our arms, O Lord; and keep watch over these, my three."

When he stood up, a finger on his lips to match the others, what swelled to bursting in his heart still clamored for expression.

"Take good care of my family, Tilda," he said, inadequately.

"Yassah, I does what I kin."

After he had gone, it seemed to Flora that a light that had not been there before lingered in the room. In the alcove, where Tilda spread her bed at night, the maid, busy at her everlasting picking up, crooned softly to herself;

"When Israel dwelt in Egyp' lan' . . ."

And down in the street, the slanting rays of the sun had a better brightness.

Brightness was needed. The next day the wounded began to come into Richmond from Williamsburg. Williamsburg? Then, the line at Yorktown had not held? No. When McClellan finally decided to strike, the supports to the line were withdrawn and all were ordered to fall back. It was too thin a line to hold. Most of the troops stationed there got away safely. A few had been taken prisoner.

Prisoners? But the South had no men to waste that way. No, but that was how it happened sometimes. The commanders knew what they were doing. One must believe that. Yes, surely, but hearts had a way of sinking before one's better intelligence or faith could rally. Williamsburg was bravely fought; but, it, too, was part of a withdrawal. Out there in the sloughs and swamps and thickets, Stuart's cavalry was guiding regiments to new stations, trying to keep them from miring in the bogs or drowning in the Chickahominy, still swollen from spring rains. When the weather was worst and the night was blackest, there he'd be himself, singing like a madman, his voice carrying where a light couldn't:

"Swing your partner to the RIGHT.
Skip to my Lou, my darling!"

The action out there must have been awful, and was most dispiriting to hear about, no matter how those in the thick of it felt. McClel-

lan broke through at Yorktown. Gunboats ascended the York River
and took White House on the Pamunkey. Another Lee estate in
Yankee hands. On the other side of the Peninsula, Norfolk was
taken. The Confederates sank their ram, the *Virginia,* hoping to
block the harbor passage. It didn't . . . much; and what was the
sense in sinking ships, when ships were what was needed? New
Orleans had now fallen at the mouth of the Mississippi. The block-
ade began to look pretty complete. What was the use of planting
cotton or harvesting it, if it couldn't be sent where there were mills
to buy it? Hold fast to what you have, ladies, of silks and laces and
sugar and spices. When what you have is gone, where is more to
come from? How are we going to clothe and arm and feed our soldiers, to say nothing of ladies?

The first gunfire—big guns—was heard at Richmond. Southern
guns at Drewry's Bluff. The Yankees had come up the James River
that far, but they wouldn't go any farther. They didn't. A few bold
people ventured out to the fort on Drewry's Bluff, to see the Yankee
flotilla. Not many. One day it became known that President Davis
had ordered the most vital documents at the Capitol packed and
moved away. His family, too, seemed to have left, because he came
to church on Sunday alone. Polite, charming, as always.

"Good morning, Mrs. Stuart. I am glad to see you out this fine
day."

But alone. As lone a man as anyone could picture.

The Careys went back to South Carolina.

"I promised Peter I would if he sent word," Lucy said. "I promised. I don't want to go and it isn't for me. It's young Peter. His
father wants him safe. He is possessed that young Peter must grow
up to be all that he once hoped to be and knows now, somehow, that
he never will be. He isn't scared. He just knows. Isn't that a state
of mind? No wonder he can't be half-civil to anybody. Good-bye,
darling."

On the last two days of May there was a battle at Fair Oaks, on
the York and Pamunkey side. General Johnston had at last seen a
favorable opportunity for making an attack. Just to show how things
work out, the man sent to hold the Yankee line was General Sumner,
colonel of the First Cavalry when Johnston had been lieutenant-
colonel. Johnston's attack jolted the Federal forces, but how badly

it was hard to say, consternation taking a new turn when Johnston himself, severely wounded, was brought to the capital the last day of May.

General Lee, who had been away in that part of the state the Yankees and some of the inhabitants now called West Virginia, and had just returned to Richmond, was given command of the defending army. He made a quick review of the situation, and requisitioned picks and spades for a change, instead of guns, from the quartermaster command. He put the trenching tools into the hands of soldiers of high and low degree and his order was brief and unanswerable.

"Dig!"

King of Spades, they called him those days; but the men dug manfully, until there were two lines of entrenchments all around the city except on the river side.

Entrenchments—around Richmond, the Confederate Capital?

"Dear Lord," the anguished citizens prayed, "send us light in this hour of darkness. Lift this awful burden of fear from our hearts. Show us a way back to hope and belief in ourselves and our cause."

Chapter 7. *A Stuart to the Rescue*

On a fair June morning of that same portentous year, the air heavy with the scent of honeysuckle distilling its juices under a summer sun, General J. E. B. Stuart rode southward toward General Lee's headquarters near Richmond. Blitheness of spirit, compounded of fair skies, of youth—he had turned twenty-nine now—of bodily vigor and a mind refreshed, not by rest—for, though he rode at a leisurely pace for him, an undeniable urgency had sent him to seek a personal interview with the commander—but by a general sense of high adventure, compelled him to sing. No need for caution. The Nine Mile Road they called this by-way and there wasn't a Yankee within that distance or more. So he let himelf out at full volume.

What he sang was of no consequence. He snatched the tunes at random from the soft air. This morning early it had been his privilege to sit his horse on a bluff overlooking Fredericksburg and watch McDowell's main army begin its withdrawal northward. There would be no union now of his forces with McClellan's. He had been called back to the defense of Washington.

"Oh, Lemuel, my love; oh, Lemuel, my beau . . ."

To be sure, he, Stuart, had had nothing to do with that withdrawal beyond observing it. It was the result of General Jackson's drive up the Shenandoah Valley, whipping McDowell's right flank before him all the way to Harper's Ferry, and so giving Washington a taste of the panic that shook Richmond. Now, God bless that dour, devout, rampaging commander of the First Corps!

"You say it is impossible to advance? Forward, MARCH!"

Stuart had had no part in the roaring, boring drive; but God grant . . .

"Rock of Ages, cleft for me . . ."

Behind him, on a horse too old and placid to mind human whimsy, rode his choice of escort for today, his favorite escort on all solitary rides, the banjo player, Joe Sweeny. An itinerant musician, he had drifted into camp the winter before and had speedily become almost indispensable. He rode with the reins of his horse caught on the pommel of his saddle, held there by one bony knee on which he cradled his banjo, playing as he jogged along a light, sensitive accompaniment to the General's singing. The tinkling notes sparkled like the silver trim of the instrument.

"Molly Bawn, why leave me pining,
All lonely, waiting here for you?"

A group of infantrymen, throwing dice near the road, turned their heads to listen. One of them rose, and walked to the edge of the glade.

"It's him," he said to the others. "Remember how he sang us through that ford on the Chickahominy?"

"That ford?" another objected, joining his comrade. "Them fords, I say. That blasted river was running wild, but it never stopped him, did it?"

Their voices carried. That had been a bitter business, that time

on the Peninsula, pulling men out of lines they had thought to defend with their lives, drawing them back and forth this way and
that, but always retreating, never advancing. A bitter business. All
softness had been ground out of Stuart in that one week. Now God
grant that finally he might be instrumental in driving out the invading army! They had no right to bring their guns and their hired
mercenaries into Virginia, to coerce a proud, free state.

A bitter business. It had been good, when the defending lines had
at last been established, to pull out his cavalry and take it northward, if only on outpost and observation duty. To breathe unpol-
luted air, to set up camp and rest the horses—and eat the contents
of picnic baskets the good ladies of the little wayside towns up the
road to Fredericksburg brought out to them, to wash up and brush
up on a Sunday and ride to church, then off to some hospitable mansion for a bountiful dinner and an afternoon and evening of whatever bright-eyed companionship might fall to a man's lot. Good for
a man to dance and sing and joke and flirt a little, against a time
when . . .

> "I been to East, I been to west,
>   I been to ole Verginny;
>   Ob all de gals I eber saw
>   Cynthia's as good as enny.
>   Oh-oh, Cynthia . . ."

He held up his hand to Sweeny in a sudden order for silence. They
had turned into a lane leading to the farmhouse he sought. A bit
farther along he pulled up before a spacious veranda. As he did so,
a courier came out the door with the importance of couriers generally, favored Stuart with a start of surprise, saluted smartly, and
without a word of explanation, wheeled and turned back into the
house.

Stuart dismounted slowly. Apparently, thinking only to add his
personal observations to the general dispatches about the withdrawal
of enemy forces to the north, he had ridden into other business brew-
ing at headquarters, something that seemed to involve him. Naturally, he had no idea what the business could be.

But was that strictly true? After that bitter week on the Peninsula,
he had included in his report to Lee his views on the disadvantage of

too much defensive action, had given his opinion that the Southern armies generally were better at offense. He hoped that an offensive campaign might be begun before McClellan became too firmly established in his lines and before the men in their own forces, new to soldiering, lost heart. Already desertion was threatening.

He had written his views in a warmth of feeling not to be denied. Almost immediately then he had the misgivings of a cadet turning in an examination paper. His opinion had not been invited. General Lee had far too many advisers as it was.

Through an open window a firm voice issued a command: "Ask him to step in at once."

"Would you care to undertake a special reconnaissance for me, General Stuart?"

Lee's way of giving an order: "Would you care? May I suggest?" No lack of firmness but always a punctilious courtesy. Time and stress might frost his hair and the new closely trimmed beard. The same combination might some day dim the lustre of the fine brown eyes that looked so paternally on this young and, by comparison, rather gaudy general officer; but General Lee would no more abandon manners than he would wear his coat unbrushed. On this busy morning he had taken time to ask about Stuart's family, about Stuart's own well-being, how were the Lees in Stuart's brigade acquitting themselves, had he had a report on the recovery of Williams Wickham of the Fourth Virginia, wounded at Williamsburg? He had discussed McDowell's withdrawal and sighed enviously with Stuart over Stonewall Jackson's march. Now this prelude to an assignment of unknown challenge.

"On the Peninsula, sir?" Excitement beat its wings in the shaded parlor.

"On the Peninsula."

Where else? An attack was shaping up. His letter to Lee had been kindly received. No, that was presumptuous. Lee had been planning all the while to move when time and the conditions were right, but sober reasoning would not keep Stuart in his chair.

"Great day . . . excuse me, sir. I will ride wherever you send me."

A smile touched Lee's lips, shone in the depth of his eyes.

"Let me explain what I have in mind."

He spread a map on the table. Stuart had one like it in his saddle bags, but marked differently. McClellan had not yet set up his head-quarters when Stuart had ridden north to watch McDowell. He noted now a red circle on the Chickahominy and marked it mentally on his own map. McClellan's quarters commanded the center of a line facing Richmond from the east. His left wing, reaching down toward the James River, was pretty well defined. It was the right wing about which Lee was uncertain, knowing neither its exact position nor its strength. Since his plan was to attack the invaders, not directly out from Richmond, but in a sweeping movement north of the Chickahominy, he must know about that right flank. How far had it been extended? Its purpose seemed to be to guard McClellan's supply base on the Pamunkey—no show of feeling about White House—but how many men had the General assigned to guard duty? Could the supply line be broken or even temporarily disrupted?

Lee sat back to let Stuart make his own study of the map. Stuart checked the marks, fitted them to his picture.

"Sir, have I your permission to choose my men?"

"Yes, of course," Lee said. "This may prove a desperate as well as an exciting ride. Take plenty, but," his eyes glowed again with subtle, appreciative humor, "do leave me enough cavalry to serve this army."

"Yes, sir. I will want both Fitz and Rooney."

"I have no sons or nephew in the army, Stuart, only near, dear relatives under arms. I think either would be disappointed if he were not given the opportunity to ride with you."

Stuart bent to study the map again, and laughed over something he saw.

"Sir, with your permission . . ."

Never was a march finally more hedged about with caution.

You will return as soon as the object of your expedition is ac-complished. While endeavoring to execute the general purpose of your mission, do not hazard unnecessarily your command or attempt what your judgment may not approve.

Heigh-ho! Caution a plenty. He had no mind to lose a man to the

Yankees; and what he might bag on the march, besides information, tickled his fancy considerably.

Take only such men as can stand the expedition . . .

The pick of his scouts—John Mosby, Redmond Burke, Will Farley. Fitz Lee with all of the First Virginia Cavalry and four companies of poor Wickham's Fourth, Rooney Lee with part of the Ninth Virginia and four more companies of Wickham's, Will Martin with a couple of hundred men from the Jeff Davis Legion and the South Carolina Rangers, Lieutenant Jim Breathed of Kentucky, second in command in the Stuart Horse Artillery, with a 12-pound howitzer and a rifle gun; and how Pelham and the rest would groan and carry on when they found out what they had missed!

The success of the expedition depends upon its secrecy.

Just before two o'clock in the morning on a misty night, an aide who had kept vigil touched Stuart's shoulder. He sat up, waking fully and at once from deep, dreamless sleep. The next instant he was on his feet, and the aide was rousing the others.

It was a strange reveille and a stranger assembling. No bugle broke the pre-dawn stillness. No order was heard except Stuart's steady word to those about him: "Gentlemen, every man must be in the saddle in ten minutes." Out of the dark the horses appeared. Stuart mounted and led the way to the road. His aides fell in behind him. Ten minutes after that the headquarters detail was moving northward over the Brook Turnpike.

The cavalry brigade, to insure forage, was camped in three places along the line of the Richmond, Fredericksburg and Potomac Railroad. At Kilby's Station Rooney Lee's command waited in line. At Mordecai's, Fitz Lee was having trouble with his. Silence was broken by grumblings and mutterings. The First Virginia was not willing to be the tail of any man's kite.

"Nothing personal intended, sir," Fitz Lee said, his salute a mere shadow of movement.

"Surely not," Stuart agreed, exultation mounting for no reason. "You may wait, if you wish, till our dust settles."

The column moved on at a fast walk. Dust muffled the rhythmic thud of the horses' hoofs. At first dawn a full chorus of birdsong made as much clamor as several brass bands. Men cocked their ears, picked out favorite or well-known trills, then relaxed, and, being able soon to see one another's faces, raised the first question. Did anybody know? Anybody have an idea? Why, having seen Old Man McDowell off for Washington and having marched south to join Lee's main line, were they now moving northward again? Lee's orders, somebody said. Grins cracked dusty faces. Lee's orders, with Stuart embroidery. But nobody in his right mind could have dreamed that they were off to plant one or more burrs in the tail of Leviathan. Had anybody guessed the truth, by late afternoon nobody would have cared, all being near to insensibility when they swung off their weary mounts on a pleasant farm place thirty miles north of Richmond. Nothing had happened. They'd seen nobody. Nobody much had seen them. Riding fools, that was all.

> *If you want to have a good time,*
> *You must jine the cavalry.*

Hell!

It was a curious ride—that first reconnaissance in force—much of it as unreal in the experience as it was later in the telling, although it became desperately real for James Ewell Brown Stuart and his thousand men before it was finished.

Himself, for example, at the end of that long first day, sitting upright on a straight chair in the parlor of Hickory Hill, the Wickham place, asking politely about the progress of Colonel Williams Wickham toward recovery; and almost immediately, or so it seemed, Rooney Lee, who had ridden there with him, shaking him by the shoulder, wishing him good morning and asking if he had enjoyed his night's sleep.

"If you're serious about reveille at dawn, sir, we'd best be going."

Riding back to camp then in the misty pre-dawn dark with Colonel Rooney of the Ninth Virginia, asking himself whether it might not be wise now, or even the right thing, to tell someone under him the program for the day, but deciding that the time had not yet come. Old Jack had a maxim about that: "If my coat knew my plans, I'd take it off and burn it."

Breakfast was almost formal, with Fitz Lee and Rooney and Will

Martin his guests at table, all munching their bread and bacon and drinking their coffee in unusual and thoughtful silence. No questions. It could have been an early morning's start on a day's hunting, except for nearly a hundred campfires glowing in the pasture and bacon sizzling in as many frying pans, and the sound of horses champing corn.

"Hear the brutes," Fitz Lee said finally. "A person might think . . ."

What a person might think he did not elucidate, seeing Stuart with his watch in his hand. He had ordered a half hour for breakfast, with a good watering and thorough feeding of the horses. He did not mean to allow one minute more.

Assembly gave Stuart his first doubt. A handsome, well-ordered line, as if it had formed on a village green. Every man in his saddle, ready, all waiting on his command. Had he any right to take them where he was going? Even under higher direction? All very well to set off on such an adventure, with a handful of men as willing as himself, knowing the hazards, but a thousand of the South's finest? Not knowing?

Fitz Lee kneed his horse to a position close to Stuart and saluted.

"The First Virginia would appreciate it, sir, if it might lead the advance today."

Not knowing. Not even asking.

"Lead off," Stuart said. "Column of fours to begin with. Right turn. The direction is east—the road to Hanover Courthouse."

They knew now. They knew even before Stuart took his three leaders aside and told them the general plan. There could be only one objective, riding eastward toward the sea. They were going to scout Little Mac and his grand army. Singe him, too, a little bit, maybe, if they found an exposed portion. Easy now, caution warned. The chances were a thousand to one that they'd feel the singeing if they got too bold. Caution? If caution had prevailed, they wouldn't be here in the first place. Leave all that to Stuart now. He knew what he was doing.

> *Mr. Frog would a-courting ride,*
> *Sword and pistols by his side—hmmm!*

But Stuart knew little more, really, than the men in the column. He had a map in his mind and in his sack. He had his orders. He was to discover the strength of Mac's army north of the Chickahominy. There was only one way to discover it—to feel for it. How else would he know? There was a hazard—rather, a certainty of conflict. Contact must be established, and that meant conflict. That was why he had a thousand men. They might have to fight their way out of an entanglement. He would do all he could to avoid entanglement, but there was that chance; and the farther he took his force, the graver the possibility.

He had a plan—a diagram, rather. Persistently it shaped itself into a circle beginning and ending at Richmond. If he could ride all the way around McClellan, he could present a worthwhile report to his commanding general and really mark a map for him: "The Yankees are here and here and here, but not here or here." It was a big "if," he knew; but that was his plan. He could say later that this had led to that and the other; but the idea was in his mind from the beginning. If his colonels had demurred over the first half, if the men in the column had faltered, the circle diagram might not have been so sharply clear and enticing; but there was no faltering, just a mounting willingness.

"We must feel for the enemy," he said; but today's road for a while looked as empty as yesterday's. Occasionally a buggy or a carriage or a mule and rider waited to see the column pass. Good, loyal Virginians all, their word to be trusted, but their information hardly. They had seen no Yankees up this way; but they could not be too far off, Stuart knew. Forward, then, feeling for them—just feeling.

Hanover Courthouse, where Patrick Henry had practised law. A few buildings scattered along both sides of the road; and sharp in Stuart's nose was the smell of smoke from that ambush at Dranesville the winter past. Short of the town he slowed the column to a dragging walk, a halt, but kept the men mounted and ready.

Up from a roadside ditch then came his ace of scouts, John Mosby. He had tied his horse in the woods and gone on into the village on foot.

"Bluebirds," he said. "Not many. Scouts, vedettes, but bluebirds surely."

"We'll take them," Stuart promised.

He sat watch in hand, while Fitz Lee and the First Virginia drifted down a side road to the far edge of town. He ticked off a quarter hour. He raised his hand to send a line of skirmishers forward, men who could bring a squirrel down from a leafy tree from as far as they could see the tree. They spurted forward, raising whorls of dust; but ahead of them, in the village, a rifle cracked and Mosby's bluebirds flew off, smothered in dust of their own raising. Stuart's main column sat impotent and watched them go.

"Let them run," Stuart said grimly. "Fitz will get them."

But, when the column, crestfallen, disappointed, rode through the town, there was no sign of Colonel Fitzhugh Lee or his crack regiment. Nothing but those damn Yankees riding lickety-cut down an unobstructed road. Nothing to do but watch them go.

Cherish the men you do take . . .

Send a scout to look for Fitz Lee. Take the rest of the column forward at a walk, to ease the men's impatience and his own, and wait. The Ninth Virginia filed down the road, the detached companies of Wickham's Fourth. Will Martin came on with his Legionnaires. Another few minutes and he must halt them all.

Where was his lost regiment? Where was Fitz Lee? He turned his head to listen. At first only the hum of a summer morning drawing toward noon came to him, a subdued rustling—no, it was not wind. There was no wind. A morning more still had never been made. He turned his horse now, in time to receive an offhand salute from Mosby. Behind the scout came the first platoon of the missing troopers, Fitz Lee riding ahead, recognizable only because of a white star on the forehead of his horse. Mud was drying in cakes all over him. He was still combing it out of his beard.

"Beg to report a stretch of bog, sir," he said punctiliously. "Five hundred feet in width, of unknown depth . . ."

It could have been worse, much worse; still Stuart did not like it. He had felt the enemy, but hardly. He had lost the first skirmish of the day to Virginia mud. He had not counted on losing to anything or anybody.

"Forward . . ."

The morning was spent. They rode easily, steadily under a mur-

derously hot sun, the direction southeasterly now, toward Totopotomy Creek. The thought of water dried some throats and moistened
others, but it was quite possible that a halt at the creek would be
for something other than rest.

Just beyond a crossroads smithy, a brash handful of bluecoats, no
more than a foraging detail, swarmed up out of a wheatfield and,
dizzied either by the heat or the sight of men in gray riding down
upon them, rode head-on to meet the advance.

"Form fours! Draw sabres—CHARGE!" Stuart roared. These
should not get away.

Dust came up on the road and alongside like an explosion. Swords
flashed and pistols barked. The ripening wheat went down in blocks
where the Yankees slipped from their horses and tried to hide.

"Get those horses!" Stuart bawled. "Spread out . . . surround
them."

The bag was twenty-five men and a sergeant—and their mounts.
But again some had got away—the lieutenant commanding the detail and another. Stuart marked the line they took through the wheat
—southwest—and turned to address the captured sergeant in time
to witness a strange reunion. Fitz Lee had ridden up, to see what
the shooting and the roaring meant. He had by now managed to
get the mud off his face. The Yankee sergeant's grim, sweating features broke into a grin. The hot faces of his squad brightened.

"Godfrey!" Fitz cried. "You blessed old sinner!"

"Howdy, Lieutenant," the sergeant answered respectfully.

"My men, General Stuart," Fitz Lee explained. "Served with me
in Texas. Have I your leave?"

"Captives to the rear," Stuart ordered. "Have the men's wounds
dressed, Colonel Lee." A half dozen sabre gashes were bleeding
freely. "Question them. As to the horses, two men to one where
possible. Save the best."

Here and there in his column, he could spot the first signs of distress from heat and unrelieved marching. The Yankee horses were
fresh and strong. He might need them all for replacements. He
could use many more.

My men. Part of his brain dealt with that as the captives passed,
following Fitz Lee, granting Stuart brief recognition. "We mighta
knowed," the sergeant put it. *My men.* A year of fighting, some of

it brutal and deadly. A year in which cleavages of friendship and family and beliefs had widened and walls of hostility had hardened and set. Still a man like Lee could say with a throb, "My men!" It wasn't only young and tender women like Flora, then . . .

My men. Another part of his brain dealt with it differently. The Second Cavalry of the old army, the Fifth Cavalry of the new. Regulars. He was touching, just touching, the edges of McClellan's right.

Totopotomy Creek at high noon, running clear and cool, the bridge sound and unguarded. Stuart led his advance across. The troopers dismounted on both banks, unbitted and unsaddled their horses, washed off their own sweat and munched on whatever they carried with them or had gathered by the way. Stuart sat against a tree, his watch in hand. No Yankees in force north of the Totopotomy. That much of his report was complete. The Fifth Cavalry was somewhere ahead, Fitz Lee had learned. All the cavalry of McClellan's right was commanded by General Cooke. Hm!

Two miles ahead now, by the road they followed, was a village called Old Church. Here roads from two ferry landings on the Pamunkey met and crossed. Provisions for McClellan's right must move by wagon over those roads. If Stuart knew his father-in-law, a strong guard, stronger than any force yet encountered, would be stationed at the crossroads. He stood up, pocketing his watch.

A half mile short of Old Church, he formed fours and set skirmishers.

"Will you fall back now?" Rooney Lee asked. "It is not right for you to expose yourself, if there should be fighting."

No, it was not right. Whatever the outcome, he must carry the report to General Lee at High Meadows. His the praise or his the blame. He drew off to one side, fell back a little, but not far. He would give the command to charge. Right down the road, was his directive. Nothing would be gained here by side-stepping or encircling movement. Boldness must be the way of it.

Yankee outposts got wind of their coming and carried the word. The guarding troops had time to form in line—on foot behind a barricade.

Forward . . . trot . . .

The carbines of the skirmishers fired a short volley.

"Draw sabres . . . CHARGE!"

Galloping now, man and horse pounded past. Pistol fire ahead was hot and heavy, but in seconds its volume was inaudible against the fierce yells of the mounted men bearing down with their sabres out. No line, without stout entrenchments, armed only with revolvers, could hold against that charge. Wild exultation pounded in Stuart's heart. He rode forward, just behind the crest of the attack and arrived in time to see the Yankee line break and the men run for better cover, in time to see one of his own horses without a rider, troopers in gray forming a hollow square around it and their fallen comrade, but not to know who the man might be, in time to rally the advance squadrons and halt them while his second line, the chafing Legionnaires and Rangers, went on to rout the Yankees if they formed again. Minutes later wild yelling told him they had found their fight at last.

Five more minutes and the dust began to settle at the crossroads. Will Martin, flushed and breathless, made his report. His Legionnaires had taken five Yankee companies, man and horse. Also the guidons. They would hang them up in Richmond presently, for others to see.

Rooney Lee reported the loss of one man—a company captain.

"Will Latané," he said soberly, "commanding my first squadron. Will you give an order . . . about him?"

"We'll carry him home," Stuart said.

Fitz Lee now had caught up with the advance.

"My regiment," he said, still lost in old sentiment, "is stationed less than a mile away. May I scatter them, for my own satisfaction and your greater glory?"

The First Virginia pounded past, raising the dust again, only the steeple of the church that gave the crossroads its name rising above it. When it settled, while company captains assembled their troopers, and the captive men and horses were being counted, Stuart took council with himself.

You will return as soon as the object of your mission is accomplished.

He had now most of the information that Lee wanted. There were no Federal troops in force in the territory he had scouted. The skirmish at Old Church had been a matter of routing a strong outpost. He waited for sounds of battle from down the road where Fitz Lee had gone. There were none. A courier came pelting back with a report. Fitz had found the Fifth Cavalry's camp but it had been abandoned. Quite recently. He had caught a few stragglers. Supplies were still there. Should he . . .

"Only what is loaded," Stuart ordered, "in wagons with animals to pull them, and the captured men and horses. He will hold his force ready to move—on short notice."

And now he must give the command. Retreat or advance. He weighed the cost of each. Could he retreat? Ahead, at any of several places, he might come up against the main strength of McClellan's army. He had managed so far to avoid a hard, pitched battle. Could he avoid one if he went on? Could he, if he turned back? From each small engagement men had ridden off with information about him. He had no doubt that troops would be sent to halt him at every point of vantage on the road back. The bridge over the Totopotomy and every other creek on the watershed. The Yankees would look for him to return the way he had come. Nobody would or could imagine his daring to advance.

"Nobody," Rooney Lee agreed soberly when Stuart called him and Martin to a consultation.

Opposition seemed then to have been what Stuart needed to clarify his purpose. He would go on. By choosing guides who knew roads and byroads, he thought he could still keep outside McClellan's lines. He was moving now through plantation country, where the people were his friends, not Little Mac's. There might be some fighting. He would try still to avoid major engagements. Nine or ten miles farther along they would cross the York River Railroad, Mac's main supply line from his base at White House. If they could reach it and tear up a stretch of track, McClellan, at the very least, would be seriously discommoded.

"It would be a pleasure," Will Martin conceded, his face as soberly apprehensive as Rooney Lee's, "if we can do it. You are the one to say, of course. We'll go wherever you lead us."

They would and they did. But not one, not even Fitz Lee, as

daring as any man alive, would have thought he could take better than a thousand horsemen down the road that lay ahead and bring any of them back alive. When John Esten Cooke carried Stuart's order to advance to Fitz, he touched it up a little.

"I think the quicker the better, don't you?"

"Right," Fitz said. "Move on at a trot."

Move on at a trot. The afternoon was passing. Sunlight, which had been a burden, was something to be measured now in precious hours. Nervousness made itself known in little ways. At one point, through a break in the trees, snow-white tents shone dazzling in the distance off to the southwest.

"Mac himself, do you reckon? Are we going to take out after him now?"

"Hope not. From what I hear, accommodations at the old Capitol Prison are not too desirable."

No grumbling now about bringing up the rear. Trouble was as likely to come from that quarter as any other. A little farther along, the road to Tunstall's Station, on the York River Railroad, branched; and Stuart sent his scouts with a patrol down the righthand fork, to be between the main column and McClellan. The rear guard heard the rustle of movement and took fright.

"Yankees! Here they come!"

Stuart, not willing to ignore any alarm, had two pieces of artillery in position before he discovered that the fright had been caused by the scout patrol. Hot words of rebuke were in his mouth, but he swallowed them, and laughed.

The main road lay close to the Pamunkey. Only a fringe of plantations separated the troops from the river. People on the plantations who saw the long line pass stared incredulously, then waved handkerchiefs, aprons or hats and cheered; but they didn't know much about any Yankee soldiers. There were boats on the Pamunkey—Federal boats—at Garlick's Landing two miles away. Not many soldiers, however, just those who handled freight at the warehouse or drove the wagons. Wagons passed most every day on any road leading west.

Stuart picked two squadrons that had seen no fighting and sent them with a guide to the landing. They were to bring off horses in particular. The need for them was plain now. Other plunder must again be easy to move. Burn the rest. The men swung away, cheering.

Tunstall's Station on the railroad. A Yankee guard kept watch.
"Form platoons!" Stuart snapped.

The stranded garrison must have thought Lee's army had come suddenly upon them. The roaring attack scattered the defenders like a wind blowing through dry leaves. Some of the platoons in Stuart's line had only railroad tracks left to attack. They went for them with deadly intent, but lacked tools. The best they could do was to hurl spare ties and fallen trees across them. Stuart sent a wrecking detail down the line to burn a railroad bridge. Before it disappeared, a locomotive whistled, coming from the east. There was a final heaving of rocks and logs into the right of way; and then the cavalry fell back under cover of trees, leaving a scattering of sharpshooters flat in the long grass beside the tracks.

The train came on. Either the engineer saw the litter on the tracks or he was in the habit of slowing down for Tunstall's. The train came almost to a stop. Behind the locomotive a string of flatcars carried what must have been a full regiment of infantry, going up to join Mac's army.

Being human and alive, they had been loaded vertically, but that had been all the consideration shown them. Their heads stuck up like the tops to so many poles, and the few miles they had ridden had been uncomfortable enough. As the cars slackened speed, from each one a few nimble bluecoats dropped to the ground, to feel its solidity under their feet, to stretch their legs, to escape confinement. Soon most of the cars would have emptied, but somewhere in the line waiting under the trees sat a trooper with a nervous finger. A pistol popped.

One shot was enough. The engineer of the train, who, in view of the deserted depot and the trash on the tracks, must have already smelled a rat, opened the throttle. The wheels began to roll faster. The men on the ground raced to get aboard. A few made it. More fell back, in as much danger from the grinding wheels as from the blaze of fire now coming from the long grass and the trees. In another minute not a Yank was left standing aboard the train or alongside. Whether those who went down had been hit or had dropped for greater safety would not be known until a count was made. On the train the heads that had been like the tops of poles disappeared. The cars looked empty.

It was an odd thing about those men. When first seen, even more when they jumped down, to find what ease they might, they had been men. Now they were reinforcements for McClellan, and the Confederate troopers blazed away at them ruthlessly. Will Farley, the scout, aimed his rifle at the locomotive and brought down the engineer, but the fireman must have jumped at once to take his place. The train, steadily gathering momentum, roared and rattled away. It would reach the bridge well ahead of the detail sent to burn it. A short while later a desultory pop of rifles told of its safe passage.

Stuart, his own pistol smoking, heard a song in the humming of the rails:

> Got to get out of here, got to get out, got to get out.
> Got to get out of here fast. Got to get out of here now.

Over to the east a column of dark smoke that he had been observing began to fade and dwindle. Garlick's Landing—the warehouse burning. Good work! A mad thought crossed his mind. If they could wipe out the stores at Garlick's Landing, why not raid the main base at White House? Give the place back to those who owned it? He had his answer in the song of the rolling wheels:

> Got to get out, got to get out . . .

White House must wait for another time.

Forward, then, to make the most of remaining daylight. Fours, where the road was wide enough. Twos only when absolutely necessary. Must try to close the line. Had the guns come up? Not yet, but they were moving. The horses were beat out.

So they were. The raiding party brought in a string from Garlick's and it was a problem to put them where most needed. Besides the horses, there was a bunch of mules. These, added to a number serving the garrison at Tunstall's, furnished mounts for the prisoners, two to a mule. Rough laughter greeted the bucking and spills and the general awkwardness of the riding.

Forward, over a road worn into deep ruts by heavy hauling through mud. The line in spite of urgent watching, straggled and spun out. Supper halt was made at first dark, in another desperate attempt to close it. Talleysville the name of the town. A small Federal hospital had been set up there. Stuart's guards delivered the badly wounded among the Yankee prisoners, touched their hats respectfully and kept in the clear. A sutler's store did not get off so well. Flour was seized, for hasty biscuits, molasses, bacon, coffee, butter for the biscuits, tinned beef, tinned sausage meat. The horses, unbitted, blew hard, fed and watered sparingly while the men gorged. Some of the troopers, after a long hot day with practically no food, went off at once into the bushes and were sick. Others waited until later. It was midnight before the rear guard and the guns came up, and Stuart, who had counted his squadrons as faithfully as ever a Cyclops did his sheep, put the advance back into the saddle, and started for the Chickahominy.

The moon, one day past full, was a pale orb in the western sky and the first light of day was showing in the east when the advance reached the river, and halted. A ford they had expected to use for crossing had been washed out by a freshet. Singly and in bunches, the tired troopers slipped from their weary horses and slept where they fell, bridles over their stiff arms. Stuart, hearing about the ford and riding up to take a look for himself, had to pick his way among the insensible men. He himself had slept the last few hours in the saddle, John Esten Cooke on one side of him, Taylor Dobson, another aide, on the other, to catch him if he swayed, or to waken him if need arose; but one thing could be said for a nearly impassable road. It was as hard to mount a pursuit as a retreat over it. Still, this frothing flood could be his ruin.

"Has anybody tried to cross?" he asked.

Rooney Lee shucked boots and blouse and plunged in. He was a powerful swimmer, acquainted all his life with Virginia rivers. He reached the far bank and pulled himself up, blowing and puffing. He waited only long enough to ease his lungs, and swam back but shook his head at Stuart's unspoken question. It would be folly to try to take the column across here. Only one man in a hundred might make it. There was Forge Bridge downstream or Long Bridge up the river a way. Forge Bridge was the nearer.

Forge Bridge—the river ran in two channels, the north one narrow but swift and deep, then an island overgrown with brush, and a second stream, wider and shallower. Of the two-sectioned bridge, the first part in some other hard-pressed retreat had been destroyed. Only two stone abutments, with a few boards dangling, still stood. The condition of the second part was not immediately discernible, nor was it so important. The shallow south channel could be crossed by way of a swampy ford.

A pontoon bridge was set up first over the deep north channel. It was a rickety affair at best, its plank floor moored from the old stone piers to a single skiff anchored in midstream. A man could cross on it, swimming his horse alongside. One man at a time, at a slow crawl. Stuart strung Fitz Lee's First Virginia along either side of the road leading to the river and sent a trickle of men over; but he knew, if some better way could not be provided, he had lost his final engagement to the Chickahominy. The sun was well up now, another hot day on to boil.

Near by stood an abandoned warehouse, once belonging to a smithy, from which Forge Bridge had its name. Will Blackford's engineers had already borrowed a few boards from it for the pontoon effort. They went to work now to tear the warehouse down, to get at its long beams.

Stuart, his ears, like everyone else's, bombarded by the pounding and rending of the old timbers, stationed himself at the bridgehead, to encourage the floundering efforts at crossing still in progress there. Each trooper, before trusting himself to the swaying pontoon, stopped to offer his place to Stuart.

"Will you go now, sir?" It became a plea.

Stuart each time shook his head.

"Soon. I'll cross in time."

He went over just ahead of the men bringing the first long beam for the new bridge. They were not any too soon. The makeshift bridge was all but gone. But it held the men with the beam. Stuart prayed them across, he felt afterwards. Balancing the heavy beam, settling it into place, was done in solemn, strained silence, broken finally by strong oaths of thanksgiving. The beam reached, with only inches to spare. The men who had carried it divided and worked at lashing it fast as another beam came, and another. Now they were ready for the cross timbers.

The flooring advanced a foot at a time. The last piece went down. Jim Breathed and a gun crew rolled the mounted rifle on to the boards. It came across. The howitzer followed. The bridge, it was known now, would hold. The first men crossed, two by two, leading their horses. If an alarm came, they would mount; but it was better now to lead, to save the strength left in the animals for the ford. No time was lost because of the walking.

The Ninth Virginia was over, the Fourth, the Jeff Davis Legionnaires, the South Carolina Rangers. The prisoners came next on their balking mules. Finally after a time that must have seemed fully as long to the men standing guard as it had to Stuart watching from the island, the first of Fitz Lee's regiment began the march through from the rear. Whatever their tension had been, they saluted smartly, even gaily now as they passed Stuart.

And now Fitz himself sat beside Stuart, watching his squadrons pass. A small delay held up the last one. The men were arguing with a detail of engineers, reluctant to leave the bridge apparently until the last trooper had crossed. Stuart whistled to them, and Fitz Lee started back, to break up the parley; but the men were already scattering and most of them came on, leaving a mere half dozen, whose object now could be seen. They were piling tinder to fire the bridge.

The tinder caught. A second, fiercer crackling was the flooring of the bridge. Flames shot up and the men scampered. Just as they reached the middle of the span, running hard, a shot whistled over their heads. They ducked and ran on. Beyond the flames a group of horsemen galloped down the road, firing as they came.

"Great God!" Fitz Lee said.

Safety had been by a margin of minutes.

Safety. They lost one gun at the ford. What was one gun? They had lost a few horses in the course of the long march the day before. What were a few horses? They had taken enough to replace them five to one. Every man was now south of the Chickahominy, even poor Latané.

"But they're sure enough spent," Fitz said, as he and Stuart rode past. "Their nags, too."

Stuart's answer was to give Fitz his final orders. He was leaving his command to the latter now, and riding on to Richmond alone. At the washed-out ford upstream at dawn he had sent young Taylor Dobson on to Lee with a report of the situation as it then stood. The chief result of that now would be that Lee could find no rest until he heard the end of the story. Stuart must give him that in person and quickly. For the commander's peace of mind and for the map of McClellan's army as he only could outline its position.

"You will camp over night at Charles City Courthouse," he said to Fitz. The friendly hamlet was only a few jumps ahead. "And come on tomorrow at the best pace you can manage. Keep flanking parties alongside, but you know. It's about thirty-five miles now, as I reckon."

Over the James River Road. He doubted that they'd see a bluecoat.

"And you'll snatch some rest yourself, I hope," Fitz said. "Mind that Yankee horse you're riding. Don't let him scent his stablemates."

"I'll handle the horse," Stuart told him. "You mind your job now."

High noon of another day; and he was dismounting before the porch at High Meadows. A little stiffly. Another scar on the saddle, but he still had the saddle.

"General Stuart reporting to General Lee, if he is at liberty."

General Lee's hand warmly clasping his, and the brown eyes bright with relief and something more.

"Well done, sir! Very well done! You will take a little refreshment now and some real rest? After that, I may have a question or two; and then . . . will you ride with me into Richmond? There are others, I am sure, whose hearts are even more anxious than mine has been the past few days."

Chapter 8. *The Most Anxious Heart*

His name, even more than Stonewall Jackson's, was now on everyone's lips.

"Have you heard about Jeb Stuart? Took his entire brigade all the way around McClellan's army and brought them back without a scratch. Man, oh, man!"

Panic fled. Hearts lifted. The wildest stories multiplied. Johnnie Chesnut, General Chesnut's nephew, with the South Carolina Boykin Rangers, had ridden one of the captured horses on the way back. At one point, when the Yankees were dangerously close, it had bolted and carried him right into a nest of them. He couldn't hold the brute and finally didn't try. Just waved his hat and yelled, "Stuart, Stuart!" and the Yankees had scattered.

From Virginia, from the Carolinas, from Georgia, recruits rode into Richmond, seeking service under Stuart.

"Let them come!" Stuart said, laughing. "They carry baskets of this and that from home and always ride good horses. Let them come and welcome!"

Only a few, in whom caution had outlived inspiration, called the ride a hare-brained adventure, profitless, and a sinful waste of man and horse. Men just as old in years gave them back hot answer.

"If we fight this war by West Point tactics purely, the game is lost before it is begun. Will you throw away the South's one great advantage—hot-headed, reckless gallantry, the spirit of adventure, the readiness to lead a forlorn hope? I, for one, should be proud to serve under General Stuart."

If Wade Hampton felt that way, why should anyone else object?

"*Ma povere petite*," Stuart said to Flora. They had a rare hour alone in each other's company. "Did you, too, shake a little, thinking of us off there and a hundred thousand Yankees between us and here?"

"I didn't know," Flora said. "I never know, until everything is over. Will it always be that way?"

Looking at him so near, seeing his high, proud swagger, his clear, unlined forehead, his eyes, hearing his laughter, she thought, like people everywhere, how young he was. Much too young for all he was doing and enduring, or even receiving. He had not lived enough beforehand. They had not finished anything together.

"The value of such operations is secrecy," he quoted from his orders, still laughing.

"That's what I mean," she said. "Can you tell me now where you will be tomorrow?"

He was startled by the question. Tomorrow he would be moving his cavalry westward, to screen the march of Jackson away from the Valley, to join Lee before Richmond. Nobody was supposed to know that Jackson was leaving the Valley.

"*Ma povere petite,*" he said again and kissed her. "Sing to me."

"Here in this parlor?" she protested. "With people coming in all the time, you waiting to be summoned? My guitar's upstairs."

The truth was that her throat was closed against song, but this man she loved had never learned to accept a refusal. Certainly not from her.

"You can sing without accompaniment. I know," he reminded her. "You won't oblige me?"

"What do you want to hear?"

"Anything," he said. "Any of your favorites."

A strange song came to her. A favorite with both of them, but plaintive, when she would have liked it to be light and gay.

> "*When the swallows homeward fly,*
> *When the roses scattered lie . . .*"

But it suited Stuart's mood as well as hers. Restlessness went out of him. He nodded in time to the music. Boyishly he laid hold of a fold of her dress and smoothed it between his fingers.

> "*When from neither hill nor dale,*
> *Chants the silvery nightingale.*"

"Autumn," he said, "and the leaves falling. Everything peaceful. Will you write out the words for me and teach Sweeny the tune?"

"I will write out the words," Flora said, "but I will not teach

Sweeny the tune. The melody is not suitable for a banjo." And their hour was over.

People were calling now from the street, "Stuart, Stuart!" The way they did outside of any house where he happened to be. They had called him out so from President Davis's mansion, not to speak to them, for they wouldn't stop cheering to hear him, just to show himself, to wave his hat, to laugh, and finally in a kind of fright—the only kind he would own to—to roar for his horse and mount it and ride away.

"Such howls can change over night," he said to Flora. "I still think a man wanting to keep his mind on his duties would do well to avoid this town."

But he liked the cheering. He would make a stand, touched with swagger to cover doubt, against disapproval or opposition; but he was most truly himself and happiest when surrounded by love and favor.

"Go out and show yourself," Flora surprised herself now by saying. "Don't run out the back way. Go . . . but tell me good-bye here, first. Wait, I've a little something for you upstairs. I won't be a minute."

She had made him a shirt, a fine, white one—a courting shirt, she teased. Where was the fun in sewing coarse cotton shirts for men who, though worthy and deserving, still were strangers? Might she not once in a while turn a seam with love pricked into all the stitches?

"Promise me you'll wear it yourself," she said. "Don't give it away even if somebody else seems to need one."

"I'll keep yours and give the others away," he promised.

Which was just what she wanted him to do. People, out of the overflowing fullness of their hearts, were again showering him with presents. Old ladies with eyes so dim that they could not sew to a line, young girls who had not acquired skill and perhaps had no Rachel to teach them. Some of both ages and all between would be in that crowd outside, disregarding utterly most of the rules they had always lived by. A few would stand aloof, their eyes filling with tears or their faces quiet and worshipful. Such an expression of still emotion Flora had seen even on the face of Mary Lee on one occasion.

But women of self-possession, who cloaked thankfulness and admiration with dignity, were few. Many of those silly pieces out there would actually run after Stuart when he rode away. One day—this was outside Governor Letcher's mansion—a girl reached out with her hands as if to snatch at him as he passed—his boot top, anything she might touch. Stuart stopped his horse, caught the girl's hand in his, then bent down and lightly kissed her smooth, flushed young cheek. The crowd burst into wild hurrahs. The girl stood rooted, her hand to her face. She could not know how simple and natural a thing that had been for him to do. He closed every letter he wrote with kisses for all. Once he had written, "I almost said kiss Tilda, but she'd hardly know what to make of that."

He was the people's idol. They honored him, they loved him, they embroidered flags and knit sashes for him. He was their champion knight, their beau ideal. They needed him. Was she going to be selfish about that?

She would try not to be. She took his good-bye kiss now and walked with him to the door, but went no farther than the threshold. She stood there, a slight, erect figure in simple sprigged cotton, watching. When Stuart appeared, the crowd surged forward. When he mounted and rode off, they surged after him. The overwhelming emotion of it turned Flora's knees to water. She fled back into the house and dropped beside the stiff hall tree, her head on her arms where minutes before his hat had lain.

Prayer was fashionable in Richmond on the days that followed. At St. Paul's, at St. James's, at St. John's, citizens knelt in deep, helpless entreaty while in the streets outside heavy guns and ammunition wagons rolled, and out on the Peninsula a monster seven-headed battle roared. Prayer was one release, another was the common practice of gathering at night on the high ground about the Capitol, to watch for the flashing of the guns, to listen and try to tell where the fighting went on.

"Malvern Hill. Jackson, I say. No, sir, Longstreet. Well, God grant those are our guns speaking loud like that."

But nobody ever knew how things had gone until the day after.

"I see by the paper that young Pelham, of the Stuart Horse Artillery, held the Yankees off yesterday till Jackson and Longstreet were in line. A Stuart man? Well, of course, sir, he held them off."

"Dear God," Flora prayed, "open my heart wide. Make me willing
to share him with these, his people, to give him to them if that must
be. They were his people before I came into his life. He is theirs as
much as he is mine, I know. I've known it always but . . . oh, God,
give me acceptance, but . . . but take care of him. Guard him
because, whatever my portion, I do love him terribly." And then,
groping, she would add, "Show me the way of duty. Guide me."

All her life before this, she thought, duty had been so clearly defined. Most people might think she could see where it lay now, but
that was different. A fearful battle was going on out there where the
guns roared. The Seven Days Battle it was called afterwards. Seven
days were a speck of time, measured against eternity; but these were
an eternity in themselves while they passed. Before evening of the
first day, the wounded were coming to Richmond by ambulance and
railroad car; and any woman strong of heart and body with the least
compulsion of conscience knew one thing she could do.

From the time of her first settling in Richmond, Maria Brewer had
worked beside her doctor husband in various hospitals. Timidly now,
still feeling her way, Flora offered her help.

"I don't know much about such nursing," she said. "All I've experienced is children's hurts and ordinary aches and ailments, but if
you'll show me . . ."

"You know worlds more than most," Maria answered crisply, "or
you're not your mother's daughter. I was hoping you'd offer. Could
you leave the children part of each day with Tilda? She could bring
them to our house."

It wasn't the children that made Flora hesitate. They were always
safe with Tilda. Maria studied her pale face, her beseeching eyes,
and added a precaution.

"Just don't let your imagination get the better of you. That and
. . . your stomach's pretty steady, I seem to recall."

More than devotion or sentiment, a woman entering a makeshift
hospital then or later needed a steady stomach. The one to which
Maria took Flora on the second of the Seven Days had been a barn,
used formerly for the accommodation of thoroughbred horses. Most
of these had now gone into service, along with the owner and his
sons. Those remaining had been put into smaller quarters.

"More and better air and light than we get in a church," Maria said, detailing the advantages of the barn. "Plenty of straw for pallets and we don't need to be afraid of spoiling anything."

The wounded lay by twos in the stalls, those needing more exacting surgical care on cots, but most on straw-filled ticks on the floor. It wasn't the gray faces of the men and it wasn't their wounds that called for a steady stomach, though Flora saw more mutilation in one day than she'd ever heard of in all her life before. It was the smell, the unspeakable stench that came even through doors and windows before one entered the building. And this when help was still to be had for "toting and washing up."

"Gangrene," Maria explained. "That and chloroform and iodoform and plain filth and blood. Some people who can take everything else faint at the smell of blood. There's so much . . . are you all right?"

"Yes," Flora said tightly. "Just give me something to do."

Her work that day was all with clean dressings and new bedding, but she came home at the end of it feeling too soiled for her own endurance.

"Tilda," she begged, "have you a washing kettle over at the Brewers'? Can you manage—I am going to have to put on every stitch clean every day at this rate. If you can wash my things, I'll press them out; and, after this, I'll wear just one long petticoat."

"Miss Flo', one petticoat's not decent. I don't keer how much I warsh. Mist' Jimmie and lil Miss Flo' kin fotch me chips."

"It isn't only the washing, Tilda. If you could see what I saw . . ." but she wouldn't talk about that now. She would not even think about it. She would rather put the children to bed, and finally sleep herself, to rest until morning, when she must return to duty, but wearing only one long petticoat, with a short one for decency. No more. She would not ruthlessly tear her extra garments of cambric and lace into strips for bandages. Not yet. But she would save her petticoats and chemises so that she would not need to replace them, using good cotton so badly needed to make the wounded and the dying comfortable.

Every morning she set out, fresh and fragrant and new; and she couldn't help noticing that, no matter what sort of shambles the stable seemed to be on any particular day, those on the cots or pallets who could observe brightened to see her coming and looked after her wistfully when she went away. Even on days when help failed or proved insufficient and she had to pin back her skirts and take up lye soap and scrubbing brush to clean some noisome mess, she would emerge, holding still an aura of crushed blossoms. The extra hours needed to achieve this miracle were made possible by the memory of Stuart's lips at her ear, saying, "You smell so sweet, my darling. So sweet!"

"Don't tell them who I am," she asked of Maria when she first went to the hospital. That would, she felt, take from the selflessness of her service. So she was called variously Doc's Sister, Mis' Brewer's Sister, just Sister or even Miss Brewer, until one day a new patient called out her true name and anonymity became impossible.

When the wounded first poured into Richmond, by far the most were Confederates, with only a trickle from the other side; but when the battle reached its awfulest and communication lines became disorganized and broken—Stuart's men sacked the Federal supply base that week at White House, putting a gunboat to flight with their artillery—when the lines became entangled and broken, almost as many wounded Federal troops had to be cared for at Richmond as born Southerners, and for a longer stay usually. Because a Confederate soldier, as soon as he was fit to be moved, could be sent to his own home or to that of a relative or friend. A Yankee had to be kept until he was exchanged or billeted to a prison.

The day after Malvern Hill, Flora, carrying a tray of dressings, made the morning rounds with Maria and Dr. Brewer. They had finished the cot patients and were beginning on the pallets, when stretcher bearers brought in a man so far gone that they laid the stretcher on the floor and one of them made signs to the doctor to come and take a look. The man on the floor was wrapped in a blue coat, and a blue cap had been placed on his chest. A rude tourniquet had been applied to his right leg above the knee, but not before blood had caked his trousers and filled his boot.

"But he ain't dead," the bearer said, "and he asked for you, Doc."

Charles Brewer took charge at once. The stretcher bearers left.

"Maria," Charles called in a minute, "Maria!"

"Yes, dear. The operating tent? I'll see to it. Sister . . ."

The man on the floor opened his eyes. Flora stood near, pale, with her tray of dressings.

"Miss Flo'?" he said thickly, and fell back into unconsciousness.

"It's Hosky," Flora said, still not believing it. "Maria, it's Hosky."

"Yes," Maria agreed. "We'd better hurry."

"Maria," her husband said, "I need you here. Send Flora."

To look for Mrs. Smith, Maria's first assistant. To look over the operating tent. To come back then, with Mrs. Smith, to finish the morning dressings. When Flora returned to the stable, Hoskins had been taken away; and when she saw him next, he was a still form on a cot, heavily asleep, pale, needing a shave, groaning, muttering.

"He'll pull through," Charles Brewer said. "A sound, well-rooted tree can lose a limb and still . . ."

"Charles!" Maria said in warning.

It was Hoskins who told Flora his leg had been taken off below the knee.

"Imagine me a peg leg," he said, more in wonder than protest. "First cannon ball I ever stopped, Miss Flo'. Don't wonder the Injuns hate cannon. Should a run myself if I'd heard it coming. Time you know . . ."

"Hosky," Flora said, "they let me watch you on condition that I would not encourage you to talk. I just want to say it's an awful way for you to be here, but I am glad to see you."

She took his fist between her two hands and squeezed it hard. He tried to return the pressure and swore.

"Got as much stren'th as the frayed end of a rope," he said. "Doc's going to put a revolver handy—cold and empty, of course—and when I can handle it, I'll know I'm coming out. Nice fellow, Doc."

"Very nice," Flora agreed. "A real brother."

The next day Flora had her name back, in part at least. It was "Good morning, Miss Flora," and, "Thank you, ma'am, Miss Flora," from cot to cot. Soon they would know the rest of it.

"How you been, Miss Flo'?" Hoskins asked.

"I'm fine, Hosky."

"That's good. You look all right. Not as pink as I remember, but all right, considering. You worrying some, Miss Flo'?"

"Hosky, what do you think?"

"Yeah," he said, "I know. Bunch o' hotheads." And a minute later, "Tell General Stuart for me he's still hell on a horse."

"Oh, Hosky, you've seen him . . . out there?"

"Sure. Just. He was pulling leather and the poor brute under him all over dirty soapsuds. How many does he kill in a year?"

"Hosky, hush! Don't pretend to me. You like him as well as the rest."

"Not that much, mebbe. I'll admit he looks good some ways." He laughed ruefully. "Too damn good right now for us. Take that ring-a-round-a-rosy he did a couple a weeks ago. Made us look awful foolish, didn't it?"

Presumably that was true. The glory of Stuart's ride was that it made the Union cavalry seem impotent, by comparison.

"Hosky, tell me about papa. How is he?"

"The old man? Fit and fine, but," Hoskins hesitated, "he swallows hard, thinking about that ride. 'Helped to train him,' he says, kinda proud, same time he's sorrowing. But I tell him you can't teach lightning how to flash. You can't stop it, neither. Nor you can't catch it. Still and all, it comes hard right now. You know what they're saying in Washington? Your paw's too old. Mebbe he'd do better in a quieter spot. 'Recruiting service,' he expects and swears some."

Oh! Was her heart going to break open afresh and bleed again?

"Miss Flo', you asked and I told you. Don't you worry too much. Your paw's a thinking man. He studies things out. If a man can do that, things come out more right than you ever thought they could. That goes—even for a peg leg, mebbe."

Yes. If amputation could make a philosopher out of Hoskins. Still, it hurt. Such an issue as this she had in a way foreseen, and its result. Still, it hurt that her husband's glory should be her father's defeat. However . . .

"It may be easier finally," she said, "if he is far away from here."

"Yeah," Hoskins agreed gloomily, "you're mebbe right. How are we doing right now, Miss Flo', do you know?"

"Yes. Not so well, Hosky. McClellan, I hear, has been driven back to the James River and it looks as if his grand attack had failed."

Strangely, Hoskins brightened.

"They'll be handing Mac a transfer order, too," he guessed. "That's how it goes, Miss Flo'. We been outridden and now we been out-generaled. You got the best of our men, to start with; and, until we get organized . . . shucks, I'm talking too much. Laying here like this, it don't much matter. Tell me about the kids, will you?"

She drew their pictures for him as best she could.

"I wish you could see them, Hosky."

"Yeah. I never did see the boy. He can set a horse already, you say?"

"After a fashion, Hosky. We did the best we could without you. Some day—this can't go on for always—you will have to finish the job."

The next day Hoskins was holding the heavy black pistol in two hands. The day after that he could manage with one, and Flora had news for him.

"Dr. Brewer has put your name on a list of wounded, Hosky, who are able to be moved to a Northern hospital whenever there is an exchange. General Stuart, too, was in town yesterday, for a short half hour; but he took time to write to Custis Lee, General Custis Lee, President Davis's military aide. He said for me to tell you that all he asked was that General Lee demand full value in exchange, not to let you go cheap."

"Did he now?" Hoskins ducked, to hide a grin of pleasure.

"And all I ask," Flora went on, "is that, when you get back behind your own lines, when you are well . . ."

"You mean when they get my leg whittled to fit?"

"Yes, when you are up and about, will you promise to look up papa or mamma, whichever is nearest? Help them to find you, Hosky. They'll want you with them."

"What good will old Peg-leg be to them, I wonder?" Hoskins asked. What good?

"You can tell them about us, Hosky. They'll want to hear. About Maria and Dr. Brewer and Johnnie. Johnnie's a wonderful soldier, they say, Hosky. Colonel of his regiment now, but I told you. And about the babies and me."

"The Old Man will want to hear about you, first of all," Hosky said. "And about *him*. Miss Flora, if you had it to do all over again . . ."

"Yes, Hosky. You tell them that I am well and happy. Tell them that General Stuart is not only a dashing officer, a great and brave soldier, but also the most tender and loving of husbands. Say that we are both well and very happy in each other."

"Miss Flo', would you write that down? I might forget."

"I can't, Hosky."

"No? Then give it to me a piece at a time, so I'll get it straight."

When, in the course of a few days, he was gone, she could add thanksgiving to her prayer for grace:

"Thank you, God, for sending Hosky. I will be braver now."

The summer of 1862 blazed on. As Hoskins had foreseen, General McClellan was superseded in command by a man named Halleck, who, before the end of July, ordered McClellan to withdraw from the Peninsula. Of this General Halleck nobody knew much; but the Confederate armies, exhilarated though battered, were not likely to hold him in much awe after his first address to his armies. His headquarters, he stated, henceforth would be in the saddle. Laughter swept the ranks on both sides.

To the north, again threatening the Valley and the upper Potomac, another general succeeded McDowell, a man named Pope. He opened his campaign with the announcement that he intended to subsist his armies on the land and would kill without mercy any noncombatants who fell into his hands, in revenge for the slaying of Federal guerrillas. Jackson with his foot-cavalry, Richard Ewell with a mixed division of foot and horse, and Stuart, a major-general now commanding two brigades, one under Fitz Lee and the other under Wade Hampton of South Carolina, were dispatched to teach him better manners. The three generals were together in Richmond late in July for a council; and Stuart arranged a meeting between Flora and Stonewall Jackson, to show one to the other, but which one, Flora afterwards could not say surely.

"Why do they call him a Cromwell?" she demanded. "Because he prays before going into battle? Cromwell never had such gentle speech or kindly eyes."

"Ha!" Stuart said. "You should march with him when he is in a hurry."

That night he had the ladies at Mrs. Duval's in stitches imitating the Southern Cromwell.

"Such a gay young man, your husband!" Mrs. Duval said now.

Again warm contradiction rose to Flora's lips, and was suppressed. Did any of these women who found him such jolly company know that he carried with him wherever he went detailed maps of the countryside and studied them whenever he had a half hour to himself, that in the same haversack he carried full lists of all the men in his command, even the troopers in the ranks, together with their home towns or counties, and those names and places he came soon to know from memory as he knew the maps? Alone with Flora that evening, the fun over, the gay young man turned her to the light, and, frowning, traced an arc on one cheek with his finger.

"Shadows," he said, "under your eyes. Is it the heat or the hospital?"

"Neither," she answered, using his tactics of laughing a bad thing away. "Fatigue, maybe, from waltzing with Major von Borcke. He has never learned to reverse." The strangest of all the volunteers who asked to follow Stuart's banner, a man who had served in the Prussian army, and had crossed the sea to share in what seemed to him the greatest military adventure of his day.

"Don't waltz with him," Stuart advised. "Hold out for a quadrille. Buck leads a beautiful European figure called 'The Lancers.' But stick to business now. How about those shadows? I've no time to worry about any of you down here being sick, no time to come take care of you. What would you think of spending the rest of the summer in the mountains? I've a letter in my pocket now from Alec, complaining that you haven't been that way in a year."

Flora didn't want to leave Richmond. Now that things were quieter, others did, on the least excuse. The weather usually. On the other hand, she would not want to worry Stuart. She offered a suggestion. Was he going to be near any of the old places—Orange, Culpeper, Fairfax Courthouse?

"Not now," Stuart said sternly.

He meant that, even on the old lines, the fighting now was more desperate.

What made up Flora's mind finally was little Jimmie's having a fever—a combination of heat and cutting his molars. He would do better in the country, Charles Brewer said, where it was cooler and he could have good milk to drink.

So, she and the family were settled in at Laurel Hill when Jackson drove Pope back at Cedar Run, when Stuart lost his hat and cloak and haversack and almost lost his freedom when Federal scouts came after him where he slept on a farmhouse porch, waiting on a meeting with Fitz Lee, due there that morning. Stuart's pickets, thinking the

Yankees were Lee's men, let them get almost to the house before they knew better. They had time then only to fire their pistols in wild warning and Stuart had the half minute he needed to mount a horse and run; but he lost everything he didn't have on him when the warning sounded.

"Even his cape," Flora complained. "What will I do about that? I've flannel for a lining, but good gray cloth is scarce and expensive. Never mind. I'll manage."

"I'm sure you will," Alec said, looking at her strangely. "The boy's plain lucky, that's all. I hope his luck holds."

"He, at least, is certain that it will," Flora said.

Alec did not answer. Poor Alec! Old Man Alec, even Stuart called him at times, and only half in jest, blithely adding any business he wanted handled or any need he wanted supplied to the load his brother carried. Old Man Alec—he played a prosaic, inglorious role these days; and Flora thought it chafed him a little, though he would have resented the imputation if she spoke her thoughts.

Salt was needed, wasn't it, he might demand impatiently, or, more probably, with that glimmer of near fun in his eyes. Farming had to go on. More than ever in places like this lower end of the Valley, where there was no fighting, to make up for destruction in those parts of the state being trampled and picked clean by two armies. Soldiers had to be fed, and so did other folks. Horses—where would the cavalry be without horses? Magistrates were needed, to administer civil law. There must be men at home, if only to look out for the families whose men were away, sometimes lost forever. More widows and orphans all the time, it looked like. There Alec would recollect what he was implying and change the subject.

Dear Alec! So patient with his mother, grown a little querulous now over diminishing substance. Even at Laurel Hill it showed signs of diminishing that summer of 1862. Alec, so generous in his welcome to Flora and her children, but looking at her so strangely now. Was he beginning to worry over things? Alec? She wouldn't allow it on her account.

"Alec," she said impulsively, "what I wanted to talk to you about today is this. James says in his letter that he is sending his pay warrants here; and I thought . . . please, I know things are scarce and growing scarcer; and four people extra to care for must make a dif-

ference. When things have to be bought, like flour, for example, or
a piece of machinery or harness, will you let us share a little in the
cost?"

Alec sighed, but, in doing so, relaxed a little; and his eyes said he
was pleased. Or just amused?

"Ts, ts!" he said. "You four don't consume what James alone did
when he was growing up. Now caring for you is all we can do for
him; so you must allow us the pleasure. Mother is very happy to
have you and the children at Laurel Hill. She looks better than she
has in months, I think."

Perhaps. What she had said to Flora was still a reproach: "I don't
think Jemmie would have come through his second summer in that
town. After this you must come in May and stay through September."

"She spoils the children frightfully," Flora told Alec, "even allows
them to dig in her garden. I'm sure she didn't indulge her own to that
extent."

Alec murmured something about a grandmother's privilege.

"But I'm glad you brought up the matter of pay vouchers," he said
then. "The first one is here. With your permission, I should like to
turn them all into cash—gold, if attainable. War does queer things
to the value of currency. If you have no present need for the money,
let me keep it in a safe place for you. You will need it most when
you return to Richmond, I am afraid. I suppose you are planning to
go back?"

"Alec, I must. It's not nearly so comfortable and it does cost, but
every so often James comes down on staff business, even if I can't
visit him at camp. It feels nearer. And he wants it, too; so—September
at the latest."

Chapter 9. *Salute to a Major-General*

The summer of 1862 in Virginia was hard on horses. Before it was
over it became routine for the cavalry corps to ride around a piece
or all of a Yankee army, overturning its system of supply, making its
commanders, one after another, look foolish. It was an enlarged corps

now, the mountain men of the Laurel Brigade, led since Turner Ashby's death by Grumble Jones, making the third division. General Jones was harder than ever to handle since his elevation, aided and abetted in mutinous objection by recalcitrant subordinates such as Colonel Carey; but he was every inch a fighting man, as were all in his command; and Stuart by then could forgive most faults if a man showed daring and resourcefulness.

Selected men from all three brigades took part in the raid that brought down General Pope finally. A handsome job the cavalry made of that bit of retribution. Fifteen hundred men set out from headquarters on an afternoon in late July to burn a bridge—at Catlett's Station on the Orange and Alexandria Railroad, over which the Yankees kept sending reinforcements and supplies to Pope's army. A grim business from the start, no matter how blithely reported. A thunderstorm met the column head-on before they'd got well started. From then on the rain never stopped. They should have turned back, knowing well what the mountain runs would be like before and behind them. But they didn't turn back. They went on. In the stormy dark they silenced the Yankee pickets, rode, then, between the outposts and Pope's main lines; and, while one detail raided Yankee headquarters, another rode off to burn the bridge.

The first detail captured General Pope's tent, his dress coat and hat, his dispatch book, his orderly, several members of his staff, including a Yankee major who had made a bet that he would spend Christmas in Richmond. They took three hundred other prisoners and as many tip-top, blooded Yankee horses; but the expedition was counted a failure because General Pope was not in his tent that evening, and because the second detail failed to burn the bridge. They carried tinder, but a bale of it wouldn't have set fire to timbers soaked by rain from above and submerged below by Cedar Run in full flood.

General Jeb Stuart lay on his back on the floor in the room at Mrs. Duval's in Richmond, his two-year-old son astride his chest; and his eyes shone as he made detailed report of this and other exploits to Flora.

"You make it sound like fun," she commented. "I suppose it is now, but . . ." She knew, for example, what he implied by silencing outposts.

"The sky dripped ink, I do believe," Stuart said, not disputing her judgment. "Blackest night I was ever out in—except one. That night in Kansas, after the fight with the Cheyenne, when I sat on my saddle from midnight to morning on the banks of the Big Blue. Remember?"

"I remember everything," Flora told him.

After Catlett's Station in July, there was the Second Battle of Manassas in August; and, whatever the other glories of that exhibition of valor and resourcefulness, the cavalry's part again was a raid —this time on the Yankee warehouses at the Junction. They captured food enough to fill Lee's hungry army to bursting, almost enough shoes for his infantry, and a great shipment of blankets and overcoats that the Yankees had sent on in preparation for a stay over winter.

"They eat well up north," Stuart observed, his eyes still shining. "And they make good shoes. The overcoats are the wrong color, but they will be worn with proper gratitude, I am sure."

Flora thought of what Alec had said to her in the spring of 1861. "If we cannot equip our fighting men, we are in a sorry state." But Stuart was so triumphant over Manassas, which was a creditable performance after the "failure" at Catlett's Station, that she would not raise a doubt in his mind, even if she could do so.

And now the cavalry was resting. Where? Doing what?

"Here and there," Stuart answered evasively. "Doing the usual. Drill, breaking in new mounts. Fitz Lee has the worst worn nags out to pasture. We keep occupied."

Camp routine. But what for amusement in the long, quiet evenings?

"That," Stuart said, "is where a man like Sweeny comes in handy. He goes through camp organizing minstrel bands. You'd be surprised at the talent he turns up. This, too, is the time the man who can spin a yarn wins his laurels."

"And at headquarters?" Flora persisted.

"Oh, Lord!" Stuart groaned. "Times like these are when my aides go dancing and courting. I never know where to look for the rascals when I need them."

She would have wagered a fair sum that he did know.

"Well," she said, "so much for the young men. Finally what about the older folk—old married men like you and Captain Blackford, for example?"

"To keep track of the bachelors, we act as chaperons," he told her.

"A rare chaperon you make, I am certain," she said. "Are the girls pretty?"

"Very. No matter what happens to other crops, Virginia comes up continually with a fresh supply of pretty girls. They're pretty," he teased, "and sweet as sugar, and, in their charming way, our most devoted patriots."

Were they, indeed? Seeing that he had pricked her, he set his son off on the floor and took a hassock beside her chair.

"You don't mind, I hope, if occasionally I tread a measure with one of them? They lead a lonely life—for pretty girls—between dancing parties and rare courtships. Some of them already have lost lovers. Many more will. But they don't complain. They have the most beautiful, undivided loyalty. I wish . . ."

"You wish I could have an undivided heart?" she asked. "How old are these girls? Sixteen? Eighteen? Twenty at the oldest. It's easy to have an undivided heart at eighteen. It is living that draws one this way and that, taking a piece off here and another there. Oh, darling, I don't mean to complain, either. It has been a good summer for me, too, but a long one. No matter how we plan, we are still too much apart. Each time seems longer and farther. I don't mind your dancing with the pretty girls. I want you to dance. But I wish I could be there, too—part of the time."

He caught one of her hands and reached for the other.

"Poor, jealous little wife!" he soothed.

"Only because I am so far away," she insisted. "My heart is where you are, but I am not. I'm sorry, but—well, there it is. Our young years are going fast; and we've had so little time together."

She was twenty-six now to his twenty-nine. It was frightening to think about.

"You look mighty pretty with dewdrops on your eyelashes," he told her.

"Ah!" She tried to pull her hands away.

"How would you like," he went on, "to put on your best bib and tucker and walk with your beau to Pizzini's Palace of Sweets for a treat? We could leave . . ."

"I been to Pizzini's," Little Flora piped up. "I like Pizzini's."

"My mistake," Stuart said. "We'll hire a hack and all go to Pizzini's. This once.

"Just as well," he added presently. "I would like to leave an order with my tailor. We could stop there on our way."

Oh! And she had been about to add to her complaints a word about her best bib and tucker being a little rusty, her shoes especially; but if he needed a uniform . . .

"Not for myself," Stuart informed her. "I'll let you in on a secret. I'm ordering a dress coat for General Jackson. A Christmas present. He can't refuse it and he'll have to wear it."

"Oh, Stuart!"

"He looks more like a scarecrow every time we meet. I've got to do something about it. Ready?"

She was ready, or almost.

"I'll make a bargain with you, sir. You can order the coat you need for yourself and give it to another, if you will ask the tailor at the same time for enough gray cloth for a new cape, suitable for a major-general of cavalry."

It was Stuart's turn to look crestfallen.

"But I thought—I hoped you were taking care of that, my darling."

"I am. I will. I have fur and I have lining, but I've been at my wits' end to know what to do for the gray cloth."

"My pet!"

"You won't need it right away, I suppose. I'll try to have it ready when you come again."

"If it turns cold, I might send for it."

"It would not be ready then. You must come for it, sir."

When would he come? From where? The question was in the eyes of both over the brave, bright, sad or foolish talk. Would it be from Maryland? In September Stuart's cavalry crossed the Potomac into Maryland, riding with Jackson's corps into the town of Frederick. The first march into enemy territory; but, before the triumphant entry could become anything so solid as possession, before the cheers of welcome died down, word came that McClellan, still commanding the Army of the Potomac, had seen an opportunity to divide Lee's armies and already had a sizable force at Harper's Ferry, set to swoop down on the Shenandoah Valley.

Nobody waited to learn whether the rumor was true or false. Jackson turned his infantry about and marched them to Harper's Ferry. Stuart gathered his cavalry, and never did that corps ride harder than it did to reach the key mountain passes and hold them. Hold them against Union forces sent to reinforce McClellan and open a road through the mountains to Lee's other army corps marching to unite with Jackson.

By the grace of God and the stubborn will of Stonewall Jackson, with some bloody fighting in the heights around, Harper's Ferry was retaken. It was a hard thing to do, but nothing to the big blaze that broke out afterwards along Antietam Creek near Sharpsburg. For two days there a battle raged so fiercely and ruthlessly that, when the second night fell, neither side knew which had won, though Lee waited in position another day to see whether McClellan could renew the attack. When he did not, bravely and sensibly Lee took his men back south of the Potomac.

Of the bloody fighting along Antietam Creek, one hour was a part that Stuart would never forget. Riding hard himself with a new order for General Longstreet from General Lee, he saw on the slope of a hill facing a hot angle of the Yankee lines a young colonel of infantry posted behind a tree—a sapling not more than half the officer's girth—giving firing directions to a deep line of riflemen hugging the ground behind him. Something familiar about the colonel made Stuart stop, and then he knew. It was John Cooke. He was in an excellent position to direct the fire of his men, but his post was suicidal.

"Get back!" Stuart yelled. "You fool! Get back!"

The colonel of infantry recognized him or his anxiety and waved his cap. A Yankee ball tore it from his hand. At once a blaze of fire from the line on the ground poured down the hill. A lull followed, in which John Cooke now waved his handkerchief at his brother-in-law and, as best he could with motions, urged him to ride on about his business.

Stuart rode on, including in his business a report to Longstreet on the foolhardiness of one of his colonels. When evening came and he could get back that way, he made it his further business to ask for news of the 14th North Carolina Infantry. It was a regiment reduced by then to a remnant of its former strength. A brave charge down the hill that it had held so ably had climaxed the day and among those who had fallen had been its young commander. He had been carried off the field more nearly dead than alive.

The next day in response to a dispatch from Stuart, Charles Brewer came up to see what he could do. John Cooke was still unconscious, a possible brain injury to be dealt with in addition to a fractured skull and other wounds.

"I'm taking him home with me," Dr. Brewer said. "I don't know that it will help. It won't hurt. Maria said to bring him if I could. Will you come? I'll need reinforcement if he should die in my care."

But Lee was by then preparing his retreat. The cavalry with all its able leaders was never needed more. The best Stuart could do was to give Brewer an address at which he could be reached in case of a further crisis. It seemed a strange address under the circumstances: Care of Colonel Dandridge, The Bower, Charlestown, Virginia.

"I make it headquarters when I'm working from the top of the Valley," Stuart said stiffly to a question in Brewer's eyes.

"It sounds delightful," Charles said drily, and pocketed it.

Two days later Johnnie was on a bed in the Brewer parlor, his head so wrapped in gauze and cotton that it was hard to know who he was until he blinked his one exposed eye and managed a crooked grin. But that was not at first. At first, if he wakened into near consciousness, the one eye had no knowledge of who ministered to his needs, and the mouth was set and grim and opened only to shout an order or a warning: "Look out! Here they come. Ready . . . FIRE! Ha! That did it. Reload . . ."

Charles Brewer, measuring out an opiate, happened to look at Flora.

"Here, here!" he said. "I thought you were a practised nurse. I'll call Maria."

"No," Flora said, shaking her head to relieve a dizziness. "I'll be all right in a minute. I just happened to think. I didn't realize until now that it could be like this."

She had prattled to Stuart about pretty girls and dancing, and he had taken her out for a sweet.

"It can be like this or worse," Charles Brewer said bluntly.

Later in the day he told her that he had seen Stuart at Sharpsburg.
"If you want to write to him, I think this will reach him."

She took the paper and read the address without flinching.

"Thank you, Charles. I will be writing, of course."

But not immediately. She could not put coherent words on paper
while Johnnie tossed in delirium. Even when he was better, when he
could manage the crooked grin, Flora's letter to Stuart was hardly
more than a plea:

"Oh, my darling, do guard yourself a little—for all our sakes. A
part of me goes with you everywhere."

The letter reached Stuart just before he took his cavalry out on the
maddest ride of all so far. It was safe in his pocket, a talisman, as he
sat his horse on a moonlit night under the trees of The Bower, listening to the beating of hands and feet and the gay lilt of fiddle music
coming from the lighted windows and open door of the house, watching fairy creatures clothed in thistledown swing past the windows,
all encircled by gray-clad arms, dark heads and fair so close together
that a man could just about make up what was being said, unless the
power of speech had been lost temporarily. Behind him in the darkness and farther away, the red eye of an occasional campfire winked
at him and from that direction more song and louder laughter drifted
to his ears. The abandoned fun and lightheartedness that some
people thought were the chief character of Stuart's men. He knew
better. Let them sing and laugh and dance and make light or serious
love while they could. Tomorrow they'd all be riding hard again.

North—to burn another bridge or try to—on the Cumberland Valley
Railroad this time, north of Chambersburg, Pennsylvania. Horses
were to be collected on the way, well-fed Yankee horses, and prisoners to be taken, to be used as hostages to obtain the exchange of
Confederates held in the North. All to be done, according to the
orders, with the usual caution.

Caution was the way of it the following night, when the column
slept under guard at McCoy's Ford on the Potomac, crossing into
Maryland at daybreak the morning after. Northward then toward
Hagerstown, passing quietly to the rear of a Federal force six regiments strong moving over the Old National Road, detouring around

Hagerstown with smothered groans. The Federal advance base, with its warehouses full, but strongly guarded. Exercising judgment and prudence.

Into Pennsylvania then by way of Mercersburg, the advance guard supplied with quartermaster receipts to pay for a purchase of shoes, and one of Stuart's aides carrying a worn slipper belonging to Mrs. Stuart, which he was to match with the best footgear obtainable. The purchasing detail bought out several stores, paying for each item carefully and correctly. The storekeepers stared at the paper offered, but thought best not to raise an alarm.

Another detail sent out through the green countryside brought back horses by the dozen. Draft horses still wearing their collars. Well fed, well kept; and the troopers who brought them in looked now almost as sleek. They had dined at various farm houses before taking the horses. The farmers did not complain about the food consumed, of which there was abundance, but did grieve over the horses. The troopers grieved with them. It was too bad, they agreed. McClellan owed them better protection. Laughter, the laughter of sudden, easy fullness, rolled up and down the column.

The lights of Chambersburg at last through the rain at nightfall. Wade Hampton, commanding the advance, rode in and took possession. Stuart followed. It was at Chambersburg that the draft horses proved invaluable. Without them it would not have been practicable to load so many wagons with army overcoats, underwear, socks, five thousand new rifles. It was to be hoped that the rich booty would compensate for another failure to burn a bridge. It proved to be of riveted iron, noncombustible, indestructible. But here they were, and so . . .

Morning, again, and Stuart smothering a laugh to see his men in line all in new blue overcoats and all with eyes west and south. They thought the mission was over? He smiled, then his teeth flashed in a grin. He raised his gauntleted hand and turned them about—on the road to Gettysburg.

> Should it seem to you more prudent to continue on to the Potomac instead of returning along the line of your advance . . .

It was eminently more prudent to take a new and unforeseen route back. By now telegraph wires were humming. Stuart rode a piece of the way with young Captain Blackford, going over a map, marking roads, outlining his plan to return by way of some ford farther down the Potomac. Near Leesburg, probably.

It was a zig-zag course the column followed—a few miles east, a few miles south, east again, south again, picking up roads wherever they found them convenient, following them until expediency dictated another turn. It was a bold course, through open country; but they met few travelers. People did not travel except from necessity over roads likely to be blocked by the movement of troops and supply trains, and the Union forces had either been where these roads led or were expected. This Stuart learned from the few travelers he did meet. He stopped them all and held them while the horses grazed and the men stretched. Some he held longer. The information given was not too clear or conclusive, but time and again it served as a warning and prevented undesired conflict.

Zig zag east, then south, then east and south again, taking a seemingly desultory path for the Potomac and home. No more plunder. The column was now five miles long, with loaded wagons and led horses drawing it out. Stuart, if the length of the column worried him, showed no sign.

Fortune still smiled on him. The rain of the night before had dampened the roads. No dust called attention to his march; and, if anyone from near by looked on, the blue coats of the troopers stopped question. With only routine rests, the column moved on. It reached Emmitsburg and the Maryland line at nightfall. Forty miles stretched between it and the Potomac and safety.

At Emmitsburg there was a report of a detail of scouting Federal lancers. Stuart held his command in check, to let the Yankees get away, then sent a small force to net any stragglers slow in pulling out of town. The captives told him most of what he needed to know. A force of Federal cavalry led by a General Pleasanton was now pursuing him from the rear and was just five miles away. Ahead General Stoneman had five thousand men guarding the main fords of the Potomac.

"Forward, at a trot . . ."

No halt was possible now, not even the shortest bivouac. The nodding men must sleep as they rode. By morning they must be where the Yankees would not expect to find them. Rest could be had only as chance offered.

Morning brought the advance within twelve miles of the Potomac. Stuart rode with Rooney Lee and a Captain White, who had volunteered to show the way to a ford named for his family. It hadn't been used lately. Roads had been let go to grass, but he could find it and Stoneman might not know of it.

A swing off the road now, west and southwest, heading at last directly for the river. Through woods, across stubble fields and abandoned pastures. Into the open again. Too open, and a proper road. How much of this, Captain? Not much. Half a mile, maybe. How far the ford now? Two—three miles. Be there soon.

The road turned up a slight rise. Over the top came the first of a column of bluecoats. Stoneman's men on patrol.

"Easy!" Stuart said, and hoped those behind him were as wide awake as he was. "Easy. Don't hurry. Keep your revolvers covered."

All day the order had been: "No shooting. No noise. If you must fight, swords only."

The quiet now was a thing audible in itself. The muffled tread of the horses, as trained and mechanical as the sway of the men in the saddles. The soft creak of leather rubbing leather, and tension a man could feel as plainly as the pressure of a gathering storm.

Forward at the same monotonous jog. Blue coats hiding gray trousers. Stoneman's Yankees couldn't know. Forward, until Stuart could see the faces of the men approaching.

"Draw sabres—CHARGE!"

The order was lost in a wild yell, in the tumult of a gallop one wouldn't have supposed the horses had left in them. Stuart's arm at full length, his blade high and several hundred others flashing in the sun, the whole column bore down at full speed on the luckless patrol. It turned and scampered away, Stuart in hot pursuit. Uphill. At the crest, he reined in and halted the column. Rooney Lee's sharpshooters drooped to the ground, flattened themselves against the ridge and peppered the fleeing Yankees with rifle fire. Young Pelham, up with the first of his guns, sent a shot after them, for luck.

Four guns up now. Rooney Lee's men back in the saddle, making for the ford. Under better cover, but nobody knew what might be met at the river. If there were no Yankees there now, soon there would be. The scattered patrol would spread the alarm. Rooney Lee, big and quiet, as soft-spoken as ever but a little red around the eyes, asked for orders.

"Get across," Stuart said. "It's up to you to find out how."

He waited with Pelham on the hill. From the ford came presently the sound of rifle fire. A courier reported that the Yankees had occupied a quarry near the ford. Lee had ordered them out, threatening them with envelopment by Stuart's cavalry if they did not evacuate. So far they had not moved.

"We could spare a gun now," Pelham said, and sent two.

By the time the guns reached the ford, the Yankees had surrendered and Lee's men were crossing. The guns crossed, too, and took a stand commanding the ford and a canal near by.

On the hill Pelham kept one last gun trained on the road. All the column now had passed except one regiment of North Carolinians. Three couriers that Stuart sent back, urging haste, were only three more men missing. Finally Blackford said he would ride back over the road until he found the regiment, if it meant the Capitol Prison the rest of his days. In less than an hour, against the echoes of Pelham's gun, came the sound of galloping horses. The Carolinians had halted three miles off against a threat of attack from the rear and only Stuart's final order to run for their lives had turned them.

Stuart waved them on. Pelham unlimbered his gun.

When Stuart reached the far bank of the river, his men were stretched out helter-skelter under the trees, the horses, unbitted, cropping what they could find of edible brush and bark. Some of the men had been so stiff when they swung from their saddles that they could not stand, had dropped like lengths of cordwood. They had done eighty-seven miles in two days. It wasn't possible, but they had done it.

On to Leesburg then, where Stonewall Jackson walked out from his tent to greet the commander of the cavalry corps.

"Well, how do you do, Pennsylvania!"

A fighting man's accolade, and another waited for him in Richmond.

"My darling, you spoke once of praying your men across a bridge. I prayed you home safely from Chambersburg."

"I didn't suppose you knew I was there," Stuart said.

"I've a way of knowing now. When I don't hear from you for days on end."

Then it was, "Thank you for the slippers, dearest. I should hang them up for mementoes, but I need them too badly. And I'm glad you are pleased with the cape. Do you recognize the fur on the collar?"

A sleeve band from that jacket he had bought her in St. Louis in 1859. Three years ago. He didn't remember. Too much had happened since. Too much had happened recently.

"It doesn't matter, dear. All that matters is that you are here and safe. But you must try to take better care of this cape. I have just one piece of fur left. And one more plume."

Chapter 10. *Another Christmas*

Time and again that bleak December Flora said to herself, if I had only kept the children at Laurel Hill!

"Sister," Maria reminded her, "you would have come to Richmond in spite of all, after you heard about John."

Yes, that was true. Then it was, if only I had watched Little Flora more carefully! It was Jimmie who had been ailing that summer and she had spent all her thought on him.

"Flora," Charles Brewer said, "these things strike, nobody knows how or when or why."

It was a hard winter on children. Not because of any lack of food or clothing. Such things could still be managed for the little ones, through gifts or parental sacrifice. The peril was the insidious spread of disease—everything from measles to smallpox—bred in some unclean spot, incubated on unwashed bodies, carried in crowded, dirty railroad cars, released to pollute water, milk, the very air.

One evening Little Flora, who a half hour before had been singing to her dolls, didn't want her supper.

"She won' tech a bite," Tilda complained.

Flora, who had been making ready to go down to her own supper, felt the child's hands and found them warm, but not enough for alarm.

"Where does it hurt, darling?"

La Pet's hands went to her throat. Flora pressed the pink tongue down with a spoon and looked. A little red, not bad.

"There!" she said. "We won't try to eat. We don't have to have our supper right this minute. Mamma'll rock you and sing to you."

"Frère Jacques, Frère Jacques . . ."

The small body, now that she held it, did seem warm.

" *'Frère Jacques'*—Tilda, is Jimmie asleep? Get somebody else to watch him and find a shawl. Between us we can carry La Pet to the Brewers'. I can't ask the doctor to come out tonight—just for us."

"Miss Flo', is she sick den, sho' enuf?"

"I don't know. I'm afraid . . . hurry, will you?"

It might be just a cold, Charles Brewer said, when he saw the child; but it might be as well to put her to bed in their house, where he could watch her.

In the morning her fever was worse.

"I believe I'd write to her father," Charles said then.

Flora wrote, the pen sputtering in her shaking hand, though she was steady enough, tending her child. And she wrote again later, sending both letters to the War Department with a note asking urgently that they be forwarded to Stuart.

Each day Little Flora slipped farther beyond a mother's or a doctor's care. The fever fluctuated but never quite went away. Life in the laughing, happy-hearted little girl burned out like a dwindling taper, but with so much pain finally that it was a release for all when the lids could be drawn down over the unseeing blue eyes and death's chill came. Only . . .

"And you couldn't locate Jeems?" Alec said when he came to help. "You've had no answer to your letters? Did you try the telegraph?"

Yes, when she had sent word to Alec. And now she did have an answer, but it was only to her first letter: "I can't possibly be away at this time. I must leave my child in your hands and God's."

Just God's now.

"He didn't realize," Charles Brewer said. "None of us did at first."

"I don't understand it," Alec said, unhappily handling his brother's letter. "It must be that he is hard to reach right now."

On both sides of a changing boundary line, again there was a mass movement of troops. The North was once more shuffling generals. Both McClellan and Halleck had declared they had Stuart trapped in Maryland, not a man of his command could escape; and then he had brought them all and the incredible string of horses, the more incredible train of wagons, safely home. So, the North was shuffling generals and preparing, the Confederate command again was sure, for the grand attack of the year; but where? The cavalry, the eyes and ears of the army, must ride the whole length of the boundary land, watch all the gaps, all the river valleys, little and big, all the railroads, feel for the enemy, hide the movements of Lee's divisions . . .

All these things, even in her blackest hour, Flora understood. Stuart was busy, perilously, unceasingly occupied; but surely he could have arranged for one day . . .

"How can I tell him?" she cried. "How can I?"

"There!" Alec said. "Don't distress yourself so. I'll find him. I'll tell him."

But Alec didn't know what she knew. That portrait Stuart had wanted of *La Petite*. She had put off having it made, for this reason and for that. All of them valid at the time, none having any weight of reasonableness now.

"Thank you, Alec. Find him if you can."

Alec hadn't been there to see Stuart carrying the baby in the crook of his arm all around Fort Riley, to show her off, his daughter. Alec . . . she said she hoped he would find Stuart. Somehow, she knew he would not. She would have to bear this unbearable thing without his support.

She excused herself and went to look up a hair ribbon she had cut for the little one the day she was taken ill. Maria found her at an open trunk, staring dry-eyed at the absurd Garibaldi jacket of red flannel. So many hours, so many stitches put into it, and it had been worn so seldom! At Maria's exclamation, she closed the trunk and turned to the bed, where she had laid out the little one's Sunday dress, cut from an old gray cashmere of her own, prettied with scraps of lace and bows of velvet. Little Flora had been inordinately proud of it. She had worn it twice.

"Sister," Maria begged, "let somebody else . . ."

"No," Flora answered. "Let me. I must. I never shall again."

Alone. Dear mamma and papa, wherever you are, did you know I have lost—we have lost—our little girl? Maria and Dr. Brewer are here with me, and Stuart's brother, Judge Alexander Stuart; but . . . but my husband is away.

"My child," Rachel would remind her, "in the army, husbands are usually away."

But right now? When I need him so?

Coming down through the mountains by way of Upperville, making for the Warrenton Pike or some lesser road leading eastward, Major Sweeny, chief musician on General J. E. B. Stuart's many-faceted staff, kept a watchful distance this morning behind his chief. He had his banjo handy before him, but the strings were silent. So was the General, for a change. He could be, Sweeny knew. Folks who claimed he was always noisy and cheerful didn't know him. Not like Sweeny. Thinking, the General was, this morning, mulling things over, putting together the pieces of the eternal puzzle he studied. Sweeny watched, keeping his banjo handy.

He watched so closely, listening and looking both, that he was aware almost as soon as Stuart of the approach of another horseman coming from the opposite direction. Stuart raised his head, then his hand, in warning, and turned his horse off the road. Sweeny followed; but by then the horseman was in full view and they came out of hiding faster than they went in. It was young Channing Price, the latest aide Stuart had added to his staff.

"Evening," was his greeting, with a quick salute, his face breaking into a smile of happy accomplishment. "Dispatches for you, sir, and a telegram from Richmond. Major Cooke said you might be riding this way. Lucky I took off, wasn't it?"

Stuart answered that he couldn't say until he had read the dispatches, then dismounted, easing his horse to let her graze. He hesitated, handling the telegram, but finally laid it aside until he had finished the military papers.

He looked up from them once to ask if they'd like to know the name of the new Yankee general. Burnside. Had they ever heard of him? They hadn't.

"Nor I, till just lately," he said, and went on reading.

But the telegram jerked him to his feet. For a second the others thought he was going to fall over backwards. He thought so himself. His ears rang. His blood seemed all to flow away from his heart.

"I do hope," Channing Price faltered, "I didn't bring you bad news."

"It couldn't—be worse." He handed over the open message. "I don't believe it," he said, "I can't. Sweeny, you knew her—my little girl. She's dead, Sweeny. *La Petite* is dead." There, he had said it. Now it was true. "My little girl—I'll never get over it in this world."

He never would, he was sure. On the road again, duty bound, the bitter fact kept repeating itself to him: "Dead. *La Petite* is dead." And then, like Flora, he thought, "What can I say to her mother? I couldn't go to her. I can't now. This man Burnside. The movement is clear. No time to be lost, but *La Petite*—dead. I'll never hear her laugh again."

Rock of Ages, cleft for me . . .

Behind, a solemn, still watchful distance behind, Sweeny tuned his banjo, then let it fall to its former position. Not now. Not now.

Jackson's aide, young Sandy Pendleton, met Stuart outside the General's tent. It was ten o'clock at night, or thereabouts.

"The General's sleeping," he said. "He's had a busy day. I know it's urgent and he is most anxious to have your report, but . . ."

"Don't disturb him," Stuart said.

"Then, if I could offer you a place in my tent?"

"Never mind," Stuart said. "I'll turn in alongside the General."

It wasn't mischievous impulse. He needed the contact—the touch of one who never argued which came first—duty or self. Before the horrified Pendleton could imagine his intent, he turned back the far edge of Jackson's blanket and crawled under.

Eased then by the most unharmonious snoring in the Confederacy, finally he slept. When he awoke, it was bright morning and Jackson sat on a campstool before a portable table at the door of the tent, drinking coffee and reading the dispatches. Also the telegram. At least, it was there.

Stuart, forgetting the source of his audacity the night before, in a state of some confusion threw off the blanket, stood up, and began to shake himself to rights, only to find that two men were waking in him, not one. On the one hand there was the husband and father, recoiling from the telegram, the wound it had given him aching like a tooth only temporarily quieted. Opposite this man stood the soldier, a hardened veteran of war—aged twenty-nine. Jackson spoke to the soldier.

"Morning. Sleep well? I didn't. Next time you call—ah, informally —you might think to remove your spurs."

"Sir, I . . ."

Jackson waved aside the protest.

"Interesting report. Very. This man Burnside. Sounds active."

The soldier answered.

"Yes, sir. Everything I've observed, everything my scouts have seen indicates an attack. It will come from the north, and be aimed at seizing and holding a road to Richmond. There will be the usual threat to the Shenandoah Valley, but that will be on the side and easy to handle. As for the other, I wish we could keep him beyond the Potomac, but it begins to look . . ."

"The Rappahannock," Jackson said, "is much easier. We'll have the high ground. Fredericksburg? Let him try it. Hope he does." He took up the telegram. The ache in Stuart jumped.

"Did you read it? You know?" he asked.

"It was with the rest of your stuff. Yes. I'm sorry, son. I think I know how you must feel."

Stuart could hardly have said how he felt. The numbness of non-realization, the ache that was rejection, a drawing, tearing . . . Jackson stood beside him, gripping his shoulder, each lean, nervous finger making itself felt.

"I have a child myself now. A daughter, newly arrived. Did you know? The mother takes it hard that I have not seen the baby. And I don't know when I shall."

The mother took it hard. *Ma povere petite* . . .

"Sir, if you could spare me for a day?"

"General Lee," Jackson reminded him, "must know what you have told me as soon as possible. Will you leave it to another to make your report?"

"I . . . no, sir. I must make it myself."

The father ached. Forever after he would pull up short when he saw a girl child at play. The mother would take it hard, but the soldier still must stay.

In Richmond, they said to Flora that she ought to go away now, somewhere to rest and try to forget.

"Will you come with me to Saltville?" Alec urged. "Ma said I was to bring you."

Not Saltville. Please. Not Laurel Hill, with its well-intentioned kindness. Not now.

Finally Charles Brewer found the place. There was a young assistant surgeon in Lee's command, a Doctor John Fontaine. His parents had a plantation not too far from Richmond, were alone in their big house, and would welcome company, most especially Mrs. Stuart and her little boy.

"On the railroad," Maria reminded Flora. "You could get back here in a few hours if for any reason you felt you must come."

Flora looked at her sister blankly. What reason now? Stuart had said he couldn't come, no matter what. "God bless you darling. My heart is with you always, but not now."

He didn't want to come, she thought. She didn't blame him, really.

"For Jimmie's sake," Maria pleaded.

For Jimmie's sake. He kept asking for his sister. Where was she? How did one explain such an absence to a two-year-old?

"All right," Flora said at last. "I'll try. Please thank Mrs. Fontaine for me . . . and say . . . next Tuesday? I think, however, I'd best keep my room at Mrs. Duval's. Oh, just in case . . ."

Before Fredericksburg, Stuart's days went well enough. Long hours in the saddle. Orders to convey to high-ranking generals, orders from Robert E. Lee that needed personal amplification. Scouts to place, to meet. Patrols to organize, to inspect. Armies to be moved. Longstreet, Hill, Jackson. His own cavalry to be stationed. A rampart of men and guns for the heights above the Rappahannock. Fitz Lee's brigade to be brought up, to form a reserve line.

"High time!" Fitz said, his horse wheeling and dancing. "Been out to pasture long enough."

Raids to make on Burnside's fat supply trains, venturing foolishly over the Potomac. Small raids of a few hundred men, with a Lee or Wade Hampton commanding. Stuart, the corps commander, not participating. His life too valuable to be risked on anything but a major venture; but his men, caught in an extremity, shouting, "Stuart, Stuart!" anyhow, frightening the opposition into a palsy.

The raids made talk all the way up and down the line. Each string of horses, each train of from twenty to fifty loaded wagons eased the problem of supply; but the greatest gain was the fighting edge they put on the men. Around bivouac fires, all—infantry or cavalry—had much to talk and laugh about, and did, judging by the sound. Stuart himself visited every unit at least once, for the pleasure the sight of his plumed hat and his cape seemed to give.

Inevitably, however, there were hours that he must spend alone—riding along a seemingly empty road, his escort keeping too respectful distance, or resting between rides in his tent. Resting? In his solitary hours two reflections haunted him.

One involved Flora. Everyone who offered him condolence included a word for her: "Do express my sympathy to Mrs. Stuart. These things fall hardest on a mother." He was troubled in his conscience about Flora. He had thought he was too busy to go to her when he first heard that his child was ill. Had he been too busy, really? Or had it been just difficult for him to arrange a leave?

The other thought was a sneaking thing, close to superstitious alarm. This was an unkind, a stealthy blow that had been dealt him. His luck had been running too high, still ran high, militarily speaking. Then this ugly jar, to remind him that no man was immune to sorrow or loss. No man who rode this earth.

One of these lonely, too meditative evenings, hearing a murmur of voices in the tent nearest his, he got up and walked over to it. The tent was shared, he knew, by Captain Blackford, his engineer aide, and John Pelham of his artillery. Theirs was a sudden wartime friendship, but none the less valid for that. Pelham Stuart found now on his back on a blanket, listening to Will Blackford, who read by poor lantern light from Napier's narrative of Wellesley's Peninsular Campaigns. Both young men sprang up at Stuart's entrance, Blackford holding his place in the book with his left forefinger. Stuart put them at ease by dropping down on Pelham's blanket, declaring he would listen, too. It was what he had come for.

But presently inactivity became too oppressive.

"Do you mean to say," he interrupted the reading, "that there is no frolic anywhere tonight within reach of you two? I hear the girls in Fredericksburg are unusually pretty, and sociable."

He knew well enough why they were at camp. A plot to have someone on hand to keep the "old man" company these days. Old man? Well, he'd be thirty soon.

"Sir," Blackford again marked his place in the book, "please remember that I have—that I am a sober, married man."

He had been about to say, "I have a wife and family."

"I think your wife would trust you, Will," Stuart answered, "and be happier for knowing that you were being well fed. They still serve refreshments hereabouts, I happen to know. Anyhow, your excuse doesn't apply to John."

"John daren't go about much," Blackford said. "He's already engaged to four girls in different parts of Virginia. A fifth might be his undoing."

"That's slander," Pelham said hotly. "It's only two—certainly not more than three. You know how it is, sir. A man kind of outtalks himself, if the music's right and there's a moon.

"But you're right about the people around here," he added presently. "They are nice. The Harts, for example, where we had dinner last Sunday. They're musical. Did you know, sir? Both girls play the harp and sing. The mother plays the organ. They belong to a musical circle that gives informal concerts almost every week. Mrs. Hart, knowing you like music, said they'd be honored if some time you could attend. I really think you might enjoy it."

The subterfuge was apparent, but the prospect of an evening of music had a strong appeal.

"Why yes," he said, "I might like that very much. I'll go with you to the next program, if I am free."

Before the words were out of his mouth, a courier came hunting him, with a message from General Lee. Barring a surprise movement on the part of the enemy, the commanding general was meeting with his corps commanders at headquarters the following morning at eight. He would be obliged if General Stuart would attend.

Stuart was surprised at the relief the summons brought him.

"Don't count on me for that concert," he said to Pelham after he had dispatched the courier. "I doubt that I shall have much free time now."

He hoped he would have none. If he were free for a day or a night, he must go to Flora. He had tried to make clear to her the gravity of the military situation which had kept him away so long; but he doubted that his best efforts at explanation had atoned for his continued absence.

"What do you do when you rest?" she had asked him often. "What do you do?" he might have asked her now; but he knew. She sat alone with her thoughts. Deep, he had called her once, and meant it. Deep as a well.

The Fontaines of Louisa County were true Virginians—kindly, hospitable, genuine. From the hour when Colonel Fontaine took Flora and Jimmie and Tilda off the jolting train at the Beaver Dam depot, Flora knew she was in good hands.

"I'm home," she thought. "It's still Virginia, but I'm home—at last."

"Mother would have come down to meet you," the Colonel said, urging the old horses onward, "but our roads are kinda in need of repair and she hates to be bounced. You're not to think now it's any trouble for you to come visiting. We live quietly, but comfortably. We're fortunate enough to have kept most of our people, and we still raise a good bit on our land, putting away fruit and garden sass and meat. Glad to have you—for as long as you'll stay. Proud to have you, ma'am."

The house was square and white among trees. Mrs. Fontaine stood just inside the door, in gray alpaca and white shawl. She looked not in the least like Rachel Cooke, but she was Rachel.

In bed at last, Flora slept as she had not done in weeks, but awoke the next morning with tears gummed on her eyelids, remembering instantly Mrs. Fontaine's words of welcome:

"You poor thing!"

Kindly meant, of course, not at all a reproach, but there it was. Flora sat up and looked about her. Jimmie was still hard asleep. A fire was burning busily opposite the bed. Somebody must have built it up that morning. She turned back the covers, slid to the floor, found her slippers and in the pleasant, fragrant warmth crossed the room to the dresser.

"Mercy!" she said.

She looked a poor thing, sure enough. Red-eyed, thin, her hair needing a good brushing—a poor, poor thing. Oh, but she mustn't be. Anything but that. A sudden giddiness seized her. She fumbled for a rocking chair, found it, and sank into it, her eyes filling again, in spite of her resolution.

It didn't come all at once. One needed to be two years old, like Jimmie, to fall into a new world and take it at face value. For several days Flora sat beside her hostess with sewing in her lap and didn't thread a needle. Then one day, as naturally as ever, she took out the sleeve of a cotton shirt, sewed a seam and turned it. For the army, she explained, and went on then to tell of the sewing ladies in Richmond.

"We have something of the sort here," Mrs. Fontaine said. "Our ladies would appreciate hearing about your distinguished friends."

"I should be most happy," Flora said, though her heart clamored: "Not yet, not yet!"

One morning she drove into Beaver Dam with Colonel Fontaine to fetch the household mail. When they reached the village and the general store that housed the post office, there was nobody around to take the horses.

"Let me hold them," Flora offered.

The Colonel put the lines hesitantly into her hands; but, when he saw how she held them—just tightly enough to warn the horses that she was in command—he nodded and went on about his business. When he returned, the horses were dozing in the sun and Flora was drinking in the peace of the little town—the red depot, the church, the single line of track spinning off into the distance, the houses scattered along the one street, which crossed the railroad diagonally.

"We've all had a good nap," she announced. "May I drive back?"

It was no great thing to do, to urge the willing, lazy animals homeward, but it felt good. When they crossed the last plank bridge and went through the home gate, a black boy swinging on it as it opened, Flora impulsively tipped back her head and whistled a bar of "Garry Owen."

And the horses bolted. A person wouldn't have believed they could. Flora had almost more than she could do to keep a semblance of control. When finally she had them checked, just short of a plunging entrance into the barn, Colonel Fontaine, who had hung on to the seat, saying nothing, let out his breath in a great gust of, if you please, applause.

"You handled them superbly," he declared, and added, as he lifted her down, shaking and shaken, over the wheel, "You're a brave girl."

But she wasn't. In the privacy of her comfortable room, she could tell herself the truth. She was a poor thing, still. If she had been really brave, she wouldn't have to pretend. She would want to meet Mrs. Fontaine's neighbors and sit long hours with them, comparing husbands and babies and other joys and sorrows. Everybody wouldn't step so softly around her. The Colonel wouldn't hide the Richmond paper, telling about the big battle shaping up near Fredericksburg. If she were brave, she'd go out now and ask what was the news from Richmond. She would do it, too!

Colonel Fontaine waited for her in the warm, homey sitting room. "How are you, my dear? All right? Mother saw us from upstairs and had to have smelling salts. There's mail for you, Miss Flora. I should have looked sooner. Somebody's sent you a magazine."

A periodical this time, reduced in size, but with a flamboyant, literary title.

"John Esten Cooke," she recognized his scribble on the margin. "My cousin. He's probably got a piece in it."

She opened the magazine to its short table of contents; and some awful, warning voice said to her, "Hush! Not here!"

December the twelfth was a warm day, even for Virginia; but the night turned off cold. The men in Lee's several army corps, bivouacked on the hills that paralleled the Rappahannock west of Fredericksburg, slept mostly in wheelspoke circles about their fires, their feet toward the embers.

Toward morning some of the men dreamed they heard gunfire. Most of them rolled over, if there was room, and ignored the sound— a popular night haunt. But, when reveille sounded in the scanty light of early morning, from the direction of the town down below, and from the river and the canal that ran beside it, and from the river road, which ran from the town southward between the river and the hills, big guns were really booming. The Yankees must be coming over or trying to. A man couldn't see. The valley was filled with fog. Never mind. The fog will lift soon enough.

Before it did, before proper daylight came, from the woods where most of Stuart's cavalry had been guarding the rear of Longstreet's and Jackson's corps, Boots and Saddles sounded; and in the spooky half-light then one could hear the mounted troopers riding past, leaving rear guard positions to take battle formation on the hills near Hamilton's Crossing, on the right end of the line. The next thing the gaping infantry saw was couriers racing by, and then came young General Jeb himself, his cape swinging, his feathers waving, his teeth flashing as he shouted a "Halloa" to someone he knew, but not stopping. On his way to tell Jackson, then Lee, that his troopers were in column formation on Jackson's right, Pelham's guns also in place.

The fog was rolling when Stuart pulled up at Jackson's tent. Stuart was in time to share morning prayer. Jackson's petition was reverent but brief. When he stood up, his eyes were blue steel, giving off sparks. Old Blue Light! God save him!

General Lee took things more quietly. He recognized all the advantages that were his, but he had to look for possible bad turns, as well. The fog was really lifting now and melting. The sun shone on the town and the river and on Burnside's regiments crossing a pontoon bridge that had been finished in the night. The Yankee guns were booming more busily now. It would be up to Longstreet, occupying Marye's Heights above the town and a sunken road at their base, to stop the bluecoats from crossing or, failing that, to pin them down before they advanced too far. It would be the work of Jackson, supported by Stuart, to cover all routes and lines leading south. It was Lee's belief that, if Burnside got enough men over the river, he would make for the railroad leading to Richmond. Men must be stationed along the right of way, ready to tear up the tracks if that threat developed.

Stuart galloped back with final orders. All day he rode up and down the Confederate lines. Never, he knew, would he see such another battle panorama. A beautiful, terrible spectacle. If Burnside had searched the map for the best possible place in which to hurl an army to destruction, he couldn't have chosen better. Longstreet couldn't check him at the pontoons. Too many Yankees poured into the town, replacing any who fell by two to one; but finally that did not decide the issue. After a couple of hours of bitter trying, Longstreet pulled back his men to their protected positions and waited. Waited until the bluecoats were in full view and short range, then turned his cannon and his rifles loose. Wave after wave of men were sent against that fire. Wave after wave, they staggered, fell, and broke.

When Burnside then tried a feint to the south, Jackson's guns and Stuart's, directed by Pelham, took care of that. When evening came on, the two armies stood almost exactly where they had when the day began; but the town of Fredericksburg was in ruins, and the streets, the gardens, the fields, even a short stretch of the river road—every bit of open ground—was carpeted in blue. Toward sunset, knowing that the battle had been won, Jackson had wanted to break from his position and drive the Union forces back into the river. He might have succeeded; but, looking at that spread of color, he held back the order. He would not cover the blue with Southern gray—not for any ground that might be gained.

All through the night, men stationed in the sunken road, their rifles still resting on the stone parapet that guarded it—John Cooke's 14th Carolinians were there—could hear moaning from that mass of fallen ones. By morning it was more than some of them could endure, and a Georgia boy named Kirkland went over the stone wall in the direction of a cry. The Yankees saw him, but not a shot was fired. Others followed.

That was Sunday. All of Sunday and Monday were given to a truce for picking up the wounded and burying the dead. The cavalry, on orders to keep unceasing vigilance, patrolled the lines, to make sure the truce was kept, to watch the enemy for signs of movement. Monday morning, visiting the sunken road, Stuart heard that John Cooke had been wounded again, not so seriously this time, but enough to send him back to Richmond, a hospital case. As Stuart turned away, his informant looked at him curiously.

"Excuse me, but have you seen yourself, sir? Looks to me like bullet holes there in your cape, and something's taken half the fur from the collar."

Stuart wore the cape, when in action, held by a short length of chain. Once during the battle he had felt a slight jerk.

"How it missed you I can't see," the man marveled; but Stuart, ruefully examining his loss, was facing Flora willy-nilly, at last. She might have been perched there on the parapet, so plainly could he hear her reproach and warning:

"Darling, I have just one more piece of fur, and one more plume."

That evening, when his scouts reported that the Yankees were pulling back over the river and had made preparations to destroy their pontoons, he rode again to General Lee's tent, this time to ask for a twenty-four hours' leave.

"Will that be enough?" Lee asked.

"Yes, sir. Twenty-four hours, and a horse, if you know of one."

At the Fontaine house near Beaver Dam on Tuesday morning, Flora in her best black silk dress and her coat and bonnet sat with Mrs. Fontaine, waiting for Colonel Fontaine to bring up the buckboard. Tilda and Jimmie had gone down to the barn with him for a last visit with the kittens there, of which Jimmie was to select one for his own, though it was no kindness to take a kitten to Richmond now.

Except that Flora did not mean to stay in Richmond. Just long enough to give up the room at Mrs. Duval's and get a message to Alec. She was returning to Saltville, after all, but didn't mean to stay there, either. Any refuge would serve until she could get clear away. If railroads were still in operation, she would return to St. Louis, to her aunt over the river in Illinois; but that could be settled later. Just let the final resting place be far!

Naturally she had not discussed her plans with the Fontaines. She hoped she had covered her misery decently. The day the magazine had come, if she remembered, she had managed finally to smile and to say, "I believe, after all, this was meant just for me."

There was a poem in the magazine. Stuart had written it. Oh, it wasn't the poem, or John Esten's misplaced humor that hurt. He wrote right sensibly for him.

"I thought you might like evidence that your Stuart at last is coming up out of the unhealthy low spirit that had us all worried here. It isn't much as a poem. It's still melancholy; but it is a good sign, don't you agree, when he can think romantically once more?"

It was a wretched bit of versifying:

> *It may be on some happier day,*
> *When our land once more is free,*
> *That I shall press your hand and say . . .*

She couldn't read it all. She would not. She could see Stuart struggling over the rhyme. Fairly biting his tongue in two. But for whom? It was really more than she could bear. Everything was more than she could bear. She was not brave. She had exhausted now every false semblance of courage. This brutal, senseless, dreadful war! It was not for such unholy slaughter that she had wanted her Stuart to be a soldier. She was running away. It was, she knew, a cowardly flight. Stuart would be shamed. No. He no longer cared for a poor thing like her. He—if she did not run, she would go mad.

The battle of Fredericksburg gave her an excuse for escape from the Fontaines. She was needed in the Richmond hospitals. Her sister relied upon her.

"My dear, of course," Mrs. Fontaine said, agreeing, perhaps, too promptly. "You must visit us again later. Any time—just any time."

And now the Colonel was at the door, his watch open.

"No hurry," he said, as Flora started up. "There's a gentleman outside asking for you. Will you see him?"

A gentleman asking for her? John Esten Cooke seeking forgiveness?

A gray horse with drooping head stood near the gate. The rider was flicking dust from his boots. His cape swung forward. She saw the bullet holes, the ravaged fur. She turned faint. She steadied. And suddenly she was running that way—running, running, running.

Chapter 11. *Happy New Year*

The room over Christmas and into the New Year was at a Mrs. Alsop's, near cavalry headquarters, west from Fredericksburg. It was the smallest room of all and often chilly; but inconveniences didn't matter. Stuart lived there with his wife, an orderly posted always at the house to maintain contact with his command. Evenings, other officers, some with wives also in the house, came for games and music in the parlor. Flora had her guitar sent up from Richmond, and found that she could sing again. Anything but *Frère Jacques*. Never that now. Never again.

The best hours were hers and Stuart's, when alone. Tilda and Jimmie remained with the Fontaines, who were only too happy to keep them, to make possible this holiday, which Stuart and Flora both needed. Flora would not have believed, after what she had passed through—Stuart, too, for that matter—that their love, their absolute oneness, could know such complete restoration. It was the grief they shared, their terrible loss, the near loss—only Flora knew how near—of everything that worked the miracle. Alone and together at last, they went back over the days and weeks of separation. Slowly. A piece of the way, like an army marching, then a halt, to examine an experience, to hold it.

The winter light coming in through narrow windows was meager, the glow from a lamp with a china shade, which Stuart had "borrowed," not much better. Sewing a new fur collar to the gray cape, raveling threads from such margins as she thought could be opened and closed again, to darn the bullet holes, were exacting tasks. Flora pricked her finger often, bringing blood. Stuart, watching, would see the bright spot and snatch at her hands, kiss the prick, then hold them, and her, until the reason for anything was forgotten. She had not known such tenderness since—since that other world they had once shared.

Flora was settled in the new room well before Christmas Day and so could attend the Christmas dinner that Stonewall Jackson gave Generals Lee and Stuart at his headquarters. To the amazement of all, he was living in a house. According to Stuart, he had moved under a roof to nurse an earache and found he liked the life of a Sybarite. The dinner, featuring ham and turkey, made the description appropriate. General Jackson, resplendent in his fine coat, bowed low over Flora's hand, and told her in his gentle, mountain boy voice that she was welcome. He was only sorry Mrs. Jackson was not present to share the hour with her. General Lee, handsomer than ever now that his hair was nearly white, kissed her cheek; and those were surely things to remember beyond ham and turkey; but what she really treasured was the smiling pride in her husband's eyes, when she made her early excuses and rode back to the boarding house, escorted by Major von Borcke and General Fitz Lee.

The next day Stuart crossed the Rappahannock to raid Yankee supply depots and, if he could, stir a few painful memories on the part of Burnside, who had not retreated far enough to suit anybody. It was a full scale raid, all the cavalry brigades and Pelham's batteries participating. They left in high spirits, making great promises. They were gone five hair-raising days, but returned almost unscathed on New Year's day, bringing two hundred Yankee captives, as many horses, and twenty loaded wagons—and tales to tell that would outlast the winter. They had been in and out of Burnside's lines. At one place, while his troopers tore up railroad track and burned a bridge, Stuart took time to issue fresh orders to the details Burnside had sent in pursuit of him and scattered them forty ways for Sunday. That done, he had wired the quartermaster general in Washington a complaint about the mules in Burnside's train. They were scarcely fit to pull his wagons over to the Confederate lines. If their quality did not improve, it would not pay him, Stuart, to come again. The new year, 1863, began well.

The cavalry rode into Fredericksburg, laughing and singing; and the girls pelted them with late-blooming roses. At the Alsop gate, Stuart, ruddy and triumphant, set Flora up on his horse and laughed at the patient animal's look of weary inquiry.

"What do you think of your husband now, ma'am?" he demanded, but did not wait for an answer. "My turn to give a feast, I think. You furnish the fixings and I'll provide the meat."

The meat was a quarter of young mutton, served with brown gravy and hot mint sauce. The men talked about it for months. Some never forgot.

On the twentieth of January it rained. Every run came out of its banks; the roads were hub deep in mud. Burnside over the river was replaced by a man named Hooker. Fighting Joe Hooker—but he couldn't move man or horse with any gain, under prevailing conditions. Later it began to snow. It snowed for three days, and the fighting was over until spring.

Everyone turned to the building of winter quarters. Log cabins sprang up where tents had been. Some were content still with canvas walls, but set them around mud-plastered chimney stacks. Wooded hillsides were stripped of their trees. Walking down a company street with Stuart one afternoon, Flora was seized with a mad desire for a cabin.

"Could we . . ." she began; and Stuart knew instantly what she wanted.

"They're rarely uncomfortable," he said, but hesitantly, so that she knew he, too, was tempted. "Not weather-tight, I'm afraid, the wood as green as it was when Riley was new." He stiffened suddenly. "No. Not for you. Not now. You'll be warmer at Mrs. Alsop's. And safer."

The winter passed too fast. Almost immediately it was March; and Fitz Lee, who early in January had again taken his brigade and as many horses as he could herd into the Orange-Culpeper area, to seek forage and also to keep an eye on the fords of the Rappahannock and the Rapidan, sent word of activities in that region that called for more watching than he and Grumble Jones could well manage. Flora knew from the way Stuart looked at her that it was Beaver Dam or Richmond or Saltville for her now. Probably Saltville, and, her heart warmed by the promise of another child, due in October, to replace, she hoped, *La Petite,* she thought she would be content to go. Stuart seemed even happier than she over the promised child, and, after he knew, doubled his tenderness toward her.

She would be content now at Laurel Hill, she thought, because she had been shown in a wonderful way how rich and full life could be even in the hard circumstance of war. If fear threatened again, she would remember, and count her gains, not her losses. It was as if in these few months she had at last reached full maturity. It was a good feeling.

However, that she would again know fear was certain. It touched her once with its cold hand in these close, but happy quarters. Stuart, not intending it, was responsible. Going over everything with her then, trying to straighten out all the tangles that had come into their living, he told her how in the past year, when his life was repeatedly in hazard, he had asked Alec to buy some life insurance for him, to care for Flora and the children in case he should fall in battle. It had been difficult and costly, but old Alec had managed.

Flora's throat closed in the old way.

"Stuart! That doesn't sound like you—to plan with such a thing in mind."

"Something told me that I must," he said.

"But I can't even contemplate it," she protested. "I won't. No wonder Alec looked at me so strangely when I was there last summer."

Still what she didn't like was that Stuart had harbored such a thought. To brighten her mood, he changed the subject.

"It's a thing we have to face," he said sensibly, "and then forget."

To help her forget, he offered another view of the future—a home somewhere for all of them, a house bright with firelight and lamplight, filled with the chatter of little ones. Himself coming in from a long day of work to her in that home.

"Well, that's better," she agreed. "Where will it be, darling?"

He pondered that.

"I know where it won't be," he said finally. "Nowhere in the enemy country. Never that for me or any of mine. You must promise."

Virginia, she thought. Still and always Virginia. Well, let it be Virginia then, if only Stuart should live out his days beside her there!

"You wrote a poem," she said slyly.

He flushed to the roots of his hair.

"So, that's where that miserable paper went!"

"It wasn't written in my honor, I think," she continued. "Still, I hope there was a thought of me in it."

"There is always a thought of you," he assured her.

Yes, she could live anywhere now in better peace.

That was March. In April camp was farther to the west; and Flora, Jimmie and Tilda with her now, was a guest for two weeks of new-found friends, named Grinnan, at Brampton. She was there when Mrs. Jackson came to visit her husband, bringing the baby daughter that he had never seen. The General took a room for them at a place called Yerby's, about ten miles from Guiney's Station on the Richmond, Fredericksburg Railroad. It was told on Stonewall that, after he had the family installed in the room, he knelt for two hours by the baby's crib in silent adoration.

Everyone, from General Lee down, went to call on Mrs. Jackson. By the time the Stuarts took their turn—they must bring the boy and that was an order, Stonewall said—Jackson had learned to carry the baby without fear of doing her bodily harm; but the spectacle of the six-foot fighting man cradling this human fragment in one arm, the long baby dress trailing to his boot-tops, made Flora's nose twitch. Laying her hand on Stuart's arm, and looking up at him, she found that his eyes, too, were wet. Oh, my love, does it hurt so still?

Immediately then, he stooped to pick up his son and hold him where he could see the baby.

"Give her a big hug and a squeeze," Jimmie offered cordially; and Stonewall Jackson retreated in terror.

Smiling, Flora turned to Mrs. Jackson. What a plain little creature she was! No, that wasn't fair. She was not strikingly beautiful, but she was far from homely. Dark, a little sallow—the baby was only a few months old. Her dress—green silk, shot with gold—was not too becoming. Perhaps she had heard her husband called drab in appearance and wanted to compensate. More probably nothing at all was wrong with Mrs. Jackson, except that, when a man stood out boldly and proudly on a hero's pedestal, one was likely to feel a little dashed by the first view of the woman who held his heart.

Really? Was it like that always? Did people look so at Flora Stuart? Yes, they must. What could a person do about that? Nothing. Carry one's head high. Remember who one was, and smile.

A few days later alarm, like a blaze spotted in dry timber land, broke out on the Rapidan near a plantation seat called Chancellorsville. Fighting Joe Hooker had crossed the river. But he couldn't—not there. That was the Wilderness. A battle couldn't be fought in such a place. Hooker must be mad to contemplate it. He'd get his armies hopelessly entangled. A Virginian could hardly make his way through the Wilderness, knowing the paths. But nobody waited to hear the full truth behind the alarm. In haste, with short leave-takings, women and children were bundled on the cars and shipped south. Flora was back at Mrs. Duval's by the time the guns began to roll.

The battle of Chancellorsville was to Flora the sound of guns going by, the sound of men marching, some of them reinforcements for General Lee, some General Winder's home guards—clerks, tradesmen, former soldiers, retired for illness or bad wounds, but useful now to defend the capital at close hand while the regulars held the enemy far away. Again there was a short time of panic, when the word spread that General Stoneman commanding Yankee cavalry had swept around the eastern end of Lee's lines and was headed toward the weakened defenses of Richmond. He failed to penetrate Lee's entrenchments and breastworks; and, blessedly, the people praying in the churches never knew how close he had come. Four miles, Yankee reports said afterwards. Four miles.

People praying in the churches. Men studying maps of northern Virginia, their faces troubled. It did seem, in spite of bravery and sacrifice and brilliant leadership, that each year the fighting came closer. The Potomac, the Rappahannock, now the Rapidan. Country that had been held tolerably safe now invaded. That was a long line for Lee to hold—from Fredericksburg past Culpeper. He'd hardly dare loosen his grip anywhere—right, left or center. Though the fighting, if that was true about Hooker and Chancellorsville, would be hottest on Lee's left. All depended then on who commanded there. Jackson? Yes, sir. Stonewall Jackson, with his Stonewall Brigade and the rest of the first corps, and Stuart's cavalry in support—Stuart himself and Fitz Lee directing their movements. The trouble lifted measurably. The line in that case would hold. Still, it did no harm to pray. About all a person could do, waiting.

To James Ewell Brown Stuart, hardly out of his saddle in two days and two nights, the first dark and furtive and filled with secret movement, the second ablaze with fighting that could not stop with sundown or the dark, the battle record was also a matter of patching together pieces, though of a livelier and more lurid hue. The quiet tensity of his final interview with Lee and the corps commanders, his final orders left no doubt as to the seriousness of the coming conflict. Not that Stuart had exactly entertained doubts before that meeting. It was his report, based on Fitz Lee's reconnaissance and one hot lick from Yankee skirmishers, that had produced the order to evacuate noncombatants wherever possible all along the line. He had lost no time packing Flora and the boy and Tilda on a train. All the visitors were gone now, all; and a man could settle down single-heartedly to the work of driving the Yankees out of Virginia. For keeps this time, please God!

A half hour after the conference he was on the road, a brace of aides in town to take and carry orders, his own orders warm in his pocket and even more firmly settled in his head. It was General Lee's opinion, formed and held without the help of any mustache-chewing worriers in Richmond, that Hooker would not attack his right, anchored at Fredericksburg and firmly entrenched, nor his center, though the Yankees might make a feint there to drive the Confederates back, if possible, into the Wilderness, but his left, which his own reconnaissance told him was lightly and loosely held.

Ha! Fighting Joe Hooker was due for a surprise. It was toward this end of the line and Fitz Lee's camp that Stuart rode now, stepping aside for a word to General Hampton to move his brigades, all but a small force left to serve the right flank, westward now in a scouting and screening pattern, defiling into the roads that led to the fords—Old Mine Ford on the Rappahannock, Eley's and Germanna Ford on the Rapidan. Not to stand or give battle unnecessarily, not to provoke an engagement, just keep Hooker generally occupied while Jackson moved his infantry out of position east of the Wilderness over the Old Plank Road to a rendezvous on the other side. Hi-ya! Any other infantry couldn't make it, but Jackson would be there tomorrow morning. He could count on that. Hooker wouldn't.

A breath of song, formless, tuneless, wordless, rose to Stuart's lips.

Old Joe Hooker . . .

He smiled it away. Not yet, but presently.

The first day and the first night were like that. By the next morning Stuart was able to make a report and knew just where he could reach Jackson with it. His cavalry was coming up in force now on the left, Fitz Lee at the far end of the line, to observe all enemy movement in that quarter.

"I will close on the flank and help all I can when the ball opens. May God grant us victory!"

Jackson's answer came back so fast that Stuart could catch the flash of flint on steel in his eyes and hear his jaws snap: "I trust that God will grant us a great victory. Keep closed on Chancellorsville."

Keep closed on Chancellorsville—all day that was the tune that sang itself in Stuart's ears as he rallied his troopers to the support of Jackson's corps, standing off Hooker's advance. Let nobody say it was easy going. All fought long and hard and bitterly. High and low, men fell. General Hill was among the wounded, though Stuart at first felt the loss of his aide, Channing Price, more grievously.

Toward four in the afternoon the valiant work of all began to tell. They had turned or were turning Hooker's right, pushing it back and away from the center. If that was where Hooker had his most strength, victory was coming.

Keep closed on Chancellorsville. Catherine's Furnace on the Old Plank Road. General Lee, come to get the feel of things himself, seated on a hardtack box, taking from Stuart Fitz Lee's jubilant report: "The enemy's right wing entirely in the air." Fighting Joe Hooker!

Lee's eyes shone and color touched his cheekbones, but he looked still at the whole picture.

"Find me a road," he said, "screened from their guns and I'll strengthen your position, General Jackson, all I can."

He rode off one way and Stuart another, the latter pelting away to find Fitz Lee, who through two winters of foraging had come to know every brush pile and cowpath in this tangle. Jackson's corps could do with reinforcement. The fighting in places went on undiminished, where one side or the other burst open a hornet's nest. Hooker had good men in his right wing. He had not sent a boy to carry water.

Dark, and Hooker, feeling the loss of power on his right, had stopped punching at the center of the line. Stuart from the plantation seat of Chancellorsville wrote a brief report and looked about for someone to carry it to Jackson. Young Major McClellan, of the Virginia McClellans, volunteered.

"Don't get lost," Stuart warned him.

He should have concerned himself with another's safety. He might have known that Jackson, on receipt of the message, would, like Lee, but with less caution, ride out to see for himself. He would ride out, not knowing, as Stuart did, that still in unexpected places and, often for no reason except jumping nerves, guns blazed away. When midnight passed without McClellan returning, Stuart worried a little, but still about the wrong man. Another hour, and the young man showed up, dejected, dazed, on a foam-flecked horse. By his looks, by the way he stood, dismounting to rest the horse, shaking himself out of a kind of stupor, Stuart knew that something awful had happened. At last it was said.

"General Jackson . . . started this way. Two patrols—nobody knows why—fired. At each other, I reckon. The fire came from two sides at once. The General."

"Only wounded, I hope," Stuart said. McClellan nodded. "Bad?"

His arm, McClellan said. He was able to walk away, but an ambulance had been summoned.

"He sent you a message. Orders, sir."

They were brief: "Take command. God bless you!"

Command? What about General Hill? For the first time Stuart heard that General Hill had been wounded. Then, of course, until Lee could be reached and could give his orders, the command was his, Stuart's.

He struck a match and looked at his watch. Two o'clock. A few short hours until daylight. No time to heft the stone that was his heart. No time to do much thinking. It was not to be supposed that Hooker would take the defeat of the day before without some attempt at recovery. By morning he would be pouring new men into that end of the line. The diminishing fire at the center might indicate that regiments from there were already moving. Meanwhile, Stuart could not know or find out whether the reinforcements Lee had promised Jackson were on the march. He must act with what he had, and promptly.

He scribbled a note to Fitz Lee, telling him the situation and his hastily conceived plan of action. At daybreak he would move the whole line forward, to clear the country of enemy all the way to the river, before Hooker could begin any opposing action. Then he himself set out to study his line.

The review was not calculated to raise his spirits. Fifteen thousand disorganized, battle-weary, footsore, hungry men. Old Blue Light was a wagon hunter when it came to the enemy's supply trains; but his own got left behind always if it was a case of which came first—fighting or eating. His infantry in the small hours of that morning, the third day of May, 1863, hadn't enough guts left to throw a stick at a cat. They hadn't eaten since day before yesterday.

And now that they had heard that Jackson was hurt, bad enough to die, maybe, they dropped in the dirt and gave up.

But Stuart was not leaving a choice to them. He was everywhere that early morning, his horse thudding over the woods roads, his cape flying, his plume waving. He set the infantrymen up on their blistered feet and dressed them into line with a flow of language Old Blue Light hardly had. He roared at them, he laughed at them, he coaxed them. He set his troopers at their heels to herd them. Would they cheat Old Jack of victory now? He wouldn't allow it.

Morning came; and there they stood, bayonets fixed, the cavalry with sabres ready, the artillery under General Alexander deployed on high ground to take care of any far shooting, and Stuart himself out in front of the Stonewall Brigade. Would you believe that was where the line sagged worst? Brave men. It was said to be a sentence of death to be elected to that proud company and no man lived to reach higher than a captaincy. They would die for Jackson, but would they fight for another? The big boy on the big horse wasn't asking. Morning came, full daylight; and out flashed his sword. He roared an order: "Forward CHARGE!" he tipped back his head and followed with a line of song. He had the words, the tune to suit him then. The sound carried from here to beyond:

> *"Old Joe Hooker, won't you come out of the Wilderness?*
> *Won't you come out, out, out . . .*
> *Old Joe Hooker, won't you come out tonight?"*

They caught the Yankees flat, some of them still sleeping. They ran over them, through them, around them. The ragged line pushed on—and on.

An hour of that and they flagged a little. Just in time, a feel of new power came up behind them. Two brigadier-generals whose men had helped hold the center of the line the day before, Lafayette McLaws and Richard Anderson, rode up to Stuart, saluted, and asked for orders.

By eight o'clock there wasn't a Yankee with any fight in him left south of the Rapidan. Yankee bacon and sidemeat were sizzling over fires and going—half raw—down hungry Confederate gullets; and Stuart, his eyes red-rimmed now, but still flashing, was receiving Robert E. Lee's congratulations.

Stuart thanked him and said he was ready now to turn over the command.

"I'm afraid," Lee answered, "I must ask you to keep it for a while."

That took the wind out of Stuart. Infantry? Before this day he had not commanded so much as a platoon.

"You don't want it?" Lee asked.

What Stuart answered was a matter for speculation forever after. He himself could not be sure what Lee said exactly or what he answered that day. If he was offered Jackson's command and refused it, it was, some said, the only act of self-abnegation on his record. More likely, if he was offered Jackson's post and refused it, it was because he didn't want it. He was a cavalryman. By now he knew it.

So did Robert E. Lee.

In Richmond, Chancellorsville was, first, the rolling of guns through the streets, and then, the trains of wounded coming home. Dear God, so many wounded, so many dead! If the war should end tomorrow, would there be anybody left? Before the question found an answer, Stonewall Jackson came, to lie in state in the Capitol, the braided left sleeve of his uniform coat empty, his face too still, his sleep at last quiet and unbroken. But what turned Flora fairly to stone was Mrs. Jackson, shrouded in crepe, clinging to the arm of her brother. How could she endure? Tomorrow and tomorrow and tomorrow after that? It called for more bravery than any mortal woman could muster.

Chapter 12. *"I Thought We Were Invincible"*

Ever since the late summer and fall of 1861, when, following the first battle of Manassas, he had set up his quarters at Fairfax Courthouse but slept by choice out on Munson's Hill, overlooking the valley of the Potomac and the cut stone and marble shining against green trees, which was the city of Washington, James Ewell Brown Stuart, militarily speaking, had been ruled by one dream. He would not rest content, he would not call himself or the South victorious until that proud city had been humbled. Take it? Perhaps not. But surely it was not beyond possibility that the arrogant men who now possessed it could be frightened into conceding that there could be two just sides to any argument and, because of differences that could not be reconciled, there should be two nations where formerly there had been one. Panic—that would do it. It was probably the only thing that would bring them to their senses, make them sit down and discuss a treaty of honorable separation.

He was always sure that this could happen and that he would have his proud share in the accomplishment. Lying now on a cot bed—it had been a cot ever since Charles Brewer had given him one and read him a lecture on how easy it was to contract rheumatism and how hard to be rid of it—under a tent fly on Fleetwood Hill near Culpeper this June of 1863, following the rout of Hooker at Chancellorsville, he thought perhaps the time had come. He was ready. The cavalry was ready. Ten thousand strong and all together, for a change, under his direct command. Lee's orders: "Keep your cavalry together."

"Stuart, it is said, has twenty thousand men in training near Culpeper. The speculation is that he is preparing for another grand ride."

Ah, the newspapers! Without them, a man would never know the magnitude of his greatness or the depths of his unworthiness. He wished he might have had twenty thousand instead of ten. At that rate, he'd have taken on the task of cowing Washington, unaided.

After Chancellorsville, he had asked permission to raise several more brigades of horse. He had mentioned Rosser, Wickham and Carey for promotion to the command of them. Lee nodded.

"I remember. It is to your credit that you have officers like them to call upon. Keep them ready. We may have need of them. Later. Right now . . ."

Stuart couldn't have his extra brigades. Men weren't to be had to fill the ranks. The heaviest losses at Chancellorsville were in the infantry. Those gaps had to be closed first. Stuart must make his present five brigades do. Bring them up to full strength, certainly, but . . . by the way, Lee was ordering John Imboden to report to his command.

Probably because he couldn't think where else to place him. John

Imboden and the West Virginia Guerrillas. As unruly a lot of fighting men as any army had ever known. Having John Imboden added to Grumble Jones and Peter Carey at this point of assembly was—well, maybe, healthful. Kept him from basking too comfortably in the friendship of men like the Lees or Wade Hampton or Galbraith Butler. Contrariwise, such friendships bolstered him against veiled or open antagonisms, if he had been one to fret over such trifles.

He wasn't, of course. Men's tempers were short when they handled their lives recklessly. Should have been the other way round, but it wasn't. Take Peter Carey now. He'd never told Pete that he had put his name down for promotion. He was not sure that Pete would have accepted the reward from him. The devil take that kind of obstinacy, anyhow!

Heigho! He must be aging, weakening somewhere, when such things began to matter. What mattered more was his pride in his cavalry corps. Ten thousand strong—well, more nearly nine thousand five hundred—but just about as right as cajolement, inspiration, reprimand and drill could make a body of men and horse. Next week, in a fine military gesture, he would present them to Robert E. Lee. It wasn't Stuart who was planning a grand ride this time. It was General Robert himself. That was why he had to have solid ranks in his infantry. He'd be ready soon to break away. Northward through the Shenandoah Valley, across into Maryland, on into Pennsylvania. He had not revealed to anyone of those with whom he discussed his general plan how far north he meant to march. Far enough to create a general Northern panic. Somewhere on the far side of the Pennsylvania line he would force a decision in battle.

Lee had no doubt that the decision would favor him and the South. To those who demurred, asking what if Hooker turned about and marched on Richmond, he said he had thought of that. Stuart's cavalry would guard his right as he took his command north, protecting all the passes through the Blue Ridge, screening his movements from the enemy, and would keep an eye simultaneously on Hooker, pestering him, prodding him, drawing him away, urging him northward, too, by a safely distant road, planting in Hooker's head, before the call came, the idea that it was Washington in danger now, not Richmond.

A proud assignment for a proud corps. It merited, Stuart thought, a parade. It had been a long time since he had staged a grand review. Too long, perhaps. This might be the best way to wind up training, let the men see themselves as a unit, let others see. Lee and Longstreet had said they would attend. Stuart had set the day. The men had been permitted to invite relatives and wives and sweethearts. There was room for all. The parade ground was a wide, level stretch near Brandy Station on the Orange and Alexandria Railroad. The railroad had agreed to run a special train and halt the cars there, to provide the spectators with seats in full view of the whole proceeding.

Flora was coming. Probably her last visit to camp this year. She had agreed willingly this time, finding no protest, to spend the summer at Laurel Hill, to await there the birth of the baby in the fall. Dear girl, brave girl, for all that she was subject at times to the upsurging of wild fears. A sweet wife, a devoted mother—she deserved a soldier's best. And she should have it. By autumn surely . . . he turned on his side, and went to sleep, smiling.

The review was magnificent. Only those not present had anything to say to the contrary.

"Such a beautiful day! Isn't it beautiful?" Flora rejoiced—so often that finally the Brewers and the Fontaines, who had made themselves her guard of honor, laughed at her.

"I never attended a parade that began so early," Maria yawned. "Do you know what time it is now? Five minutes before eight. And most of the men danced half the night away in Culpeper. It's a wonder they turned out."

"Probably thankful," her husband suggested, "that they weren't turned out earlier. It takes time for a single march past of ten thousand men."

Flora hardly heard them. Her heart, she thought, had never been so full. She had not wanted to miss a single bit of anything. Reveille had wakened her and after that she had been like an excited child, wanting everybody to hurry, hurry. They'd be late. They weren't, of course. Fortunately for her, others were as excited as she was, with less reason, naturally. By eight o'clock, assembly had been completed for spectators as well as the five brigades. The train of cars was in place, people swarming over them from roof to rail. She and her party held a place of honor in the Fontaines' carry-all, from which Charles Brewer had sternly ordered the horses to be removed. He would not chance a runaway. Everybody, Flora thought, so good to me now. She had never felt better in her life, or happier.

Eight o'clock on a fine June morning. The five brigades stiffly dressed in line—a line that was a mile and a half long. It reached clear across the field to a small branch at the base of a ridge of low hills. On the hills the batteries of the Stuart Horse Artillery were stationed. The sun, bright, but not yet hot, picked up flashes of metal everywhere. A breeze held company guidons out straight and swirled the heavier regimental banners. A fanfare brought the long line smartly to attention. The commanding general rode out upon the field.

"Stuart! Stuart!"

A cheer broke from the spectators, followed closely by a sigh. Lee was not there. At the last minute other duties had prevented his attendance. Even those who had heard he would not be present were disappointed afresh; but nobody, Flora knew, was more disappointed than Stuart. He had considered postponing the review, then had realized that he could not do that. Too many people had come up just for the day. None of that disappointment, however, showed in his manner now. He rode a tall bay horse, under absolute control. The plume on his hat had been freshly curled. He had for himself this year a new uniform coat, the buttons brightly shining, new gauntlet gloves of creamy doeskin, his boots oiled and shined, the gold spurs flashing.

"Dear God, he is a major-general," Flora thought, as if before this she had entertained a doubt, "but he still looks so young!"

So young compared to the division commanders who rode with him—Wade Hampton, who was much older, and Fitz Lee, who was his own age. Young, compared even to his aides, some of them just into their majority. Imperishably, immortally young. With his small personal retinue, he rode the length of the line. As he passed before each brigade, the brigadier-general waiting, with his staff, fell in behind Stuart. This continued to the far end of the field, where all turned in a pretty sweep past the left flank and began the march up the rear.

That completed, the brigadier-generals returned to their posts and

Stuart rode on to the reviewing stand—a knoll near the center of the parade. A little ahead of his escort always, he mounted it and for a brief minute sat there alone, so alone that Flora gave a sharp gasp. Charles Brewer looked at her in startled inquiry. She shook her head at him. She couldn't stop now to explain to him an old dream. The march past had begun.

Beautiful, solemn, dignified, the first march past. At a walk, the intervals clean and sharp and orderly. Then again, at a trot; and, as the first platoon of each column reached a line with the reviewing stand, a sharp order sent the horses into a gallop. Sabres came out and up. The rebel yell split the sky. Finally, though order was never lost, the whole field seemed a melee of dust and pounding hoofs and flashing swords and hoarse cries in chorus. When Beckham's batteries added a salvo of blanks for a final flourish, women fainted —from hunger, weariness, excitement, alarm. Flora's cheeks flamed.

"Thank you, God—for letting me see."

A magnificent show, with only one flaw, the absence of Lee. The thing was that, after that, there was always some circumstance, large or small, to mar the record. Two days later, when Lee did review his cavalry corps, asking to have the ceremony shortened and no galloping of the horses, please, because he was making ready now to begin his march northward, Grumble Jones was late in bringing his brigade into line. Pure recalcitrance and Stuart covered the delay, but the day lacked, to him at least, verve and glitter and sound.

General Hooker was pleased to supply the lack of sound. That night his cavalry came over the Rappahannock by three different roads and in the small hours of the morning roared down on Stuart's camp. His critics said afterward that, intent on display, he had failed to station sufficient guards on the river roads. He had his pickets and outposts in position; but, when night fell, there was no sign of the enemy across the river. This was just a well-covered and well-executed surprise attack. The Yankees were learning. They were bringing up better men. In the thick of the fighting, Stuart noted one lot, in particular, wearing special uniform—black hats with rolled brims, and blue shirts with long red neckties streaming back over their shoulders.

"Custer's command," Tom Rosser told him. "George Custer. He

was in my class at the Point. Had a taste then for high jinx and fancy clothes." He hesitated, and went on. "I'll be glad to singe his feathers for him, if you give me leave."

"We'll give him our special attention henceforth," Stuart promised.

He wasn't joking. He could never joke about the battle of Brandy Station. He nearly tasted disaster there. Not until Beckham had his guns in position for telling fire, did the tide change. After that the Yankees soon had enough. Withdrawing, they left close to a thousand men behind, wounded, dead or captive; but Stuart, too, had lost six hundred, among them Rooney Lee, with a bullet in his thigh.

Lee begged to remain with his command. A few days by ambulance, and he knew he could ride again; but the surgeons said, "Better not." It should have been Richmond for him then, but nothing would satisfy his wife but that he should be taken to Hickory Hill, her home, instead. She cried, and Stuart gave in. A week later the Yankees surrounded Hickory Hill and made Rooney prisoner. It would be a long while before the Confederates satisfied their terms for an exchange.

This was a telling blow. Big, easy-going, genial Rooney Lee, never thrusting himself forward, but always there. Steady as a rock. He could hold a ford or a bridge while an army crossed and turn in, smiling, after the last man was over, not before. Stuart must march north now without him.

The march north began two weeks later than planned. Two weeks over the middle of June made a difference. The sun was higher and hotter. Men and horses tired sooner. Still, good progress was made. The cavalry rode the eastern slope of the Blue Ridge, between Lee's infantry and Hooker. There were skirmishes at most of the passes, but the cavalry came out of each victoriously, spoiling the enemy's reconnaissance and taking few losses, although at Upperville Heros von Borcke took a bullet in his throat and nearly choked and bled to death before a surgeon saved him. Stuart sent him under guard to Richmond, but could not stop longer, to show the concern he really felt. Personally he was watching Hooker, balancing, judging his movements. If he could pull out in pursuit, harass him, herd him in the proper direction, execute a really "grand ride" that would paralyze him and those over him, Lee's march had double the chance of a triumphant finish.

Stuart was always sure that, if he could have taken all his cavalry, his plan would have succeeded. Lee, thinking of the safety of his infantry, said no. Two brigades must be left to guard the mountains and screen his advance. With the rest, Stuart could turn east, keep close watch on Hooker, parallel his advance into Maryland, if possible, if not, cling to the rear of his army, doing the damage possible, collecting provisions and so on. If or when it looked too difficult to remain close to Hooker's flank, he was to abandon all idea of a separate advance and turn west to join the main army. It was expected that, considering the relative speed of cavalry and infantry on the march, he would arrive in Maryland about the time that Ewell, leading Lee's advance, crossed the line farther to the west. Stuart was to keep in communication with Ewell. Always.

These were the orders that he tucked away as, minus two fighting brigades, he set out about midnight of the twenty-fourth of June. Finally his success or failure would depend on what turns of circumstance he met and how he met them. On good or bad fortune. If his luck held . . .

It didn't. It rained that night, and every day for three days following. On the twenty-eighth he had reached his old camp ground at Fairfax. One day's ride in his best style would have taken him farther. The rain was an excellent screen but bad in every other way. The men were already miserably uncomfortable, and their horses hungry. Forage in that part of Virginia was failing.

Perhaps he should have turned back then. He couldn't. Hooker was still moving northward. Fitz Lee and Rosser took over the scouting, and Stuart was able to send a message back to Lee, giving him the position of Hooker's command, converging now on Leesburg, making ready to cross the Potomac, Stuart close on his left and rear.

It was his last report to Lee. He could not give even this messenger explicit directions as to where to find the commanding general. As for General Ewell, with whom he was to keep in constant communication, he could more easily have located a particular jack rabbit on a Kansas prairie. Somewhere on his left and probably north of him now, well ahead of cavalry protection.

Under these generally unfavorable conditions, but still with high hope of success, Stuart crossed the Potomac into Maryland. He was as close as safety allowed to Hooker. His men could light their fires from the embers left by the Yankees. If only there had been time to let the horses graze!

There was never time enough for anything. At a place called Rockville, they captured a train of one hundred and twenty-five wagons and took four hundred prisoners. A glorious thing on one of the old marches. Not this one. No men to spare as guards. They had to parole the prisoners and let them go.

On the second day after crossing the Potomac, they learned from prisoners that Hooker was in Frederick, Maryland, and Ewell was already in Pennsylvania. Stuart was now on Hooker's right—between him and Washington, but hardly between him and Lee. The cavalry tore up some railroad track, for what inconvenience that might create, and rode on.

North, as directly as they could. No chance now of moving west to contact their infantry. North, and keep feeling for Ewell. Just keep feeling.

They began to pick up pockets of Federal cavalry. They pulled out of each skirmish in good style, but every brush diverted the march a little more to the eastward. Bad, though not necessarily disastrous; but the column had begun to straggle. Men and horses were tiring. If they won an engagement, they couldn't follow up with an attack. They couldn't harvest their best opportunities.

On the first day of July, in a very fog of weariness, they made their stubborn way to Carlisle, Pennsylvania, and began a slow shelling of the town. Why? There was food in Carlisle, and they were hungry. More hungry than tired, maybe. When they had taken the town, they would fill themselves, feed their horses, and load what remained into the one hundred and twenty-five wagons, empty now, but still with them. Steadfastly Stuart had held to his belief that Lee would have use for the wagons. And then? Then, perhaps an hour or two for shopping. Every man in the command had carried a list of wants from Virginia. Stuart had two—Flora's and Maria Brewer's.

Sitting his tired horse, watching the not too effective bombardment of the town, he became aware suddenly of a stir in the ranks behind him. Looking that way, he saw the men, by squadrons and platoons, sliding from their horses, dropping on the ground, their bridles over their arms. The horses, sighing, lowered their heads and browsed over the trampled stubble. A messenger—it looked like one of his own, though mounted on a plow horse—seemed to be giving some word as he passed along the column. He worked his clumsy mount up to Stuart, saluted groggily, and spoke in a kind of raven's croak.

"Beg to report . . . I found them, sir . . . the army."

And Stuart remembered. A scout, sent east from Dover. This morning or was it yesterday?

"Hid my horse in a hayfield. Borrowed this one. Slow, but . . ."

"The army you speak of? Stick to your report, man. Where?"

"Gettysburg, sir. We come too far."

"Never mind that now. Early's command? Ewell?"

"All of them, sir. There's been some fighting and you're to come at once. General Lee's orders, sir."

Stuart jerked himself full awake. He sent the messenger on the plow horse back down the lines to meet General Hampton at the head of the rear guard and turn him by the nearest road to Gettysburg. He got his own tired, hungry men up off the ground and back on their jaded horses and turned them, too.

On the morning of the second day of July, the second day of the battle of Gettysburg, he reported at last to General Lee, with whom things had gone even worse than they had with Stuart. Lee was ill, a victim of the old camp malady that spared nobody—dysentery; but he sat his gray horse as proudly as ever there on Seminary Ridge, looking over the little town and its ring of smoking hills; and Stuart took from him there the one reprimand Lee ever gave him:

"Well, General Stuart, you are here at last!"

At last. His cavalry, for all he knew, asleep in roadside ditches all the way north to Carlisle. Not all asleep. They roused to give battle when danger threatened; and they were wakeful enough when at last the order came for them to cover the retreat.

Lee's words then to those who commanded under him were gentle enough: "Never mind. It's all my fault. I thought we were invincible."

Chapter 13. *"I'd Rather Die"*

The baby was born in October, a girl, beautiful, with silky golden hair—it would turn darker, everyone said—and the bluest of blue eyes. A perfect baby, sound and well. All babies born that fall and winter were not so blessed. That the child was healthy and proportionately well-behaved, that she herself came back to full health soon after the birth, Flora credited to her good fortune in having a safe retreat like Laurel Hill, still supplied with home-cured meat and milk and butter and fruit and vegetables, though a little short on such staples as flour, for example. She felt shame, remembering how once she had wailed that she had never felt so alone. She was surrounded by staunch friends—well, if not exactly surrounded, still she could name a number.

Alec telegraphed to Stuart the news of the baby's arrival, and Flora followed the message with frequent reports. He couldn't come, and this time she was able to accept the fact. He was busy recruiting new brigades and getting them into fighting shape. No parades now. Just battle training. A Federal army under General Meade had followed Lee's retreat into Virginia. The new general seemed indisposed to try a grand assault, but a person could never be sure. The cavalry was busy, playing fox and geese around his flanks, making themselves out to be more numerous and deadly than they really were.

Stuart seemed in wonderful spirits. Whatever bitterness he might have tasted in Gettysburg, he, like most others, had swallowed up north. He had no explanations to make, no apologies to offer. He had no comment except the necessary written reports, in which he spoke feelingly, as always, of "my brave men." The cavalry swung back over the Potomac with undiminished swagger, the Richmond papers again marveling that they could frolic as they did. A little of that, a taste of welcome, and then into the saddles again for whatever offered.

Plenty offered. Neither Richmond nor Patrick County saw anything of J. E. B. Stuart that autumn. Part of the time he rode in active command of Hampton's division, Wade Hampton being out now with wounds. Rooney Lee was still a prisoner, Colonel Chambliss taking his brigade. Stuart spoke of Chambliss often in his letters, and of Rosser and Wickham and, now and then, Peter Carey. There were, besides, two new men, whom Flora could not identify—Gordon and Young. His new aides, Majors McClellan and Venable, were all any commander could ask. Finally, in an exchange of troops with the Confederate army in Tennessee, he had the inexpressible joy, he wrote, of welcoming Lunsford Lomax. It seemed to Flora that she could hear his jubilance clear down in Saltville.

She herself sang softly, under her breath, these days, looking forward to a visit from her general. Surely by Christmas, at the latest, he would find a way. The christening, she wrote him, would wait on his coming.

"I mark off the days one by one," she wrote, "until I can show you your daughter. Oh, my darling, wherever you are, whatever you are doing, God keep you and return you safely to us soon."

Just riding around and up and down, he said afterwards, harassing General Meade. Sometimes carrying things off with a high hand, sometimes taking grave risks. Flora studied each letter he wrote, to get its full import.

Toward the end of November, the weather turned bitterly cold; and, by some sign mutually recognized, the fighting of the weary year of 1863 was over. On a late afternoon in December, Flora, wiping light frost off a window pane that looked out toward the lane leading to the house, thought she heard someone singing, and, rubbing harder, sharpened her ears to listen. The sound swelled, became clearer:

> "In the sweet bye and bye,
> We shall meet on that beautiful shore . . ."

"Stuart!" she cried, and ran for the door.

Almost immediately, from the second floor, Mrs. Stuart called querulously, "Flora? Is that you keeping the front door open? We'll all catch our deaths."

Stuart, dismounting at the gate, heard the protesting cry, looked up at the house, smiled as if it had been a bar of longed-for music, then saw his wife, and hurried forward. As his arms went around her, suction brought the offending door to with a bang that neither heard. Was it cold in the house? It was like spring outside.

"So long," Flora murmured over and over. "So long!"

"*Ma povere petite!*" Stuart spread his cape across her quivering shoulders. "*Ma povere petite!*"

He knelt now beside the baby's cradle. He had greeted his mother, brushed his clothes and warmed himself. He would eat later.

"My stomach has learned to wait its turn," he assured both solicitous women.

The baby first. She had slept through his arrival but was awake now, stirring, expectant, but not demanding. The best of babies!

"Beautiful!" Stuart knelt, worshiping, his left arm around his three-year-old son. Flora sat on the far side of the room, studying fondly the two brown heads, so blessedly together. By God's grace and so long as He willed it, her menfolk. Reassured as to that, her eyes went on to trace more particularly the lines of Stuart's back, the square set of his shoulders, the bend of his long arms—oh, even the soles of his boots. When a woman had had only memory, or a flat, black and white purported likeness or a phantom image to contemplate for months on end, reality was hardly to be grasped all at once.

"Did you come alone?" she had asked earlier.

Stuart had made a face before he answered.

"Venable or Mac will be showing up some time—too soon, I'm afraid."

When they came . . . but she would not think of that.

Presently it was time for Jimmie to have his supper and be put to bed.

"I'll take him down to Tilda," Flora said to Stuart, "if you don't mind waiting here?"

"What a question!" Stuart dropped back on his heels and drew the boy close. "I'll take a hug and squeeze for good night, young man. Does a kiss go with it? I should say it does. That was a big one. Now, off you go. Mommie's orders."

By the way he didn't turn to look at her, Flora knew that his eyes were wet. Her own filled as she led Jimmie away. As they left, a fretting from the cradle made her pause. She heard Stuart get to his feet. The cradle creaked and the fretting stopped. Before it could begin again or Jimmie could raise a question, she hurried on to the stairs; but her ears, sharpened to catch the least sound, picked up footfalls and a fancied subdued crooning:

"*Frera Jocko . . . Frera Jocko . . .*"

"Papa's singing," Jimmie said. "To the baby?"

"Yes, darling, yes. Let's hurry now, and see about that supper."

"James has changed," his mother said; and so did others, provoking Flora to a denial of what she herself felt to be true, though she could not define the alteration, unless it was that he was more tender when moved to tenderness, gentler, when that mood was on him.

Or, he could be harder than Flora had ever known him to be, when that mood came. Rooney Lee was still a prisoner, his wife desperately ill and begging to see him. Letters had gone to Abraham Lincoln. Custis Lee had offered himself in Rooney's place, he having no wife or family. But all pleas had been denied.

"I can't talk about it," Stuart said, his eyes like banked fires when a wind fans the embers.

"Yes, he has changed," Flora said firmly, ending argument. "He's older. He'll be thirty-one in January. And now, wouldn't you like to know what we've decided to call the baby?"

Virginia Pelham Stuart. A proud name for a lady to carry all her life. A name with sound and deep meaning. Just saying it told all anyone needed to know. Virginia . . . Pelham . . . Stuart.

"I declare, I never saw the like of your husband, Mrs. Stuart. It seems impossible that so much vitality could be packed into one human frame. After all he's been through, too . . ."

That was Richmond in February. Flora and the children were visiting the Brewers, who could wait no longer to see the baby. Charles wanted to see Flora, as well.

"Fine," he pronounced mother and child, "but better accept that invitation from the Fontaines. Richmond's no place for you now."

No place for anyone whose home or whose work was not there. Maria bore up well. And Lucy Carey, her children still in South

Carolina, had returned. She was, amazingly, nursing in the hospitals. Flora wouldn't believe she could until she saw her—a pale, soft-spoken Madonna whom sick men followed with their eyes whenever she moved among them.

"She has a deft touch," Charles Brewer said, "but if she were of no account that way, it would do the men good just to see her. Confidentially, I think her inspiration was her husband. Pete came tearing down when he heard she was here, determined to send her packing, and fell in love all over again, seeing her in this new guise. Then it was her turn to use a few sharp words. You should have seen that redhead back down. 'I'd crawl on my hands and knees to her, doc,' he said to me, 'but it wouldn't do a bit of good. Only way I can get her attention now is to be kissed by a Yankee bullet. I'm going out to find one.' And I shouldn't wonder if . . . forgive me, sis. A clumsy joke."

Flora understood about Lucy. She had been desperate to see her husband, no matter what had passed between them at the meeting. Flora was in Richmond herself, not because of the Brewers, but because Stuart these days was in and out of the city, his cavalry headquarters between there and Fredericksburg. It had been no light matter to get herself and the two small children and Tilda ready. There had been some question about bringing Tilda, but the girl herself settled that by going to Stuart.

"Effen de chillun's away, dey ain' too much to do roun' yere," she argued. "Reckon dey kin git along without me."

"Reckon they'll have to," Stuart said. "Anyhow, you're Miss Flora's girl; and whatever happens, you are to stay with her always. Always, do you hear?"

"Yassah. Dat's wot I tell her an' ev'ybody."

So, here they all were in Richmond. Stuart and Fitz Lee together were also there—on military business. And here was this party at the home of Mrs. Admiral Semmes. A starvation party. Meaning you went after supper and danced and sang and played charades and there was fun, but no refreshments. The stage was being set now in the back parlor for a charade, and Major-General Stuart had the honor of being one leg to a stile on which sat the prettiest girl in Richmond that winter. He did not carry off that honor with his usual aplomb. Either he had his mind on some other problem or the general construction of the stile was at fault. Presently there was a rending crash in the back parlor. It looked from up front as if one end of the stage had collapsed. And so it had. Fitz Lee finally scrambled out of chaos to make a statement.

"Kindly keep your seats, ladies and gentlemen. There is no cause for alarm. We've had a misadventure, merely. I am sorry to inform you that General Stuart has been found guilty of a soldier's most serious offense—sleeping at the post of duty. For his sins he has now been banished to the audience and I will carry on in his place. Ready in a jiffy."

He disappeared; and the laughter and applause that followed him greeted Stuart next, as he came out of the wreckage, ruddy, unperturbed, laughing with the rest, and crossed the room to Flora's chair.

"Did you?" Flora asked.

"No," Stuart said. "Of course not. I was smothering under that curtain."

But suppose he had dozed off? Suppose . . .

"Dear," Flora said, "it's a charming party, but we can't stay. That is, I can't. Would you want to send someone else home with me?"

Stuart shook his head. He was ready to leave at any time. And then, clear as an alarm bell, Flora heard their hostess in the hall, welcoming another guest.

"Good evening, Major Venable. What a pleasant surprise! That is, unless you've come to break up my party."

And Venable's reply. Had he been correctly informed? Was General Stuart present?

1864—the end of April. Beaver Dam now, and Tilda had been out gathering pokeberry shoots for greens.

"I never thought I'd see the day," Mrs. Fontaine said, viewing the pale green tufts with deep suspicion.

"You gotta bile 'em an' dreen 'em," Tilda explained. "We only feeds 'em raw to Yankees. Dey's pizen raw but real nice cooked."

"Tilda," Flora said, "you didn't . . ."

"No'm, I ain' seed nobody—man, woman or chile. Ef dar wuz sojers, dar wouldn't be greens. I stay close lak you say—found dese in de woods pasture."

It seemed strange here in this quiet place to have to caution

Tilda about soldiers, strays from either army. So far, none had been
seen, but Stuart himself had given the order. "Don't go off alone,
afoot or driving. Keep Tilda and the children under your eye. Don't
be afraid, but stay close."

Don't be afraid. The battle line was no nearer than last year's. It
was a surprise crossing of the Rapidan that had called Stuart away
from Richmond in February, but it hadn't amounted to much. The
raiders had been driven back. Their aim might have been merely to
draw attention from another thrust at the capital, made this time
by a man named Dahlgren, who had a mad idea that he could get
through and hang the leaders of the Confederacy. He hadn't succeeded. The city's defenses had held, and Dahlgren had died with
his threats in his throat. Still, you never could tell. General Lee was
taking no chances. With Stuart's cavalry riding patrol and furnishing
intelligence, he was again massing his armies south of that long line
reaching from Fredericksburg to the fords of the Rapidan. Beaver
Dam was now a base of supplies, with a warehouse and a guard.
That was why Stuart had spoken of soldiers.

The battle lines were no nearer, but nobody could deny that there
was a different feel to the situation. Without being downright afraid,
a person could be apprehensive. It was, Flora and many others
thought, the new Union commander. That General Grant who had
mounted stubbornly to the top Federal command out west—Forts
Henry and Donelson, Shiloh, Vicksburg, Chattanooga—had been
moved east. Was he the seventh or the eighth to take over there?
He didn't look like any of the things one heard him called—brutish,
dissolute, brilliant, inexorable. He seemed from printed photographs
a fairly young man, not young like Stuart, but much younger than
General Lee, his hair and close-cropped beard dark, his forehead
smooth, his eyes straightforward, his expression pleasant, if anything
in particular.

It was just a feeling, but it was there. There was this supply depot
at Beaver Dam. And Stuart had been given a third division of cavalry. It was not known yet whether Rooney Lee or another would
command it. Rooney had come home in March, not well and grief-
stricken over the death of his wife and both his children. Everything seemed—well, chancey, for want of a better word. Flora sent
Tilda now back to the kitchen to wash and "bile and dreen" her

greens, while she fed the baby and then went to sit with Mrs. Fontaine on the front porch and wait for the Colonel and Jimmie to come back from the village with the Richmond paper and the mail. She tried not to watch the road, but at the first sound of wheels was on her feet and out on the lawn.

As the wagon rattled past her and on to the barn, Jimmie called an ecstatic greeting and waved a bulky object, all but spilling himself overboard as he did so. The thing proved to be a wooden stool, as stubby-legged as Jimmie himself. A guard at the warehouse had made it for him.

"And did he say, darling, 'My, what a grubby little boy!'" Flora asked, kissing his cheek.

"No'm. He said . . . you tell her," Jimmie commanded Colonel Fontaine.

"He said," the Colonel obeyed, "for little Jeb Stuart, Junior."

And then Jeb, Junior, trying to sit his stool with his legs crossed as he'd seen men do, did go overboard; and everybody had a big laugh, the Colonel showing him finally how to prop himself against a wall before he tried again.

"Any news in that letter you've read three times?" the Colonel asked Flora.

"Nothing special. You asked if Stuart knew General Sheridan, the new commander of Northern cavalry. He says, 'Of course, I know him. He was at West Point when I was. We were not close friends, but I remember him well. A dark, stubborn little fellow, with bad bursts of temper. I thought he had gone into the infantry; but, then, I've promoted many an infantry captain to a horse myself.' He sends his love to both of you."

Colonel Fontaine looked after her thoughtfully as she took Jimmie into the house, to clean him up for dinner.

"I think we'll lose the Richmond paper, mother," he said. "It says the campfires at night north of the Rapidan are too many to count. I tell you, I don't like that man Grant having command."

Nor did anyone else south of the Rapidan.

"One thing I hold against him," Fitz Lee said, as he reported to Stuart at Spotsylvania Courthouse three days later, to receive final instructions before Stuart rode west to make sure that A. P. Hill's

corps was tucked in tightly against Dick Ewell's on the left end of
the line, where Lee again was certain the first thrust would come,
"is that he keeps his supply trains too far to the rear. Used to be I
could count on a percentage of their corn. Now, how am I to feed
my nags?"

"I don't know," Stuart answered, "but it seems to me I've been
hearing that question or one like it from you for a long time now.
Hold the line, fellow, will you, while I'm gone? You've got Lomax,
Wickham, Gordon . . ."

"I know whom I have of our own," Lee said. "What for infantry?"

"Anderson," Stuart began. "Heth . . ."

"Enough. We'll make out. Hurry back, will you?"

Simultaneously, on a shared impulse, their hands went out and
gripped hard.

"Good-bye. Watch yourself now."

Fitz Lee leaned far in his saddle until his friend and commanding officer was lost to sight among the trees. He'd never been so
sorry to see the back of anyone.

If he had not ridden the route so often of late, Stuart would not
have recognized the countryside. It was not possible to encamp
armies, even one's own, on land without destroying it. Everywhere
was ruin, and a kind of dead, barren blight. Things could hardly
look worse if the enemy had broken through. They'd find lean pick-
ings if . . . but they had not broken through and they would not.
The line was too thin, the divisions too extended; but the men were
full of fight.

General Robert E. Lee welcomed him warmly.

"I hardly hoped to see you in person, sir. Your reports have been
a great help and say without words how you've been busy."

"Riding my picket lines, sir. I like to every so often."

"I know."

"And I thought I might perhaps be of service to General Hill,
having fought over this territory several times now and knowing
the roads."

Fitz Lee knew them better; but, in view of late news on the right
end of the line, which Stuart had just left, only Fitz would do as a
substitute for himself there; and he felt that he wanted to discuss
personally with General Robert this special report.

"You are sure you have no other news for me, Stuart?"

"I have, sir. A force of Federal cavalry, its size undetermined," his scouts said it was thirteen and a half miles long in column formation, "but probably considerable, Sheridan commanding, has been observed near Fredericksburg, making ready to move southward, is probably doing so now."

"Another raid on Richmond?" Lee suggested.

"A raid in force if the reports are true."

"They must be halted."

"Yes, sir. We will divert them, if possible, hold them as we can. But we lack the strength for a prolonged battle. We shall need infantry support."

Again they studied a map together, Stuart showing his cavalry posts.

"I will relieve each brigade of yours as I can," Lee promised. "And if all goes well and I can spare a regiment or two of foot, I'll send them. Have you any preference?"

"The nearest," Stuart said, unhesitatingly, knowing who that would be.

Off then, to play wilderness scout to A. P. Hill's corps, led still by men calling themselves the Stonewall Brigade.

"Old Joe Hooker, won't you come out of the Wilderness?"

No doleful malingering this time. They took up the song with a roar.

On the back track finally, stopping for a word with Tom Rosser, settling his brigade in line against nobody knew how many times its number, cautioning Rosser to get his horses in a safe spot to the rear, to be ready when needed.

Halfway back to Spotsylvania he had a scrawled line from Fitz Lee: "I think you'd better come fast now."

Faster than fast. At Todd's Tavern old Fitz sat, peering through the trees as if he hadn't stirred since Stuart had left. Stuart charged him with it, laughing.

"You fool!" Lee said. "You ultra-ultra jackass! Listen now."

Sheridan's column was already on the Telegraph Road south of Fredericksburg riding for Richmond. It numbered anywhere from ten to fifteen thousand men.

"They must be halted," Stuart repeated.

"Right!" Lee agreed. "You say how."

Stuart took out a scrap of paper and began sketching roads, all sharply clear in his mind. He spotted each of his five available brigades—one to ride to the rear of the Yankee column, one to either side and two in front. He sent for the young brigadiers and, for once, there was glory and death enough to go around. They assembled their commands and rode away, shouting. They rode away to harass the Yankee column from the rear, cut the rear guard away if they could, then pull out for safety. They rode to take watch beside the pike and charge the Yankees marching and so, off-balance. Across the line of Sheridan's advance they dismounted and hid in cross ditches, and had their rifles and pistols ready for the hot fire of ambush. Fitz Lee took command of one of those death-before-dishonor brigades up front, Stuart took the other. Each had the support of one piece of artillery.

For two days this went on. They slowed Sheridan's advance, but they could not stop it. All the while, to the west, the battle of the Wilderness raged. They saw the awfulness of the woods on fire between them and Lee's center and left, and they had no clear idea how things were going—not until suddenly a regiment of Union infantry appeared where they had looked to meet only horsemen. Then Stuart knew. Grant's army had been checked on the Rapidan and he was shifting his line.

Behind the Union lines, vast wagon trains and herds of cattle and mules were hurrying eastward. The two friends looked at each other gravely. The situation, bad enough before, was worse now. Stuart sent a courier to the commanding general with this report. But, that routine duty performed, he still faced disaster. Where would his infantry reinforcements come from now? The Wilderness was still afire.

His courier, returning, brought Lee's acknowledgment of the news and word that, to make more rapid the movement of men and guns, Lee's engineers had begun to hack a road through the blazing forest. It seemed to Stuart an impossible thing to attempt and he sent young Henry McClellan to Richmond with a warning to General Bragg commanding the defenses there. Major McClellan would tell Bragg how desperate things were.

Hours later, enough supporting infantry had made its way out of the Wilderness to enable Stuart to give full attention once more to Sheridan's column. By then part of it—some said the main force—had got by to the south and, instead of continuing on to Richmond, had turned west, making apparently for the line of the Virginia Central Railroad, Lee's supply route for the center and left of his armies. Mention was made of Beaver Dam.

The warehouses, Stuart thought, Flora and the children. The reserve supplies—Flora and the children. No, he told himself. He must keep his mind cold and clear and settled on the military problem. He did not think Sheridan would send his main force so far out of line, but he could spare a brigade. He, Stuart, must know. Again he turned over to Fitz Lee all his cavalry available except one brigade, Gordon's, and with that one he set out across country toward Beaver Dam.

A map was in his saddle bags, a sharper, clearer one in his mind. A side road to Davenport's Bridge over the North Anna. Not obstructed. No enemy cavalry. Another south from there. Another. . . .

He and Gordon and the brigade rode out the night, unopposed except by mortal weariness. Morning came with the reddest dawn Stuart had ever seen. Then he realized that dawn could not come from that southwesterly direction. The glow was fire. He was too late.

Still he must know. A mile or so farther, tongues of flame now showing where the warehouses burned, dawn spreading a pale light over all the sky, he halted the brigade under cover of trees, the men falling from their saddles like sacks of coal, and started on alone.

Gordon rode after him.

"Let me, sir, please. I beg. I insist."

"No," Stuart said. "Stay with your command. I order you."

A minute later there was another.

"It's just me, sir. Reid Venable."

They could smell the fire now, then the reek of food—good bacon and hams and flour burning to soot and cinders. There was no shooting. No, that would have been earlier. A little later, the sergeant commanding the warehouse guard stood in the road, his pistol cocked, but dropping now at the end of a limp arm.

"It's you, sir? I coulda dremp' . . ." He shifted the pistol and saluted raggedly. "All clear, sir. All clear of enemy, that is."

"Who set the fires?"

"We did, sir. Orders of General Lee, in case of enemy in force approaching. They come in the night, sir, by train. Stopped down the line to put water in the locomotive. We got word. We set the fires then."

"Did they come on?" Stuart had to know. "Did you see them?"

"Yes, sir, they come on. Two trainloads, one right behind t'other. But when they seen the stores all gone up in smoke, they held a pow-wow and pretty soon they began backing down the line again. Reckon they backed all the way to where they come from. We . . . we hid, sir."

Of course. The only thing to do. Two trainloads. Two trains seized. More supplies possibly, going to the front. They'd backed out, gone. Less than a mile away, over Stuart's right shoulder as he sat now, a white house stood back from a country road, among trees. There the most of everything that made life worth living slept safely. Thank God for his family's safety. That, at least. He opened his saddle bags and took out his map. He had to instruct Gordon on how best to rejoin Fitz Lee. Scanning the map, he thought he heard a moan.

"Yes, sir. They had prisoners. I don't know where from. They dumped 'em. Abandoned 'em, sir, wounded, not knowing . . . we put them in the depot, sir."

"I'll send help," Stuart promised.

He dictated his order for Gordon to Venable.

"Tell him," he concluded, "I'll join him within the hour. I won't tarry."

"Yes, sir." Venable turned his horse, then turned again. "Please give my regards to Mrs. Stuart. Tell her I am with you, if you remember."

"I'll tell her. She will take comfort from it, I am sure."

In the big house among the trees, only the children, creatures of habit, still slept. Mrs. Fontaine, wakeful in the night, had seen the fire first. She roused the Colonel. They had wondered what to do about waking others, then had concluded that the grown-ups might better rise and get into their clothes. Also, it would be well to warn the servants before they took fright on their own account.

All had watched from upstairs windows until the fierceness of the fire subsided. Then, since there was no further alarm, Colonel Fontaine apologetically unbuckled the belt with pistols that he had put on at the beginning, and went out to see that his stock was being fed.

"I don't suppose anybody is ready for breakfast," Mrs. Fontaine said, but went to the kitchen with Tilda.

Flora, on the point of following, stepped out to take one more look from the front porch, then lingered, because she thought she heard a horse down the road. When the rider appeared, she was glad to see his gray uniform but did not think of its being Stuart because of the dragging gait of the horse. Not until he turned at the gate; but then she was halfway down the path.

How tired he was, she thought, as he leaned from the saddle to kiss her, but not nearly so tired as his horse. He would not dismount, could not take time for breakfast. He had to rejoin his command. He asked about the babies and Tilda and the Fontaines, about their alarm in the night. All over now, he said, the enemy gone, and told her what had taken place. He told her how he happened to be near. Just chance. On his way to Richmond now. He told her how the battle of the Wilderness had gone, so far as he knew. He had no doubt that Lee would throw the Yankees back now at Spotsylvania, and that the cavalry and General Bragg would save Richmond.

A quiet, married talk. Would she be going back to Laurel Hill soon? He thought that the best place now for her. She must not think she was ever a burden to the family.

He told her about the wounded men at the Beaver Dam depot. If later in the morning she could go down and help them? She promised she would go right after breakfast. He all but forgot Reid Venable's message. They laughed about that. He leaned from his saddle to give her good-bye. This time he held her chin in his hand a few seconds, studying her face, before he kissed her.

Their words were what they had been countless times before: "Good-bye. God bless you and keep you, my darling, my darling!"

Within an hour after overtaking Gordon, Stuart was riding knee to knee with Fitz Lee and hearing the latest intelligence. Tracking Sheridan from the rear had amounted to riding fairly close to Gordon and Stuart. The main Federal column was bearing south still, but

well to the west now of the Telegraph Road, making apparently for
a bridge over the South Anna River. That would be the Mountain
Road, a thoroughfare leading from Louisa and points west into Richmond. Leaving Gordon's exhausted men to the duty now of reconnaissance from the rear, Stuart, with Lee, turned the rest back to the
Telegraph Road, his best chance to reach the capital in time to help
Bragg. Wishing that he might know Bragg's strength, he sent him
word of his position and plan. If Sheridan got to the defenses first
and attacked, the cavalry would make an assault from the rear. If
this proved to be only a diversionary raid and Sheridan turned about,
to rejoin Grant, the cavalry would pursue. He hoped that the message would put Bragg on guard without indicating the failing
strength of that promised cavalry.

It took the column all day to reach the Telegraph Road. Everywhere there was evidence of Sheridan's march in trees felled for
obstacles, in bridges down. When the weary horses staggered into
Hanover Junction, where the Virginia Central and the Richmond-
Fredericksburg railroads crossed, there was no pursuit left in anybody. The men fell out and down by squadrons. Fitz Lee slipped
from his horse and settled himself on the ground against a tree.

"You can sleep until . . ." Stuart began. Fitz snored.

Well, presumably Yankee horses also must rest some of the time.
Stuart looked at his two aides and picked McClellan to stand guard
over Fitz. He was to rouse the sleeping General at one in the morning, then report to Stuart, who, with Venable, would ride a couple
of miles farther—to the next town, if they could. They made it; but
it seemed to him that he had hardly settled himself there under half
of Venable's blanket before Henry McClellan had him by the shoulder, telling him that Fitz Lee was up and making ready to move.
Before Venable and Stuart were clear of the blanket, Mac had it,
dead to the world and all its wars. A courier arrived from Fitz Lee.
He was marching. Stuart left the courier to watch McClellan until
his nap was out, and turned his horse south.

A dreary march for a Stuart, not like any in times past. No need to
order caution or silence. The men rode in a half stupor, between
sleep and waking. Poor devils, they couldn't even feel how hungry
they were.

Near Ashland, they roused to the smell of smoke off to the right.

Scouts reported a warehouse burning, six miles of the Richmond-Fredericksburg tracks destroyed, and a handful of bluecoats making nuisances of themselves still in the town. Two companies of the Second Virginia rode off, followed by subdued cheering. A half hour later they swung back into line, leading a huddle of prisoners.

Men of the First Massachusetts Volunteers. No time to question them in detail, but Stuart had no doubt now that Sheridan's main line was advancing on his right. The incident, indicating the approach of action, roused his men further. There was talk, even laughter back through the files now.

At seven o'clock the first of the column, crossing the South Anna, reported rifle fire off to the right. Gordon, carrying out his orders for rear guard molestation. Good boy. Hold them, fellow. Hold them if you can.

At eight, Stuart halted the march. He had reached a crossroads, marked by an alehouse known as Yellow Tavern. Here the Mountain Road from Louisa and the Telegraph Road from the north joined the Brook Turnpike, leading into the city of Richmond. They were only a short distance from the "Outer Defenses," those ditches Lee had dug in the spring of '62; and, on neither the turnpike nor the Mountain Road was there a sign of Yankee cavalry. The impossible had been achieved. Stuart's cavalry was between Sheridan and the capital.

The situation called for study. Stuart lacked the power to go forward and risk a head-on battle with Sheridan's advance. The best he could do was to put his men in a favorable position to strike from the side when Sheridan came on, as he must do presently, if he meant to attack. He sent a final message to Bragg. "My men are now between the enemy and the capital. They are tired and hungry and their horses in poor condition, but both are magnificent." Bragg was to relay the message to Lee, if he could.

Next he ordered his battle formations. Half of his force he ordered into a ditch paralleling the Telegraph Road, Wickham commanding. The others under Lomax formed behind a rail fence and a little creek, almost at right angles to the Wickham line and facing a small patch of woods. It was a thin line to take the first assault, but it was backed by another ditch deep enough to hold reserves, and covered by guns on a small hill near by.

Just before noon Stuart rode both lines, to have a word with the men himself. Halfway down Wickham's position, the colonel of a mountain regiment whipped his hat off a thatch of copper hair, to wave a greeting. Stuart halted.

"Pete! Where did you come from?"

Incredible the sudden flow of warmth around his heart. Peter Carey, with a dismounted horseman's awkwardness in boots, came up out of the ditch.

"Thought a few hundred men might help out here," he explained. "Not much fighting cavalry can do up yonder." He nodded his head northward. "Kind of tore themselves to pieces day before yesterday at a spot called Mule Shoe, out from Spotsylvania, but the Yankees got hurt even worse. We're holding. We're holding all right—everywhere."

"Pete! Glad to see you." How glad! A conflict of impulses churned in Stuart. His expression was equally incoherent. "Pete, I've wanted you to know. I've had your name up for a brigade since Chancellorsville. Not my fault . . ."

"Pshaw! It doesn't matter now. Does it?"

No. Somehow it didn't. Stuart rode on, whistling softly.

At four in the afternoon, out of the woods forward of Lomax's line, a round of shot came over the hill where the guns were. The shot dug up the turf. The gunners stiffened. Stuart rode up to them.

"Steady!" he shouted. "Steady there!" In the woods he could see men moving.

"Sir," Venable reined up alongside, "ought you to expose yourself so?"

"Why, I don't reckon there's any danger." But Venable's face was so white that he turned and rode away with him. "Look!" he said in a minute. "You don't need to stay by me. Find something better to do. Go help Lomax. That's where we both are needed. You take the far end of the line and I'll take the near. See you later."

Before he reached the rail fence, his guns on the hill had been silenced. Whistling again, he pulled up between two troopers of the First Virginia.

"Watch it now," he said quietly. "Here they come."

They came in three waves—beautiful formation—sabres flashing, horses—stout, well-fed horses—at a gallop, pennons flying—no, red neckties streaming back over their shoulders. Custer's men again.

Three waves, roaring forward. He had no idea his first line would hold. The creek, the fence broke the impetus of the charge, but did not stop it. The first wave was through. Oh, God lend strength to my reserve! If only he could have kept to the hill, where he could see! But the first wave of blue had smothered now everything that stood there when the charge began. Oh, God of battles . . .

The second wave pounded past—the third. By some grace, he and the men to either side were out of the torrent's path. One of the troopers grinned.

"Give it to 'em, boys!" Stuart shouted, emptying his pistol, bringing one man down, winging another, he thought.

Still the blueshirts swept by. He loaded his pistol, clenched his teeth and prayed. Evening was near. God send the darkness soon! The fury was all behind him now. He listened and caught a change in the roar of it.

"They're coming back!" he yelled.

God bless Wickham, Lee, Pete Carey and the rest! The Yankees came back faster than they had advanced—one wave, two, three. Now there were only the stragglers, men who had lost their horses. He fired at one—a big, heavy-shouldered man. His pistol clicked harmlessly. Empty again. The trooper turned.

The blow took Stuart just below his belt. That was all he felt—a blow, but heavy enough to snap his head forward on his chest. His hat, which he had never lost in the wildest gallop, flew off his head into the dirt. One of the troopers at the fence hurried to pick it up.

"General, sir," he faltered, handing it to him, "are you hurt?"

"Why, I'm afraid so," Stuart said, his voice strange in his own ears.

Both troopers sprang to his help then, one taking hold of the mare's bridle. She shied. That was when pain came—a tearing, searing pain—all the agony he had ever heard in the groans and sighs of a dozen battles. No mortal man could endure it.

"Take me down, please."

They eased him out of the saddle, bending under his weight. They leaned him against a tree.

"But he can't stay there," one of them said. "I'll get another horse."

He found a broad-backed, stolid beast, as willing to stand still as to move. Stuart managed to mount. He bore the ride, but was glad to be let down again.

"A doctor," he ordered now. "General Lee . . ."

Doctor John Fontaine came with an ambulance. He called for whisky.

"I never," Stuart began in protest.

"You must now," the doctor said. "You need it."

The whisky sent warmth through him. A hot day, as he remembered it. Had it turned so cool, with evening?

Fitz Lee came at a tearing gallop. His face was chalk white above his beard.

"Bless you!" Stuart said. "It's your fight now, fellow. Go back. Anything you do will be all right, I know."

Others came.

"Go back," he ordered. "You can't do anything here. Go back. I'd rather die than be whipped."

There were fewer interruptions now, fewer sounds. The ambulance had left the battle behind. There was just the jolting—and the pain. How long could he endure it? Was there no help? Yes—way off at Beaver Dam. She could have helped. Just the touch of her hand. He wanted her as he had never wanted anyone before. He must have said her name.

"Yes, sir. We'll do what we can, sir."

"Mac? What are you doing here? Fitz Lee needs you. Go back!"

He must have lost consciousness finally. When he awoke, Charles Brewer stood beside Doctor Fontaine. He was being lifted out of the ambulance. Oh, God, the pain again!

"Where . . ."

"Home. Richmond," Charles said.

"Flora?"

"I will send a telegram," somebody promised. He didn't know who it was.

The long night. On waking, the same question.

"She should be on her way," Charles said.

But he didn't know about the railroad tracks, the Yankee cavalry.

"She will get through," Charles said.

"I hope so. I would like to see her."

He didn't say once more, but he knew it was that.

President Davis called and they let him enter the room—a tall, ghostly presence in long, black frock coat.

"I came to tell you what I think you'd want to hear. Richmond is saved. Again. You gave us time to call up reserves from south of the city. The enemy is withdrawing."

"My men," Stuart said. "My brave, magnificent men."

Tears rolled unchecked down the President's gaunt cheeks.

Major McClellan reported, and Reid Venable. With quiet efficiency they took down his orders. So much to be settled when a man was going away—forever.

"Charles, how long have I?"

"I don't know. You've borne up amazingly well, but I don't know."

God's will be done. He would have liked to see Flora again.

A preacher and a prayer. A song—"Rock of Ages." Soon now.

He slept. He dreamed. He was riding down a country lane. Ahead of him danced a little girl in a dimity dress tied with blue ribbons. Her bright curls bobbed as she skipped and twirled. He rode up to her, leaned over and snatched her upon his saddle. She squirmed and pulled away, laughing.

"You . . . tickle!"

"*Ma pet . . .*"

At Beaver Dam pallet beds covered the waiting room of the red brick depot. It had seemed best to care for the wounded men right there. About noon of the first day a train from the west had come through, heard of the raid, hesitated and backed off, the engineer vowing he didn't like the looks of things and he'd feel safer back as far as Louisa, at least. Two passengers got off the train in disgust at such cowardice. One was a Mr. Carter from Hanover County, the other a Reverend Dr. Woodbridge on his way back to Richmond from visiting his son, who was in Rosser's brigade. Both of them wanted to get on to their destinations. Dr. Woodbridge had been to some pains to reach the railroad. They would not backtrack now if they could help it. They held to the opinion that the train would return presently with, they hoped, another engineer. They would then resume their journey.

"No reason why it shouldn't a gone on in the first place," the telegraph operator and agent said—back at his post after a night in the woods. "Line's clear as far as Hanover Junction."

If the train reappeared, if there seemed any certainty that it would go on through, the wounded men would also be put aboard. They needed medical attention badly. That was how they had come to be taken prisoner. They were traveling south by ambulance under guard when Sheridan's outriders overtook them, then, finding them more care than their importance justified, dropped them off in this place, to meet whatever mercy Fate had in store for them.

"But they're doing all right now, ma'am," the agent assured Flora the second morning. "Leastways, they're still alive. Mr. Carter and the Reverend say they had a real quiet night on the benches. No, ma'am, no trains and no word of any. I figure they're fighting down yonder." He motioned toward Richmond.

She thanked him, took from Colonel Fontaine a basket of dressings she had made the evening before and went to see for herself.

"We rounded up another pail or two," the sergeant of the warehouse guard said at her back. "They's plenty of water this morning."

Time passed swiftly. It had been agreed the day before that, while this state of affairs lasted, Flora, knowing most about hospital duty, would take charge in the mornings, helped by ladies of the neighborhood. Then Colonel Fontaine would take her home to dinner and the children—she couldn't be away from the seven-months-old baby longer than a few hours—and would bring Mrs. Fontaine back to watch through the afternoon.

The third morning began much the same as the second. Still no trains; but all morning, it seemed to Flora, the station agent's telegraph key made an unwarranted amount of fuss. She was tempted to ask him what was being said back and forth while nothing happened; but, knowing little of the ways of the telegraph, she concluded that he was just trying to see with whom he could communicate, and let it pass. Suddenly the click-click-clack was still; and the man was standing in the door of the waiting room, gawping at her with as witless an expression as she had ever seen on a human countenance.

"Do you want something?" she asked impatiently. After all, it wasn't easy to minister to a room full of floor pallets.

The agent disappeared. A few minutes later Colonel Fontaine came for her.

"Time to go, Missus," he said.

"It can't be," she protested, but was glad enough to follow him.

When they reached the plantation, it was still not quite noon. She made a laughing remark about cheating and hurried on to her room. She freshened herself, washing her face and hands in cool, scented water, then fed the baby. Mrs. Fontaine came in as she was putting the child down.

"Dinner ready?" Flora asked, but one look at Mrs. Fontaine's face told her that wasn't it.

"My dear," Mrs. Fontaine began.

"You've heard," Flora said. "It's about General Stuart. Tell me."

There was a telegram. The agent had tried to give it to her and quailed. Then Colonel Fontaine had lacked heart. At home, his wife said, "Let her feed the baby. Then we'll tell her."

An hour wasted. Another, added to all that has passed since . . . the telegram had come from Richmond by way of Lynchburg and Gordonsville. Why . . .

General Stuart wounded come at once.

Nothing to indicate just when or how badly.

"I must go to him," Flora said. "Right away. Please help me."

"Yes, dear," Mrs. Fontaine answered. "The Colonel has gone back to town, to see what can be arranged."

About two o'clock in the afternoon, a locomotive, drawing a tender and a passenger car, chugged to a standstill at the depot. Flora was waiting, with the children and Tilda.

"I can't leave the baby," Flora said. "So, I had as well take Jimmie. Whatever happens is for all of us. We must bear it together. Tilda . . ."

"I's comin'," Tilda said. "I promise de Gin'ral . . ."

"Bless you. He'll want to see you, I'm sure, as much as anyone."

"That's the way to talk," the Colonel said. "Don't give up hope before you set out."

No, of course not. He was alive when Major von Borcke sent the telegram. If she hurried . . .

The train had a new engineer—a young man, shy, but eager to help.

"I ain't ever run an engine," he said, "but I fired one off and on for a couple a months. I ain't afraid if you ain't."

"I'm sure you can do it," Flora said. "Please hurry, will you?"

"Don't let anything happen," Colonel Fontaine urged.

"I'll do what I can, ma'am. I'll do my best, sir."

The journey was not far in miles. If the trains had been running properly she could have been in Richmond by four or five o'clock that afternoon. And strictly speaking, she was not alone. There were her two gentleman escorts. Mr. Carter, to be sure, rode in the engine cab most of the way. He could, he said, keep a lookout for the young engineer, and help fire the boiler. Dr. Woodbridge remained in constant attendance.

He said, "I'll be glad to offer a prayer."

"Please do," Flora answered, but couldn't remember later a word of his earnest petition.

The baby claimed her attention part of the time. At seven months she was able to make her wants and discomforts known, and she was not nearly so docile as she earlier had promised to be.

"I'm afraid, Tilda, we are not bringing her up very well. We must begin soon to use a little discipline."

"Miss Flo' . . ." Tilda's lower lip shook ominously.

"Now, Tilda!"

"Yassum."

Jimmie was enchanted to be on a train. He mashed his nose against the grimy window and shot questions back over his shoulder to anyone who would listen.

"I'll take him with me, Mrs. Stuart," Dr. Woodbridge again.

"Thank you. I'll sit with him a while. Later, when I'm tired, maybe . . ."

What did she think? With Jimmie she counted telegraph poles. Each one brought her that much nearer. To what? The poles were too many. They blurred.

She went dry-eyed the whole way. That was strange for her. In a thousand anxious days and nights she had soaked many a handkerchief and pillow cover with her tears. Was it because she had shed so many tears in the past that she could cry no more? Or was it because she knew that whatever was to happen was now done? Tears and prayers would not alter it. The tears that had gone before had been largely anxiety and fear. Anxiety she still felt, but only for Stuart's comfort, his peace of body and mind. As for the other awful possibility, well . . .

If this was the end—much of the time she thought it must be. They wouldn't have sent for her if the wound had not been serious. If this was the end, she thought, what a waste! So young, so vital, so brave, so proud, so dear! Then she saw him as he had looked the day before, riding a tired horse. It was the first time she had really seen what others had noted earlier. "Jeems has changed, seems to me. General Stuart has changed, don't you agree?" A stiff determination backing his courage, even his laughter and song.

Was the South going to lose this fight? Some said it had been lost with Vicksburg and Gettysburg. Some said places didn't matter. It was money and men. The North had suffered great losses, too. They wouldn't tolerate that forever. But they were richer up there, had more to draw from. If the South lost, could Stuart bear it? He would have to, like anybody else; but truly he would be a changed man then. Did she want to see that?

Yes, oh, yes. She wanted him. At any cost, in any way. He was hers, her own. Anguish tore at her, but still no tears. Then she thought, how wicked to go on like that. How wicked to lose hope. Wounded, the telegram said, not dead. With his youth and his strength and his great will to live and serve, oh, he would surely recover. She would believe that now—steadfastly.

At Hanover Junction, an official of the Virginia Central moved the engine and car to the tracks of the Richmond-Fredericksburg Railroad. He told her the news from Richmond was good. Stuart was holding his own. It was believed now that the wound was not serious. However, his report, whatever its source, could have been true only hours before this. At Ashland the engine ground to a final halt. There were no more tracks, and, of course, no telegraph wires.

"But I must go on," Flora said. To Mr. Carter, to Dr. Woodbridge, to anyone who would listen.

"Mrs. Stuart, it really isn't safe."

"I must."

"Yes, ma'am."

Word was spread that she was there, wanting transportation to General Stuart's bedside. Within an hour an ambulance appeared, drawn by two mules and driven by a trooper in homespun gray, with another, armed, on the seat beside him. Mr. Carter had found the ambulance. It had been sent to carry a wounded officer to Richmond. Who the officer was or of what command, Flora never knew. At the time, she could neither protest nor inquire.

"There's a bed made up inside," Mr. Carter added, thinking that she could rest.

"Thank you. The children may be ready for sleep before we arrive."

"Mrs. Stuart," the good man was truly distressed, "there are people here to whom you could entrust the children. They'd be proud to do for you and the General. It looks like rain—a storm coming. Do you think it wise . . ."

"No," she said, "but I am not afraid. God, who has brought us so far, will take us the rest of the way. I know how to ride in an ambulance."

Dr. Woodbridge went on with her. Unthinkable that she should not have male escort of suitable station. Afternoon was darkening into early evening when the driver slapped the lines over the mules' backs and yelled, "Giddap!" Her heart skipped a beat. Hosky . . . if only . . .

The early darkness was the storm coming on. A half hour beyond Ashland, the rain began, a shower, then successive downpours. At intervals the ambulance halted.

"Jest makin' sure o' the road, ma'am," one of the men up front called.

They went on. Thunder rolled and crashed. Tight curtains kept out the rain but not all the sharp brilliance of the lightning. They stopped again. There was talk between the driver and someone alongside.

"We'll be here a few minutes, ma'am." The guard stood at the ambulance step. "Got to take a different road. Driver's gone to get directions. If anybody wants to step out, the ground will hold. Rain's slacked up some."

Dr. Woodbridge left the ambulance and, after him, at a nod from

Flora, Tilda with Jimmie. While they were gone, she held the baby and fed her.

"Bedtime, my precious," she crooned, her cheek on the soft curls at her breast. "Sleepy time for little things."

The child was asleep when she laid her on the stretcher bed. She went to the ambulance step herself then for a breath of air. No farther. Everything outside was inky black, except for pools of light made by a few lanterns. The men carrying them could be soldiers. It wasn't always possible to be sure. Thunder rolled, but it seemed farther away, and she wasn't sure all of it was thunder. Some of the roar and some of the lightning could be guns. It was like those evenings when the people of Richmond sat on Capitol Hill, making a picnic—no, theirs were anxious hearts, too.

The ambulance must turn here because ahead were the battle lines. She went back inside. By the time the others returned she had opened the hamper of food that the Fontaines had insisted on sending. Dr. Woodbridge and Jimmie ate a good supper. Tilda ate a little, but not until Flora had done her best with some cold chicken and bread and had drunk a little milk. A few minutes later, Jimmie slept at the other end of the bed.

"My dear?" Dr. Woodbridge urged compassionately.

Flora shook her head. Not now. Not yet. Outside there was considerable splashing, she thought. Had they picked up an escort? Dr. Woodbridge said yes, that had been one cause for delay. About to add more, he faltered, speech shaken from him by the abruptness of the next stop. There was a terrific stamping and backing and balking; and nobody called back to say why.

"I'll go see," the good parson said.

"Bridge gone," he reported presently, "but we're all right. There's a ford downstream the cavalry's been using. We'll try that. What I started to say was we're in good hands—mortal ones. A colonel of cavalry commands our escort. Said he knew you and General Stuart. Carey is the name."

Peter Carey? It was Peter! The ambulance pulled up at the ford to the accompaniment of rifle shots and curses. Peter's voice rose high above the others.

"Fools! Don't you know enough to challenge before you shoot?"

His head came through the rear curtains and he asked hoarsely, fearfully, "Flora? You all right? Infantry guards at the ford. They never know . . ."

"Peter . . . Colonel Carey . . . oh, bless you for being here!"

"That's all right, honey. I wanted . . . I saw Jim yesterday. Before it happened. He was looking fine. He'll make out. We . . . everything's all right all around, dear. I'm taking you through the ford. Sit tight. Here we go!"

They descended a steep bank. They wallowed through the river. What river was it? The Chickahominy. The army had a joke: "How many Chickenhominies . . ." The ambulance swayed and rocked. Was that water around her feet? Then it all but stood on end and the water ran out the back. The mules were climbing the far bank.

"All present and accounted for!" Peter shouted. "Good-bye, girl. Give my best to Jim when you see him. Chin up all the way now!" And to the driver, "All clear. Keep those mules stepping. When you meet sentries on ahead, the password is . . ." he gave it inaudibly. "And tell them whom you have as passengers. Good-bye. Good luck!"

It was ten o'clock by Dr. Woodbridge's watch when they passed the guards at General Lee's inner defenses. It was after eleven when the ambulance pulled up before the Brewer house on Grace Street. Peter Carey had known where they would find Stuart. Dr. Woodbridge left the ambulance first, but Flora was close behind him.

"My dear . . ."

She saw why he had tried to stop her. The street was dark, the front of the familiar house without a sign of light. They were too late. Stuart was gone.

Gone. She moved past Dr. Woodbridge's arm. She stepped down into the street and up on the sidewalk and stood there, facing the house. Why had she come? Stuart was not there. He was nowhere now in all the world. A great, hollow emptiness took possession of her. Tilda came timidly from the ambulance. She took a few steps and threw herself, sobbing, down on the stoop. The driver, the guard, Dr. Woodbridge stood with bowed heads. They could mourn. Richmond, the South, would mourn like that. The world would mourn the passing of one so brave, so rare. Only she would know true bereavement.

Never to feel the touch of his hand, the strength of his arms, the warmth of his lips again! Never hear his gay greeting. To be denied now the sweetness of a last leave-taking! No, she had had that. Some strange prescience had sent him to Beaver Dam two days before.

"Good-bye. God bless you and keep you, my darling, my darling!"

And from that dark house where he had stood his last watch, almost audible,

Ma povere petite!

No, not that any more. Mrs. Stuart now. A soldier's daughter, a soldier's wife, at the last a soldier's widow. "It isn't as if you didn't know. . . ."

The door of the house opened. Someone was there with a light. Flora raised her head. Chin up all the way, girl! And stepped forward to meet whoever waited there to receive her.

Author's Note: *Farewell, My General*

When it comes to acknowledging the help I have had in assembling the material for this book, I face a list of sources so long and so complex that I hardly know where to begin.

Perhaps with the military aspect of the story, since for a long time that threatened to be almost an insurmountable difficulty. Simply because we no longer have any semblance of a mounted cavalry force. Statistics I could gather without end, but establishing the color, the rhythm of movement, the picture was harder. For a long while my best source was the history of my grandfather's cavalry regiment, compiled from the journals of the company officers. Finally, however, by persistent inquiry and exploration, I came to correspond with Colonel Hamilton Gardiner, Retired, of Salt Lake City, an authentic and living cavalryman, who was of great help in directing me to various others. Notably, he introduced me to Colonel W. J. Morton, Librarian at West Point, who was good enough to send out here to St. Louis on an inter-library loan Philip St. George Cooke's book on Cavalry Tactics in the 1861 edition. I am sure Colonel Morton was doubtful as to my ability to learn much from this volume; but, where purely intellectual absorption becomes impossible, I practise a sort of general osmosis, which serves a novelist even better. From the best of sources —General Cooke himself, whom I have long admired—I learned terms, movements, drill, maneuvers and formations. I almost think I could pitch camp.

In this field, too, the Public Information Officers of both Fort Riley and Fort Leavenworth were helpful. However, for cavalry records of the two posts I had to go to the National Archives at Washington. The same courtesy prevailed there and my information on the two cavalry regiments that figure in the first part of the story is direct from the actual records of those years.

For library help of a special nature, I must mention the Collections of the Kansas State Historical Society, my chief aids to an understanding of the history of Kansas as a territory. Also at this very time my own Missouri Historical Society in St. Louis most opportunely purchased a collection of letters in manuscript written by George Bayard, the "overambitious young second lieutenant" in J. E. B. Stuart's company of the First Cavalry. Since these letters were uncensored, they offered priceless comment on life at the two Kansas forts from 1856 to 1860. Also some sidelights, not always complimentary, but illuminating, on our hero himself.

In Virginia, I am indebted to Mr. John Cook Wyllie, Curator of Rare Books, at the Alderman Library at Charlottesville. Also to Miss India W. Thomas of the Confederate Museum in Richmond and members of her staff. They opened all the files for me. There I was privileged to examine the scrapbook kept by Stuart in his early army days and to read several unpublished letters, notably one in which on a note of typical, high-pitched excitement the young lieutenant writes home of his marriage: "I came, I saw and I was conquered by the eldest daughter of Colonel Philip St. George Cooke." And, of course, the case which holds the Stuart uniform, his boots, his sword, his field glasses, his gauntleted gloves, his hat and all, was good for hours of study.

In letters quoted in Chapters 2 and 5 of Part III, I have borrowed a few short passages from a volume entitled "Letters of General J. E. B. Stuart to his Wife, 1861" published by the Emory University Press of Emory University, Georgia. I thank Miss Margaret M. Jemison of the University Library for graciously transmitting to me the University's permission to use these words.

For help of a more personal nature, I owe thanks to Dr. Averam Bender of St. Louis, author of "March of Empire" and other works on western history. He is engaged now in writing a biography of Philip St. George Cooke. We piled our books and papers on the same long table in the library of the Missouri Historical Society and traded notes freely. Another gentleman equally generous was Mr. Lonnie C. Elmore of Snowville, Virginia, who for many years has made a study particularly of the locale of Stuart's youth. He was generous with maps and letters, and gave me some bits of information I could not have obtained elsewhere.

I had also some most enjoyable and profitable correspondence with a few members of the present Stuart and Cooke relationship—notably the present Mr. Philip St. George Cooke of Richmond, son of General John Rogers Cooke in the story. In addition, Mrs. Virginia Waller Davis, daughter of Virginia Pelham Stuart, was most kind, as was the alumnae secretary of Stuart Hall, where Flora Stuart in later years served as Principal. Miss Balluf, the secretary, gave me the names of a few alumnae, who answered my letters of inquiry generously. I recall in particular Miss Esten Duval of Charlottesville, Mrs. Peyton Cochrane of Staunton, and Mrs. Anne Pendleton Forrest of Cuckoo, Virginia—near Beaver Dam. Unfortunately for my needs, most of these people remembered my heroine as an older woman; and I was still on my own when it came to recreating Flora Cooke Stuart as a young woman of nineteen and the early twenties. There I still owe most to Jeb Stuart himself, with his crosses for kisses and his reiterated "My Darling Wife."

It was a long campaign—mine—meaning the writing of the book, taking me even on a tour of all the roads and battlefields in Virginia, though that was a pleasant adventure mostly, thanks to the excellent park service of the state. In that connection I might say that if anyone visiting Chancellorsville recently has picked up a red morocco spectacle case, it is mine. I dropped it there among the autumn leaves.

And now finally, with friends and strangers rallying to my aid, with my editors admonishing and advising and directing and applauding, the book is done. The historic background is as accurate and as complete as the framework of the story allowed. I regret certain omissions of people and events. The character of Flora Stuart is my own creation—not altogether imaginary, but fashioned after deep contemplation of the facts available. Also my own is my interpretation of the character of General Stuart, to whom I offer homage as a matchless soldier, but in whom I was even more interested as an impetuous, high-spirited, loving and lovable young man.